DRAGON KING CHARLIE

THE DRAGON MAGE BOOK 3

SCOTT BARON

"The path that leads to truth is littered with the bodies of the ignorant."

- Miyamoto Musashi

CHAPTER ONE

"Off with his head, Sire?"

"No, Bob."

"Impale him on a pike, then?"

"No. Jeez. What is it with you?"

"A king must rule with an iron fist, and as your adviser, I advise you to at least flay some of the skin from his body. Or remove a few fingers. One must keep up appearances, after all."

"For the last time. No flaying. No bodies on pikes. And no beheading."

"So, the finger option?"

"And *no* chopping off fingers."

The pale man sighed. "Very well. But your reluctance to punish wrongdoers in the manner befitting a king of this planet in this era makes you appear weak. We've only been here a few months, now, and your king act is somewhat lacking."

Charlie pinched the bridge of his nose. *It's going to be a headache kind of morning, isn't it?*

His, friend, aide, and adviser was right, as he often was in such matters. But then, the alien space vampire had seen a lot in

1

his day, including more than a fair share of royals in action. Of course, it was natural he'd have been around a lot of royalty, what with his murdering them regularly during his life as a deadly assassin.

Funny that so dangerous a man, one who had killed silently across the systems of his distant galaxy, would adopt the persona of a meek adviser to the king. But as Bawb knew firsthand, being underestimated often meant the difference between life and death. Namely, his life, and the deaths of those who foolishly took him for a lesser man.

It also loosened lips when people felt you were not a threat, and despite the fact he could easily take out anyone in the castle grounds––with magic or without with equal ease––he kept his skills secret. Bawb was merely King Charlie's unassuming aide, feared by no one.

"Bob, how about we assign the man to hard labor, cleaning the moss from the lower dungeon's stones? That's a pretty shitty job, and one that will put him out of sight for a few weeks. By the time he is seen again––exiting the dungeons, no less–– people will naturally assume the worst."

"And if he tells the truth of what happened? That you had a goat thief simply scrubbing stones as punishment––while receiving food and board, I might add––what's to stop others from taking a cue from him and assuming their king will let them get away with crimes, and perhaps even worse offenses?"

"Because we'll spread rumors of torture, performed by an expert from distant lands. One that leaves no marks but breaks a man's will. He'll look normal and act normal, but everyone will just think he's putting on a strong face. A nice misdirect, if you ask me."

The Wampeh assassin turned royal aide couldn't help but smile.

"You *have* been paying attention," he said with a note of satisfaction.

"Hey, you've done this far longer than I have. When it comes to misdirection and subterfuge, why not learn from a pro? And I can't think of a better teacher than the Geist, the deadliest and most successful assassin for thirty systems."

"Thank you, Charlie," he replied with a grin. "And it's far more than thirty."

"Okay, so that order of business is taken care of. What next?"

"Now we discuss taxes."

"Oh, God," Charlie groaned. "I almost wish we were still on the run from Visla Maktan and his Council of Twenty goons. At least then we were *doing* something."

"Yes. Most notably, fleeing for our lives."

"Well, yeah. But besides that bit, we were doing okay. I mean, the slavery thing sucked."

"Which you remedied when you shed your restraint collar."

"And the whole being captured by pirates thing was a bit of a mess."

"Though you befriended them and became a pirate yourself."

"And then there were the years of gladiator training with Ser Baruud, though I actually rather enjoyed that, despite the bruises and bleeding."

"True, you excelled in that area, and your spell-casting is more than adequate. And your bond with the Zomoki—"

"Dragon. Use the local terms."

"Fine. *Dragon*. It was enough to lead you to Visla Maktan's attention, and our current situation."

"Right? So stuff was a pain there, but at least it was an interesting pain. This? It's great being king and all, but I swear, some days I could die of boredom."

The Wampeh flashed his pointy-toothed grin and laughed. "You wanted to come home, Charlie. You said it was a dream of yours since your ship crashed in my galaxy. And now the rest of us have all been thrown exactly where you wanted to be. *Your* galaxy. *We* are now the ones in a strange land, while *you* are home."

"Yeah, home all right, but a few thousand years too early. Still not sure how that happened, no matter how many times I go over it."

"Ara said it was likely the residual origin energy of this world lingering on the equipment you salvaged from your ship. When the Council detonated their Ootaki-fueled, magical world-ending device, it combined with the power of the blue supergiant in that system. With Ara's panicked attempt to jump clear of the blast, all of that magic blended together, and here we are."

"It's a theory, yeah. And Ara's been working with me to try to devise a spell to not only get you guys back home, but also to move all of us forward to the right time. Like a stretched rubber band returning to its normal state."

"A lot of work. And even the Wise One has never experienced an event of this order."

"No, that she hasn't. She said she felt some strange traces of residual magic when we first arrived, but that's faded. You'd think an ancient space dragon with a shit-ton of magic flowing through her veins could simply jump home in a snap. So if *she* can't do it, I'm not getting my hopes up."

Bawb stroked his angular chin in thought a moment. It was true, Ara was a very old, and very powerful dragon. 'Zomoki' in his home galaxy. Her inability to solve that problem was more than a little disturbing.

They were settling in to their new lives on Charlie's home world of Earth, but the people were primitive, even if Charlie explained that was just because they'd arrived a few thousand years before his own timeline.

At least they were living in luxury. Having quickly dispatched the former king upon their unlikely arrival had everything to do with that. Word of the event spread quickly, and nearly no one had made a move against Charlie since the king had fallen that fateful night. Death by burning and eating, courtesy of an enormous dragon, was not an end anyone craved.

And so it was that Charlie became King Charlie. Bawb was his loyal aide, Hunze his domestic servant. And Leila, well, she was his queen, though she was in no way amused at the title being thrust upon her.

"We have to keep up appearances," he hissed to her when the servants of the castle showed them to their bed chamber.

"No. I am *not* sharing sleeping arrangements with you, Charlie."

"I'll sleep in the anteroom. There's a couch there. But we *must* look the part or the natives will talk."

"Let them talk, then."

"Come on, Leila. After all we've been through? Help me out here. Pretend to be queen, and we'll live in comfort while we sort all of this out."

She reluctantly agreed, and after a few months of their odd living arrangements, had even grown accustomed to their charade. As queen, she had power, but not the responsibility of the king. Not in this place and this time. Charlie, on the other hand, was busier than he'd been in years. In fact, only designing and building his employer's spaceship had been as demanding. But that was enjoyable work. This? This was mind-numbing. But as Bawb had pointed out, it was better than the alternative. That alternative being slavery, abuse, and likely death.

"What next?" he asked his adviser when they finished going over the taxation records.

"Public requests from your people," he replied. "Shall I begin showing them in?"

"Just kill me now," he groaned.

"Excellent. Death by public service it shall be. I'll fetch them straightaway," Bawb said with a laugh.

Charlie watched his friend exit to fetch the first peasant

come to make a request of their liege. "It's good to be the king," he grumbled, sarcastically.

CHAPTER TWO

Lunch was hearty, consisting of cured meats, some cheeses, and dense bread. For Charlie, access to comfort foods—even if they happened to be a few millennia too early—was a godsend. He hadn't realized just how much he missed good old-fashioned Earth food until he had stacked a massive amount of goodies between two thick slices of bread, fresh from his kitchen's ovens.

"Is His Highness certain he would not like a hearty stew instead?" Thomas, the head cook, asked. "Cold meats like this, it is an *unusual* meal."

"Are you kidding?" Charlie said. "A good sandwich is the perfect lunch. Portable, handheld, easy to eat. And your bread. Oh, man. Kudos on the bread."

"*Kudos*, Sire?"

"Uh, it means well done. Slang from my homeland."

"Ah, I see. Thankee, Sire."

"Of course. All it really needs now is a good mustard and it'd be perfect."

Thomas looked pensive.

"What is it, Thomas?"

"Well, it's just that the burning must is not a popular item in these parts. Far too strong a taste for most folk."

"Have you tried making a sweet mustard? Maybe with honey or mashed apples. I know the Germans are famous for their Bavarian apple mustard."

"I admit, I have not. If you wish, I can fetch what we have from the cellar. It is strong, but we do have fresh apples on hand."

"Excellent. Let's give it a go."

Thomas hurried off, returning shortly with a sealed container of incredibly pungent mustard, as well as several sound apples.

"Okay, let's try this," Charlie said, grabbing a knife and quickly peeling and chopping up a few apples, reducing them to chunks.

He then mashed them and stirred in the thick mustard, stirring until the texture seemed about right.

"Moment of truth," he said, scooping out a dollop with a piece of bread. "Oh, yeah. Now that's good. A little strong for my taste, but still, hits the spot."

"Hits what spot, Sire?"

"Sorry, figure of speech again."

Charlie opened up his sandwich and spread a layer of the condiment across the bread, completing the creation, then slicing it in quarters.

"Here, try it."

"It is *your* repast, Sire. I couldn't take—"

"Oh, just try it."

"As you wish," his servant said, reluctantly taking a bite. His eyebrows wavered in surprise as the flavors and textures rolled across his palate and tongue as he chewed. "This...why, this is wonderful, Sire!"

"Told ya."

"The lettuce with the cheese? And the meats and mustard?

I've not had its like before. A most excellent creation. I shall tell the others. The King Charlie Loaf shall undoubtedly become popular with the people."

"Glad you enjoyed it so much. But do me a favor, will ya? Just call it a sandwich."

"A what, Sire?"

"Sandwich. Humor me. Now, if you'll excuse me, I don't want to keep Bob waiting."

"Of course. Thank you for gracing us with your visit."

"Always glad to be in a happy kitchen," Charlie said through a delicious mouthful.

The kitchen visit was a high point of the day for the new king. After lunch, unfortunately, Bawb had tasked him with hearing still more requests of his subjects. And they certainly did love to talk.

Fortunately, the Wampeh had cast a powerful translation spell on each of his friends upon arrival in the strange land. It followed Charlie and the others wherever they went, not only allowing them to understand the locals, but also projecting outward, allowing the locals to understand them as well.

Some days, he didn't want to hear another word.

Charlie had already listened to over two hours of his people's concerns when a cattleman shouldered his way past Bawb to see the king. The Wampeh was unable to fully hide his musculature, but the meek act was honed to perfection, and this particular man was somewhat of a bully, always seeking to intimidate others, even when it served no purpose.

"Oh, pardon me," Bawb said when the burly man bumped him in passing.

The rancher knew better than to show open hostility toward the king's aide, but intimidation was his goal, and from the flustered dandy's reaction, he felt he had achieved it. Bawb, as always, was silently pleased that his reputation as a pushover was reinforced yet again. Underestimated was always a good thing in the assassination trade.

From their posts at the entrance to the room, Captain Sheeran's men quietly mocked Bawb, and not so quietly when he was not around. He was the king's man, however, so to his face, at least, they had to show respect. Privately was another thing entirely, and to their delight, this new incident would give them fresh fodder for their amusement when their boring shifts as the king's guard were completed.

Some might have thought to take advantage of the new king's reliance on unfamiliar men for protective details to overthrow him. But his enormous beast with its periodic flybys overhead quickly put those thoughts far from men's minds.

Ara was the only dragon any of them had ever actually seen, and she was an impressive specimen at that. They may have been spoken of, but that was always in legend. Until her arrival in their lands, they had been chalked up to long-dead monsters of a bygone age. Mere stories used to keep children in line.

The deep red dragon that protected the king was undeniably far more than just a story, and her affinity for––and apparent connection with––the king was clear to all in the realm. Sometimes, the king would even fly atop the beast, surveying his lands from great height.

The king never spoke aloud to the dragon––at least, not that anyone ever observed––though it was clear it heeded his commands. And if any so much as lifted a finger at him, it was a given they would face the same fate as the prior king.

Namely, being burned alive and eaten whole.

The thing about Ara was she was a very patient creature, having lived as long as she had, and would only speak aloud in the presence of her closest friends, and even then, only when absolute secrecy was assured. And she knew how to apply just the right show of force from time to time to keep the people in line and Charlie safe.

The burly rancher had no interest in challenging his new king. He just wanted reparation for the damages inflicted by the queen's pet.

Baloo had grown like a weed in the short time they'd been Earthbound, and with his spike in size came a ravenous hunger. He was a good boy, and fiercely loyal to his mama and those dear to her, but he was nevertheless just barely removed from a wild animal. And a large, deadly one at that.

Charlie directed Bawb to count out some coin from the coffers and sent the man on his way, quietly asking his Wampeh friend to remind him to have another talk with Leila about letting Baloo run free. There was food aplenty, but his appetite for a hunt was getting expensive.

"Refreshment, Sire?" a musical voice asked.

Charlie noted the protective glance the assassin gave the room when Hunze entered with a tray of beverages. He took his oath to protect her seriously, and despite his timid act, heavens help the man or woman who tried to harm a single golden hair on her head.

She looked rather plump in her loose attire, but rather than added weight, the garment hid the rest of her decades-long growth of hair, braided and woven around her body to keep it from getting underfoot.

Back in her own galaxy, Hunze was a priceless slave, her race, the Ootakis, possessing the ability to store magic in their hair. Their unique gift led to them being one of the most sought-after commodities in the five hundred plus systems lorded over by the Council of Twenty. And hers had never been shorn, making it exponentially more powerful.

The Council had planned on harvesting her hair to power a magical weapon, but Bawb had saved her from them when her ship was destroyed. She was no longer a slave, and, fortunately, those who sought her golden locks were in a distant galaxy. She was finally safe.

A strange thing happened when she had first experienced the warm rays of Earth's yellow sun. Hunze actually *felt* her hair growing stronger. Something about the odd radiation from this blazing star in a galaxy far from her own was reacting with her physiology in a powerful way. Ara was feeling good as well, but Hunze's hair was almost radiant in its power absorption.

Given time, it might even build enough power to end wars and build societies, but Ootaki could not utilize the power they carried. Nature's little joke on the peaceful, golden-haired species. So, they became slaves, hunted down and raised in captivity, their hair taken from them when its stored power was needed. It lost potency that way, but was still more than enough for most magic users' needs, and to make the loss worthwhile.

Upon her first arriving at the castle, Hunze had found herself besieged by good-willed house staff. Gwendolyn, the head chambermaid, was convinced her naturally yellow-toned skin was actually a sign of the foul liver humors––known as jaundice to modern medicine––and constantly tried to force a dreadful milk thistle concoction on her.

Charlie sipped the chalice of wine she had brought him. It really was quite good, he had to admit. Perhaps not a fine Cabernet or Brunello, but quite tasty all the same. Bawb even partook of a bit, though despite their friendship, it always weirded Charlie out a little, seeing red on the Wampeh assassin's lips.

Wampeh. Sounds a lot like vampire. And for good reason. It was only a tiny fraction of a percentage of his race that had the gift, but Bawb was one of the few. Those who could take another's power by drinking their blood. It was incredibly rare, but for those few with the ability, it was a ticket to immense wealth and influence. Of course, now they were on a planet with no magic users around for him to feed that part of his hunger. Bawb would just have to suffice with regular old food and drink.

If that meant no more magical attacks on him or his friends, he was just fine with that. For the time being at least. Both he and his king couldn't help but wonder how long things would stay tranquil in their new home.

"That's the last of them, Sire," Bawb announced an hour later, when the final villager left the chamber.

"Oh, thank God. Guards, you're dismissed."

The two restrained their obvious relief and trotted from the room.

"I hope you wrote all of that down, Bob, because there's no way I'm remembering all of it."

"Of course, Charlie. I'd be a rather poor aide if I didn't."

"About that. We really need to find you something less menial."

"Absolutely not. This role allows me not only great freedom to observe the goings-on around the grounds, but also to command a modicum of obedience and respect, when the need arises."

"I see. Walking quietly but carrying a big stick."

"Another of your clever analogies, Charlie. You really should write them down one day."

Charlie chuckled to himself. "Yeah, Bob. I just might do that. Now, what say you we go see what's up in the training grounds? I desperately need some fresh air."

"A lovely suggestion," Bawb replied. "Lead the way. *Sire.*"

CHAPTER THREE

The familiar sounds of clashing steel and grunting combatants was welcome music to both Charlie and Bawb's ears. The assassin was, well, an assassin, and had dedicated his life to the deadly arts. Charlie, on the other hand, had been a decently proficient fighter, but his original calling had been space engineering. Until he was sucked through a wormhole, enslaved by aliens, and sold off as an unwilling gladiator.

He survived, thanks to both his own perseverance and moxie, as well as the years of training he received at the hands of Ser Baruud, one of the most legendary gladiators to ever earn his freedom.

It had been hard going, but the daily training and constant combat drills had drawn out his hidden talent for it, as well as honed the skills he'd already practiced while back on Earth. In fact, it was Charlie's gladiatorial prowess that had landed them back on his home world—via a very long way around.

Today, however, he and Bawb were in a much different position. That of spectators, a king and his aide observing his men as they lumbered through the rote drills devised by Captain Sheeran and his men.

The troops were practicing swings and parries. Their form left more than a little to be desired.

"Wow," Charlie said.

"You said it," Bawb agreed. "They look even less elegant than last time we saw them train. They lack agility and grace. And look how they telegraph their swings."

"I know. It's almost painful to watch."

They had observed the men's practice several times in the months since Charlie had abruptly seized the crown and become king, but had thus far refrained from interjecting in the goings-on of the captain and his top men. They were newcomers, and until they were well situated, it made no sense to rock the boat.

Today, however, Charlie had finally had enough.

"That's it. I have to say something," he said, walking across the dirt to the combatant's square.

"Are you sure?" Bawb asked, his hesitance only minor. He, too, wanted to step in, but to do so would mean shedding his carefully crafted persona.

"Yeah. Hold my wine," Charlie replied, handing him the chalice he'd carried with him.

"Sire, it is a pleasure to see you join us," Captain Sheeran said with a strained smile. It was most definitely not a pleasure.

Ever since his former king met his fate at the hands of Charlie's dragon friend, he had carried out his duties to his new liege, but under duress. He kept up appearances, though, and for continuity of the king's guard, that was vital.

"Thank you, Captain Sheeran. I was just commenting to Bob that it seems the men could perhaps use a little more training in basic movement and body awareness before continuing with fight instruction," Charlie noted. "I would be glad to make a few suggestions, if you don't mind. Things that might serve them well in the long run."

"Oh, I assure you, we have trained hundreds of men in this manner, and it has always served us well."

Charlie smiled and bit his tongue as he chose more respectful words than initially sprang to mind.

"I mean no disrespect to your methods, Captain, but it seems the men rely more on brute force than finesse, which leaves them at a disadvantage in individual skirmishes. And I'm sure you can see that more than a few of the men have the tendency to telegraph their attacks."

"In training, Sire. But bloody battle is a far different mistress," the captain replied.

"Of course. But some refinements could help more of them return home intact."

The air fell silent as the men ceased their training, watching their captain and their king. Captain Sheeran quickly glanced at the faces of his men. His jaw flexed, but he said nothing.

Charlie couldn't help but notice. In fact, even a blind man would have seen the painful restraint on the man's face.

"Do you have thoughts on this?" Charlie asked.

"No, Sire."

"Please, Captain, speak freely. We all want what is best for the men, here. There is never repercussion for honest discourse."

"It's just warriors should handle the training of warriors. *Sire.*"

A slight titter of laughter rippled through the men.

"A reasonable position. So, you don't think my opinions have value in that arena?"

"Sire, I mean no disrespect, but what can the king know of real combat? You have your dragon fight your battles for you. It is hardly the same."

A murmur spread through the assembled men.

Oh, damn. He went there, Charlie thought, both shocked and amused. He cast a glance at Bawb. The assassin grinned with amusement.

"Perhaps my liege would indulge the captain and his men with a demonstration?" the Wampeh suggested.

Charlie held his smile in check, but the thought had been crossing his mind as well.

"I would never dream of laying a finger on my king," Captain Sheeran said, his back stiffening at the very prospect of sullying his position.

"Oh, I don't think that will be a problem," Charlie replied with a little smirk, then turned to the gathered men. "Gentlemen, the captain and I will be putting on a little demonstration. I wish it to be clear, I have requested he fight me as he would any other, with no fear of reprisals or displeasure." Charlie turned to face the captain. "Do not hold back, Captain. There will be no repercussions for striking me. In fact, if you manage it, there may even be a reward."

Charlie began to strip from his robes. The ceremonial garb was an annoyance he put up with at Bawb's request. When meeting his people, he had to look the part, after all. But now he was free of them, embracing the lightness of body that accompanied his trousers and tunic.

"That goes for any who would care to challenge me. Land a blow and you shall see additional coin in your pocket. Any takers? Come, now. These swords are dull, don't be shy."

Five of the cockier of his men stepped forward, dulled training weapons in hand, flashing confident smiles at their leader. The captain nodded his approval.

"Very well. Who's first?" Charlie asked with a grin, picking up a training blade from the rack.

The first man's battle cry was more impressive than his assault. He fell quickly, his attacks far too aggressive, leaving him terribly off-balance. Charlie feinted right, then moved left, knocking the man to the ground with the flat of his blade.

"Next."

The second met the same results, though he at least managed to throw a few awkward swings, which Charlie easily dodged, again feinting right, then moving left, his footwork a little bit awkward on his weak side. The captain felt his confidence grow as he watched and studied.

Two more men went in similar fashion, though Charlie refrained from ending the fights quite as quickly as the first pair. He wanted to give the men more than just a show, but also a learning experience as well. It was more about his men becoming better fighters than his own ego.

The final man actually held his own decently for a series of attacks and parries, but once again, Charlie positioned him with careful footwork, then feinted right before slipping to the man's left, sweeping his feet out from under him as he landed his swing.

"Well done, Sire," Captain Sheeran said.

"Oh, please. That was just the warm-up. Come, now. Let's show them how it's done, you and I."

The captain picked up a training sword, a knowing grin lurking behind his lips.

He and Charlie circled each other a moment, then he launched a series of rapid attacks.

Shit, he's actually pretty good.

Charlie was hard-pressed to defend himself for a moment, retreating and regrouping before launching an attack of his own. The two went back and forth for a few minutes before the captain saw what he had been waiting for. The predictable feint. The king's weakness.

Sheeran swung, then positioned himself as Charlie feinted right, then moved left. The captain struck hard and fast, aiming for the king's vulnerable flank.

But the king wasn't there.

A look of shock passed across the captain's face for the

briefest of moments before he felt his sword wrenched from his hand as his body was spun and flipped through the air, landing in the dirt with a dusty thud. His sword arm, he was distressed to note, was held at an odd angle, the king applying the slightest of pressure to his wrist, causing pain to radiate from his hand to his shoulder.

Despite himself, he let out a small cry of pain. A young guard, distressed by his captain's cry, rushed forward, charging the king.

"No, Owen! Do not——"

But it was not a problem for Charlie. He merely shifted stance, easily sending the youth flying through the air and landing in a pained heap.

"Stay your hand. All of you! This is your king!" Captain Sheeran called out to his men.

The stunned soldiers' shoulders relaxed slightly at his command.

"Are you all right, Captain?" Charlie asked as he helped the man to his feet. "I hope I didn't wrench your shoulder too hard there."

Captain Sheeran brushed himself off, shocked at what had just transpired.

"Please forgive him," he said, nodding to the lad getting back to his feet. "I've known him since he was a boy, and I'm afraid he has more loyalty than sense."

Charlie grinned and patted him on the shoulder. "Of course, Captain. Totally understandable. You know, it actually felt nice to have a little bit of a surprise thrown in there." He turned to the assembled troops. "And I hope this serves as a lesson for you all. You will not always fight man-to-man, and you will not always be at an advantage. You must keep your wits about you and your eyes sharp, for danger can come from any direction."

The captain faced his men. "Okay. Back to work, you lot. The king will be making some alterations to your training shortly."

The men trudged off to their duties, the looks on their faces as much of respect as shock at what they'd just seen the king do.

"You were faking," Sheeran said when they were out of earshot.

"I'm sorry, what?"

"Your feint and counter. You faked it with each man you fought. You knew I would notice the weakness and attempt to capitalize on it."

Charlie grinned. "Indeed."

"Clever," the captain admitted.

"Things are not always as they seem, Captain. A lesson all would be well-served to remember. This applies to life in general, but especially to battle."

The captain silently studied his new king a moment.

"May I return to my men, Sire?"

"Of course."

Sheeran turned, then paused. "You are definitely not what you seem, my liege," he said, then walked away.

"He seems a bit disgruntled," Charlie said as Bawb helped him back into his robes.

"Well, you did just show him up in front of his men. But in so doing, I believe you have won their respect, and with it, I feel they will be more likely to heed your commands in the future. And I mean as a man they respect, not just a stranger who has seized the crown."

"I hope so. But I didn't mean to upset the captain. He's been here forever, and that's the kind of man you want on your side."

"Well, then. I think, perhaps, you will need to address that further."

"Yeah. But *after* we eat."

"Yes, sustenance would be good," Bawb agreed as they walked back to the king's reception chamber.

Many eyes watched as they went, and not all were friendly.

CHAPTER FOUR

"Are you sure you wouldn't be better served leaving him alone for a bit? I'd imagine after you so easily dispatched the Captain of the Guard in front of his men, he'd benefit from a little time to stew in his own juices," Bawb suggested.

Charlie didn't slow his pace down the castle's stone hallway, his footsteps hushed against the floor by the soft soles of his boots. Another trick he'd learned from his assassin friend. One that allowed him a modicum of stealth in the walls where everyone greeted him with "Sire" or "my liege." Stealthiness provided him brief respite from the attention and had now become second nature.

"I'd rather deal with any hard feelings as soon as they arise," Charlie replied. "When I was lead engineer on the *Asbrú* project, I had to oversee dozens of often socially awkward science-brained people. Managing their mood swings was a daily task."

"But this is a military man. And a man of some violence, it would appear."

"Yes, but it's best to let people air their grievances and let off steam rather than risk it festering. Trust me, Bob, this is the right move."

They arrived outside the thick wooden door to the captain's quarters.

"Very well. I shall leave you to it, then."

"Thanks, Bob. I'll meet you in the dungeons afterward."

"I look forward to it," he replied with a mildly unsettling grin.

Of course, being a space vampire with a penchant for flashing his pointy teeth when he and Charlie were alone—teeth that could be retracted if he really wanted them to be—it was only natural to feel a little discomfort from the gesture.

Charlie knocked twice on the hefty lumber and waited.

"What is it? I told you not to disturb me," Captain Sheeran's irritated voice said as the door swung open. "Oh, it's you, Sire. My apologies."

"May I come in?"

"Of course."

Charlie had been in the man's chambers before. He lived a rather Spartan lifestyle, with few creature comforts, but the space was still cozy enough, with the dark wooden furniture and small fire in the hearth. The selection of weapons hanging from the wall would have been merely decorative in any other's home, but Charlie suspected the captain had put them all to good use over his lengthy career.

"What can I do for you, Sire?"

"I wanted to thank you for joining me in the demonstration today."

"Anything for the kingdom," he replied.

Charlie noted he said *kingdom*. Not king.

"I also wanted to discuss the addition of some new training to add to your regimen."

"Whatever Your Highness wishes."

"No, Captain, I want this to be a joint process. I value your input and experience, and am not trying to usurp your long history with the men. It's just that where I come from, we do things a little differently, and I saw an area in which the men's training could be improved. It does not reflect on you or your service. I hope you realize that."

"Of course, Sire."

He was saying what was expected of him, but Charlie wasn't buying it.

"Look, I've watched you for a long time now. Since the day I first arrived, actually."

"When you wondered if you might have to fight me," Sheeran stated, plainly.

"Yes. If your king had commanded it, you and I would have fought. But things went a bit differently than any of us would have expected, eh?"

"Your dragon saw to that," he replied, his face unreadable.

"Yes, she did. But you acted wisely, and your men lived because of it. That was restraint and wisdom I saw that day. It was one of the main reasons I asked you to stay on as head of the guard. You're a smart man, Captain. Smarter and far more capable than most in the castle, in fact."

"Flattery does not suit soldiers."

"No, but honest discussion does." Charlie paced the room, admiring the weapons on the wall. "Look, I understand what it feels like to have your martial skills bested. Believe me, I've had it happen to me countless times, and it's never fun. But it is a learning opportunity."

"Your skills are indeed, surprisingly formidable," he reluctantly agreed. "I'd not wish to face the man who trained you."

"There have been a few who did, you know. Basic training, and some Krav and Silat in my free time, but for this style, Ser Baruud was the man's name. A gladiator slave who earned his freedom. One of the deadliest fighters I've known. I do miss training with him," Charlie said, momentarily lost in memories.

"But he is elsewhere."

"Yeah, you could definitely say that. I doubt I'll ever see him again."

"You could perhaps return to your lands," he dared suggest.

"I would if I could, but that's just not an option. We're stuck here, so we have to make the most of it. And that's what I was getting to. Making the most of things. Ser Baruud was already far superior to any in his realm when we first met, but he saw something unusual in my style. And you know what he did? Rather than drill it out of me, forcing me to fit into a fixed mold, he watched, and learned, and eventually adopted the parts he found useful into his own training."

"As a warrior would. We strive to improve."

"Exactly! That's the thing. I greatly respect your talents, Captain, but even the most skilled fighter can always learn new tricks."

"Even you?"

"Especially me. I learn every day."

"But who teaches you now? You said your teacher was far away."

"That's, uh, *complicated*."

Charlie walked to the weapons collection once more, plucking a sword from the wall, giving it a few swings, then replacing it in its spot.

"Good balance."

"It has served me well," the captain replied.

Charlie reached deep within his robes and removed a long dagger and its scabbard from its hiding spot. It wasn't his favorite, but he'd carried it with him from the distant galaxy where he'd procured it.

It was a Tslavar design, gentle curves and scrollwork in the pommel, the blade possessing the faintest of glows. It wasn't a true enchanted blade––only a fool would part with such a thing––but there was a little power to the weapon. It would hold its edge after even the most vigorous use. And it would never rust or tarnish.

He held it out to the captain.

"I brought this from far, far away. In this place, it is one of a kind. Ever sharp and true."

"I don't understand."

"I want you to have this. As a token of my faith in you. To thank you for all you do for the *kingdom*."

Charlie made sure to emphasize the last word. The captain's loyalties were to the realm and its people, not the man wearing the crown. Perhaps that would change one day, but for now, faithfulness to the kingdom would suffice.

The captain hesitated, then took the dagger, slowly pulling the blade from its sheath. The faint glow made him catch his breath.

"A magical blade?"

"I'd keep it sheathed unless you truly need it. Too many questions otherwise. And it's good to have a few surprises up one's sleeve, is it not?"

The captain admired the blade, turning it over in his hands. "Yes, Sire. That it is."

"Excellent. I'll leave you to it, then. Places to go, king stuff to do, you know. I'll draft up some new training to incorporate in the men's regimens. We'll start adding it in tomorrow."

Charlie left the man, turning his back to the disgruntled soldier with a deadly, magical blade in his hands. His senses were on edge, and he was ready to move, if need be, as he walked out the door, but even if he did have ill intentions, the captain would not stoop so low as to stab someone in the back, least of all the king.

Charlie walked away from the old soldier's quarters wondering if he'd made headway with the man, or merely better armed his foe.

Time would tell. Hopefully in a bloodless manner.

CHAPTER FIVE

Charlie dove to the side, rolling across the hard stones as the small blade flashed through the space he had been occupying moments before. His boots scrambled for purchase on the dusty floor, digging in and gripping the rock face as he launched himself into a counterassault.

He spun in the air, throwing a diversionary attack while positioning his body to land in a solid defensive stance, weapons held ready.

Another blade, this one longer, swished through the air. Charlie deflected it with a sparking parry of his own weapon, then turned his focus to the foot-sweep spell welling up in his mind. A counterspell blocked it, but that instant of surprise and reaction gained him a momentary advantage. One he pressed to the best of his abilities.

Charlie eschewed both weapons and magic, opting for a good old-fashioned tackle, pinning his opponent's arms as best he could in the process. He could still be cut, but not by anything so deadly as a full-force swing.

The two men hit the ground with a dusty *wumph*, wrestling

one another as they struggled to be the first to achieve the mount position. A sharp pain shot through Charlie's shoulder, and despite his best efforts, his body reacted of its own accord, twisting ever so slightly to escape the nerve attack.

That was all his deadly opponent needed, quickly trapping his arm and pushing with his hips, flipping Charlie onto his back. The fight continued, the men discarding their long weapons and scrambling for their smaller ones concealed on their persons. The point of a deceptively small—yet quite deadly—dagger pressed into Charlie's neck.

"Shit. You got me," he grumbled, ceasing his struggles.

Bawb laughed, pushing the hair from his sweaty brow as he climbed back to his feet.

"But that was better, Charlie," he said, reaching down to help his friend up. "Much better."

"But you still got me."

"Yes, but I've been doing this a *lot* longer than you."

"Well, yeah. But still."

"You improve greatly every day. And, Charlie, you are becoming quite proficient in casting without a konus or slaap. It was a well-placed surprise attack. The magic imbued within you from your bond to the Wise One is growing stronger. And with it, your control."

It was true. While Charlie had no problems casting his spells using either his wrist-worn konus or brass knuckle-looking slaap, it was the internal magic rather than that stored in those devices he had been cultivating. Ever since he and his dragon friend had accidentally merged their blood years prior, something had been growing within him. Now, it seemed, it was transitioning into something new. Something he could tap into without any external aid. A good thing, too, as the great iron content in many parts of the castle tended to unexpectedly disrupt magically charged devices. As with old Earth tales of iron restraints binding witches, it seemed some truth lay behind the legend.

Internal powers, however, were far less affected.

Charlie wiped the blood from his left arm. A small slice from one of Bawb's blades. Most men would have been covered in little scars from all of the 'lessons' he had been taught, but Charlie had the healing powers of the waters discovered in the Balamar Wastelands still strong in his body. The wound was slight and would be healed by nightfall.

While the human suffered minor cuts regularly, the deadly Wampeh was still too fast for him to land a solid hit on. They trained with steel––unenchanted weapons were the order of the day––but Bawb was at no real risk, though his friend was improving rapidly.

In the safety of the remote part of the castle's dungeons, the pair could train in earnest, sealed off from both prying eyes and attentive ears, the thick stones shielding them from unwanted scrutiny. They even used magic in their sparring without fear of discovery.

The assassin had accepted that he would never see his home––or home galaxy, for that matter––again. It posed him some unique issues. No longer bound by the rules of his own world, he found a strange bit of freedom afforded him. Freedom to break an oath of his sect. The Wampeh Ghalian never shared their deadliest secrets, but here, in this alien galaxy, he had decided that oath held no sway.

As such, Bawb was not only training Charlie in martial combat, but was also teaching him the basics of the deadliest of spells. Assassin spells known only to a handful. Charlie's nascent ability to cast with his own power was not a threat yet when it came to them––they required a significant amount of magic to be cast, and without a konus or slaap, Charlie could not yet access them. The intent to kill had to be there as well, and the human had remarkable grasp of that elusive element of spell casting.

Even experts could always learn more, however, and it was Ara who had helped Bawb down that path, teaching him to cast without saying the words aloud, relying instead on his internal connection with the spell and his visceral drive behind it. After their dangerous escape from the distant galaxy, and the Council of Twenty's destruction of the entire planet of Tolemac in their pursuit, she had felt he was worthy of her trust.

For the Wampeh, being taken under the wing of so great and respected a creature as Ara, the Zomoki of legend, known to some as the Wise One, was a dream he never would have allowed himself to believe could come true. He listened intently, studying her every lesson and practicing as he hadn't since he was a novice.

It was drastically different, her silent casting. He could already cast incredibly quietly, being an assassin, but to do so without so much as a single vocalization was something entirely new, even for him.

"How is Hunze's training coming along?" Charlie asked, slipping into a clean tunic.

"Quite well, for an Ootaki," Bawb replied.

The Ootaki were a naturally peaceful people, and it had taken several weeks for Bawb to convince the young woman to learn at least the basics of self-defense. She had acclimated well to the new planet. Being in a galaxy where her hair no longer made her a target for theft or abuse had done wonders for her confidence. Her shell of cautiousness was finally shed, at least every so often.

Being one of the king's personal retinue also helped. The other servants were kind to her out of necessity at first, but once they got to know her, with her sweet and open demeanor, they soon came to the realization that they would have treated her

SCOTT BARON

the same regardless. In short order, Hunze had befriended the majority of the castle's inhabitants.

Not because she was Charlie's friend. Not because of her priceless, magic-storing hair. But because of who she was. Charlie just hoped she would never again know the strain of being returned to her former slave life. And with Bawb watching out for her, heaven help any who tried.

CHAPTER SIX

"I hear you showed up the captain today," Leila said, tearing off a thick chunk of fresh, crunchy-crusted bread and mopping up some sauce from her plate.

Charlie delayed his reply a moment, chewing his food a few extra seconds while trying to decipher whether the olive-skinned woman was actually annoyed, or just curious. While she'd been a very pale green back on Visla Maktan's world, where she was born and raised as a slave, here, on Earth, the yellow rays had––as Charlie had thought they might––tanned her other worldly skin to a more Mediterranean olive. All the better to fit in with humans, fortunately.

He washed his food down with a liberal drink of wine. *Nah, she's not upset,* he decided.

"Bob and I were taking a stroll after a ridiculously long day of hearing requests and complaints from the people."

"It's your job, Charlie. You took the crown, after all. Comes with the territory."

"I know, but if I knew being king was so much work, I would have let Bob do it."

"That's a funny thought. Far too public for him. He loves misdirection and a degree of anonymity, you know."

"That I do."

"Speaking of our Wampeh friend, I see he and Hunze aren't joining us tonight," Leila noted. "Everything okay?"

"Yeah, he's just been taking a little extra time with her to go over some basic defense stuff. He's kinda super-protective of her."

"Tell me about it. But it's sweet. The deadly assassin and his pet," she said, tossing a chunk of meat to Baloo, where he lay quietly at her feet.

"You've gotta stop feeding him at the table, Leila."

"He's a growing boy."

"Who could take your hand off if he wanted. He's getting huge."

"He's well-behaved. Aren't you, Baloo?" she said, scratching him between the ears.

Baloo looked up at his mom lovingly. He was a sweetheart of an alien wolf-looking creature who was fiercely protective of those he considered his pack. Charlie was glad to fall into that category.

"Still, it's a bad habit. Which leads me to the next thing. I've had some complaints about him killing livestock again."

"Baloo, what did you do?" she scolded, jokingly.

"Seriously. I'm the king. We can get him his own game to chase around the castle grounds, but he's gotta stop roaming and taking out farmers' goats. It makes the locals upset."

"I know," she relented. "It's just, he gets that instinctive thing running through him when he's out in the woods. He's a born hunter, after all."

"Which is a problem, sometimes."

"I know," she replied. "He listens to me, but sometimes even that isn't enough to stop him when he's on the hunt. I'll try to keep him in check as best I can. Promise."

"Thanks."

"Of course. Now, what about your run-in with Captain Sheeran? Did you really manhandle him in front of his men?"

"Only a little. And I let him make a good show of it first. The others I took out pretty fast."

"Others? Charlie, you know you have to tread carefully. We're still new here, and you *seized* the crown. The old king is barely cold, you know. It's going to take time to be fully accepted."

"Technically he's fully digested by now. I'm sure Ara pooped his bones out weeks ago."

"That's disgusting."

"But accurate. I mean, she did eat him, after all."

"Fine," she relented. "But you know what I mean."

Another little piece of meat made its way to Baloo's eager mouth under the table. Leila flashed an amused little grin at her friend.

"You don't need to worry about the captain, by the way. I visited him after our demonstration. I think the talk went pretty well, all things considered. We're going to start integrating some more modern training techniques into his regimen."

"There you go, changing things on the poor fellow after humiliating him in front of his men."

"I didn't humiliate him. It was a teaching demonstration. And despite perhaps denting his pride a little, the captain is a warrior. He understood my point about everyone benefiting from new viewpoints. We never stop learning, you know. This is just an opportunity for him to become even better at what he does."

The serving help brought out a warm bread pudding and placed it on the table before the king and queen.

"Thank you, Daria. It smells delicious," Leila said, savoring the steam rising from the dish.

The shy woman smiled, curtsied slightly, and hurried back to the kitchen.

"At least the household staff are comfortable with us," Charlie noted. "I think the previous king wasn't much of a fan of creative cooking. Our being here gives Thomas a little freedom to try new things."

"Yes, and Hunze has been watching and learning. It's all such a novelty for her, a galaxy in which nothing is magic-powered. The concept is so entirely foreign to her. I mean, it is to me, too, but for one raised not only in captivity, but also specifically for the magic she stores, well, it's got to be quite a head-spinner."

"And have you felt the ripples from her hair when she lets her emotions free? She's gotten so much stronger here. One thing for sure, my planet may not possess magic beings, but those from your galaxy seem to greatly benefit from our sun's rays."

"Funny to think that the people of this kingdom have never even seen outside these mountains and valleys, let alone other worlds, or systems."

"To be fair, you never left your world, either, before we fled."

"Yeah, but I knew what was out there. That it was possible. To them, it seems an impossibility."

The king and queen enjoyed a more relaxed discussion of the marvels they had discovered since their arrival over dessert, followed by a small glass of fortified sweet wine.

The serving staff cleared the table, and Charlie and Leila retired to their chambers, her chambermaids trying to help her remove her attire.

"Ladies, really, I can do this. I've been dressing and undressing myself my whole life."

A blush and look of shame flashed across both their faces.

"Not that I don't truly appreciate all of your help," she quickly added. "You've both been doing a fantastic job. Really, top-notch. Now, please, go have some dinner and enjoy yourselves tonight. That's an order," she added with a wink.

The chambermaids' smiles returned to their faces as they left their queen to her own devices. She was odd, and her refusal of their services was disconcerting, but she was a good woman and treated them well. As is the case among servants, word of her treatment spread, and was met with appreciative nods.

The thick door closed behind the pair as they left. Charlie padded over to it, locking it soundly behind them. He felt they were safe in the castle, but old habits die hard, and that meant King Charlie and Queen Leila would die hard as well. He walked across the chamber to the smaller door in the far wall.

"All right, then. Sleep well," he said, then walked into the adjacent room for another night on the surprisingly comfortable couch. Within minutes, he was sound asleep, enjoying the sensation of flying above his kingdom. Whether it was all in his mind or was him tapping into Ara as she hunted was unsure. Whatever the case, it was comforting, and he had come to enjoy the frequent dreams.

CHAPTER SEVEN

In the dark surrounding the castle, the faintest of sounds of footfalls would occasionally present themselves to the most strained of ears. But no one was listening, and their passage went unnoted. Invisible, the Wampeh assassin snuck deeper into the woods, following an impossible route through crags and boulders, skirting bogs and fallen trees, until, finally, he arrived at his destination.

The rocky face was sheer, the backside of a granite hill that had fallen away many millennia earlier. The resulting formation was a slope that dropped away to the jagged boulders below. But halfway up the near vertical face, a small cluster of trees hung firmly to the soil, growing strong in spite of their precarious home.

It was there that Bawb had chosen when he had given the lands surrounding the castle a thorough once over in the days following their arrival. One tree in particular had caught his eye, and since he began tending it, its bark had grown dense and healthy.

He slipped back the hood of his shimmer cloak, the magical camouflage making it appear as if just a head were floating in the air. It was such a familiar bit of magic for him that the use of it was second nature, pulling almost no power from the konus he wore on his wrist.

In times of the most dangerous infiltration, he would also use one of the more esoteric spells at his disposal. One that would hide his reflection, and even shadow, should he lack his shimmer cloak. But it was a power-hungry spell that would easily drain a lesser konus dry of its stored magic.

The Wampeh pulled a small flask from his cloak and set it aside on the nearby flat rock he used as a work surface. He then bent close to the tree, casting the slightest of illumination spells, far too faint to be seen unless you were right on top of it. His fingers ran along the almost invisible seam on the low branch.

If you didn't know where to look, it would appear as any other. Only, this had been his project. His secret experiment, spurred by one of Charlie's seemingly random comments months prior.

Wood could not hold a magical charge in his galaxy. Everyone knew that, so no one even bothered to try. But the strange human from a distant land knew no such restrictions, and great innovations were often made by those simply unaware what they attempted was impossible.

He had taken his sharpest blade and carefully split the tapering end of the branch, gently prying it open until the heartwood showed. The gap was roughly a foot long, and into it he pressed a thin rod of magically charged metal. It had been a konus days prior, but with the help of Ara's magical flames, he had managed to forge the band into a rod without losing its magic-storing properties. The result was a foot-long, pencil-thin device.

Wrapped tightly around it was a single, powerful strand of long, golden hair. A gift from Hunze when he confided his project to her. The immense power of her freely given strand was super-charging the konus rod as it shared its energy.

He had then pressed the split wood tightly together around the rod, wrapping the protruding remaining length of the hair around the outside of the branch, allowing it full exposure to the planet's nourishing yellow sun. With a final series of precise bindings to hold things in place, he set to work maintaining his experiment, returning to it every few days to tend to it.

Bawb was making a wand, growing the power directly into the wood, as Charlie had offhandedly suggested. The idea, though unheard of, was intriguing, and from what he could sense after several months of healing and growth, it had been a good one. The wood was sound and strong, reinforced with ample power, constantly upping its charge from the bit of exposed hair that still fed into the branch itself. The tree's absorption of the planet's rays also added to the effect in an unforeseen way.

But Bawb had taken to visiting at night, now that there was actual power being handled. Better extra safe than having curious eyes stumble upon his treasure.

The Wampeh gave the branch one more going over, and—once satisfied with its health—carefully unsealed the small flask he had put aside. With great care, he dripped the smallest amount of the iridescent waters contained within onto the healing split of the branch. The Ootaki hair glowed faintly when it contacted the water, channeling its healing power deep into the wood.

He then poured a small amount onto the roots of the tree, as he had done a few times prior. Healing and strengthening the entire organism, not just the appendage he had commandeered.

The waters were scarce, most of their hastily filled containers having been lost during the battle at the Balamar Wasteland before they fled and accidentally arrived on this strange planet. But even here, far from home, the powerful waters would harm Bawb just as easily as they would heal others. It was a rare weakness the Wampeh possessed, and every time he used a portion of their stash, he put himself at risk.

But the tree was healing nicely, and this would likely be the last time he would need to tap into the priceless water reserve. So little remained, he knew it was vital to save it in case a true healing emergency arose.

He held his hand over the damp wood, careful not to touch it with his bare skin. Combusting would not be a fun way to end the day.

"Yes," he murmured, satisfied with the power he sensed being given off by the branch. "That's coming along nicely."

If Charlie was right, the magically charged piece of tapered wood could be a fantastic amplifier of power. A directional conductor of magic the likes of which konus and slaap users had never seen. And all because it had been created with living wood, its powers imbued into every cell of the plant surrounding its magical core.

It was amazing no one had ever thought to try it before, but sometimes it really did take outside eyes to see what was obvious to them but overlooked by all others.

Bawb silently cast a masking spell, hiding the tree's blossoming power from any who might seek it out. He knew they were the only ones who might sense it, but nevertheless, he hadn't lived as long as he had by not being overly cautious. He then slid the hood of his shimmer cloak over his head and vanished into the misty night air, silently beginning his long trek home.

CHAPTER EIGHT

A small cart rattled along the dark, rutted path, its wheels bumping and lurching with every rock and hole they encountered. The small pony pulling it moved on steady hooves, well familiar with the road and its hazards. The cart itself was a light burden, carrying a single load—a small goat, its foreleg splinted and bound.

A lone woman walked beside the pony, gently stroking its side as it labored. She was something of a local version of Leila—at least in her former life. An animal healer and woman of the land. Though a good decade older than the now-queen, she was still quite spry and healthy, even for the time and place.

While life on ancient Earth could be hard, if you had the good fortune to be well-fed—which she was, for the grateful locals paid her not only in coin but in food, as well—and avoided serious injury, you could live to a ripe old age.

Of course, that was decades away. She was in her late thirties, which was still her prime, so long as no malady befell her.

The pony whinnied and bucked at movement in the shadows.

"Come on, Toby, keep moving. We're almost home. Gotta get this little one fed and tucked in with the others."

The little goat had been attacked by a wolf, apparently. While its sibling wasn't so fortunate, this little one had managed to escape with his life, having slid under a stump, where the farmer had found the bleating creature some hours later.

She knew it hadn't been the queen's massive beast that had caused the injury. She'd seen its handiwork before. It didn't maim. It killed. And when it killed, it ate all but the bones—and sometimes those as well. No, this had been a run-of-the-mill wolf, and with any fortune, she'd have the youngster healed and back with the rest of his herd in no time. And Farmer Griswald would surely pay her a handsome bonus of potatoes and carrots for her troubles.

"We'll make a nice soup," she murmured to her jittery companion. "But don't fret. I'll save some carrots for you, my friend."

Toby stopped abruptly, eyes wide with fear. A pair of dark figures stood in the middle of the track, blocking their way.

"Please step aside, if you would. I've got to get this injured little one back."

More shapes materialized from the woods on either side, quietly making their way to the road. There were nine of them, and she was surrounded.

"I have no money. And this old pony won't fetch any coin," she said, attempting her most stoic voice.

The men were not impressed.

"That goat will make a nice supper."

"Please, it's just a little one. There's hardly any meat on its bones."

He scoffed. "We'll take whatever we want," the man who seemed to be their leader said. "And I see something else I think will suit us just fine," he said, moving closer.

"Leave me be! Stay back!" she shouted, her voice echoing in

the night.

Her hand reached under her pack where it sat on the cart, pulling a small knife. She brandished it at the bandits, swinging it side to side.

The men just laughed.

"Oh, lassie, you think that wee thing worries me?" the ruffian said, moving in quickly and grabbing her by the wrist.

He plucked the blade from her hand, looked at it a moment, then tossed it into the woods.

"Just a little thing like that?" He laughed, a wicked grin blossoming on his grimy face. "Well, I've got something bigger than that to pierce you with. And I think you——"

That was the last he said. The small knife protruding from his forehead where it had pierced the bone and sunk deep into his skull seemed to have interrupted his train of thought.

Before the man staggered back a pace and fell into a heap, she could have sworn that was *her* knife. But that was impossible. It had been thrown into the darkness.

And from that darkness a new threat emerged. Appearing seemingly out of nowhere amidst the bandits, a man in dark attire now stood. He threw aside his cloak, freeing him for ease of movement, then drew a faintly glowing blade from his waist.

"The Ghost!" one of the bandits gasped before his head was nearly separated from his body in a single stroke.

Rumor had been floating of a strange apparition in the night. One that wandered the lands, protecting the people of the realm, dispatching those who would cause them harm. Of course, the group of roving bandits had taken it as just another fairy tale told to scare away people of their ilk. An apparition disposing of entire bands of dangerous men, then disappearing without a trace? Impossible.

The impossible was rapidly dismantling the incredulous ruffians with deadly efficiency, moving in ways no human could possibly move.

They were right, in a manner of speaking. Their attacker was, indeed, *not* human, and perhaps one might even have gotten the briefest of glimpses of the pale hunter's pointed canine teeth poking from between his lips as he smiled with deadly pleasure.

Any close enough to witness that, however, would join their departed friends straightaway.

Like a whirling dervish of death and destruction, the apparition flew through the men, but did so without making a sound. The only noise that reached the night air was that of dying gasps and the sound of bodies hitting the soil.

The Ghost, as locals had taken to calling him, stood among the dead, surveying his handiwork, then wiped his enchanted weapon on a dead man's tunic before returning it to its sheath. With the blade's glow concealed, the road was once more quite dark but for the moonlight.

The woman stood stock-still, not daring to so much as breathe as she watched the apparition quickly remove all valuables from the men, then throw their bodies to the side of the road with such ease she knew he could not possibly be human. Finally, he pried the small blade from the dead bandit's forehead, wiped it clean, and placed it in the woman's small cart, along with the rest of the seized booty.

There were assorted deadly implements, all of which could be sold or traded, which she was surprised to be given. Then again, from what she'd seen, if he'd wanted her dead, no amount of weapons would keep her from him. But then he truly surprised her, tossing several small pouches of coin he had taken from the fallen men into the cart as well.

"I don't understand," she blurted. "Are you *giving* this to me?"

The shadowy figure merely gave a little nod of the head and a salute farewell, then pulled his cloak tight and literally vanished right in front of her, melting away into the night.

CHAPTER NINE

It wasn't sadism. At least, not the traditional variety.

Charlie had made good on his promise, and early the next morning he joined the men in the training courtyard. Most were not thrilled to be required to rise quite so early, nor were they happy that their first order of business was not going to be strapping on light armor and swinging swords, but rather, going for a run in the hills around the castle.

Mind you, the hills were just that. Hills. Not peaks, mountains, or any other sort of brutal, towering land mass. But for soldiers accustomed to getting their cardio from hefting steel rather than moving their legs, it was enough to make their lungs burn and their limbs feel like wet noodles.

In assessing the men, Charlie had realized that before he could even begin to get into some of Ser Baruud's techniques, he would first need to implement some of his own torture from his days in basic training.

First, he put them through a basic warm-up routine, including push-ups, sit ups, and jumping jacks—which the men had never seen before, and found ridiculous. That is, until they became winded after less than a minute.

With the group sweating and gasping for breath so soon, Charlie decided to skip the rest of the planned warm-up, opting instead to take them out to run that first mile, but slowly, so as to help them limber up and avoid injury.

Grumbles from the men reached his ears. Things along the lines of, "Why is he making us do all of this?" and "Isn't this useless when we need to train in fighting, not child's play?" Then there was Charlie's favorite: "It's easy to come up with all of these torturous things when you're sipping wine on a couch.'"

Charlie walked the ranks, surveying the men. They seemed of decent fitness––Captain Sheeran had made sure of that––but they just needed a little tune-up to reach their next level of potential. And what better way than with some motivation?

He took off his regal robe––which he hated wearing, anyway––and stripped to his tunic and trousers. Dressed like the others, albeit in cleaner clothing, Charlie began a quick warm-up, bouncing on his feet and loosening up.

"Okay, you lot. We're going for a little run," he said, sliding a water skin over his shoulder. "I want each of you to take water with you, and shed any extra gear. Believe me, you'll thank me later."

The men looked amongst themselves with confusion. Was the king going to train *with* them?

Captain Sheeran had a pained look in his eyes. "Sire, may I speak with you a moment?"

"Of course," Charlie said, stepping out of the men's earshot.

"Sire, are you certain you wish to do this? My men are perfectly capable of carrying out your directives without your needing to join them."

"Sheeran, there was an old saying where I came from. 'Leadership requires just two words. Follow me.' I won't ask the men to do anything I wouldn't be willing to do myself."

A curious look passed across the captain's face. "But if you take the men without arms, you will be at risk. At least allow a few their weapons."

Charlie thought on it a moment. "I'll tell you what. That's actually a very good idea."

"Thank you, Sire."

"So, what we'll do is this. Have however many men you feel are needed accompany us on horseback. They can bring extra water and perhaps some food as well, in case anyone gets low blood sugar while we're at it."

"You wish for blood-soaked sugar, Sire?"

"What? Oh, no, no. Nothing like that. What I mean is, pack some fruits and dried meats as well. Perhaps a few extra swords too. That way, should we need them, the men will have access to additional arms. Would that put your mind at ease?"

"Actually, yes."

"Good. And, Captain, I do appreciate your concern with my safety. You're a credit to your position, and I thank you for it." He turned and surveyed the men. "All right. We're going for a little stroll. I know this is new to you, so if you feel you can't keep up, stop and catch your breath, and we'll gather you on the way back."

Charlie knew the men's pride would not allow them to do any such thing.

"Captain, I'll see you and your retinue on the trail shortly."

"Aye, you will, Sire."

"Excellent. The rest of you, with me," he called out, then started off at a very easy run.

It was the first time many of the men had done a run of any distance since their youth, so he made a point to go easy on them this first day. Once they'd gotten over the initial soreness, he'd start upping the pace and mileage.

By the time they returned an hour later, the men looked as if they'd been dragged through hell and somehow crawled back out the other side. The exhausted troops collapsed to the ground, chests heaving, clothing drenched with sweat.

Charlie wasn't even breathing hard.

Wow. Just four miles in over an hour, and they're all toast. Not the fittest of soldiers, I dare say. Okay, I think I'll need to adjust training plans downward a bit more than I expected.

The following day, per Charlie's instructions, the captain had the men do a light jog around the castle. Charlie knew the real pain would hit them the following day, as delayed-onset muscle soreness always did, but at least getting them moving would reduce the impending agony somewhat.

"Okay, listen up," Captain Sheeran called out when they returned, the aching soldiers moving a bit more freely now that their aching limbs had warmed from the exertion. "The king has a new task for you today."

Groans rose from the ranks.

"No, it won't be more running," he added, to the men's delight. "The king wishes you to work your *other* muscles. Every man grab an axe and assemble here in ten minutes. We are heading into the forest."

The men hurried off to do as they were told. Young Owen, loyal to the captain, stepped in close to his commander.

"The king is sticking his nose where it doesn't belong, Captain. And the men are not happy with it."

Sheeran merely grunted. "Best get with the others," he finally said.

"Aye, Captain," Owen replied, and went to join the men.

When all were ready, they began their new task. Deep into the woods they trekked, the trees Charlie wished for them to fell already marked with ribbon tied around them.

"When did the king have time to do this?" one of the men asked.

"I hear he sometimes rises with the sun and goes out alone. Must've been one o' them times, I reckon," another replied.

Captain Sheeran strode to the head of their ranks. "All right, you lot. The task is one you should all be well familiar with. Chop down the trees marked with ribbon, then section them every seven feet. Once that's done, partner with one of the others and carry one of the logs back between you. Is that clear?"

"Yes, Captain," the men shouted in unison.

They set to work with vigor. This was more like it. Swinging hard metal, building their arms and backs for battle. This was useful for fighting, unlike that ridiculous running about. They would likely use the logs to build some sort of battlement, or maybe a siege weapon.

When they returned to the castle many hours later, a great many shovels and spades sat waiting for them.

"His Majesty wishes a hole be dug for each log," Bawb informed the captain. "Three feet deep. Have the men hew the top until it is flat, then place each one upright and secure it with stones and dirt in the hole."

"I fail to see how this is a job for soldiers," Captain Sheeran grumbled. "Men of action should train for action. There are laborers for tasks like this."

"Perhaps. But it is the king's command. I merely relay his wishes, but if you would like to take the matter up with him personally, I'd be happy to pass along your request."

Sheeran forced his ire down. There was no sense arguing with the foppish, pale man. Why the king kept such a weak-spirited aide was beyond him. But they had arrived to the kingdom together, so there was obviously some history between them.

"I will make it so," the captain finally replied.

"Excellent," Bawb said with a grin. "He will be quite pleased. And tomorrow, he requested the men have a recovery day consisting of only a short run around the castle. After that, he wishes them to have the rest of the day to gather their strength.

The following morning, he shall meet with you and instruct as to the new training regimen the men are to begin."

The king's aide then turned and left the men to their labors.

"What did he mean, new regimen?" Owen asked the captain.

"Honestly, lad, I do not know."

CHAPTER TEN

The first week of Charlie's strange new training regimen had left every last soldier sore, exhausted, and more than a little disgruntled at the new king's seemingly insane tasks for them. Some were more vocal about their displeasure than others.

"Standing atop a pole in the ground? For hours?"

"I know, but he is our king," the captain replied. It was becoming a regular utterance.

"And holding cups of water? It makes no sense. That's women's work."

"Yet the men keep failing as if they were as weak as one," the captain hissed, eyeing the king as he walked among the men. "Now keep your voices down and your gripes to yourselves, lest you draw the king's ire."

"I'm not sure he should even *be* king," Owen said, quietly.

It was a thought that had passed through all of their minds at one time or another since Charlie seized the throne from their former liege. But with the mighty dragon on his side, and an apparent talent for combat only recently revealed, none dared move on those impulses.

"Captain? A word, please," Charlie called out to him.

Captain Sheeran gave Owen an odd look, then walked over to the king. "Yes, Sire?"

"The men. How are they doing?"

"Not terribly happy, if I'm to be honest about it, Sire."

"No, not that part. I know they're not happy. *No one* is happy during basic training. But that's not the point. The point is drilling the basics into them. Preparing them so they will *instinctively* survive when they'd otherwise fail. Making them realize they can do more than they previously thought possible. So tell me, it hasn't been long, but do they seem stronger to you? More agile?"

The captain thought about it a moment. It had only been a week, but the men actually did seem to be moving better, and fewer were tumbling from the poles when they'd perform that particular task.

"I think so, Sire," he said. "Fewer are falling, and it seems that they are recovering from the runs faster."

"Excellent."

"But, Sire, when will they begin training in combat once more? These are men of action, and I fear this is not helping morale."

Charlie paused a moment.

Shit. Hadn't really thought about that. Different time, different life. Of course they'd react differently than the people of my Earth. Stupid, Charlie. You've gotta fix this.

"You're right, Captain," he said. "My thanks for bringing this to my attention. I may have been a little overzealous in changing training schedules around on them. What would you suggest as a means to keep the men engaged, while also improving their fitness with the new exercises?"

Sheeran stroked his chin in thought. "Combat training. That's what the men always look forward to the most. If we incorporate that back into their routine, I think it will go a long way toward easing unrest."

A smile slowly spread across Charlie's face. "If it's fighting they want, then it's fighting they'll get."

"Thank you, Sire. I'm sure the men will like the change."

"I don't like this," Owen said, adjusting the belt holding his wooden sword in place on his hip. "No armor? Wooden weapons? What sort of fighting is this?"

"I don't know, but the king himself is leading the demonstration," the grubby soldier at his side said.

"It was luck and tricks that beat Captain Sheeran the other week. This time we're ready. This time, we get him back."

"Whoa. Watch that talk, and keep your voice down. You want to get us both thrown in the dungeon?"

The younger man reluctantly shut his mouth, but the dislike still burned in his eyes.

"All right," Charlie called out to the assembled men. "First training group of the day, and I see you're all outfitted with your short swords. Good."

"Sire, but these are mere wooden sticks. And they are a good deal shorter than our usual weapons."

"Yes, that is true, but I've watched your fighting styles and noticed you expend a lot of energy with swinging and blocking those enormous blades. Now, there are obviously times where, tactically, that is the best option. But there are also times where you may be at an advantage if you surprise your opponent and opt for a shorter blade. It will require modifying your armor to allow for more freedom of motion in the shoulder joints and across the hips, but I think you'll find the new techniques you will be able to employ well worth the slight bit of additional vulnerability."

"Less armor?" the men murmured.

"I understand your concerns, but allow me to show you what

I mean. Captain, please have one of the king's guards over there come attack me."

"Sire?"

"They're in full armor. The usual makeup of plate and chain, if I'm not mistaken."

"You are not. But—"

"Don't worry, Captain. I'll be fine."

"But you have no weapon, Sire. And no armor."

"I have this," he replied, waving his short, wooden sword. "Now, if you please."

Sheeran hesitated.

"If I wasn't clear, that *is* an order, Captain."

The soldier turned on his heel. "You. Simms. Attack the king."

"And don't hold back," Charlie added. "I'll be fine."

The men whispered in disbelief. "It's madness. He'll be cut in half!"

Owen's dark gaze flicked from Simms to the king. "All the better, then," he said, quietly.

"Now, notice the restriction of Simms's hips? The way he has to sort of lumber when he moves?" Charlie ducked a wide swing. "Please, *do* try to actually hit me. That's the entire point, after all."

The men continued circling one another, Charlie effortlessly dodging the armored man's increasingly energetic attacks. Seeing how easily the king could evade him, Simms had finally begun trying in earnest, hoping for at least a glancing blow, if only to prove his worth to his king.

"See here?" Charlie said, slipping under a high attack and jamming his stick into the shoulder joint at the rear of the man's armor. "With a long sword, I could not have made that move. But with this," he waved the wooden implement. "The shorter weapon, in this case, is the deadlier one."

Simms tried to surprise him, dropping an elbow toward the

king, but Charlie kicked the back of his leg at the joint, sending him to one knee. From that angle, he easily stuck his short sword in the small gap between the helmet and armor.

"Again, an angle a long sword could not reach. And see how much easier it would be with more freedom of motion in the joints? Now, obviously, in melee battle with multiple attackers, you'll want your armor. But these modifications should allow you to have the best of both worlds. Mobility, *and* protection."

He turned to the men. "Let's have four more of you join in. The rest of you watch closely. This is your first lesson in the use of the short sword, similar to a gladiator's gladius."

Four men stepped forward and began circling, unsure if they should attack with full force, then remembering how easily the king had moved through their number when first he showed his true skills.

One by one, they attacked, and Charlie easily evaded them, landing blows as he did.

"No, no. Not one at a time like that. In battle, there is no honor. Only survival. Save honor for your daily lives. It would do you well to remember that you cannot live honorably if you are not alive."

Watching from the sidelines, Bawb couldn't help but smile at that. Charlie had used one of his lines, and quite well at that.

The four men with wooden swords, and one in full armor, attacked at once, hoping to overwhelm their adversary. Charlie used their momentum against them, pivoting and sending them careening into one another, all of them tumbling to the ground in a heap.

"This is one of the problems with an uncoordinated attack. Even if you have superior numbers, an agile enough opponent can use your strength against you."

Charlie's gladiatorial perceptions sensed something off. He spun, dropping low and casting a silent *kika rahm* spell just as his hands connected with the midriff of his surprise attacker. Owen flew backward nearly twenty feet, tumbling to the ground.

The captain snatched him up angrily and dragged him to the king. "You dare dishonor yourself and attack our king from behind?"

"He said there is no honor in battle," Owen said plainly. He was entirely unrepentant.

Charlie laughed loud and hard, defusing the tension. He was actually rather annoyed, but he knew the effect his laughter would have.

"Oh, that's wonderful," he said. "Well learned, uh, *Owen*, isn't it?"

"Yes, Sire."

"Very well done. You have potential. I can see it. But I think that's enough demonstration for today. Now, let's get you all to work. I've shown the captain and his assistants the moves I wish you to work on. If you excel at them, we will progress to sparring this afternoon." He looked across the expectant faces. "All right, then. Get to it!"

The men split off into groups to train, the captain pulling Owen aside for a few private words before sending him to join the others. Charlie casually walked over to Bawb. The Wampeh was not amused.

"You used magic, Charlie."

"I know. But I don't think anyone noticed."

"They didn't, and believe me, I was watching. But you might not have been so lucky, and while they may tolerate you as king, for the moment, a wizard ruling them would likely lead to an unpleasant outcome."

Charlie sat quietly a moment. Bawb was right. He had to be more careful. But one thing that had happened stood out.

"Bawb?"

"Yes?"

Charlie held up both arms. They were bare. "No konus. No slaap," he said.

"I noticed that, too, Charlie. It seems your own powers continue to grow."

"I still don't get it. We're back on my planet, and no one here is magic."

"No, but you are bound to a mighty Zomoki."

"Ara's doing this to me?"

"Not directly, but I suspect the unique rays of your system's sun is increasing her power, much as it is flowing into Hunze's locks. And in turn, that is flowing into you. But you must keep these abilities hidden, Charlie. Never let your enemies know your full potential."

"I know. But these are my men, at least."

"And more than one could very possibly stab you in the back one day. It would serve you well to remember that."

"Always such a downer, Bob."

"It is one of my most endearing traits, I am told."

Charlie laughed and turned for the castle. "Come on, let's see what Thomas has in the kitchen. I showed him how to make a hoagie the other day."

"Hoagie?"

"Trust me, you'll love it."

The deadly assassin chuckled, shaking his head, then followed the unlikely king on his quest, not for gold or power, but a hearty sandwich.

CHAPTER ELEVEN

With her king busy helping train the troops for several weeks, Leila had begun to feel her own stirring need to do something more with her days. Castle life was fine and all, but the novelty had quickly worn off.

Essentially, she was beginning to climb the walls.

"I don't need all of this," she said to the armored man riding at her side.

"You are the queen. You must travel with the queen's guard to protect you."

She glanced at the dozen men riding with her on her outing to the neighboring farms of the realm. Plodding alongside them was her faithful four-legged companion. He had been a tiny little thing when she rescued him, but Baloo had rapidly grown into a strapping mountain of an animal.

Leila gave a little whistle, and Baloo trotted up close, his enormous head rubbing Mom's leg. He was so tall now that she could scratch his ears while still mounted on her horse, a stoic animal that had fortunately become accustomed to the giant canine.

Something rustled the leaves. A rabbit or fox, most likely.

Baloo's ears stood up straight. He looked at Leila with questioning eyes.

"Oh, all right. Go get 'em, boy."

Not waiting for any further encouragement, he took off in a flash, a blur of dark gray fur vanishing into the woods. At least it wasn't another farmer's goat, she reasoned.

"You were saying something about protecting me?" she said as he trotted back from the woods just minutes later, specks of blood on his muzzle, but nothing more.

"Well, I––"

"I realize it's your job, so go ahead and do your duty. But really, I think I'll be fine."

They rode for a while, cresting a few hills and crossing streams as she visited farms along the way. Most of the crops were growing well, but a few seemed to be having problems.

That was more her father's area of expertise––Leila had been the animalist at Visla Maktan's estate, while her father handled the grounds––but she had learned plenty from him growing up.

"Let's head over there," she said, nodding to a particularly shoddy-looking series of fields.

"Wouldn't Her Majesty rather visit a more, *productive* farm?"

"Why would I do that? They're not the ones who could use my help," she said, nudging her horse onto the muddy path toward what appeared to be the main farmhouse.

It was more of a hut, truth be told, but Leila found the small structure warmed her heart, reminding her of a simple, happy life with her father on the visla's grounds not so long ago. Before she was forced to flee.

The man of the house came rushing out, followed by his wife and daughter. A few others continued to work, glancing up with curiosity. Apparently, they were seasonal help, exchanging their muscle for room and board.

"My queen? To what do we owe the honor?" the farmer blurted, his face flushed.

"We were just riding by, surveying the lands, and I noticed your farm appears to be having something of a rough time at the moment. What happened?"

"The pigs, they've been rooting the fields when they should be in the hills looking for mushrooms. With the extra effort required to repair the damage they've done, some of the crops didn't come in on time, and the land is angry with us for it."

She scanned the fields. Indeed, the soil in several areas appeared unhealthy, their crops blighted and lacking nutrients.

"Have you burned the crops and turned the soil?" she asked.

"I'm sorry, did you say *burn*?"

"Yes."

"I––no, we've never burned them. We use every bit we can, and––"

"Burn the ones not faring well or past harvest," she said. "Sometimes a touch of fire and death is all the soil needs to be renewed. I believe this will help alleviate some of your problems."

"But the lost crops––"

"Don't worry. I'll request some neighboring farms send you a portion of theirs to tide you over. Enough to see you through the replenishing period."

"But, their crops? Won't they be selling them at market?"

"Yes, but helping their fellow farmers in a time of need is what good people do. And one day, they too may find themselves in need of assistance. At such a time, I'd expect you to return the favor."

"Of course. Gladly!"

"Good. Then it is settled. I'll make the arrangements, so do not fear going hungry. Now, how about your crop rotations? Have you replanted in opposite fields?"

"Not for several seasons. It was extra work, and things seemed to be growing well enough."

"That's also likely a part of your problem. Rotating crops is vital to ensure the soil is kept healthy and not overused. A little burn off, a little rotation, and I think in just a few months you should recover from this bump in the road."

The confidence in their new queen's voice gave them hope where there had formerly been none. Most unusual, the newcomer. Unusual, and knowledgeable.

"Majesty, if I may ask, how does my queen know so much about farming?"

Leila climbed down from her horse and glanced at the pigsty, where a dozen large sows were making quite a racket. She then began removing her riding coat and finery.

"My father worked the land," she replied. "Much like you do, though he also used a konus often enough."

"A what?"

She realized she had brought up magic, a no-no in their new home.

"Uh, a farming tool where I come from," she covered. "Anyway, I learned by watching him work the land when I was a girl."

"You were a commoner?"

"Do not speak to the queen this way!" her guard barked.

"No, it's okay. There is no offense taken from a genuine question," she said, stepping in. "Now, to answer your question, you could say I was a commoner. Not royalty, that's for sure. My father worked the land, and I tended the animals. Speaking of which, let me have a look at your pigs. I may be able to help with their troublesome ways. I'll be right back."

She placed her coat on her saddle and walked right for the pigs, ignoring the mud sucking at her boots, to everyone's dismay. The sows were rowdy, all right, but her gift with animals seemed to carry over to those of this world.

"You need to stay out of the fields and help find mushrooms," she scolded them. The pigs squealed with discontent. "Hey, I'm just relaying what's expected of you. You're damaging the crops, which costs the farmer time, money, and food. But if you'd rather keep acting up than help out, I'm sure the farmer could fetch a good price for you lot at the butcher."

The pigs fell silent. They may not have understood what the strange greenish-toned lady was saying––not exactly, anyway–– but the gist got through.

"Good. I'll let him know," she said with a satisfied nod, then walked back to the waiting men.

"I don't think you'll have any problems from the pigs anymore," she said. "Now, let's see about getting this replanting going."

She unbuttoned her regal dress, drawing gasps from the women as she did. Her guard were also in shock, but having never experienced such a situation, had no idea what to do with a defrocking royal.

Leila whipped off her dress, revealing comfortable trousers and a simple tunic worn underneath. Her guards let out a sigh of relief.

"Right. Let's get cracking."

Her lead guard had dismounted when she had, and now quickly strode up to her. "A queen does not work! And in mud, no less!"

"Well, this one does," she replied, picking up a spade and walking into the fields.

The farmer, his wife, and the rest of the residents of the small plot, all fell in and followed her, ready to break soil as well as a sweat alongside their strange new queen.

The workers were shocked, but not nearly as much as the ladies of the farm, who were also in awe, but shared smiles among themselves as well. The queen was one of them, and had endeared herself to the family and earned their respect, not with words or gifts, but her actions.

Hours later, muddy and glowing with the joy of a good day's manual labor loosening her muscles, Leila cleaned up as best she could with the women of the house, then mounted her horse. Baloo was off in the woods again, but she knew he'd come along soon enough.

"Okay, I tied ribbons to stakes in each of the fields you should burn. Once they've smoldered out, turn the soil and let the ash sink in. They should be ready for a new planting come spring."

"But the ground is damp, and the crops may not burn."

Their queen gave them a knowing smile. "Don't worry. Just stay clear of those fields. I'll have a friend take care of it."

With that, she and her guards rode off, leaving the farmers to chatter and replay the day's events among themselves. Leila's reputation would strengthen after today, and her standing in the land would grow. Villagers and farm folk talked, and she was sure to be a hot topic of discussion.

CHAPTER TWELVE

The royal procession slowly made its way back toward the castle, the queen's guards flanking Leila on the dirt road. She had managed to clean off nearly all of the mud and muck from herself before donning her dress and coat, though her trousers had acquired a decent layer of dirt. As a result, she had to shed them, stowing them in a saddle bag for proper cleaning back at the castle.

A happy smile was plastered to her face. It had felt *good* working with her hands. This queen thing was getting old, and fast. How anyone could live such a passive life was beyond her.

From the woods, a familiar, furry shape came trotting up to join them. His snout, she noted, was bloody yet again.

"Baloo, what did you get up to? That's not from a rabbit, is it? I know you're a growing boy, but no more killing livestock, you hear me?"

The enormous canine looked chided, understanding his mother's tone, if not every word spoken. The men couldn't help but grin. Their new queen certainly had a way with animals, and since they'd been on her protective detail, they'd been witness to a number of unusual situations. Least of which was her scolding her huge and deadly pet.

"Oh, Charlie is going to be so upset. Another dead goat, I'd wager." She turned to the youth assigned as her aide for the day's ride. "Would you please make a quick ride around and see what he killed, and if possible, whose it was? I want to send them payment for their animal."

"Of course, Highness," he replied before racing off into the woods.

"Fearless lad, that one," the head of the guard noted.

"Why do you say that?"

"Well, he just saw a bloody beast strut out o' those woods, yet in he plunges, carefree as can be."

"Well, it was only Baloo," she countered.

"Aye, but who knows what else might be lurking there."

He had a point. There were plenty of dangerous creatures in these parts. Fortunately, *her* dangerous creatures put the others to shame.

Almost as if on cue, an enormous shadow passed overhead, circling the party as they rode. All heads turned skyward, watching the mighty, red dragon as she soared above before coming in low, flapping her mighty wings and landing beside the road in a cloud of dust. The deep green Magus stone hanging around Leila's neck beneath her clothes flashed a momentary warmth, the power-storing gem having become attuned to the Zomoki's power and even absorbing a little trickle of it over the time they spent together.

Ara had fared well since arriving on Earth. Better than well, actually, the solar system's sun's rays were doing her enormous good, and her scales were a resplendent, deep, shiny red. Ever since her rebirth after drinking the waters from the remains of Visla Balamar's kingdom, she had been buzzing with power and health. Now, it seemed she was gradually adding to that.

Much like Hunze, she was very positively affected by the

yellow sun's radiation. A constant slow feed of power was healing and nourishing her. Even when she settled into a cavern in the distant mountain range for a nap, the planet's absorbed radiation still trickled into her, though at a minuscule rate.

Her giant, golden eyes watched the procession approach. She was careful not to speak with others present, but made eye contact with Leila, giving her a slight nod. The guards were still reticent in her presence. She may have been their king and queen's pet, but several had been present when she burned the prior king alive and swallowed him whole, horse, armor, and all. They were glad she was on their side, but she still terrified them.

Another aspect of her relationship with the king was the bond they shared. None would dare raise a finger against him, lest they face the mighty dragon's wrath, for she would always come when the king called for her. In fact, some said she knew when he wanted her, arriving even if he didn't say a word. And when he spoke to her, it seemed she understood every word he said.

She was his guardian, and all who encountered the dragon were awestruck.

Except Baloo, it seemed.

The giant canine bounded through the field, letting out a low, rumbling yowl, playfully nipping at her massive feet. Ara's eyes held a look of love and amusement as she played back, gently knocking him over with her tail as he bounced and leapt through the air with his limitless energy.

"Come on, Baloo. Leave Ara alone. We're going home."

He was a little too worked up to notice Leila's words, but Ara didn't seem to mind. Baloo was part of their unlikely little family, and she adored him as much as the rest of her friends.

Friends. Had anyone told the mighty Zomoki she would befriend a Wampeh assassin, a half-Alatsav girl, and a man from a galaxy far beyond her own, she would have laughed.

Or eaten them.

Or both.

But life works in strange and unexpected ways, and the unlikely allies had become far more than just that. For the first time in hundreds of years, Ara felt like a part of something. A family.

"Hey, Ara," Leila called out. "I was wondering if you could do me a little favor. That farm just over the hill? They had a run of bad crops and have several fields that need a good burning before they till and replant. If you wouldn't mind, I'm sure they'd appreciate you torching those for them. I marked them with ribbons on stakes, so they're easy to spot."

The dragon rose to her feet, looked in the direction Leila had mentioned, and took to the air with a single flap of her wings, the wind nearly knocking several men from their horses.

"Our king and queen are allied with fearsome beasts," one of the younger guards said, awed by the sight.

"Aye. But the big one there has much more self-control than the queen's beast. None have seen it hunt in these parts. Wherever it feeds, our lands remain unscathed. And protected," he added, watching her fly over the rise.

"Lucky for us," his friend said.

"Aye. And heaven help any who would take up arms against us."

CHAPTER THIRTEEN

The farmer's fields soon lay smoldering. The Zomoki's flames had made quick work of the failed crops, despite any lingering dampness in the soil or plant matter. Dragon's breath was not something to be trifled with, and Ara's was strong, even by those standards.

Once she'd assisted Leila with her little project, she took to the skies, soaring high above the kingdom. Though they could not share her vision as she flew, Ara and Charlie's bond nevertheless allowed them to communicate silently across increasingly larger distances.

"Everything looks good from up here," she told him. *"I helped Leila out with a little side project, as well. It felt nice getting a good burn going."*

Charlie tried to keep his attention on the men pleading their case before him, despite the voice in his head. He was king, and he was expected to adjudicate over such matters. Ara had been listening in, as she could do when he opened his ears to her mind.

"It seems like a simple solution. The stream moved due to heavy

rain the other week, and when it did, their property lines changed. If they were foolish enough to use something as impermanent as that as a legal boundary, then it's their own fault, and they should have to live with their foolishness."

"Always the understanding one, aren't you?" Charlie replied as the men pleaded their cases.

"It's simple logic. You needn't waste so much of your time on trifles, Charlie. You're the king. Act like it."

"I am acting like it. But I'm also new to these lands, and if I can foster a bit more goodwill from the locals, then all the better. Now leave me alone for a bit, I need to pay attention."

"Fine. I'm going to hunt. I've discovered a wonderful type of beast across the sea."

"Wait, where are you going, exactly?"

"Don't worry, Charlie. I'll be back shortly. You forget, I can easily exit the atmosphere as I please, which means it takes little time and little energy to circumnavigate the globe, if I wish."

"Ah, yes. A dragon-shaped ICBM hurtling through the skies," he replied with a silent chuckle. "All right, then. Go hunt. We'll catch up later."

"Indeed, we will. Have fun listening to peasants."

"Have fun eating furry things."

Ara felt their connection sever as she pushed herself high through the atmosphere, until she was comfortably in a low orbit above the Earth.

It really is a rather lovely little planet, she mused, then began her descent to the far away land she had discovered in her explorations.

She had stumbled upon the vast, golden plains of grain and unusual beasts while searching out new places to bask in the sun a few days prior. She had been lying in an enormous open expanse when a rumbling roused her from her slumber.

What could that be? she wondered, lifting her head and craning her neck.

What she saw was impressive, even for a space dragon from another galaxy.

"There are millions of them," she marveled as the ground shook and the skies filled with dust.

The herd, if something so massive could be called that, consisted of beasts that were somewhat similar to cows, she supposed, but much darker, and furrier, with tiny, curved horns atop their thick skulls. The creatures were very stocky up front, possessing dense muscle that allowed them to charge up hills and over obstacles with ease.

Ara swatted one with her tail, quickly roasting it and swallowing it with relish.

"Oh, these are delicious!" she exclaimed. "And there are literally *millions* of them."

It was true. Centuries before European invaders had deposited the forebearers of the men who would nearly lead to their extinction, the great plains of the continent were teeming with what settlers would eventually call buffalo. Only a handful of indigenous people were on hand to hunt them, their kills not making so much as a dent in the population.

Ara had watched the natives—primitives with what appeared to be some sort of nature religion shaping their beliefs. Whatever the case, she was not concerned with them as a possible threat. And now that she had this wonderful food source, she needn't hunt anywhere near Charlie's realm, sparing the locals any unfortunate frights.

She filled her belly with several more of the beasts, then took to the skies, breathing deep, sniffing out the freshest, cool waters, bubbling up from below the surface. She found a large cavern in a desert patch of land farther west. The tunnel went down and down, and as it did, she felt the crystalline properties of the cave's walls soothing her body. It was in no way comparable to the waters of the Balamar Wasteland, but it felt nice, just the same.

So many things about Charlie's homeworld had restorative properties to her kind, it seemed, and she was delighted for it. Crawling under a low overhang, she squeezed her way into the next chamber.

"Ah, there you are," she cooed, spotting the burbling source of the small flow.

She bent and drank deeply, the waters cool and fresh, untainted by any pollutant and charged with minerals and the sun's rays that filtered through the planet's crust. It was just the sort of place her kind sought out to lay their eggs, or in rarer cases, to lay their heads down for a nice hibernation for a few years. A long time for men, but a mere nap for creatures who lived as long as the Zomoki did.

But that was not on the menu today, and Charlie was expecting her back, so Ara made her way back to the surface, taking to the skies once more. A quick hop outside the atmosphere and she was dropping back to her friend's kingdom in no time. No sooner had she dropped below the clouds than she felt their connection once more.

It had been growing stronger. What had once only worked when they were in each other's company had expanded, and significantly. Just one more unusual thing she shared with her unlikely bonded friend.

"Glad you're back," she felt him say.

"Back and sated. I really should bring you back one of those beasts to try. Quite delicious."

"Thanks, Ara, but maybe we'll do dragon barbecue another time. Thomas made up something special tonight, and I wouldn't want to offend him."

"Of course not."

Ara settled down just outside the castle in a glen she had more or less taken for her own. At this point, everyone was accustomed to seeing her there, so her arrival didn't cause the commotion it had in their first weeks on the new planet.

Charlie looked out the window and admired the beauty of his unlikely new home. Then he made his way to join the others. He was sure they'd have plenty to tell him over dinner, as they so often did in their strange new home.

CHAPTER FOURTEEN

Thomas had laid out an impressive spread. The local farmers, it seemed, had been benefiting from an unusually robust harvest. As such, the new king and his friends were the beneficiaries of the bounty their cook whipped up, the man enjoying the freedom of menu selections his new king allowed.

"Whatever you think," Charlie typically told him. "You're the expert, after all."

For Thomas, the contrast to the previous king was drastic. *That* royal had insisted on a very particular selection, and if things strayed from his menu of choice, more often than not the poor chef would find himself berated. Cooking for King Charlie, however, was a joy.

"Oh, Thomas, that smells wonderful!" Leila said as a bowl of steaming stew was placed in front of her.

"Thank you, Highness. I was trying something a bit different today––with the help of His Majesty."

"Hey, don't look at me. This is all you, Thomas. And she's right, you know. It smells wonderful."

"Thankee, Sire. It was that butter and flour thing I saw you mixing up at lunch the other week."

"Oh, the roux. It doesn't have to be butter, you know. Any fat will do in a pinch. But yeah, it really rounds the flavors nicely, I think."

"Your tarragon and chicken—what did you call it? *Chowder?*"

"You've got it right. Chowder. Well, of sorts, anyway."

"It was a revelation. And since then, I've been experimenting."

"And we're quite happy being your test subjects," Bawb said, appreciatively sipping a hot spoonful of the stew. "You've made some impressive changes to your cooking regimen, Thomas."

The man beamed with pride. It was a night-and-day difference, this new royal entourage. The former king was always a bitter man, but when his queen succumbed to an illness a few years prior, he had become even more difficult to please than before.

"Sarah! The bread!" he called to the kitchen. A moment later, his baking assistant brought out a piping-hot loaf of multi-grain bread, baked with rosemary in the crust.

"Oh, my!" Hunze exclaimed when she took a bite. For the often-quiet young woman to blurt out her surprise, the bread must have really reached her on a visceral level. "This is divine, Thomas. The aroma, the crunch of the crust. I think it may be your best yet!"

The cook blushed. The slightly yellow girl was so pure and innocent, her appreciation genuine and untainted by false flattery. She absolutely loved baked goods of any type, and had been spending more and more time in the kitchens of late, watching and learning.

He was never quite sure of her exact status on the king's staff. She had been introduced to the household as a servant, but given her close friendship with the king's adviser, and the fact that she dined with the king and queen regularly, he suspected she was perhaps something more than just a servant girl. Whatever she was, however, she was a delight.

"I can smell that all the way out here," Ara noted. *"I remember his output when you first arrived. Your cook is definitely benefiting from your influence."*

"Ha, thanks. You know, if you want, I can save you some," Charlie replied.

"Though I am quite satisfied from my earlier meal, I would actually appreciate that. A little taste of something new would be nice."

Charlie laughed to himself. *"It'd have to be a little taste. Given how big you are, a full serving for one of us would be no more than a drop on your tongue. I'll ask Thomas to bring you a dish."*

"Thank you, Charlie."

"Thomas, a moment, please," he said, calling the man over.

"Yes, Sire? Is everything to your liking?"

"Absolutely. In fact, Ara thinks this smells wonderful. Would you please bring a small tureen out to her? I know she's enormous, but even a little taste would be a treat."

"Of course, Sire. It would be my pleasure," he replied, hurrying back to the kitchen to fill a dented, older vessel with the stew.

Thomas had been terrified of Ara at first. The sheer size of the dragon, with teeth that could rip him to shreds with the slightest of effort, made his bowels loosen––a visceral, primal fear response in the face of a true apex predator. It was hard-wired into his DNA, a survival instinct honed over his species' evolution. But as he spent more time around the king's mighty pet, he gradually became more comfortable with her.

The thing was, she seemed to understand him when he spoke, her giant, golden eyes showing far more intelligence than any beast of the woods. And when he had first served her an herb-encrusted goat, roasted specifically for her pleasure at the king's request, she had been exceedingly careful taking it from him. Her spatial awareness and care for his well-being was not lost on him.

Now when the king asked him to bring her a taste of something, he would make the trek to see her alone, unafraid, and actually a bit happy at the prospect of giving a treat to so mighty a creature.

It would be a little while before the next course was served, so he took the opportunity to carry down the tureen of stew while it was still hot. The path was clear, and Ara, knowing her new friend would be bringing her a sample, had moved to just outside the castle walls. Her sudden appearance there had startled some of the guards atop the parapet. For such an enormous creature, she could move quite silently when she wanted.

"Hello, Ara," the cook said as he stepped outside the walls. "A little treat from the kitchen tonight. I hope you enjoy it."

Ara lowered her head to the ground and opened her mouth, slowly. She could have just picked up the tureen and dumped its contents with a flip of her tongue, but she felt it was important to build trust with the human.

Thomas leaned into her mouth, no longer afraid she would eat him whole, as he had feared the first time the king had requested he feed his pet. The contents pooled in the middle of the dragon's enormous tongue, and he stepped clear. Ara then gently closed her mouth and savored the new flavor.

"This is indeed delicious," she told Charlie. *"Please, give Thomas my thanks when he returns to you."*

"Will do," Charlie replied.

Ara smiled and nodded to Thomas. One day, perhaps she'd speak to him. But that would be some ways away. For now, she kept that ability secret. As the Wampeh often noted, one should not give up an advantage lightly.

"Well, then. Hope you liked that," Thomas said, then waved his farewell and headed back into the castle walls.

Ara quietly rose to her feet and returned to her favorite glen to turn in for the night.

CHAPTER FIFTEEN

Leila was famished from her hard day's labors, tucking into her stew with gusto, mopping up the dregs with thick slices of bread. Charlie, Bawb, and Hunze watched, sharing an amused glance.

"What?" Leila asked, noting the attention.

"Nothing," Charlie said with a chuckle. "You're just making quick work of that. I'm glad we've got another course coming."

Leila slowed down, self-consciously eating at a more ladylike pace.

"I was hungry."

"I could see. Busy day?"

Her eyes brightened. "It was wonderful. I helped a farmer with their pigs, and—"

"With *pigs*?" Bawb interrupted.

"Yes, pigs. They were acting up, and had damaged some crops. So I had some words with them."

"And they'll behave, now, I assume?" Charlie asked.

"The animals of this world seem to be more receptive than many from mine. I'm confident they'll not be a problem moving forward," she said. "Plus, the threat of becoming dinner may have helped," she added with a grin.

The group laughed merrily, even Bawb the assassin finding her threat to the porcine troublemakers amusing.

"It's impressive, really," she continued. "These people work so hard and persevere in the face of adversity, despite not having any magic to aid them. It's so much effort from each of them, and on a daily basis, no less, but they don't give up. It's inspiring. Their methods are a bit lacking, though, but with a little guidance, they could be so much more productive."

"Ah, now I'm seeing why you were so hungry today. Always eager to help. You decided to get your hands dirty, didn't you?" Charlie said with a warm smile.

Leila blushed slightly. "Well, with just a little nudge in the right direction, their crops would be much more bountiful. And now they should hopefully not have to work quite as hard, while achieving better results."

"Work smarter, not harder," he said.

"Exactly. And I may steal that line," she added.

"Yours for the taking," he said, the two sharing a lingering look.

Bawb broke the moment, interjecting as he was wont to do. "A queen does not work in the dirt, Leila. It is just not done, even on this world."

"Well, now it is. And don't worry, I won't make a regular thing of it."

"People will talk."

"Let them. If all they can hold against me is helping my—I can't believe I'm saying this—my *subjects* be more prosperous, then that's a pretty good bit of gossip, if you ask me."

"Perhaps," Bawb relented. "But what of Baloo?"

The freshly washed beast raised his head from his spot beside his mama.

"What of him?"

"He can't keep eating livestock, Leila. Another goat today, I hear," Bawb noted.

"How did you know about that?"

"I have my ways. But the point is, whatever goodwill you have earned from your little outings, his jaws are negating on a regular basis."

Charlie sighed and pinched the bridge of his nose between his eyes. "Bob, make a note to pull some coin from the coffers. We'll ride out to see them tomorrow to pay the owners and apologize for Baloo."

"A king does not apologize," he replied.

"Well, this one does."

"No. This one does not," Bawb replied, a steely look in his eye. "Some lines even you must not cross. To do so lowers the legitimacy of the crown."

"But I—"

"No. That is final," he said.

Charlie looked around, but he knew Bawb would not make such statements if any staff were within earshot.

"He's trying to make amends for Baloo's actions, while addressing the concerns of the people *before* they become complaints," Hunze said. "Surely that is a kingly thing to do."

Bawb sighed, but slowly nodded his acquiescence. "A king *can* make reparations," the Wampeh finally relented. "But through an envoy, not in person. And, yes, he can even *signal* or hint at an apology, but the king does not—must not—explicitly apologize for such trivial matters."

"Good enough for me," Charlie said.

Hunze reached over and squeezed the Wampeh's arm warmly, and Charlie could have sworn, just for an instant, a small bit of color appeared in the pale man's cheeks.

"So, Bob. It's been a few months, now. What have you managed to suss out in the royal records?"

"The books are a mess, for one," he grumbled. "They rely heavily on taxes, yet have seemed to spend those revenues most frivolously, and with nearly all of the benefit going to the largest land owners, but not trickling down to the average citizens. It's not sustainable."

"Sounds familiar," Charlie said with a wry grin. Thousands of years hadn't changed the games of the ultra-wealthy, it seemed.

"Across both of our galaxies, this happens far too often. And I hear the tax collectors can sometimes be a bit heavy-handed as well. The former king was respected, and ruled with a firm hand, but he was certainly *not* loved. But we're in a grace period at the moment. Things are a bit up in the air now that you've arrived. You've shaken things up, and in a good way, for the most part."

"So, the natives aren't too restless, then."

"Not terribly. And as you've already noted, Leila is rather adored. Her actions are most definitely not those of a queen, but then, that may well be contributing to her acceptance by the locals. And your guard seems to be over their initial displeasure at your means of seizing the throne."

"Hey, to be fair, the old king didn't give me much choice," Charlie said.

"He's right. That man was threatening all of us," Hunze noted.

"Exactly. So they didn't have much reason to be upset about it," the king said.

Bawb shook his head. "No, Charlie. Your taking the throne by force was not the problem. Having Ara do it for you was."

"Ah, that."

"Yes, that."

"But you have since proven yourself a warrior, and they undoubtedly realize you would have defeated the king on your own anyway. They were loyal to the man, nevertheless. It just takes time to build new allegiances."

"And Captain Sheeran? He seems to be coming around, though, admittedly, he wasn't thrilled about the new training regimen."

"He's a tough nut, Charlie. You bested him in single combat, and you have his respect for that. But I fear he may never be a true ally. Time will tell."

"What about the men? I mean, if they are coming around, but Sheeran isn't, where do they stand? I don't want to have loyalties split between us."

"They're getting used to the new training, though it was very hard on morale at first."

"To be expected."

"Indeed. But now they are over that first hump and are seeing rapid improvements in both their fitness as well as abilities, and their confidence is growing daily. They are still loyal to the captain, of course, and they may not have liked the change, at first, but you've made a lot of progress."

"I guess that's all I can ask, for now. So we're good, then?"

"I think so, yes, though the castle's staff is a bit shocked at some of Leila's changes to the grounds."

"Hey, I'm just trying to brighten things up a bit," she said between mouthfuls. "Just because the place has been this way for decades doesn't mean it can't be updated. And now that the basic work is done, the new gardens should bloom in a few months, though that giant stump is still in the way and messing up the flow."

"It was a rather large tree, from what I can gather," Bawb said. "It broke in a storm a few years back from I've been told."

"Well, I may have to just burn the cursed thing to get it gone, but its roots are just so deep."

"And you wouldn't want to flood the kitchens and servants' quarters with smoke," Hunze pointed out.

"True," Leila replied. "You've been spending a fair amount of time there, watching Thomas and the others."

"Yes. I wish to learn to bake. I want to learn to be of use."

"You do not have to do this," Bawb said.

"But I want to. You've shown me a new life. One of freedom I never knew existed. If I can contribute, even in this small way, it would be a great joy to me."

"Can't argue with that," Charlie said, drinking deep from his chalice. "Bob, not to change the subject, but I was thinking, we really should make a royal trip to visit this winemaker tomorrow to commend him on his product."

"A good suggestion. The king is a figurehead in times of peace, and a visit to brighten spirits goes a long way to earn goodwill."

"Exactly what I was thinking!" Charlie said. "I like the sound of that. Spirit-brightening is always a good thing."

"And it's also an excuse to sample his other wines," Bawb said with a knowing wink.

"Well, I suppose I wouldn't be opposed to that," Charlie said with an amused grin.

The group chattered warmly the rest of the meal, laughing and enjoying one another's company. They especially delighted in the sweets Thomas had whipped up for their dessert, Hunze particularly, as she had never had such treats in her captive years.

It was getting late when Charlie and Leila finally retired to their chambers, bellies full of good food, good wine, and good conversation.

"Here, let me help," he said, pulling her boots off while she sat on the edge of her bed.

She may have put the dress back on to keep up the queenly image, but her choice of footwear was still that of an adventurous animalist from a faraway galaxy.

Charlie placed her boots together on the floor and rose, crossing to his little side room as he loosened his tunic. He paused at the door a moment.

"Good night, Leila."

"Good night, Charlie," she replied with warmth in her eyes.

He smiled, a happy feeling growing in his chest, then closed the door, leaving them both to their individual slumber.

CHAPTER SIXTEEN

Only a handful of guards traveled with the king and his aide the following afternoon as they rode to greet the favored winemaker at his grounds. The captain rode with him, of course, and his young helper came along as well, though is seemed Owen would have rather been anywhere else.

Word was sent ahead that the king and his small retinue would be visiting, along with a small purse of coin to cover costs for a late lunch. Charlie could not be seen paying for a meal, as king. He could, however, ensure his visit placed no undue hardship on his subject. Especially one who made such delicious wine.

The road passed many farms along the way, each specializing in one thing or another. Some appeared to be having a bountiful year, while others seemed to have fallen on hard times. This concerned Charlie. Leila had mentioned it previously, but seeing it with his own eyes, he couldn't help but feel for the poor farmers.

Up ahead, a pair of well-attired men were roughing up a peasant, Charlie noted.

"Bob, you see that?"

"I do, indeed."

"Looks like Danny Cooper. And the damn taxman again," Owen said aloud, quickly silencing his tongue.

"Taxman? I've not met him for some odd reason. Come on, Bob. Time to meet the staff," Charlie said, spurring his horse into a trot.

As they drew near, Owen's hunch was confirmed. It was, indeed, Danny Cooper, a man he'd known pretty much his whole life. Standing over him was an enormous brute of a man, his close-shorn head sweating in the sun. And with good reason. Beating on an innocent was hard work, after all.

At his side stood a slight man in expensive garb, watching the proceedings but not taking part.

The brains and the brawn, Charlie noted as he rode closer.

"You there. Stop beating on that man!"

"I'm just doing me job," the larger man replied.

The smaller watched the king approach with distaste in his eyes. Both seemed irritated to have their work interrupted, and obviously did not appreciate having to bow to their new king. In the few months he'd been there, he'd already made something of a mess of more than one of their projects.

"Are you all right?" he asked the man on the ground.

"I'll live," he replied, pain in his voice.

The tax collector flashed a look at his lackey, who immediately slapped the downed man.

"Enough of that!" Charlie roared.

"But he's a peasant, Sire. His kind does not dare speak to the king," the small man said.

"I decide that," Charlie said. "And as ruler of the people of these lands, all should have access to speak to their king."

His guards looked at one another in shock. The previous king would stand for no such behavior, but the new one seemed to genuinely care what his subjects thought. It was an unusual change, and they weren't certain it was for the better.

"Now, tell me. What's the problem here?" Charlie asked the farmer.

"I'm sorry, Sire. It's just, I am unable to pull in my harvest in time to pay your tax collector."

"Which could be problematic, of course," Charlie said. "But what's different from other years? I assume this isn't an annual problem."

"Oh no, Sire. Normally it's no problem at all, but this past year my eldest son left, taking to the roads to seek glory and fortune. With him gone, we've been short-handed. And when the taxman took one of our oxen to compensate for the lowered payment, well, we found ourselves without the beast to pull the plows and help work the land. The beast covered our debt, but without it, I'm afraid we just can't keep up with the taxman's demands."

The little man was seething. He glanced at his lackey, who raised his hand to strike the peasant again.

"You will not strike that man!" Charlie shouted. "What the hell is wrong with you people? You can't beat money out of someone. All you'll do is break something, and worse yet, render him unable to work. Is that what you want? For him to be incapable of paying taxes due to injuries you cause?"

"Uh, no, Sire," the brute replied.

"And you? What do you have to say?"

"Of course, Sire. Whatever His Majesty wishes."

Bawb leaned in close and whispered into Charlie's ear. "That one is going to be a problem."

Charlie looked at the bruised man, then glanced over at his fields. The ground seemed good, but it did need tilling and planting in the already-harvested fields. His other crops were also in need of attention, but in the form of a rapid harvest. Minus his son and ox, it was clear he could not possibly hope to accomplish both.

A decision was made, but Charlie wondered how well it would be received.

Oh well. Fuck 'em. I'm the king, and what I say, goes, he reasoned.

"Okay, I have a solution to your problem. You," he said to the brute. "What is your name?"

"Clay, Sire."

"Very well, Clay. I have a new task for you. I assume you wish to do your duty and collect taxes from this man?"

"Aye."

"Very well, then. Your wish shall be granted. Your new duty is to arrive here at sunrise each day to help till the soil, plant new crops, and harvest the old ones. In this manner, you shall make this fellow able to pay his taxes."

"But, Sire, I'm a—"

"I'm sorry, did you think you had a say in this matter?" Charlie said, flashing his best we-are-not-amused regal look.

"No, Sire. My apologies."

"Good. This is my decision, and you shall start tomorrow. Now, as for you," he said, turning to the tax collector. "You are not of strong back, like your lackey here. But you will find new use with the castle's cleaning staff. You are to report to Gwendolyn in the morning for your new task."

"But, Sire, the taxes—"

"Bob will oversee the allocation of taxes for the time being. Serve me well in your new positions and perhaps you shall see yourself returned to your old ones. But for now, do as you are told. Is that quite clear?"

"Yes, Sire," both men replied.

"Good. And you. Mister Cooper, is it not?"

"Aye, Sire. You know me?"

"My man Owen here does," he said, gesturing to the youth among his men. "If you have further difficulties, I am ordering you to report them to me or my men at once. This seems to have been an avoidable situation, and I would rather not have it repeated, if at all possible."

"Of course, Highness."

"Excellent. Now, if you'll excuse me, we have a winery to visit."

CHAPTER SEVENTEEN

As Charlie and his men rode on toward the winery, he couldn't help but notice the area seemed a bit sparsely traveled that day. Normally they'd have encountered at least a few of the locals on the way. It seemed the taxman's presence had frightened everyone back to their farms for the day. The adults, anyway.

A young boy of no more than ten ran out from the trees and crossed the nearby field, stopping to stare in awe at the men on horseback.

"Are you the Dragon King?" he asked with bright eyes.

Charlie leaned down from his mount. "Yes, I am. And who might you be?"

"Stuart Hopper, Sire."

"Well, Stuart, it's a pleasure to meet you. I assume you live around these parts?"

"Oh, yes, Sire!"

Charlie dug in a pouch on his hip and took out a single coin. "We're heading to the winemaker's vineyards, but we seem to have gotten a bit turned around. Might you show us the way?" he said, throwing a little wink to Captain Sheeran.

"I know where it is!"

"Excellent," he said, tossing the boy the coin. "Payment for your services, young Stuart. Now, lead the way."

The lad trotted off to the head of the procession, glad of his new job. Sheeran looked at Charlie but said nothing.

Probably thinks it's a waste of a coin. But little things build lifelong memories, and this kid's gonna think King Charlie is awesome, he mused with a little grin.

The recent rains had rutted the road a bit, forcing a detour around a particularly bogged down muddy section.

"This way," Stuart called back, running ahead along the narrower track that went around the obstructed path.

A loud crack pierced the air, followed by a rumble.

Then Stuart was gone.

"Sire!" Captain Sheeran called out, grabbing his reins and pulling the horse to an abrupt halt.

"Yes, I see it, Captain," Charlie said, taking the reins back, then hopping down from his horse to examine the sinkhole that had swallowed the poor lad.

"Is he down there?" one of the men asked.

"Of course he is," another replied. "The question to be asking is if he's alive."

"Shut up, both of you!" Charlie barked.

The men did as he commanded, and the king strained his ears as he leaned toward the edge of the hole in the path. A faint crying could be heard, but judging by the sound, he was quite a fair way down.

"Water and limestone, Sire," Sheeran said, eyeing the edges of the hole. "Rock just below the soil. It must've been eaten away by the last rains. Probably loosened things up just enough for the lad to shake them free."

Limestone did indeed run all over the region, but Charlie still had to marvel that of all times, this was when this particular section would collapse.

"Get a rope," he commanded.

"Sire?"

"A rope, Sheeran. We have to get the boy."

"But it's a long way down. There's no way our length will reach him."

"You never know until you try. Now, get moving."

The men quickly tied together the lengths of rope they had among them, then lowered the end over the edge.

"Stuart! We're lowering a rope to you. Can you see it?"

Sobs greeted him from below.

"Look up, Stuart. Grab the rope."

"It's too high," his frightened voice called back from the darkness. "And there's a lot of water down here. I don't want to drown."

Charlie began stripping off his colorful robes and coverings.

"What are you doing, Sire?"

"Getting the kid."

"But the rope isn't long enough. He said so himself."

"Captain, if the water table is high from the rains, that boy might drown down there before we are able to get another piece."

"But the king cannot go climbing down into the earth for a peasant boy."

"Yeah, he can," Charlie replied, grabbing the rope and stepping to the edge. "Don't worry, I used to boulder a lot," he said, then hopped over the edge.

Charlie lowered himself down the rope, the collapsed walls providing relatively easy footholds as he went. It was cold, and it was damp.

The poor boy must be freezing. Better hurry, Charlie.

He reached the end of the rope, his eyes searching the darkness below. "Stuart, can you hear me? Where are you?"

"I'm here, Sire."

It sounded like he was close. Maybe no more than twenty feet or so, but the rope simply wasn't long enough.

"How deep is the water down there?"

"I can't feel the bottom," the terrified boy replied. "I don't want to drown, Sire."

Charlie weighed the options and knew the cold would get him before more rope would arrive. He'd go hypothermic, then fall asleep and drown.

"Ah, fuck it," the king said. "Hug the wall, Stuart. Are you up against it?"

"Yes."

"Good," Charlie said. Then he took a deep breath and let go of the rope.

Holy fuck, that water is cold!

He sank deep, his feet not touching the bottom, then swam back to the surface, sucking in a big gulp of air.

"Hey, kid. You ready to get out of here?" he asked. "I'll give you a push up, then you grab higher on the wall, okay?"

"I can't."

"Sure you can. You just have to try."

"I really can't," the boy sobbed.

Charlie's eyes were rapidly adjusting to the dim light, and he realized Stuart was injured. His arm appeared to be broken, though the cold of the water likely kept the pain and inflammation down. But it was clear the boy simply couldn't climb up on his own.

"Sheeran!" Charlie called up to the men waiting above. "I need you to cut me a length of rope and toss it down. About seven feet should do."

"Sire, you need that to climb back."

"Just do it."

The rope dangling above them disappeared as it was hauled back to the surface. A moment later a voice called out warning, and the requested rope arrived with a splash. Charlie grabbed it before it sank and swam over to the boy.

"Okay, now listen. I need you to hold on to my back. I'm

going to tie this around you so you don't fall. Can you do that
for me?"

Stuart nodded, pale in the dim light.

He's already getting hypothermic, Charlie realized. He would
have to hurry.

As quickly as his cold hands could manage, he strapped the
youth to his back, then began climbing out of the water. The
rope now dangled more than twenty feet above his head, but
with the slippery handholds, he suddenly realized he wouldn't
be able to make it. Not with the additional weight.

Think, Charlie. Think!

He felt his feet losing feeling in the frigid waters. If he didn't
get them *both* out soon, well, it was not a way he wanted to go
out. He made a decision, hoping he could actually pull off his
plan.

"Stuart, I want you to close your eyes, okay? Close them as
tight as you can and hold on. Can you do that for me?"

"Y-y-yes, S-s-sire," the boy said through chattering teeth.

"Good boy. Now keep them closed, and don't open them
until I tell you."

Charlie waited a moment, calming his mind and focusing. It
was just like a Drook pushing a ship or a conveyance. Only he
wasn't a Drook, and the things he was about to attempt to move
were not ships or carts, but humans.

He couldn't risk trying to float them all the way out of the
cavern. He doubted he even could, so that wasn't going to be an
issue. But the bottom of the rope, that could be done. Or so he
hoped. If he was wrong, they'd both be casualties this day.

Charlie called up the spells he knew, weaving those capable
of pushing or levitating an object into a silent song within his
head. Stronger and stronger he repeated the words to himself,
letting them flow, drawing on the power within.

Come on, Ara. Let your connection be enough.

He strained with all his might until spots floated in front of his eyes, followed by an unsettling tickling on his face. Charlie willed his eyes to focus and realized it was the end of the rope brushing against him. He lunged out and grabbed the rope before he lost all concentration and fell back to the waters below.

"Pull us up!" he called out. A few moments later, King Charlie and a very cold boy were greeted by sunlight as they were pulled free from their watery peril.

Charlie shed his wet clothes, going commando under his royal robes. He wrapped his overcloak around the youth after quickly setting his arm, splinting it with some small branches, then binding it snugly.

They made a quick ride for the nearest farmhouse. The owner was beside himself with both worry and joy when he heard the tale. Stuart would be okay, and the king left him before the roaring fire in the hearth and stepped back out to his men.

"Thank you, Sire. Thank you ever so much!" the man said.

"I'm glad the boy will be all right. He was very brave, you know. His king is proud of him. Make sure you tell him after he's rested."

"I shall, Sire. But is there anything I can do to repay you? Perhaps some food? Or wine?"

"Actually, we are already heading to the winemaker just a few miles from here. Can you direct us?"

"Direct you? I'll take you. That's my brother's vineyard, Sire, and that's his nephew you just saved."

Charlie shared a little look with Captain Sheeran, then turned back to the man. "Well, in that case. Please, show us the way."

"He'll be so thrilled, Sire. So grateful," the man said. "Come, follow me. I'll take you to my brother."

CHAPTER EIGHTEEN

It had been a very good afternoon, once he had warmed from his unexpected dip. A lot of wine certainly helped with that.

Quite full, slightly tipsy, and in all-around good spirits, Charlie and his men rode back to the castle at a leisurely pace, pausing to enjoy the natural beauty of the land—and to heed the call of nature—more than a few times.

The grateful winemaker had fed them quite well, and the wines he had provided had proven most delightful. Charlie bought several casks on the spot, most heading for his cellars, but a good many were earmarked for his men, as well. If he couldn't pal around with them and make friends that way— Bawb had expressly forbidden it—he'd do it the old-fashioned way. Namely, bribery. And among military sorts, alcohol was a most welcome form indeed.

Bawb had mentioned that promoting him to tax collector, in addition to his other positions, might not sit well with the older staff members. Giving a newcomer so much oversight power in a land he was, admittedly, a stranger to, could put even the mildest of spirits on edge.

"What would you have me do, Bob? I mean, sure, there may

be some hiccups here and there, but you've got a knack for this stuff."

"Even so, it's bound to upset many people."

"So piss them off. Jeez, it's not like you can't take care of yourself," Charlie said with a chuckle, but quiet enough so the guards riding with them wouldn't hear. He may have been tipsy, but not so much so that he forgot to maintain his friend's deception.

"And if I do manage to right this taxation ship? What are your plans, *Sire*?"

He had said the last bit loud enough for the others to hear, and Charlie had taken the hint. The men would talk, and gossip would spread. This was his opportunity to ensure the message he wanted to leak out was what traveled forth on their lips.

"My plan is to help the people, Bob," he replied in a clear voice. "We can be so much more efficient in the way things are run. The old king had a lot of waste going on under his watch, and I aim to remedy that."

A low murmur among the men signaled that his words had indeed made it to their intended ears.

"We arrived in this kingdom by unexpected means, and I seized this crown when the situation forced it, but we did not come here in search of wealth. Hell, we already live in a castle. What more could we want? At what point does amassing more wealth make a king's rule any better?"

"I couldn't say, Sire," Bawb replied, pleased with the direction the king's speech was heading.

"Tax revenues will still be collected, but at more reasonable rates. What is needed to support the kingdom, of course, and enough to provide for the staff and my soldiers, naturally. But aside from those crucial things, our tax revenues can be put to so much better use than acquiring more tapestries and piles of gold."

"What did you have in mind?"

"From what we saw today, some of my subjects occasionally fall upon hard times. While their neighbors may help them when they can, it should be my obligation as king to see to the well-being of my subjects. I would put aside a fund to provide emergency services, such as food, field help, and even temporary shelter, if need be, for my people. Enough to get them back on their feet and self-sufficient. We may live in a dark age, but there's no reason for our people to suffer for it."

"No man wishes to live by handouts, Sire," Bawb said, steering the conversation.

"Of course not. But a wise man also knows there is no shame in accepting help so he can once more become the captain of his own destiny."

Charlie was on a roll, and as Ara glided by overhead, he was glad for her presence, as his guards were so intent on his next words, he worried bandits might actually take them by surprise if they were so foolish as to harbor ill intent. Of course, there was also the man who was most definitely *not* at risk of being taken unaware riding at his side.

He quickened his pace a little, gesturing for Bawb to accompany him at the head of the procession, where they might talk privately a moment.

"You know, Bob, I have heard talk of a highwayman roaming the roads and woods at night."

"Oh? A problem, then?" the assassin replied, his face impassive.

"Well, apparently this man inflicts great violence on those who would assault and rob my subjects, leaving them maimed, dead, or wishing they were as often as not, while my people remain unharmed."

"Ah, I see. So not a problem, then?" he replied with a faint smile.

Charlie flashed him a grin. "So long as you keep doing this Robin Hood thing and don't get caught, I see no harm in it."

"Me? Why, *Sire*, I have no idea what you're talking about," the deadly Wampeh said with a knowing, pointy-toothed smile.

"You know, it sounds like fun, actually. Maybe I'll have to take a late-night stroll sometime. You know, just to get some air. Perhaps you'd even care to join me."

"It sounds like it might make for a nice outing. And there has been word of some unusually well-armed bandits these past few days. Men with military gear. Mayhap, we might have ourselves a little fun."

"Hang on a second," Charlie said, sobering slightly. "Military? Are these scouts? Are we being invaded?"

"No, nothing like that. Not yet, at least. But I do fear that word of the former king's fall has spread, and it's only natural that your grasp on this kingdom will eventually be challenged."

"Ugh, just great," Charlie groaned. "I'm so done with fighting."

Bawb chuckled. "Perhaps, my friend. But fighting is certainly not done with you."

CHAPTER NINETEEN

Dusk had uncorked its nightly magic, the sky's colors shifting from gray to indigo as the sun set in the west. The men were in good spirits as they left the king and returned to their barracks and families now that their liege was safely within the castle's walls.

The ride had brightened their spirits, and the exceptionally hearty lunch had found a happy home in their bellies. And now, with several casks of wine, courtesy of the king, they were sure to warm their bodies even further, singing and carousing until the wee hours.

Bawb had an errand he needed to run for Hunze, leaving Charlie to stroll the grounds surrounding the castle alone, for a change. Though he knew he should have summoned some of the guards to accompany him, Charlie opted not to, the solitude offering him a much-needed opportunity to take in his surroundings and simply *be*.

Finally, beneath darkening skies, he turned from his walk, heading back to join the others for dinner. His eyes fell upon the new garden plots. They were rather extensive, he noted. Leila's freshly tilled soil and rows of seedlings were indeed an improvement over the formerly untended ground, but he could see where the enormous stump lodged in the clay soil was giving her problems. A literal stick in the mud, so to speak.

Still, despite the dead tree's stubborn blight blocking her plans, the queen's vision was clear, and the beginning of what would surely be a beautiful garden was taking shape.

Dinner was a festive event, with a fresh cask of the newly acquired wine tapped, the contents shared liberally with not only the king and his friends, but the kitchen and house staff as well. The king's generosity, while unusual for a royal, most certainly did not go unnoted.

They filled their bellies and shared stories of their day until it was quite late, then, finally, they turned in for a good night's sleep.

It was quite late when Charlie snuck from his chambers, wearing a dark cloak and his quietest boots. He would never reach Bawb's levels of stealth, but he could nevertheless be quite silent when need be. He stopped at the cache of magical devices he had hidden on the ground floor, gathering a lone konus for himself from behind the layered shimmer spells that made the hiding spot blend in with the stone wall.

The king then unbolted the small side door and carefully stepped out into the night. His breath was visible in the cold air, the exhaled mist giving him away in the moonlight. Quickly, he wrapped a scarf around his nose and mouth, effectively stifling his exhales until he once again blended into the shadows.

All but the guards high on the walls were asleep at this hour, so he felt reasonably confident in his anonymity as he approached the stump that had been vexing Leila so. He reached out, lightly placing his hands on the long-dead wood. Silently, without so much as moving his lips, he recited a simple spell, the konus on his wrist glowing slightly in the dark.

As his connection to Ara grew stronger and stronger, his need to verbalize spells had diminished until it was gone entirely. She had been making him practice the art since they had first met, but now he was exceeding her expectations by a long shot.

He had taught the basics of the technique his Zomoki friend had shown him to Bawb, and the assassin––unsurprisingly–– had shown quite an aptitude for the new skill. It would be very useful for one in his line of work to cast completely silently by force of will alone. Such things were occasionally spoken of, but even his ancient order had not mastered the art.

Ara, however, had, and––after extracting a promise and blood oath that he would never share what she taught him with the other assassins of the Wampeh Ghalian sect should they somehow return home one day––she schooled him in the ways of casting by will. Of making a spell not with words, but with intent. The Wampeh assassin gained a new tool. One he was sworn to take to the grave with him.

But none of that concerned Charlie at the moment. What did was the troublesome stump spoiling Leila's project. She was trying to make the castle grounds more pleasant, and the project really meant a lot to her. As such, it meant a lot to Charlie as well.

He silently cast his spell. The wood beneath his hands creaked and snapped before he added a muting spell to the one already in play, weaving the two together in a sing-song manner unique to the odd human.

Ara had speculated that the rhythmic manner in which he memorized, and later cast combined spells, might have been the reason he had succeeded in feats of magic where others had failed. Whatever the case, the layered spell silenced the sounds of the stump as it tore free of the ground, hovering a foot above the freshly turned soil.

Charlie carefully directed the massive piece of wood far from

Leila's garden, setting it down against an unused area near the castle's wall, where it could dry out in coming months, eventually becoming fuel for the kitchen's ovens.

He looked at the hole in the ground where the tree's last remains had been. The ground was damp and fecund, and churning with worms. He smiled to himself as he cast another spell, pushing the surrounding soil over it, leveling the whole area into a workable surface. With all of those worms burrowing and fertilizing as they went, whatever she planted here now was sure to grow heartily.

Pleased at the result of his labor, Charlie walked back to the small door and stepped inside, bolting it firmly behind him as he walked back to bed.

Silent as the night itself, a pair of eyes had watched him from the dark, their owner most intrigued by what they had seen.

CHAPTER TWENTY

The fist that whipped past Charlie's chin only barely missed, his reflexes having to kick into overdrive to avoid the attack. The follow-up kick to the ribs, however, he simply didn't see coming.

"Again," Bawb said, his sweat-soaked hair tied back from his face.

"Sonofa—"

"Stop griping and start fighting. Now concentrate!" Bawb launched another series of empty-hand attacks, his limbs a blur of activity.

Charlie ducked and twisted, his body bending in ways that would have seemed impossible to him just a few short years ago, even with Rika forcing him into shape before their failed mission launched.

But that was years ago, and now, after Ser Baruud's lengthy training, combined with the Geist's painful drills, moving as was required to flow with combat was as natural as breathing.

Breathing. That thing that became hard to do when a punch landed in his solar plexus.

"Shit," he managed to gasp as he dropped to one knee.

"Better, but there's room for improvement," Bawb said, tossing a water skin to his sparring partner.

Charlie caught it despite his spasming diaphragm, downing several big gulps before forcing himself to slow his intake. Both men were shirtless, having long since soaked their tunics in the increasingly stuffy confines of the smaller dungeon area they'd relocated to.

Charlie's punishment for one of his subjects had been to clean the dungeons. It seemed like a good idea at the time, and indeed, the man was repenting his actions with every layer of blood, grime, and filth he removed. But it also meant he and Bawb had to constantly switch training spaces to avoid unwanted eyes from learning the pale man's true martial prowess.

"You really think I'm getting better?" Charlie asked, wiping the sweat from his brow.

"Yes, I do," Bawb said. "Though you have a long way to go, yet, before I would consider you a worthy adversary."

"Gee, thanks."

"I mean no offense by it. You simply asked for my honest assessment. And believe me, I'd wager that you could more than hold your own against even the most talented agents of the Council of Twenty. And you are definitely far more skilled than any on this planet, from what I've seen."

"Well, there's that, then," he replied.

Footsteps sounded outside the heavy door, then the latch ground open.

"I thought he was cleaning the big room today," Charlie hissed.

"He is. Or was supposed to be," Bawb said, jumping into the shadows and vanishing, as he was wont to do.

"Hey, fellas," Leila said, walking into the room, Baloo at her side. She sniffed the air, and wrinkled her nose. "I think this place could really use a window if you're going to keep using it like this."

Charlie rose to his feet and jokingly sniffed his armpits. "What? Are you saying we stink?"

"I do not stink," Bawb said, sliding from the shadows.

Charlie laughed, his pumped muscles tensing under his skin as he did. Leila couldn't help but notice. She quickly looked away, examining the impromptu training space instead of her shirtless king.

Baloo plodded over, and moments later Charlie found himself wet with slobber where he'd formerly been covered in sweat. Baloo gave a small yowl, his tail wagging like a giant fan.

"Hey, okay!" he laughed. "Enough, already. I know I'm like a giant salt lick, but come on, Baloo."

He grabbed the massive animal by the head and distributed a healthy serving of ear scratches until Baloo's rear leg started spasming with a mind of its own. The leg's owner leaned into it, eyes closed with bliss.

"He's ridiculous, you know," Charlie said.

"Maybe, but he's my boy," Leila replied.

At the sound of his mama's voice, Baloo opened his eyes and looked at her with anticipation.

"It's okay, Baloo. We're just talking about you," she said. "Charlie, there was something I wanted to ask you."

"Oh, and here I thought you had just come all the way down here to cover us with slobber. I notice that Bob has somehow avoided the drooling dog treatment."

"Baloo and I have an understanding," the Wampeh said. "He doesn't slobber on me, and I don't eat him."

"You wouldn't!" Leila said with mock horror.

"Of course not," Bawb said with a grin. "Far too much fur to be worth the effort."

"So, you were saying?" Charlie asked.

"Ah, yes. I wanted to know, did you pull out that stump?"

Charlie wiped himself off with a rag. It was better than dog drool, he figured. "I can neither confirm nor deny tha—"

"That was foolish, Charlie. Not pulling the stump, but there's no way you did it without using magic."

"A little konus never hurt anyone."

"But if someone saw you—"

"It was late. No one did."

"But why risk it? I mean, I get it, you miss using your magic, but it's just not like you to take such an unnecessary risk. You have to be more careful. It was a dumb thing to do."

He paused a moment. "It was, I suppose. But I know this garden project means a lot to you, and I just wanted to do something to help. Sorry."

Leila paused, at a brief loss for words as color flushed her cheeks.

"I, uh—"

"And I was hoping you might plant some of those Tsokin berries out there. We've been out of coffee for weeks, you know."

Bawb winced. "Yes, we are all quite aware. Why in the worlds you traded the last few bags of beans to those bright-eyed explorers I will never know."

"Because they were full of piss and vinegar, Bob."

"Piss and vinegar?"

"It's a saying. What I mean is, they were adventurers, off to face danger. To see the world, heading to all corners of the globe."

"Charlie, a globe is by its nature round."

"Yes, Bob, I know. Again, a figure of speech. And as for why, I thought rather than just give them safe passage and a bed for the night, why not do more than what any other king would do? With the dried berries, they could plant their own, you know. I explained the process, so in theory, they could be brewing up their own cups in a mere year or two from now."

"In some distant land."

"Precisely." Charlie paused, a thought flashing through his mind. "Holy shit."

"What?" Leila asked.

"I just realized, what if they actually *do* plant the Tsokin berries along the way?"

"Then the plants would grow, obviously."

"Right. But that means Tsokin berries might actually *be* coffee. We're here, thousands of years before my time, and I brought them with me when we fled your galaxy. What if I'm the reason coffee exists on my planet? What if coffee came from outer space?"

"It does seem a strange, but entirely possible scenario," Bawb said. "But that doesn't make your use of magic any less foolish. Even if it was to help Leila."

"Yeah, I know. I just thought she'd like it, is all," he said, slightly dejected. "Anyway, I should go clean up and get back to king stuff."

He slipped into his damp tunic and headed out the door.

"Charlie?"

"Yeah?"

"Fool that you may be, thank you, all the same," Leila said.

Charlie gave her a little smile and headed out the door, Leila watching as he left. Bawb couldn't help but notice that her eyes lingered on him a bit longer than in the past. "Come on, Baloo, let's go," she said a moment later.

"Hmm," the Wampeh mused, then followed his friend to clean up and return to his official business.

CHAPTER TWENTY-ONE

Leila spent the next week planting her garden, including a special section for Charlie's Tsokin berries. Or coffee, if that was indeed what they were. The implications of his traveling through not only space, but time as well, all for the universe's grand plan of becoming the man who brought coffee to the planet was an amusing twist not lost on either of them.

Her castle labors had required her to temporarily cut short the daily outings to visit the farmers in the area, but she nevertheless made an effort to see as many as she could over the course of the week. Charlie was right. As rulers of the land, one of their concerns was the well-being of their subjects, and as odd as it felt being a queen, that part of the job came naturally to her.

"Karl, I'll be heading out for a stroll shortly," she told the sandy blond guard tasked with leading her entourage.

"Of course, my queen," he replied. "I shall ready the men."

"Thank you. Your attention to your duties is greatly appreciated."

Karl kept his smile to himself as best he could and went to fetch the men. Leila had grown on all who interacted with her over the months. At first, they were more than slightly uneasy with the odd, slightly green woman. Most had assumed she was ill and might not last the season.

But sunlight did her well, and her faint green skin darkened to a warm olive complexion within weeks, and with it, her overall appearance shifted to the picture of exotic, but Earthly, health. Added to that, she was young, she was fit, and above all, she seemed to possess a genuine care for those around her.

When word got out that she had been raised by a man of the land, not a royal, the people warmed to her even more. And when she had dug around in the muck, helping shift crops and till soil, while many were shocked that she would lower herself so, they nevertheless felt a connection to her, even if they might simultaneously disapprove. She was one of them, even if she came from far away.

Baloo took his usual place at her side as they jogged the trail to visit the local farms. Bawb had told her to ride a horse, as was expected of her, but running was something she had done all her life. It felt *good* to stretch her legs, and her rambunctious pup enjoyed trotting along with her.

The men following on foot had given up trying to keep an even pace, knowing by now that she was wont to sprint up a hill for no reason from time to time. That their queen could undoubtedly best any of them in the physical training the king had them engaging in proved to be both a source of inspiration to train harder, as well as a reason for the deeper respect they felt for her.

The guard spaced their horses out, several riding ahead to clear the way, the rest leapfrogging from the flanks and rear of her retinue. Leila just kept on at her own pace, reveling in the glory of nature. The planet wasn't so different from her own, all told, and she'd grown to appreciate it with each passing day.

"Baloo, fetch!" she said, hurling a stick as far as she could.

Her canine fur baby took off in a flash, bounding over shrubs and rocks in his pursuit. The men all laughed at his shenanigans. While the utterly enormous animal could easily kill them all, he knew them now, and so long as they didn't pose a threat to his mother, he treated them as just another part of his pack.

From the nearby woods, however, a pair of curious ursine eyes watched the woman on foot. Men on horses were a difficult meal, with all of that metal and their pointed sticks. But the woman was at ground level, and unarmed. And she wore only fabric, not shiny steel.

The bear's stomach grumbled. Yes, a meal would be good, and he could grab her easily enough the way all of the big men on horses were spaced out. In fact, any second he could just—

A massive beast with a mouthful of sharp teeth trotted back to the woman, a large stick in its mouth. Carrying the hunk of wood had exposed just how big its teeth truly were. Big, and sharp, and myriad.

Baloo turned and looked into the shadows of the woods with his piercing gaze. The bear knew from years of hunting that the humans didn't possess the vision to see him in the shadows. This new adversary and he, however, locked eyes in an instant.

He didn't bark, and he didn't growl, but for the briefest of moments, Baloo flashed his canines in warning. This woman was protected.

The bear briefly considered its odds and found itself not liking them. Not at all. This was no ordinary dog. Nor was it a simple wolf. It was far, far larger, and he found himself experiencing the rare sensation of doubt. For once, he wasn't the biggest, baddest thing in the woods.

The bear wisely turned and lumbered deeper into the trees, deciding to look for an easier meal.

"What is it, Baloo?" Leila asked, noting his stare into the woods. "You see a rabbit?"

Instead of racing off in pursuit of game as he normally

would, Baloo stayed at her side a while, trotting along with her, casually staying close as he scanned the treeline.

The farmers she passed during her walk were all glad to see her, but one in particular was thrilled at her arrival. The recently burned fields had been tilled, and the rows of replanted crops had taken shape. A few sprouts had even begun poking up through the fresh mounds of soil. And for Baloo they had even saved a massive leg bone from a steer they had slaughtered and sold at market.

"Thank you so much!" the queen gushed as they presented the gift to her canine pal.

"It's the least we could do, Majesty. With your help––and your dragon friend, of course––the fields have turned a corner and seem to be recovering their former health. We have you to thank for this fortuitous turn of events."

"I'm thrilled it's working out for you," she said, watching Baloo happily gnaw on the bone. "Now be careful, Baloo. Don't go breaking it. You'll poke your cheeks."

"Oh, Majesty, it was a fine steer, sturdy and well-built. I doubt even one as big as he could break––"

A crunching snap stopped them in mid-sentence. Baloo, however, didn't cease his gnawing, focusing now on the portion of the thick femur he had broken free.

"Dear Lord. The strength of him!" the farmer exclaimed.

"Yeah, he's a big boy, that's for sure."

"We are fortunate he is Your Majesty's protector. Any who would challenge your wolf would find themselves in a dire condition. No offense," he added, blushing as he addressed Karl and the other guards.

"None taken," Karl with a warm smile. "We are *all* here to ensure the queen's safety, and knowing Baloo will protect her to the death makes all of us glad for his presence."

She was a queen of the people and loved by all, despite her somewhat unconventional ways. She had come a long way from her life as a slave and animal keeper in a distant galaxy, but the groundskeeper's daughter had found her niche, as unlikely as it was. Leila only wished her father could see her now.

But that was impossible. He hadn't been born yet, and wouldn't be for a few thousand years.

Maybe I'll catch you next time around, she thought, the idea of somehow meeting her father again warming her heart.

If Ara proved successful in devising a spell that would help them return forward to their own time, perhaps she would see his smiling face again, one day. If they managed to move forward in time. Back to where they belonged. It was all theoretical, of course. She still had to figure out not only how to get back to the right time, but also to her own galaxy.

The odds were stacked against them, and none of them really thought they'd succeed, but working the problem at least gave them all a little sense of hope. Though the longer they stayed in this strange time and place, the more it grew on them. Leila couldn't help but wonder if one day, given the choice, they wouldn't choose to stay.

CHAPTER TWENTY-TWO

While Leila had taken to accepting her guards as an unneeded, but required, part of her daily outings, Charlie had found himself increasingly annoyed at the lack of any alone time. Me-time for the sometimes-introverted king was exceedingly rare. But all he wanted was to go out in nature alone to walk the hills and think. To recharge his mental batteries with relaxing silence, as he so often did before stumbling into this strange new life.

With a few tricks he had learned from Bawb, Charlie was able to piece together a reasonable disguise, one that he could shed quickly should the need to prove who he was actually arise. He didn't want his own guards attacking him while he snuck back into his own castle, after all. Fortunately, that hadn't happened. At least, not yet.

"*Sire*, this. *My Liege*, that. It's exhausting. I don't know how celebrities can stand it. It's overwhelming," he grumbled as he snuck out the small door at the base of the castle's wall. "I guess it just takes a special kind of person to crave fame at the price of privacy. Not worth it, in my opinion."

When he had first taken possession of the castle, a means of coming and going unnoticed was a priority for them all. So Charlie had taken Bawb's advice and started casting layers upon layers of shimmer spells, much as they had done in hiding their stashes of magical gear. It was just a faint drop of magic applied daily, building up like layers of a jawbreaker candy, hiding the door from prying eyes. But it couldn't be done all at once.

A door suddenly vanishing would draw attention. But one that just faded from notice over months, well, *that* was something they could manage, and that wouldn't draw scrutiny. Passersby would simply be confused, questioning their memory, asking themselves if there hadn't been a door there before.

He pulled his hood over his head and adopted the shuffle of a lame-legged peasant as he leaned on his staff, making his way toward the small trail he had so often enjoyed following deep into the woods. Once he was out of sight of the castle and surrounding grounds, he could switch back to his normal walk, but for now, he was a gimpy mendicant. Yet another of Bawb's assassin tricks he had found useful since arriving home.

Home, but far, far too early.

Still, beats being hunted down by a crazed cabal of evil wizards, he mused. And indeed, compared to avoiding the deadly Council of Twenty a distant galaxy away, this was a walk in the park.

Or a walk in the woods, in this case.

On a whim, he turned from his usual trail, heading toward the farmland a few hills over. It would be a good walk, but he could use the exercise, and besides, he wanted to quietly see how the farmer was doing now that he was out from under the tax collector's thumb.

He had crossed a clearing and the small stream flowing adjacent to it, and was just cresting a wooded hill when he came across a group of men walking through the woods.

He kept his hands steady, restraining himself from the instinct shouting at him to grab his sword from under his cloak.

He was just a peasant, out for a walk. With his disguised appearance, he wasn't a particularly tempting target.

Charlie simply kept his same steady pace, adjusting his course to go around the men. He'd come into view walking normally, though, so it wouldn't serve him to go back to his injured gait. The bright side was he would get clear of the men faster.

Except it looked like it wouldn't be so easy. The men saw him trudging along through the woods and began moving toward him.

Oh, for fuck's sake. Really? he grumbled to himself.

Charlie glanced at the men, taking inventory of their gear as he cataloged them with a fighter's eyes.

Far too well-armed to be mere bandits, he realized, a sinking feeling forming in his gut. *And there are more of them in the woods over there.*

Bawb had mentioned soldiers might be probing the land. Men with military gear, disguised as ruffians. He did a quick count of the men coming his way. Including the others joining them from within the treeline, there had to be twenty, if not more.

He was already regretting not wearing a konus or slaap, the possibility of people seeing him wield magic be damned. But all he had on him was his walking staff and a short sword.

Okay, I'm good, but not that good. Still, I could maybe take most of them, but the whole point is avoiding a scene.

Charlie quickly weighed his options. He was really wishing they hadn't used up the last of their ammunition for the firearms they'd pulled back through time with them, but in the early days of his kingship, he had been tested, and a flashy example needed to be made. Unfortunately, that left him without a gun.

There were a few other responses he could still go with, but the choice was made for him when the nearest of the men picked up their pace, jogging toward him.

Fuck it.

Charlie took off at a run, bolting back the way he had come. The men broke into pursuit, the rattle of their weapons ringing out as they wove through the trees after him.

Down the hill they went at breakneck speed, Charlie outpacing them, but not by nearly enough for his comfort. He reached the bottom, the ground tapering off to level, and ran straight for the little stream he had crossed earlier, vaulting to the other shore and rushing to the clearing ahead.

A slight tickle fluttered in his mind.

Ah.

Charlie spun and stopped, throwing off his cloak, shedding his disguise as he drew his sword. The men quickly formed a skirmish line, sizing up their prey.

"Stop your pursuit! I am no easy victim walking these hills. I am King Charlie!"

"Yeah. We know," the nearest man said.

The revelation did not sit well with him.

"Oh. Shit," was all he managed to blurt as the men attacked.

His adrenaline spiked, and Charlie fought like a man possessed. Since it was very literally a fight for his life, his reaction was entirely understandable. But fighting without a konus or slaap meant none of his usual arsenal of spells were at his disposal. At least, they shouldn't have been.

But things had been changing within him of late, and as he cast diversionary spells out of pure instinct, he was surprised to find them working. Nothing to give away his true power, but subtle things that were nonetheless buying him time.

Swarms of invisible flies badgered one man, another found his feet inexplicably slip out from under him despite his seemingly sound footing. Still another was knocked backward by a *kika rahm* spell silently cast just as one of his comrades bumped into him, masking the magical blow.

He was making a very good show of it, but as the men kept coming, Charlie knew that eventually they'd get the best of him.

A flash of a shadow crossed overhead, followed by an enormous crash as a pair of massive, scaly red feet crushed a handful of men, several trees shattering to pieces from the dragon's diving approach.

Ara bellowed, flames spraying from her mouth and nose as she sized up the tiny attackers, all of whom stood in sheer terror, white with fear.

"No, wait!" Charlie called out. "Don't burn them alive and eat them. I know how you love eating men whole, but I would have words with them," he said, turning back to face the attackers. "You'll all be good now, won't you?"

The petrified men nodded yes.

"You know I had no intention of eating them," Ara silently said.

"Well, yeah. But it makes more of an impression on them that way. Burning to death is one thing, but being eaten? That shit's a whole other level of visceral fear."

Ara chuckled in his head. *"I'm very curious to see how this plays out. And if they so much as lift a finger, I very well may eat a few, just to make a point."*

Charlie felt the muscle in his jaw twitch, but managed to make it look like an angry tic, rather than a laugh threatening to burst free.

"Now you lot, you listen up. You're new here, obviously. Maybe you don't know me. Maybe you thought the stories were just that. Stories. But now you know the truth, and you will report what you've seen to your captain and king."

Ara huffed a plume of smoke for effect.

"I am Charlie, the Dragon King, and this land is protected. We are not weak. We are not scared. And to invade my lands is to court your own death."

"Dragon King?"

"Has a nice ring to it, don't you think?"

"You're ridiculous, Charlie. You know that?"

"Perhaps. But look at their faces. No denying it. That shit works."

He scanned the men, too afraid to fight, and too afraid to flee. For grizzled battle veterans and soldiers of whatever land they'd come scouting from, the sensation of loosening bowels was one they hadn't felt since their first battle. In the presence of certain death, and not in the form of combat, as they had prepared themselves for, its abrupt return was startling.

"Now, go tell your masters what I have said. And do not dare tread on my lands again. You may keep your lives *this time*. Next time, you shall not be so fortunate."

The men moved, abruptly unpetrified by his permission to flee. And flee they did, at great speed.

"I don't think I've ever seen fully armed men run that fast," Charlie chuckled.

"Indeed," Ara replied. *"Well, that was interesting."*

"Yeah, it was. Did you see an army nearby, or was this just a scouting party?"

"No army that I could see, but I'll keep an eye out. There's something strange in the air, but I can't quite place it."

"Strange? Like, stranger than a few dozen disguised soldiers in the kingdom?"

"I can't say for sure, yet, but I am beginning to wonder if this planet doesn't possess its own magic users after all."

CHAPTER TWENTY-THREE

Charlie rode out from the castle later that day, still determined to visit the formerly over-taxed farmer. Only this time, when he left the castle walls, he did so with a full contingent of men, as well as a slaap in a pouch on his hip and a konus on each arm beneath his clothing.

He didn't think the foreign scouts would be foolish enough to try something again so soon, but after discussing the situation with Ara, both agreed it was far better to wear them today, just in case. She would be nearby, scouring the area, but if she couldn't be there fast enough, she wanted him protected.

"You don't have to tell me twice," he told her.

"I'd hope not. That was far too close, Charlie."

"Agreed. But I think the message got through to the surviving men loud and clear. But for peace of mind, give the region another look, will ya?"

"Of course. Ride safely. I will return this evening to discuss what I uncover."

With that, she was gone, and Charlie was on his own. Or at least, as on his own as one could be while surrounded by two dozen of their finest guards.

They rode a slightly longer route to the farmer's lands, avoiding choke points and locations the captain thought might be likely ambush sites.

"I don't know what His Majesty was thinking, going out alone, and unarmed like that," the captain griped.

"I wasn't unarmed. I had my sword."

"Against *twenty* men. If not for your winged pet, I fear we might be looking at our third king in as many months," the captain noted.

"You know, Sheeran, for a minute there, you almost sounded like you'd miss me."

"Continuity of rule is of utmost importance. The people suffer without it. *Whoever* winds up wearing the crown, it is imperative there is no vacancy of the office of king. Otherwise, chaos would reign."

"A little apocalyptic there, Captain. But I appreciate the sentiment. And you're right. The people deserve stability in their lives. Now, let's go see how things are working out for my subjects, starting with one in particular."

They made the ride to the farmer's land in good time, the sun still high in the sky, the day comfortable and clear. Several weeks had passed since Charlie had come upon the tax collector and his muscle harassing the poor man, and the transformation of not only the fields, but also their owner was noticeable.

The crops that had been lying fallow were either harvested or cut back and replanted anew. The formerly unplowed fields now possessed neat and orderly rows of sprouting plants. And surprisingly, the farmer himself was almost radiant with happiness, his color returned to a healthy flush. His cheeks had filled out a bit as well, Charlie noted.

"Sire! It is a pleasure to have you visit my farm again!"

"You seem to be doing well."

"Aye, Sire. The rations you had delivered were a Godsend, they were. Helped us regain our strength and prepare for the hard labor ahead. And with Clay's help, we've been able to get even more work done than when my son and ox were both here. The man is a marvel of nature, he is."

"So it goes well, then. He is performing his tasks without complaint?"

"Complaint? Hardly, Sire. Of course, he was not thrilled about it for the first few days, but then he discovered he had a natural gift for it, and has been greatly productive ever since. There he is, over in the field. Clay! Clay! Come greet the king!" he called out.

"You really don't have to--"

"Oh, but Sire, I'm sure he wishes to thank you for the opportunity."

The enormous man stood up tall in the field. Even from a distance, Charlie could see his changed countenance. Gone was the glowering heavy out to hurt at his master's command, replaced by a free, contented man, putting in an honest day's work.

His muscles, Charlie noted, were also growing larger and more defined. While his natural strength was suitable for the tax collector's needs, working in the fields had given them the impetus to grow even stronger. He waved pleasantly as he made his way from the field toward the others.

"And how are your finances?" Charlie asked. "Are things getting back on the right track?"

"Ah, Sire. I will have the taxes ready for you first thing in the--"

"No, no, that's not what I was getting at. I want you to take your time and build a safety net for yourself should you fall on hard times again. There is enough wealth in the kingdom for all, and overtaxation, especially of one who works as hard and honestly as you, would be foolish. I was merely inquiring to see if you still needed additional support or if you were self-sustaining now."

"Most generous, Sire. Most kind! And to answer your question, we are not only self-sustaining, but are beginning to have a surplus to sell once more."

"Good. Then keep doing what you are doing. When you have stabilized your situation, *then* we will discuss resuming taxes."

"Sire," Clay said, dropping to one knee upon arriving in the presence of his king.

Even lowered in such a manner, he was still a giant of a man.

"Rise, Clay, and tell me how this new labor treats you. What I see appears to be a changed man, if I am not mistaken."

The former thug smiled broadly. "Changed, aye, Sire. This labor, this *life,* it's harder than working for tha tax collector, fer certain, but it's so much more satisfying. I help things grow, now. And I've made new friends," he said, putting his arm warmly around the man he'd been beating for his money only a few weeks prior.

"So, no lingering bad blood between you two?"

"Water under the bridge, Sire," the farmer said. "Clay's like a part of me family now. He's a good man what were stuck in a bad job for a while, is all. Isn't that right, Clay?"

"Aye."

Charlie felt the warm glow of a job well done fill his body. His decisions had been hit and miss over his time as king, but this, he was quite certain, was a hit. He surveyed the fields once more and noticed the farmer's eldest daughter watching them. Watching_Clay, to be precise.

Ah, there's more in the air than just hard labor, Charlie noted with a little grin.

"Well, then. We shall leave you to your labors. I am glad to see you in such changed and better conditions. All of you. May your improved fortunes continue," he said, nudging his horse back to the road.

"Thankee, Sire, and God bless!"

CHAPTER TWENTY-FOUR

"You *what?*" Bawb said, anger flaring in his eyes.

"I went for a walk. And don't give me that, I know you sneak out from time to time as well."

"Yes, but at night. And I'm a Wampeh Ghalian, Charlie. Master assassins, invisible to all."

"Hey, I can be sneaky too."

"I'm sorry, my friend, but while you may have greatly improved your techniques since I've known you, nevertheless, compared to me, you are like a toddler knocking blindly through a pile of dishes. No offense."

"No offense? You can't talk shit like that and just drop 'No offense' in there like it's all good."

"But you say it."

"Yeah, but not like that. The way you do, it's like it makes the insult almost worse."

"That was not my intention, I assure you."

"Well, that's how you come off, Bob. Like a dick."

"Then I apologize for my 'dick' behavior. But we are straying from the point, here. Setting aside your foolish insistence on running around the countryside unprotected——"

"I have Ara."

"When she happens to be nearby, yes. And you're lucky for that. But had she not been present, what then? What if she were off hunting across the sea? Even she can't be by your side at all times. You must be more cautious, Charlie. Especially now that we know with some degree of certainty that the realm's borders are being tested."

"You really think it was more than a random probe? Oh, hell, who am I kidding. They *knew* it was me they were attacking." He paused a moment, mulling over the event now that he'd had time to process it. "Hang on. How exactly did they know it was me out there? I didn't pass anyone on the trail, and the shimmer shield is masking the door."

"Do you think we have a traitor in our midst?"

"I don't know. You're the subterfuge expert. Do we?"

Bawb furrowed his brow slightly. "Loyalties are hard to gauge here. Especially as you've taken the throne so very recently, and by such unusual and violent means." He thought on it a long moment. "It is possible, yes."

"Just fucking great," Charlie groaned. "That's what I need. To be watching my back inside as well as out."

Bawb headed toward the door. "I should speak with the captain about this. See what he knows."

"Okay, see if he's heard anything new. Ara's doing a sweep, so we should know if there's anything out there when she gets back. We can regroup and go over it with the others at dinner."

"Very well. I shall see you this evening," the Wampeh said as he headed off on his fact-finding errand.

Captain Sheeran was slicing strips of leather with his faintly glowing dagger when Bawb found him. The blade cut the tough hide easily, though the Wampeh's trained eye could tell it was a mediocre enchantment at best.

"I see our king has bestowed one of his finest weapons upon you. I think you must have made quite an impression to warrant such a gift," he said, playing to the man's vanity.

"It's amazing," Sheeran said. "Cuts leather like it was nothing. And never dulls."

"A useful weapon, indeed."

The captain fixed his gaze on the pale man. "What is it you want, Bawb? You're not a man of action, so I assume you didn't come to talk about knives."

"Very astute of you. No, I have come with a concern. The king has informed me he encountered a band of ruffians on the trail earlier today. From his account, they appear to have possibly been scouts from a foreign army."

"Yes, His Majesty already informed me of that. Damn fool thing he did, going out there alone like that."

"On this, we are in agreement," Bawb said with a disarmingly meek grin. "I feel it would be wise to perhaps do a little digging and see what we might find of our new intruders."

"One step ahead of you. I've already sent my spies out to scout the area. We should hear back from them any day now. Just need to give them time to do their work."

"Ah, I see. I'm glad you've dispatched men already. There were some rumblings among the men that people had been talking about forces mounting to test the kingdom's borders."

"And where did you hear this?" Sheeran asked, casually slicing yet another strip of leather.

"As I said, just talk among the men I happened to overhear in passing."

"Can't really trust what you've only heard part of."

"Certainly, I agree with that sentiment. But one must heed *all* rumors, however far-fetched, when in positions such as ours, wouldn't you agree, Captain?"

"In this case, yes. And the rumors were a bit more substantial than what you overheard. There's talk of forces mounting, possibly a new player in this game come to challenge the king. There's even talk a nearby realm has a mighty wizard among them."

"Oh?"

"Aye."

"Well, if it comes to that, I have some small abilities of my own, should they be needed," Bawb said, suppressing a chuckle.

"You're no wizard."

"Oh, heavens, no. And most who claim to be are nothing more than tricksters, but I've acquired a few novel skills in my many years of service. Enough to perhaps help persuade a would-be wizard to seek out an easier target. But I hope that will not be necessary."

"You? Going up against *anyone* in a fight? And a fake magic one at that? Now *that* I'd like to see," the captain said with a laugh.

"Ideally, that will not be the case, of course. I abhor the use of violence," Bawb replied, maintaining his meek charade. "But tell me, Captain, what should we do while we wait for your spies to return?"

"*Do*? There's nothing *to* do, especially after what happened today. I, for one, seriously doubt a full attack will ever happen. Once they saw the king's dragon, well, I think you'd agree, only a fool would attack with such a beast on our side."

"Of that we agree," Bawb said, but nevertheless, an uneasy feeling was growing in his gut. He hadn't survived as long as he had by ignoring it. "I should speak with the king on this matter," he said.

"By all means. And, Bawb, don't worry. I'll inform you when I hear something."

"Thank you, Captain."

Sheeran merely nodded, his attention turned back to the glowing blade as he turned its edge on the tough hide once more.

CHAPTER TWENTY-FIVE

Charlie wasn't hard to find. Whenever he needed to mull over a particularly troublesome issue, he'd taken to sitting in the small storage room in the corridor just up the curved staircase from the kitchen. The smells of comfort food, combined with the muffling properties of the thick stone walls, made a sort of happy place for him.

It was an odd thing, he realized—a man who had been held prisoner, enslaved, now king, and willingly putting himself in a room not much larger than his old cell aboard the slave traders' ship.

Much was afoot in his castle, and a clear head was needed if he hoped to not only survive, but do so in a 'kingly' way.

Traitors, he mused. *In my own castle. It could be anyone.*

He furrowed his brow, trying to narrow down the list of those who might turn on him. Or stay turned, might be more accurate, their having never actually come over to his side in the first place after he seized the throne.

But we don't know for sure that anyone is working against me. I mean, how would they know when I was leaving when I didn't know myself until I made the decision? And the door is hidden from all but

Bawb, Leila, and me. It just doesn't make any sense. But whatever it is, something isn't right.

He nearly jumped when the door abruptly swung open.

"I thought I would find you here," Bawb said.

"Jesus, you scared the shit out of me, Bob. Knock next time."

"Apologies. I had assumed your highly attuned ninja hearing would have known I was there," the assassin said with a sarcastic grin.

"I should never have told you about the ninjas," Charlie groaned.

"Oh, it's a most amusing tale. And admittedly, the basic tenets are sound. Stealth. Infiltration. Silent assassination. But the running across rooftops and throwing exploding packets of powder? While indeed a diversion, it seems a bit, well, primitive and unnecessary. An assassin—a *true* assassin—would not even *need* to run, let alone across a rooftop."

"Well, duh. But shit happens, Bob. And when the shit hits the fan, you'd better run."

"Your people are rather focused on fecal analogies, aren't they? The fan one is new, though I can see the need to run in such a circumstance."

Charlie shrugged off his friend's ribbing. "Okay, so what've you heard?"

"I've spoken with Captain Sheeran. He has sent men to survey the region and expects them to return within a few days."

"Days?"

"They're moving slowly, blending in, not charging across the realm on horseback, Charlie."

"Right, right. Sorry. I'm just a little wound up now that I've been thinking about it all. I mean, what if another kingdom really is trying to make a play? We've got Ara, but even so, I'd rather avoid a war."

"Well, a Zomoki—sorry, a *dragon*—should deter most attempts. But the captain had other fruit from the rumor vines.

Apparently, there is talk that there is a wizard of some sort residing in one of the nearby realms, though he has not yet verified the whispers."

"A wizard? Not a chance. There is no such thing as magic on my world, Bob. And if there were, Ara would have sniffed them out by now."

"True, though a magical assault would potentially—" Bawb stopped abruptly. "Do you smell that?"

Charlie pushed the door open. Tendrils of smoke wafted into the small room.

"Shit! Fire! Are we under attack?"

Bawb slid a slaap onto his hand in one smooth motion and made for the door.

"I didn't know you were packing heat."

"After today? I thought it prudent."

Charlie followed him down the stairs at a run, two at a time, drawing the small knife from his boot as they ran through the smoke, heading straight toward the commotion rather than away. It was what warriors did, and the duo were more than capable in that capacity.

Bawb shouldered the door open, no visible weapons in his hands—maintaining his illusion of meekness—but his arsenal of spells sat on the tip of his tongue, ready to be deployed at a moment's notice. He realized instantly what was happening, and the slaap on his hand quickly disappeared into whatever hidden pocket he'd had it stored in.

Right behind him, Charlie, likewise, slid his knife back into his boot with one fluid motion.

Hunze, Leila, and the kitchen staff were buzzing about, frantically putting out a fire in the ovens, plumes of smoke billowing out in all directions. Thomas and the others had opened the doors and windows and were doing their best to fan the air clear.

"What in the world?" Charlie said, his adrenaline levels slowly dropping to normal.

"So sorry, Sire," Thomas said. "We'll have this cleared in no time. Just a little mishap, is all."

"A mishap? Unusual for one as seasoned as yourself, Thomas. No pun intended," Bawb said.

Hunze's cheeks were streaked, not only with soot, but also flour and shining rivulets of what appeared to be melted butter. A fiercely apologetic look clouded her face.

"I'm so sorry, Bawb. It's all my fault. I didn't mean to, it's just I couldn't get the temperature right, so I––"

"So the silly lass threw far too much wood into the mix, but failed to open the flue to let the air flow," Thomas added. "But it happens. It's how we learn, Hunze. No shame in that."

"An honest mistake," Leila added, staring at Charlie. "No harm, no foul, *right?*"

"Of course not. He's right. These things happen. Not to worry," he replied.

Thomas's shoulders visibly relaxed, though his frantic fanning continued.

"So, I guess we're adding the Cajun Blackened thing to the menu now?" Charlie joked.

"I was just trying to make you all something nice," Hunze said. "I've been learning, and Thomas has been such a gracious teacher. It's not his fault. I just can't quite get the hang of it."

"But, Hunze, you really don't have to do that," Bawb said, gently wiping the flour from her face.

The tenderness of the action made Charlie pause a moment. It was still strange seeing his friend acting that way.

The deadly assassin had taken the Ootaki girl under his wing when he saved her life, and since that unlikely day, the two had grown ever closer. But so far as Charlie could tell, it seemed to be in a rather pure, and almost sweet way––though those weren't words one would usually think to apply to the Wampeh.

"It's not that I *need* to. I just wish to be of help. To bring you joy—"

"You do bring joy. You're an important part of our—"

"No, Bawb, I mean a joy created by my hands. The joy of a good meal. I had never experienced such pleasures during my captivity, and now, here with you all, well, I want to be of use. I am so glad to at long last be valued for more than just my hair."

"You *are* valued," Bawb said, gently holding her shoulders. "But this does not mean you must resort to this type of labor, though the effort is noted, and is most certainly appreciated."

Leila and Charlie shared a look. There was obviously a growing connection between the two, and one couldn't help but wonder if it hadn't developed into something more than a victim-savior relationship at this point.

The damsel and the assassin, Charlie mused. *Sounds like some kind of warped fairy tale.*

A little tingle in his head distracted him from his train of thought.

"Hey, guys, I've got something I need to take care of."

"Go on, then. We'll see you at dinner," Leila said, fanning the thinning smoke out of the kitchen.

"Great. See y'all in a little bit," he said, then headed outside, where the air was fresh, and a giant, red dragon sat resting in the courtyard.

"Inside the walls? Wow, you must've found something good to come in here."

Ara laughed inside his head. *"Nothing so exciting, but given the events of the day, I thought perhaps my presence* inside *the walls might put people more at ease."*

"And make any with ill intent think twice."

"Well, that too," she added, amusement in her eyes.

Indeed, the giant dragon served as both a comforting

reinforcement of the king's power, as well as a not-so-subtle reminder of what could befall those who would dare move against him. The way the two often sat together so quietly, the tiny human resting comfortable and secure beside the creature that could eat him in a single bite, their bond was obvious to any who looked.

"So, what did you find?"

"Not much, surprisingly. I smell something, but I didn't see more than a few campsites around the kingdom. It's quite odd, Charlie, and I don't like it."

"You'd rather we were being invaded?"

"No, obviously, but the point is, something just isn't adding up."

"Keep your eyes and ears open, then. If you find something amiss, anything, let me know, and I'll send out troops to back you up."

"I don't need backup, Charlie."

"Maybe not, but it wouldn't hurt, and it would also make the men feel more comfortable, riding out with you having their back. It's quite a confidence booster, you know. Having the mighty Ara on your side."

"Then I am glad to oblige," she said, rising to her feet. "I'm going to make one more pass over the lands, then head abroad a bit to hunt. Hopefully all will have settled back to normal by morning."

She flapped her wings, quickly lifting off and soaring over the realm. Charlie hoped she was right, but there was a nagging doubt in his mind. One that told him things would most likely not be back to normal.

CHAPTER TWENTY-SIX

Much to their pleasant surprise, an entire week passed without any major incident. There had been a few more probes at the borders, and whispers of foreign men wandering the woods made their way back to the king. But for the most part, things were relatively calm.

The thing about calm, though, is it can often be deceptive, and when Captain Sheeran's spies finally returned with news, it was not good.

"My men have confirmed the rumors, Sire. The lands to our west are moving against you. King Horgund is seriously considering invading."

Charlie glanced at Bawb. Not good news, but not entirely surprising.

"Then it will be my first real test as king, I suppose. The men have been training hard, and I dare say their fighting skills have greatly improved."

"That they have, Sire," the captain agreed. "I think they will make a good showing, whomever their opponent may be."

As much as he did not like having his methods questioned,

the captain was a practical man, and King Charlie's new regimen actually *had* made the men readier to face combat. Only a fool would let ego stand in the way of victory, so he wholeheartedly embraced the new training, pushing his men even harder, forging them into a renewed and deadly fighting force.

"Do we know their numbers?" Bawb asked.

"I should know shortly," Sheeran replied. "And, Sire," he said, turning to Charlie. "The rumors persist. Tales that King Horgund has a powerful wizard on his side."

"A wizard? Seriously?"

"I know, Sire, it seems unlikely, but this is what my men have reported."

"Very well. I trust your skill and judgment, Captain. Brief the men, and increase the guard. We wouldn't want to give them any easy opportunities, after all."

"Aye, Sire. It'll be done."

Sheeran's light armor clanked as he hurried off down the corridor to round up his men for a general meeting. They had a lot to prepare for, and whatever the threat was, he was not taking it lightly.

"So," Charlie said, turning to his Wampeh friend. "What do you make of all of this?"

Bawb picked his teeth casually, but Charlie had known him long enough to see he was slightly on edge.

"The reports are accurate," he said. "My people have heard largely the same things, both from within our borders, as well as in King Horgund's realm."

Charlie was surprised. "Wait a minute. 'Your people?' How do you have such a robust spy network when you barely just arrived on the planet?"

Bawb smiled. "You not only seized a throne, Charlie. You took possession of its fat coffers, as well."

"Hang on. Those funds were supposed to be used for the

betterment of the kingdom. I earmarked them specifically for projects that would help the people."

"And they *are* helping them. Namely, by making it easier for Your Majesty to keep them alive in the face of an enemy with unknown forces and a potentially magical ally. Don't get me wrong. It's very altruistic, your plan, but a little coin well spent goes a *very* long way in intelligence gathering. And as newcomers to this realm, that has been one of my top priorities since our first day in this castle. I have sources in all neighboring kingdoms."

"Seriously?"

"Yes. It was of the utmost importance to establish an intelligence network to know our potential enemies' thoughts. It's amazing how little it takes to convince a man to act against his king, if he perceives it as only a small violation of fealty."

"Hence the coin spent."

"Precisely. And then you have them. Once hooked, they are compromised and become a fish that cannot hope to break free without doing great damage to themselves in the process. So they go along with whatever you wish. Thus, intelligence is gathered."

Charlie couldn't help but admire his friend's proactive measures. "I have to admit it, that's pretty impressive, Bob. You're always one step ahead, aren't you?"

"Often, but not always," he replied. "Hence the need for caution. There are strange things afoot, and so long as we do not possess a clear picture of the machinations across the border, we are still at somewhat of a disadvantage."

"But their forces are still far to the west, right?"

"Yes. For now, at least. Only light skirmish squads have been popping up along the borders. But if they feel emboldened, I fear they may press closer."

"I'll ask Ara to do some low passes in that area, then. Should make them think twice about trying anything stupid."

"But men will always try something stupid, if they can convince themselves they stand a chance, Charlie. It seems to be a standard madness that is universal across both of our galaxies."

The king sighed. Bawb was right. It was probably only a matter of time before someone decided Ara wasn't *that* scary. And if that happened, armed conflict would be inevitable.

"Well, there's not much more we can do besides prepare our people. Fortunately, things in this world move so much slower than we're used to. Even if they do invade, we'll know about it days in advance, leaving us plenty of time to prepare and evacuate those in their forces' path."

"Yes, there is some benefit to being the most advanced beings in this world. A simple skree communication and we can accomplish in seconds what would take one of Captain Sheeran's runners over a day."

"So, life as normal, then?"

"For now," the pale Wampeh replied. "But we will all need to be on our guard. It is far too easy for a lone troublemaker to slip past our watchmen. Believe me, it's a skill I know intimately."

"Agreed. We'll warn the girls tonight. And have Gwen and Thomas spread word among the staff. Sheeran's got the troops covered. But otherwise, I guess we just carry on as usual. At least, until we have reason not to."

King Charlie only hoped that reason would never arrive. But he felt he would almost certainly not be so lucky.

CHAPTER TWENTY-SEVEN

The queen's guard were doubled in number when they rode out a few days later, the men far less relaxed than they usually were on her outings. Even with Baloo padding alongside her, they nevertheless scanned the countryside for the first hint of trouble.

The ride, however, proved uneventful, and as she moved along from farm to farm, the overall contentedness of the people added to the gradual release of pressure the men were all carrying within themselves. That's not to say they were lax in their duties. Far from it. But the feeling of electric tension buzzing through the ranks had lessened considerably.

The fields Ara had torched were now spotted with new growth, and the other fields, having been properly rotated, were likewise looking healthy and lush.

"Looks like they don't need much help over here," Leila noted to the captain of her queen's guard. "What say you we hop over the hill and see how the farmers over in that area are faring?"

"If Her Highness will humor me with a brief respite before

we depart, I will send scouts to ensure the road, and surrounding woods, are safe."

"Of course. I would never wish to keep your men from doing their jobs," she said.

The scouts took off at a quick ride, cresting the hill, then splitting off in different directions to make a quick loop of the area.

"Come on, Baloo. We have a little time."

Her furry friend padded beside her, right up to the laughing children waiting near the farmhouse. They were all accustomed to him by now, and once they got over his size and fearsome teeth, they had all come to love the pup.

"Hey, look what I have," Leila said, pulling out a large grapefruit-sized ball of tightly woven hide strips, formed over a hollow center.

It was something Charlie had whipped up for her one night after she had retired to bed. Baloo had been acting up a bit, his youthful energy lacking an outlet within the castle's walls. The following morning, he presented her with his version of a dog toy. One that was made for one hell of a big dog.

"You made this for *me*?" she said, cheeks slightly flushed.

"Well, for Baloo, technically. But yeah. Do you like it?"

"I do. And I just know Baloo will! Thank you, Charlie!" she said, giving him an enormous hug. "Baloo? Where are you, silly boy? Look what Charlie made for you!"

He came running, tail high in the air with excitement. There was something new to play with, and while it may not have been *Squirrel!*, it smelled really good. Leila took him outside and hefted the ball into the air. With her lifelong outdoorswoman ways shaping her into who she was today, her toned muscles had no problem lobbing it a fair distance.

Baloo took off in a shot, his massive feet tearing up clods of soil as he ran. He picked up the ball and shook it, chewing the hide happily as he brought it back to his mama.

Within five throws, he had completely destroyed it.

"Well, shit," Charlie said with a chuckle when he saw the mangled remains. "He really is getting strong, isn't he?"

"Yeah. My big, strong boy," Leila said, scratching his head.

"Okay, I'll make another. I think I know how to make it stronger."

Three mutilated balls later, Charlie finally found the trick. A metal sphere inside, holding its shape, while the rawhide protected Baloo's teeth from clanging off its surface.

"Let's see you pop that one!" he said with a laugh when he handed it to Leila before her ride.

And now it seemed his design was working, though the added weight made it a bit harder for the smaller of the children to throw. Baloo, for his part, had seemed to realize the nature of the game, as well as the fact that he couldn't play anymore if he destroyed the ball. So it was that with surprising gentleness for such massive jaws, he retrieved the toy for another toss.

Leila wandered the farm while he played with the children. None of her men were concerned, though. The slightest call and her beast would come running, always within earshot of his mistress.

The scouts finally returned nearly twenty minutes later.

"Good news, Majesty. The roads are clear for safe passage if you still wish to proceed."

"Yes. Let's," she decided.

They all mounted their horses and departed, thanking the farmer for his hospitality, as always, waving goodbye to the children as Baloo returned to his spot at her side.

Two farms, and a great deal of warm greetings from the families living on them, later, Leila arrived at a troubled plot she was familiar with from prior outings. But where it had so recently been run-down and poorly maintained, it was now a rather impressive-looking piece of land. The soil was well-tilled, the fields harvested, and not a single crop showed signs of neglect.

The farmer saw her coming––a queen and her company of guards was rather hard to miss––and walked from the fields to greet her as she dismounted her horse. He bowed, but Leila took his dirt-covered hands in hers in a warm greeting.

"It's so good to see you! Look at your farm!"

"I know. It's been something of a miracle, truth be told."

"But what happened?"

"*He* did," he said, gesturing to the utterly massive man working the field. "Clay, come say hello to the queen."

Clay put down his tools and walked toward them.

"I have to tell you, I don't know what we'd have done without his help. A gift from God, I tell you."

"Highness," Clay said, bowing politely. "Oh, and aren't you a beautiful fella," he said, scratching Baloo's cheeks, utterly unafraid of the huge canine.

"Funny, he usually takes a little while to get comfortable with new people."

"Me and dogs, we 'ave us an understanding," Clay said with a laugh. "I've raised dozens since I was a wee lad."

She looked at the massive man and laughed. "I doubt you were *ever* a wee lad."

He chuckled. "No, I suppose not."

Leila figured if Baloo trusted him, so should she. So far, her pup had never steered her wrong when it came to character.

"Our friend here says you showed up out of the blue to help him save his farm, is that correct?" she asked.

"Aye. But not exactly out of the blue. I was working at another plot just a few miles away and heard there was a fella in need of an extra hand. Well, I'd gotten the other place in shipshape, and we were in between plantings, so I decided to come and offer my help."

"Generous of you."

"Not at all. It's the least I could do. Farming's given me a new lease on life. A new purpose. I just want ta make the most of my second chance."

"What do you mean? What was your former profession?"

"I'm ashamed to say, but I was tha taxman's muscle."

Suddenly the giant man's identity snapped into place for the queen. Charlie had told them the story months ago of his run-in with the taxman and his lackey. It seemed his punishment had proven far more beneficial than punitive.

"Ah, yes. I've heard the tale."

"I'm sure there were plenty of ill things said about me. And, honestly, I deserve most of 'em."

"But you've repented of your violent ways, it seems."

"Aye, and none too soon. I hate thinking where me life might have taken me if I'd stayed on that path." He looked almost innocent and pure as he contemplated his unexpected change of fortune. "Highness, if you could, please thank the king for what he did. He could have thrown me in chains, or banished me, or worse. Instead, he saw what I *could* be. And honestly, this is tha best I've ever felt. It's a life I never thought I'd want, but the king somehow knew I'd be better for it."

"Yes," she said, thinking back to her own life, and how he had changed it so drastically, protecting her every step of the way. "He does tend to do that."

A slow and steady warmth was building in her chest. Charlie had done well by his people, even if he wasn't exactly cut out for the job. He was a king. A true king, even if only by actions rather than birthright.

"He's a good man. A good king," Clay said. "I'm sad to say I misjudged him at first. But please, m'lady. Do tell him Clay the taxman's helper sends his thanks and warmest regards."

"Of course," she replied. "In fact, I will tell him as soon as we return." She turned and slowly rode away, hiding the proud glistening that was swelling in her eyes.

CHAPTER TWENTY-EIGHT

Night came with surprising calm in the air. No reports of ruffians in the woods or armed men massing spoiled their meal. It seemed as though things had finally taken a pleasant turn for the better, which was a welcome change. Of course, that could shift in an instant, but for the moment, at least, they were enjoying the respite.

Thomas had whipped up a simple but ample feast from the neighboring farms' bounty, their proprietors gratefully sending a large assortment of their crops back to the castle with Leila's guard. Her popularity with the people of the land was completely organic and unforced, and the culinary benefits they received were a welcome perk of it.

"Wow, Thomas. This stuff smells fantastic," Charlie said, breathing in the steaming aroma of the roasted vegetables.

"Thank you, Sire. Though to be fair, it was the unexpected bounty the queen brought back from her outing this afternoon that is to be credited."

"Nonsense," Leila said. "I only provided the raw ingredients. You made them into this delightful spread."

Bawb and Hunze shared a glance, silently watching the

exchange with amusement as they tucked into the feast. They were happy for the food, whatever its source, but when Charlie placed a bottle of wine on the table, their silence abruptly ended.

"Oh, and what have we here?" Bawb asked.

"Just a little something from our friend's vineyards I'd been saving for a special occasion."

"Charlie, we saw him only a few weeks ago," Bawb said.

"Well, yeah. But do you know how hard it was to not open this? I mean, it's *good*. Even in my time."

"Careful," Bawb warned, quietly. "Eyes and ears."

Charlie looked around, but the serving staff was clear of the room. Still, Bawb was right. He needed to be careful. While dragons, and maybe even a little magic, might fly, time travel would likely get the new king and his friends burned at the stake.

"Right. Sorry," he said, pulling the cork and pouring liberally for his friends.

"Oh, that's delightful," Leila cooed at her first sip. She poured a little on a saucer and placed it on the floor for Baloo, who merrily lapped up the treat.

"Hey! Wasting wine on the hound?"

"It's not a waste, it's Baloo!" she shot back. "And he's not a hound. I've finally learned what a hound is, and Baloo is most definitely not one."

Charlie grinned. "Fine. But at least give him the regular table wine. We don't have too much of this. Get the pup drunk on the cheap stuff," he joked.

Leila rolled her eyes, amused. "My baby deserves the best."

"But as big as he's gotten, he'll drink us out of house and home in a week!"

"Now, kids, play nice," Bawb said.

The friends broke bread and made quick work of the first course before settling in to a more leisurely repast.

"So, Charlie, I rode out to the northern farms today," Leila mentioned. "They've turned things around, and their crops are looking pretty bountiful, all things considered."

"Obviously," he replied, gesturing to the meal in front of them.

"Such kind people. In fact, as it got late, one even offered lodging for me and all of the men if we did not wish to make the long ride back. He even offered me his own chambers."

"Well, you *are* the queen," Bawb said.

"Obviously. But still, it's just nice, is my point."

"Nevertheless, it is best if you return to the safety of the castle's walls come nightfall. While things may have quieted down somewhat, there is still a potential threat brewing just across our borders."

"Yeah, about that," Charlie interjected. "I was thinking. Maybe we head over there with Ara. Give them a little show of force, courtesy of our kickass dragon. That, and maybe a well-placed spell or two from one of our slaaps might be enough to convince them we are not an easy target."

"I do not think that would be a wise idea. If we give them the excuse of what could be perceived as an aggressive act, they could use that to perhaps try to rally other kingdoms to their aid against us."

"Even though they're the ones acting aggressively?"

"Yes. They haven't invaded."

"Not yet, anyway."

"That is true. Not yet. But until they do, these little skirmish parties can be written off as rogue men, and not enough to justify a military response. This world, backwards as it is at times, does have a fairly well-defined code of conduct for these situations."

"Until they're ignored," Charlie added.

"Well, obviously."

"Right. Then we all just need to be extra careful out there

when we leave the castle. That goes for all of us," he reluctantly agreed.

"I have Baloo, Charlie," Leila said. "I'll be fine."

"I am the Geist," Bawb said with a rare, cocky grin.

"Yes, yes. We all know who you are, Bob. And I have Ara," Charlie said. "We're all badasses, okay?"

"I am not," Hunze quietly said. "I possess no skill in fighting. I've tried to learn, but it just does not come naturally to me."

"Perhaps not. But you have *me*," Bawb said, a fiercely protective look in his eye.

Charlie had seen the man in action. In *real* action. Heaven help anyone foolish enough to lay a finger on his golden-haired friend.

"Bob will keep you safe, Hunze. But I think until we get things sorted with our aggressive neighbor to the west, perhaps it'd be best if you stayed in the castle walls. No sense tempting fate, after all."

"A regrettable, but wise suggestion," Bawb said.

They sat quietly a moment, each of them in thought at what might happen if such circumstances actually did arise.

"I'll be back in a moment," Hunze said, scurrying off.

"Is she okay?" Leila asked. "I hope we didn't scare her with all of that."

"I'm sure she's fine," Bawb said. "She is a gentle spirit. Our more violent tendencies sometimes unsettle her."

"But she's good?"

"Yes, Charlie. She's good. Remember, it's not only this world that is new to her. *Freedom* is something she'd never had before we found her."

"Before you did, you mean. You saved her, dude. That's pretty huge."

The Wampeh blushed slightly. For a man so entirely in control of himself, it was telling.

Before the deadly assassin could be properly ribbed about

his reaction, Thomas stepped into the room carrying a festive cake, Hunze following close behind.

"What's this?" Charlie asked. "What's the occasion?"

"The occasion is a celebration of your friendship, Sire," he replied. "A sweet reminder of the bond between you all."

"Wow. That's a really beautiful gesture," Leila said.

Baloo's nose twitched, his curious eyes coming to rest on the treat.

"Okay, Baloo. You get a piece too."

"There's no chocolate in that, is there?" Charlie asked.

"What is 'chocolate,' Sire?"

"Right. Too soon for that to be here."

Thomas sliced the cake, plating a generous piece for each of the diners, as well as one for their furry companion.

"Here's to us, then," Charlie said, taking a big bite. "Oh, this is fantastic!"

"Yes, a most wonderful treat," Bawb added. "My compliments to the chef."

Thomas grinned broadly, but his eyes were fixed on Hunze. The others turned to look at her. The golden-haired woman's smile was radiant.

"Uh, should we know something?" Charlie asked.

"Aye, Sire. I did not bake this cake. It was made by your friend, here. Hunze made it all, from start to finish."

"With your help, Thomas," Hunze said, gratefully.

"I only watched. *You* did all of the work."

Bawb seemed to glow with pride. "*You* made this?"

"Yes."

"Hunze, this is marvelous!"

"Really?"

"Yes. On my honor, it is truly delicious!" Bawb said, practically beaming.

"Thomas, thank you for helping our friend," Leila said.

"It was my pleasure."

"You must sit with us and have a slice," Charlie said.

Bawb flashed him the quickest of looks.

"Oh, thank you, Sire. An honor indeed. But perhaps I should just take my piece back to the kitchen."

"Uh, of course. And take some for the rest of the staff. I'd love for everyone to see what a talented baker Hunze has become."

"I'll bring a taste to the others, then. Thank you, Sire. Most generous."

Thomas carried his portion to share with the kitchen workers, leaving the friends to wind down their evening with laughter, banter, and the warm embrace of good company.

They all felt good, having come so far and surviving so much. And now, finally, after months and months on this strange world in this unlikeliest of times, they had finally made this place home.

CHAPTER TWENTY-NINE

The friends had stayed late in the dining hall, sharing laughter and wine. Even Hunze, who was normally a bit reserved and unsure of herself, seemed to come out of her shell. By the time they all said their good nights and left for the staff to finish cleaning the room, their spirits were quite high.

"Oh, I met someone you know earlier," Leila said as they walked to the royal chambers.

"You'll have to be more specific. I know a lot of people these days, it seems."

"Braggart," she said, slapping his arm playfully. "This one stands out. Huge man, works out in the fields over by—"

"Ah, the tax collector's assistant. Yeah, you're right. He does stand out. Massive guy, that one. You didn't have any trouble with him, did you? He seemed to be on a good—"

"No, nothing like that. He actually asked me to thank you for what you did."

"Oh? Well, that's good to hear. I guess he's still doing okay over there. I've been meaning to check back in on him."

"Better than okay, from what he says. He was lending his

muscle to a neighboring farmer when I met him. He seemed so at peace. So happy with what he was doing."

Charlie looked quite pleased with that bit of news. "You know, I was hoping he would take to the new job. I mean, it was a punishment, obviously, and his former boss was a lost cause."

"The one you have working with Gwen, cleaning the castle?"

"That's the one. Nasty temperament, that man. He actually *enjoyed* being the tax collector. But the other one—"

"Clay."

"Yeah. Clay. He seemed like more of a victim of circumstances, you know? Just because he was the biggest guy around, he sort of got pulled into a job without having a say in it. I mean, a man that size? It's only natural he'd be snatched up for hired muscle."

"And now he's farming, and quite happy about it."

"I'm thrilled. People should be given the opportunity to improve their situations, even if it's not in a way they originally thought of themselves. So, it seems Clay's doing well and flourishing. Our tax collector, on the other hand, seems as miserable as ever."

Leila laughed and threaded her arm through his as they walked. "Well, he was rather dour when he started here, and not much has changed, so I'd say that's an accurate assessment. But Clay, he says you gave him a new lease on life."

"I'm glad it all seems to have worked out for him."

"And I wanted to thank you too."

"What for? I haven't forced you into hard labor in the fields. At least, not yet," he said with a laugh.

"No," she replied with an amused grin, "but my garden is growing in nicely, thanks to you. Moving that pesky stump really allowed me to get in there and do what I envisioned. Having my own little plot to work on, it was, I don't know, *freeing*. Having something of my own, you know? And now it's starting to grow."

"It is looking quite nice, I agree."

"Well, thank you."

"Happy to help," he replied.

"I mean it. It's been a tough road, Charlie, but you've really done all you can to make this life as good for all of us as you're able."

"Just trying to smooth the transition for you," he said. "I know it must have been incredibly hard, leaving all you know like you did. I mean, we were being chased by Visla Maktan, and then Malalia showed up as well, along with those Council of Twenty ships. But I never meant to throw you into another galaxy. I hope you can forgive me for that."

"Charlie, it wasn't your doing. We arrived here by accident. And while you're right, it *was* hard leaving my home, my galaxy behind, you've made the transition as painless as anyone could hope."

"Good. It puts my mind at ease hearing that. I do still worry about you sometimes, you know. The culture shock, all of *this*," he said, gesturing to the stone walls around them. "It could be overwhelming if you let it."

They walked silently a moment, until they finally reached the thick door to their chambers. Charlie unbolted it and held it open for his queen.

"Why, thank you."

"My pleasure," he said, following her in, then bolting the door behind them. "You know, Leila, I want to thank you as well."

"What for?"

"For being my friend. For going along with all of this crazy royalty stuff, even though you didn't want to. You've been a rock star, and I honestly don't know what I would've done without you."

"You're exaggerating," she said, laying her overcloak on its rack.

"No, I'm not. I was so caught up in the escape from Maktan

and the Council that I didn't have time to process. But now, here—well, it's all been such a tumultuous experience. I mean, I'm *home*, Leila. But I'm *not* home, if that makes sense. To be back where I had been trying to go, only to arrive a few thousand years before my friends and family were even born—it's a bit of a mindfuck at times."

"I suppose it's only natural."

"Yeah, but you've been a touchstone for me. You've helped steady my ship when things were tough. Honestly, without you here, I'd have been lost, Leila, and knowing I can count on you means the world to me."

She felt a tear form in her eye as she watched him walk to his room. She felt something else as well. Something new, and warm and welcome.

"Charlie?" she said, hesitant.

"Yeah?" he asked from the doorway to his chamber.

"Come sit with me a while longer."

He placed his coat on the couch in his room and went to her side.

Come morning, his little makeshift couch bed remained untouched.

CHAPTER THIRTY

Morning broke, and the skies across the kingdom were crisp and clear, with not a hint of ill will or sound of strife. The denizens of the realm had risen with the sun, the animals shuffling out to forage their breakfast, while the farmers set to work in their fields as the glowing orb in the sky warmed their skin.

Royal staff scurried about their duties, readying the dining hall for the king's breaking of his fast. In the kitchen, Thomas and his assistants prepared a traditional and hearty repast, albeit with a few modifications to fit the king's preferences.

Both Charlie and Leila had been a little late arriving at breakfast, though when they took their places at the table, nothing seemed amiss. Well, not *amiss*, exactly, but for those with sharp eyes, there was quite a lot to see, in fact.

Bawb looked at Hunze across the breakfast table with a knowing gaze. She looked back, an amused crinkling in her eyes. They both turned and watched Charlie and Leila trying to act casual as they ate their hearty bowls of oats accompanied by some eggs, fresh-baked bread, and jam.

The change was painfully obvious, but the assassin and his friend said nothing.

As for Charlie and his queen, the two may have been going through the motions of their daily routine with expert skill, but there was no hiding the almost clichéd glow about them.

The king had a spring in his step, and he wasn't even standing. And the queen? You could illuminate the dungeon with her radiance. At least it wasn't a glow of magic origin. That would have been hard to explain to the staff. But things between the two had changed, and it was not nearly as subtle as they tried to pretend.

Charlie's eyes drifted to Leila, meeting her gaze. Sparks flew a moment, then they broke contact, each looking intently at their food.

The pale man across the table smirked and raised a lone eyebrow, eliciting a titter of laughter from the golden-haired Ootaki.

"Something funny I don't know about?" Charlie asked, causing Hunze to lose her composure and chuckle-snort. "Seriously, what's up?"

"It's nothing," Bawb replied. "So, are you two enjoying your breakfast this fine morning?"

"Yeah. It's really good. I'm absolutely famished," Leila said.

"I'm sure you are," he replied with a knowing grin.

It took a moment for the statement's true meaning to register before her cheeks flushed red despite her complexion.

"Bawb, be nice," Hunze chided, glancing at her embarrassed friend.

"Of course. I was just making small talk over breakfast."

"You never make small talk, Bob," the king noted.

"Why, Charlie, what ever are you implying?" he replied with a mischievous, pointy-toothed grin.

Charlie sighed. "You're ridiculous, Bob. You know that?"

"As I believe your saying goes, 'Sticks and stones.'"

"I should never have taught you that."

"All the better to fit in, you said."

"Yeah, on *my* Earth. Not this prehistoric version of it."

"Well, to be pedantic, this isn't exactly prehistoric."

"You know what I mean."

"I do. But you seem in such a good mood, I doubt anything I say could darken your spirits much."

"But you're going to keep trying, aren't you?"

"Me? Of course not. And I'm happy for you. For you both."

"I don't know what you're talking about, Bob," Charlie said, defending his lady's honor, though half-assedly at best.

"I do," an amused voice said in his head.

"Hey, you weren't eavesdropping through my ears last ni—"

"Nothing of the sort. And I'm happy for you two."

"You know, you really do need to work on your—how do you call it?—'poker face?'" Bawb said, looking as though he was perfectly content to keep ribbing Charlie all through breakfast.

"Boys, are you going to keep this up for the entire meal? Because if you are, I may just take this to go and eat on my horse," Leila said, her cheeks slowly returning to their normal olive tone.

"Going for a ride?" Hunze asked.

"Yes. It should be a fairly busy day, actually. One of the farmers sent word last night that they were having some problems with their flock of sheep. I've helped them get the troublemakers under control in the past, so they requested my assistance once more."

"Animals tend to listen to you, that is true. But I do hope you will be careful on your ride. The guards are slightly reduced in numbers for a few days, since that stomach ailment hit the ranks," Bawb pointed out.

"Not fun when you're stuck in armor, I'm sure," Charlie said with a little chuckle.

"My God, you're no better than a child."

"Come on, Bob. You have to admit, shitting your armor *is* kind of funny."

A tiny smile cracked the corner of the Wampeh's lips. "Well, I suppose it *is* a bit amusing. The hypothetical, of course. The reality would not be amusing at all."

"Unless it's your enemy, of course."

"Naturally."

Charlie turned his gaze back to his queen, a spark flashing behind his eyes, reciprocated in kind. "But seriously, Leila. Be careful out there, okay? Keep your eyes open."

"Don't worry, Charlie. I'll have Baloo. Even with a slightly reduced escort, I think I'll be more than safe with this good boy at my side," she said, scratching the head of the huge beast at her feet. "Who's a good boy? Yes, you are. You're a good boy."

Baloo's hind leg twitched as Leila scratched him in just the right spot, the massive paw making quite a racket as it thumped against the floor.

"I am also going to do another flyover, Charlie. I'll be sure to sweep over her path on the way out, if that puts you at ease."

"Thanks, Ara."

"Of course. There's something in the air. I can almost smell it. Something not quite right. I'm going to finally hunt it out properly. That is, if you don't need me for anything today."

"No, I'm laying low. Let me know what you find when you get back."

"I shall. Have a restful day, Charlie."

"Fly safe, Ara."

The friends finally finished their breakfast and went off their separate ways to begin the day's work. Bawb was to meet with the captain to discuss the cost of some new equipment for his men, while Hunze was planning on helping Thomas in his work, learning more of his craft.

Charlie figured he'd give the men an easy day of it and just stay in the castle. With the stomach bug running through them, they could use a respite from bouncing around on horseback. Leila, however, wouldn't be stopped. Not when some troublesome animals needed a stern talking to. Charlie walked her to the courtyard door.

"See you tonight," he said, pulling her close.

Her lips met his, a warm sparkle in her eye.

"I'll be back before you know I'm gone," she replied, then squeezed his hand and stepped out into the morning's glory.

I think I could really get used to this life, Charlie mused with a contented grin, then made his way back inside.

CHAPTER THIRTY-ONE

"Good to see you," Leila called out from atop her horse, addressing the woman approaching them on the road. "All is well, I hope. How are the kids? Growing like weeds, I would think."

"Yes, they are well, Highness. Thank you so much for coming on such short notice," the older woman said as she met Leila and her small entourage. "We've been having quite a time with the flock, all of a sudden. To be honest, I don't know what's gotten into them."

Leila smiled warmly. "I'm sure we'll get to the bottom of it. It's been a while since they've behaved like this."

"Yes, it has. Really, not since your pet tore into them have they been so difficult."

Leila kept her blush reflex under control. Baloo had, in fact, been rather fond of this particular farm in their earliest days on this world. As a result, Charlie had covered for her, paying far more than the animals' market cost to smooth things over.

He didn't tell Bawb, of course. The Wampeh would have frowned on the expenditure and reminded him a king did not do such things. But this one did. He did for her. A happy little smile tickled the corners of her lips as a warmth flared in her chest.

"I was wondering," the farmer said, "would it be possible if your pet didn't come onto the farm? I hope I do not cause offense, it's just that he makes them even more agitated than they already are."

"Oh, my dear woman. Of course. And I am truly sorry for the difficulties Baloo caused in the past."

"Water under the bridge, Highness."

Leila turned to her furry companion. "Okay, listen, Baloo. I need you to stay up here. Or go play in the woods. But don't come down to the farm, okay?"

He cocked his head, but, as always, he knew what his mama wanted. With a grumbly little woof, he trotted off to see what he could forage among the trees.

"All right, let's go see what's up with those sheep. I bet a good talking to and they'll stop acting up."

"I'll go ahead and corral the horses and open the gate, Highness," the farmer said, then headed off down a small rabbit track between the trees.

Leila and her guards carried on, enjoying the serenity of the ride down the quiet road. She had always been fond of this part of the kingdom. The hills were picturesque, the trees thick in some areas, thin in others, making for patches of bright sunlight warming their bodies after sections of cooler shade.

A little stream flowed not far away, the fresh water adding that invisible, yet comforting smell to the air that she found so soothing to her spirits. The smell of clean and healthy nature. For the briefest of instants, she flashed back to her life on Visla Maktan's estate. An entire lifetime spent on those grounds, and now, here she was, not only in a new system, but a new galaxy. And she was no longer a slave. She was a queen.

It wasn't often that she allowed herself to revel in her

circumstance, but today—and after the previous night—she gave in to it and enjoyed the feeling.

Her men were also in good spirits. Most of the others were back at the castle, suffering from an intestinal bug that was making the rounds. If it wasn't coming out of one end, it was coming out the other. The little ride with the queen not only got them some nice, fresh air, but it also put distance between them and the sick men carrying the illness.

They rounded a bend in the road, the farm visible through the break in the trees. Soon, they'd be hit with the smell of sheep. Not exactly the most pleasant of aromas, but they hoped the breeze would air things out a bit for them. In any case, their noses would be freed of the sheepy stink as soon as the queen finished her task and they rode out. With any luck, on a day as beautiful as this, she'd be in the mood to take the long way home.

The farm seemed in good condition, the fields were in order, and the animals were all corralled in their pens. The horses seemed a bit agitated, but troops riding in on their larger steeds could sometimes stir things up with the smaller farm horses.

Leila took the lead, riding through the open gate and heading to the farmhouse. She dismounted, as did her men, glad to stretch their legs a bit. The farmer walked from around back.

"Just over here, Highness," she said.

"Right. Let's see what we can do with your naughty sheep then, shall we?"

Leila reached the corner of the house and paused. She was tuned in to the animals, as always, and she didn't sense any discord among the sheep. But *something* was wrong. And not just with the flock. All of the animals were on edge. Spooked. She shifted her confused gaze to the farmer. Something in her eyes was off.

"I'm so sorry," she said with an apologetic look. "They threatened my children."

Leila felt her Magus Stone flare warm against her chest beneath her clothes.

Soldiers in strange armor rushed from hiding, surrounding her. Still more fell upon her guards, overpowering them by sheer numbers.

"Baloo!" she cried out.

A ways up among the trees, the giant canine's ears shot bolt upright. A millisecond later, he was off and running toward the farm. He was forced to weave between the dense growth of trees, not being quite big enough to simply run them over. This slowed his pace, and on one twisting turn, a metal trap snapped shut on his front leg, snapping the bone with its force.

Baloo let out a shrill howl of pain, then began fiercely pulling on the device, trying to pry the jaws open. Leila felt her heart skip a beat when she heard his cry, and the woman in need of saving suddenly threw her attackers off, her Mama Bear instinct kicking into full drive.

She kicked and punched, knocking several men to the ground despite their armor.

"Baloo!" she yelled in anguish as her boy howled.

Leila broke into a run, evading the grip of another set of lumbering, armored men as she sprinted for the hills. Moments later all she saw was blackness as she lay unconscious on the ground.

"Put her on the horse. We're to take her to the king," the man in charge of the assailants said. "Kill the rest of them."

CHAPTER THIRTY-TWO

What is that? Ara wondered as she flew low in the skies off to the west. *It smells like magic, and it's getting stronger.*

She dropped down below the spotty cloud cover, scanning the terrain. Something had tickled her senses ever since they arrived on this odd world, and in recent months it had only gotten stronger. Enough that she was finally able to get something of a read on it. To trace it. To track it down, hopefully to its source.

Ara felt it but couldn't see it, whatever it was. But she knew she was growing near. Her sharp eyes darted to and fro as she glided, seeking out anything at all that might be the source, seeing in the shadows as well as the light.

There!

She swooped down low, landing in the smallest of clearings near an overhang of rock. It was a cavern. Well, it was the opening to one, to be clear, and there was no way a dragon of her size could squeeze through the opening. But that was where the magic was coming from. It wafted up, like the teasing aroma from a baker's oven, drawing in passersby from the street. Only this passerby couldn't enter the shop.

Ara stuck her head inside, getting a better look around the rock-walled space. From what she could tell, only the outermost part was small. The rest grew larger as it traveled downward into the ground.

She pulled her head out and began carefully removing chunks of stone from the cavern entrance, enlarging it bit by bit until she might squeeze inside. The magic was still faint, which meant it was hidden deep underground. But her kind wer no strangers to those tight spaces beneath the rocks. In fact, she, herself, had been resting in such a place in a hibernation of sorts when she had been captured back in her own galaxy. And this cavern system looked far more spacious.

It was relatively slow going, opening the entrance enough to accommodate her mass, but she was old, and she was patient. Rushing might cause the whole thing to collapse, burying whatever strange, magical thing was in there.

That would leave her in her original predicament. Namely, wondering what on Earth was giving off that magic smell. After nearly an hour of meticulous removal of rock and dirt, Ara folded her wings back against her body and wiggled her way into the limestone cavern.

Dripping waters in the realm had carved a massive network of tunnels and caves over hundreds of thousands of years. Some were big enough for her to spread her wings, while others required a more compact posture to make her way through. But the magic was stronger now. Closer. Deeper, but not too much farther away.

As she progressed ever downward, following the small trickle of water at her feet, she noticed something else unusual about the caverns. There were large deposits of the mineral Charlie called iron. The one that interfered with magic from her realm.

That would explain why it was so hard to pinpoint, she realized.

The natural elements forming the winding caverns were a block of sorts.

"*Charlie. Can you hear me?*" she lightly sent, reaching out to her friend.

No reply.

To be expected, I guess.

Slowly, she moved deeper still, traveling farther and farther beneath the surface, her glowing, golden eyes scanning for the source of the magical signature she had sensed. The water at her feet actually carried the tiniest spark of the planet's sun's energy, trickled down from the surface through layers of stone. Outside in the full glow of it, she'd never have noticed. But here, muffled from all of the sun's power above, she noticed it gently tickling her feet.

Interesting.

But that wasn't the source. Not by a long shot. The amount of magic in the water was like a drop in a river. Something stronger was nearby. A tight bend required her to compress and slide on her belly through a long tunnel stretching nearly fifty meters, but when she came out the other side, she found herself in a cavern just large enough to stand to almost her full height.

Then she saw it. Sitting on an elevated rock in plain view. The source of the magic signature she'd been tracking.

No. It can't be! she thought in shock. She spun toward the tunnel. "*Charlie! Can you hear me? I found what's been giving off magic all this time. It's—*"

A magical blast triggered without warning, a daisy-chain of small rumbles traveling throughout the entire cavern system, collapsing the caves and tunnels behind her all the way to the surface.

"*Charlie! You're in great danger!*" she sent with all of her might as the dust settled around her, deep beneath the ground.

· · ·

Leaning over the countertop in the castle's kitchen, the king and his friend were enjoying a light lunch of hearty bread and meats. He stopped eating abruptly and sat up straight.

"What was that?" Charlie asked, looking around, confused.

"What was what?" Bawb replied casually as he chewed his sandwich.

Charlie strained his senses. There had been something, he could have sworn it. A visceral sense of danger, then it cut off abruptly. No trace of the odd sensation remained.

"I guess it was nothing," he said, turning his attention back to his food. It was good, but nevertheless, a lingering *something* nagged the back of his mind.

CHAPTER THIRTY-THREE

Charlie had only just retired to his chambers and was about to engage in some light stretching and a bit of meditation in the sunlight of the open window when a clanging, rumbling sound reached his ears, echoing over the hills. And it was getting closer.

Bells rang, and men could be heard rushing to arms.

"Sire!" a young page said, bursting abruptly into his chambers. "It's King Horgund! We're being invaded!"

Charlie leapt to his feet and grabbed his weapons, racing down the hallway and out onto the parapet overlooking the front of the castle. Incredibly, it was as he had been told. An army of men was marching toward him in the distance, a long trail of dust in the trees the only real sign of their numbers.

Bawb was already there, watching the advancing men.

"How did they get here without anyone seeing them, Bob? That's not a scouting party, that's a goddamn army!"

"I can see that, Charlie. And I do not know how they hid their numbers from us. Obviously, this has been some time in the planning."

"Our men?"

"We got lucky. One of the guards incapacitated by the stomach ailment had gone out for a ride to try and get his humors back in line."

"Riding a horse after stomach flu? Ouch."

"Indeed. Not a pleasant experience, I am sure. But he was tired of being idle, and it is only because he happened to go out at an unscheduled time, in an unplanned direction, that he somehow foiled their plan, stumbling upon them in a premature contact. Needless to say, he rode like the wind, calling out warning the whole way back."

"Safely inside the walls now, I hope?"

"Yes. And all of the subjects near the castle have been offered refuge, though many chose to return to their farms to protect their crops and animals."

A flush of panic hit Charlie's stomach.

"Oh my God. Leila's out there. She rode out this morning."

"Breathe easy, my friend. Her destination was far from here, and her route would not have taken her anywhere near these forces."

"But she's out there alone."

"Not alone. She has the queen's guard. And Baloo, on top of that. If all else fails, he will protect her with his life. And word will swiftly reach them. Her guard will know not to come back to the castle. Not right now. The people love her, and honestly, she is probably safer staying out there, away from the castle, until this blows over."

Charlie forced himself to take a few breaths and count to ten, lowering his heart rate and flushing the excess adrenaline from his system, as Ser Baruud had taught him in his gladiatorial camp many years ago.

"Speaking of blowing over, I think perhaps it is finally time to end this before it begins," Charlie said.

"Agreed."

"Ara, some idiot thinks he can waltz in here and invade my

kingdom. Would you mind dropping by the castle and convincing him that's not a good idea?"

Silence.

"Ara, can you hear me?"

Again, no reply.

"Hey, have you seen Ara around? I can't seem to reach her."

"I saw her this morning when the sun rose, but she left early, likely to feed. Perhaps she is hunting."

"Still? And far enough away that I can't reach her?"

"She can travel beyond your range of communication quite easily, you know."

"Yeah, but even then I can typically *feel* something, ya know? Like, we can't talk, but I sense her pretty easily."

He fell silent, straining his mind, reaching out.

"I can barely sense her, Bob. Almost not at all. I don't understand."

The Wampeh bore a grim expression on his face. "Nor do I, Charlie. But this is bad."

"No shit."

"Yes, 'no shit,' as you say. If the Wise One is unable to put an end to this foolishness before it begins, we may be forced to deal with the invaders in more traditional ways. And once that begins, I fear a great many will lose their lives, even should she make a swift return after hostilities start."

Charlie and his friend watched as the army marched closer. Hundreds upon hundreds of men, many on horseback, accompanied by pike men and foot soldiers as far as the eye could see, trailing off down the dusty road. They would be at the castle in no time.

"We have to prepare," Charlie said, rushing from the balcony, Bawb close behind.

They raced down the stairs, heading for the courtyard, when Charlie paused.

"We should get our weapons."

"We have our weapons."

"No, Bob. Our *weapons*."

"Ah, those."

"Yes, those."

"As a last resort only."

"But we could——"

"Charlie, hidden in the woods in the dark of night, we can get away with it, but if the men see you or me using magic, there is a very real possibility that, given this invading force, they may choose to side with the newcomers. These are superstitious people, and many still view magic as a dark art. They may perceive you as a threat rather than their king."

"Seriously?"

"Yes, seriously."

"But I have a fucking *dragon*, for chrissakes. That's okay, but a little magic isn't?"

"She is a mythical beast. She is beyond their comprehension. You, however, they can relate to. You are a man, Charlie. And from what I've heard over our months here, you're earning the trust and respect of the subjects. But all of that could turn if they don't perceive your power in a positive light. And believe me, you do not want a mob of superstitious people rallying against you. That can be unpredictable, a trait that is often far more dangerous than the actions of a regimented army."

"Fine." Charlie sighed and continued his downward run, taking the stairs two at a time as he went.

The staff was rushing to hide the weak, young, and old, while those of fighting age headed out into the courtyard to take up arms. Charlie and Bawb burst out of the door at speed, making a beeline for the gate's high wall. Captain Sheeran was already there, fully armored and directing his men.

"Reinforce that bit over there. No, the part where the hinge meets the stone. If they ram it, that'll be the weakest point."

He turned and saw his king approaching.

"Status?"

"Sire, battlements are armed, and the men are stoking fires to boil oil to repel invaders. We have archers atop the walls, and lookouts in the turrets. The other men are suiting up should the walls be breached."

Charlie looked at the ranks on the walls and in the courtyard. Far too few were present.

"Where is everyone, Sheeran?"

"Most were sick, Sire. Remember? You said to send them home until they felt better, so as to not spread the contagion among the rest of the men."

"A valid strategy," Bawb commented.

"Aye. Unless you happen to be invaded at precisely that time. Which we have."

"We should have been able to recall the men long before any army reached us."

"Again, you are correct. But somehow they snuck up on us, though I have to admit, I have no idea how. A force that large shouldn't be able to move that quietly."

Bawb nodded, reluctantly. "You're right, Captain. There was nothing to be done for it. These are extremely unusual circumstances." He looked at those locked inside with them. The forces seemed rather thin. "But your men still inside the walls, what are our numbers?"

"About a third of our men are here and able to fight."

"It's enough. We still have a——"

Trumpets blared from the other side of the wall, and the sounds of marching abruptly stopped. The three men shared a look, then quickly made their way up to the top of the thick wall above the gate.

Hundreds of men stood ready just a few hundred meters away. From their ranks, a lone horse rode forward, carrying a white flag atop a pike, along with the colorful banner of his king.

"A herald, Sire. Shall we fire?" Sheeran asked.

"Now, Captain, you know the saying: Don't shoot the messenger."

"Is that from your homeland, Sire?"

"You could say so," Charlie said as he watched the lone horseman ride closer. "Do you recognize the flag?"

"Aye. It's King Horgund, all right, just as we'd feared," the captain replied.

"What exactly do we know of his kingdom? Are they lacking resources? Why invade?"

"Honestly, Sire, it makes no sense. They are a fertile land, and we've never had reason to quarrel with them. But strange things are afoot, I fear."

"I am inclined to agree with you," Charlie said.

The herald stopped his horse forty meters from the wall and set his eyes on the king atop it.

"I come with a message from King Horgund. He wishes all the men here to know that he does not desire senseless bloodshed if it can be avoided."

"Then he should not have invaded my kingdom," Charlie called down to the man. "I am King Charlie, the Dragon King, and if he came here looking for trouble, I'm afraid he found it."

"And yet, there is no dragon," the man replied. "My king says it seems the myths of your realm are just that. Myths. But even so, he wishes to spare both of our forces a bloody and lengthy battle."

"So, he plans on leaving, then? A wise choice."

"No. King Horgund will achieve victory, one way or another, but he offers a means to spare countless lives. An old tradition. King Horgund hereby challenges King Charlie to single combat, the winner of which shall be declared king of both realms. A merging of two kingdoms without a war."

Charlie turned to his captain.

"Sheeran, what do we know of him?"

"Horgund's a well above average fighter, definitely, though he's a bit past his prime."

"Your opinion, then?"

"If you're asking if you can take him, I would think so, Sire."

"All I needed to know," Charlie said, turning back to the herald below. "Tell your king I accept."

"I shall tell him."

Captain Sheeran spoke up. "On neutral ground. The field by the river. Standard escort for each side. Thirty men and no more. Agreed?"

"My king expected such terms, and agrees," he replied. "At first light, then," he said, then rode back to his king.

The army turned and marched away to make camp for the night, leaving the castle unscathed.

"Well, that went better than expected," Charlie said as they descended from the wall.

"Do not take him lightly, Sire. Tomorrow will be a great challenge."

"Yeah, but I can take this guy, right?"

Bawb put his hand on his friend's shoulder. "The captain is right, though. A lot rides on the outcome, and you must prepare as you would for any other contest. Eat well, sleep soundly, build your strength. Tomorrow, you save your kingdom."

CHAPTER THIRTY-FOUR

Charlie rose before the sun, slowly centering himself as he went through his lengthy series of katas and stretches in the solitude of his chambers. It had been odd, sleeping in that space without the sound of Leila's breathing. He hadn't realized just how comforting her presence had become until it was absent.

He took a deep breath and pushed those thoughts from his mind and went through the motions once more. She was safe at some farmhouse far from the conflict, and once he defeated King Horgund, she would be free to return home to his waiting arms.

Warm and limber, the Dragon King finally dressed in his preferred attire for fighting—that is, for fighting while wearing armor. Normally he would have eschewed it entirely, opting for the gusseted crotch pants with reinforced knees and the tunic and short coat that contained myriad little pockets and sheaths in which to hide weapons. But today had to look right. Traditional. It had to be the sort of fight people expected it to be.

That meant Charlie had to wear his suit of armor and go at it the old-fashioned way. Fortunately, he had modified the metal attire to allow for a far greater range of motion, and that, along with both his pirate and gladiatorial experience, gave him something of an edge.

But armor would wait. He threw a warm cloak over his clothes and padded down to the dining hall to fuel up for the contest. Thomas was rushing about, clearly nervous at the thought of possibly having a new king that very same day. Several of his regular staff were out sick as well, which meant he had to show their last-minute replacements where things were, what they needed to do, how to prepare portable nourishment to be taken along to the contest.

"Thomas, relax. I'll be fine," Charlie said, hoping to soothe the poor man.

"Yes, of course, Sire. My apologies. I'll send out your meal straightaway."

"Thanks. And a cup of tea, if you don't mind. It's a little chilly this morning."

"Immediately, Sire," he said, then rushed back to the kitchen.

Oh, what I would give for a hot cup of coffee right about now. If I knew this kind of thing was going to happen, I would have saved an emergency stash, Charlie silently lamented. *Those tsokin shrubs can't bloom soon enough.*

Bawb was waiting for him in the courtyard when he stepped out, well-fed, fully armored, and ready to face whatever was coming. Captain Sheeran stood ready with thirty men. Charlie looked them over. Good men, for the most part, though a few of them had been less than thrilled when he had first arrived. But now those same men would have his back. Amazing how far things had come in a few short months.

"All right. Let's do this," Charlie said, mounting his horse, his men following close behind.

The road was clear—scouts had ensured King Horgund had

honored his agreement––and Charlie made good time riding to the clearing agreed upon for the contest. They were the first to arrive, but not by much. King Horgund and his men rode in shortly thereafter, dismounting and setting up their preparation area across the field.

"Not terribly intimidating looking, is he?" Charlie said, eyeing the man he was about to fight.

"But as we well know, looks can be deceiving," Bawb noted.

"Well put," Sheeran agreed. "It would do His Majesty well to remember that while Horgund is no longer in his prime, he has fought many battles and knows many tricks. I believe you will win, Sire, but do not underestimate the man."

King Horgund pushed aside his attendant and strode toward the field of battle.

"Are you ready to face your death, Dragon King?" he said with great sarcasm dripping from his tongue.

Okay, then. I guess we're getting started.

Charlie rose from his stool, took a final swig from his water skin, and took a few paces forward as well, in what he hoped was the traditional way this sort of thing played out.

"I think you are mistaken whose death it will be today," he called back. "You know, it's still not too late for you to turn and go home. You don't need to die today."

"Oh, it will not be I who perishes," Horgund taunted. "I only wish my mistress were here to witness your humiliating defeat at my hands."

"What, your lady off having a roll with one of the servants, is it?" Charlie said.

"What are you doing?" Sheeran hissed.

"Taunting him. An angry fighter is a sloppy fighter," Charlie quietly replied.

Horgund didn't take the bait, however.

"My mistress is with child, soon to bring me a son to carry on my line. But where is *your* queen? Perhaps it is *your* woman who is with another."

"He's just trying to get a rise out of you," Captain Sheeran said.

"Yes, Sheeran, I know. Now let me do my thing." He began slowly walking toward the center of the field. "My queen has no need to see your blood cover the ground, Horgund. She's sipping tea and eating biscuits as we speak."

"Are you sure of that?" his adversary replied with a knowing grin.

Something about the way he said it made Charlie's stomach feel queasy.

"You know, it can be treacherous, visiting farms so far from the castle. You never know what sort of trouble you might find," he said, pulling a hanky from his armor and dabbing his forehead.

It was not a hanky. The material was familiar, a square cut from the hem of Leila's dress.

Charlie no longer cared for norms and formality, drawing his sword and rushing the man, fury surging in his veins. Metal clashed as the two met in a fierce collision, their blades locking from the impact.

Charlie wasted no time trying to dislodge his sword, instead letting go entirely, wailing on Horgund with his steel-clad fists, viciously pounding dents into the man's armor. He rained down his fury upon him, kicking the invading king square in the chest, sending him flying backward in a rough tumble.

Horgund, to his credit, kept his cool in the face of such a furious assault, carefully freeing Charlie's sword from his as he got to his feet, dropping it on the ground and lunging straight into an attack of his own.

His sword gone, Charlie quickly drew his long dagger from his side, deflecting the powerful swings of the much longer weapon flying toward his head. They exchanged blows, the heavier sword unable to land a blow on the faster, stronger Dragon King.

Charlie fought unconventionally, throwing armor-covered elbows and knees into Horgund, targeting his head and thighs. A few shots to the chin staggered the man, and a well-placed knee caused his leg to spasm in a painful contraction. He was chipping away at the better-armed man, not even trying to recover his own sword. And that was fine.

This was visceral. It was violent. Much as he hated to admit it, it felt good.

Without warning, Charlie's feet felt unsteady on the ground, and he found himself unexpectedly dropping to a knee, and just as King Horgund's sword blurred past where his head had just been.

What the hell?

Charlie shook it off and drove upward, his shoulder catching Horgund in the chest, his powerful legs lifting the armored man clear off the ground, sending him flying backward and then crashing to the dirt once again. He was down, and Charlie had a clear shot at his exposed flank. All he had to do was make one quick little lunge with his dagger and it would be over.

Charlie faltered. Waves of nausea hit him, his legs turning to rubber. Something was very wrong. Bawb took a step forward, but Captain Sheeran placed a hand across his chest.

"No, he must do it himself."

"Something is not right," he replied, but refrained from rushing onto the field of battle. At least for the moment.

Horgund regained his feet, obviously dazed by the pummeling he had taken. His eyes locked on his opponent, clearly in distress, and he wasted no time, rushing at him, beating on Charlie's helmet with his gauntlets. The Dragon King seemed unable to defend himself properly. Most of the blows, though weaker now, as Horgund himself was dazed and quite fatigued, were landing, driving Charlie to his knees, his arms blindly flailing as he tried to defend himself.

"No! He must do this!" Captain Sheeran said, again restraining Bawb as he moved to step in for his friend.

King Horgund kicked Charlie to the ground, then turned to retrieve the long dagger from the soil. It was as good as over. The blade would find a new sheath in Charlie's chest, and the fight would be over.

Dennis, a young guard who had spoken particularly ill of Charlie when he first arrived, charged onto the field, knocking King Horgund over with his shoulder.

"Dennis, no! What are you doing?" Sheeran bellowed. "Stop!"

But it was too late. The guards from both sides leapt into action, an all-out melee breaking out all around the downed king. Dennis was the first to fall, quickly run through, a sword piercing his heart. He was dead before he hit the dirt.

"Stop this fighting!" Sheeran yelled, while swinging his own sword in defense.

Charlie tried to focus on the battle raging around him, but all he could do was lie there, his limbs unwilling to move. A pale face appeared above him, looking worriedly in his eyes. Charlie would have commented that he'd never seen Bawb that concerned before, but he slid into unconsciousness before the quip reached his lips.

CHAPTER THIRTY-FIVE

It was dark. Dark, but strange little pinpoints of light seemed to break up the darkness. Charlie slowly pried his eyes wider, the lids heavy and his senses dull. He looked around, confused.

I was on a field, he recalled. *Not in some hovel, sprawled out on a dirt floor. How did I get here?*

A figure moved in the shadows, a shaft of light bouncing across his pale features.

"What happened?" Charlie managed to croak.

"Here. Drink," Bawb said, holding a small cup to his lips.

The water was fresh and cool, and the sensation as it slid into his belly was amazing, the inner fire churning his guts temporarily quashed. His limbs were still heavy, and his joints ached, along with a fierce pounding that had taken up residence in his head. But he was alive, and still in possession of all of his limbs, so at least there was that.

"I was fighting," he said, pushing up to one elbow.

"Yes. And you were winning."

"And then I wasn't," he said, the memories coming back. "Something happened."

Bawb held up Charlie's royal water skin. "You were poisoned."

"But how?"

"Someone in the castle is a turncoat. They must have spiked your water skin just before we rode out. Had they done it any sooner, you'd have fallen ill before the contest started, and they would have been found out."

"So they wanted me weak for the fight."

"No, Charlie. They wanted you dead." He gestured to the far side of the little room, where a goat lay motionless and unbreathing. "That was from just a sip," Bawb noted. "And in less than a minute."

"You killed a goat?"

"I had to know. And whatever they used, it would have easily killed any other man. If not for the power of the healing Balamar waters still flowing through your body, and quite possibly the Wise One's blood that is bonded in your veins, you'd have met that same fate. Even so, it managed to take you out of the fight, and at the most inopportune of moments."

It was all coming back. The fight, knocking Horgund to the ground, the clear line to his unprotected flank.

"I was about to win, wasn't I?"

"Yes, you were. But then you faltered. At first, I had no idea what was happening. I thought maybe you'd just somehow stepped on uneven ground. But then, quite suddenly, you went from winning to very nearly dying."

"And you saved me."

A grim look flashed across the assassin's face. "No, Charlie. I did not. Dennis, your guard—"

"Yeah, the kid who was talking shit behind my back when I got here. I've been tutoring him on some of his fighting drills in private. A good kid, once you get past the attitude."

"He's dead."

Charlie sat silent a long moment. "What happened?"

"He broke the rules of the contest and rushed to your aid. He struck King Horgund. He was killed almost immediately when the guards stepped in."

"Well, isn't poisoning your opponent against the rules too?"

"Impossible to prove in the heat of the moment, and by then the fighting had already broken out. Captain Sheeran tried to stop the combatants, but they had already committed."

"But we were evenly numbered, Bob. And you're the Geist, for chrissakes. Why didn't you stop them? There was no reason to keep up the disguise at that point."

"No, there was not. However, before I could act, dozens of Horgund's troops rushed from the treeline."

"But we had scouts. There was no one there."

"I know. Somehow, they possess a form of magic. Something that hid their soldiers, camouflaging them to our men's eyes. Had I been the one scouting the woods, I'd have undoubtedly spotted them. But on this world, well, this type of magic shouldn't have come into play."

Charlie mulled over the implications. Ara had been right. There *was* some magic on Earth. And now it seemed they had somehow come across it.

"How many died?" he finally asked.

"Most, though many were captured, and a few managed to escape, from what I could see. I was a little preoccupied."

"Carrying me to safety. Thank you for that," Charlie said, locking eyes with the pale man.

"Of course, my friend."

"He has Leila, Bob. Taunted me with that piece of her dress. I'm afraid he got the reaction from me that I wanted out of him."

"Completely understandable, Charlie. Had it been Hunze's, you may rest assured I would have done the same."

Charlie drank more from his cup, cracking his stiff neck as his head slowly cleared. Bawb refilled it from a pitcher, and he drained it once more.

179

SCOTT BARON

"Good. Flush it from your system."

"The bastard has her, Bob. She could be dead already."

"I do not think so. The queen is very popular among the people, and to kill her—especially when no outright war is declared—would earn him more trouble than he wants. No, I think he will keep her alive and locked away. At least until the people's anger fades and they become used to their new king."

"You really think so?"

"It is what I would do."

"But what about Baloo? And where the hell is Ara?"

"I was going to ask you that same question. She is nowhere to be found, Charlie. I assumed when you were injured she would come immediately to your aid. You share a blood bond, after all. But nothing. Not a trace."

"We've got to rescue Leila," Charlie said, rising to his feet, then falling right back over again.

"We must bide our time. Learn what we can about our enemy. We must not be foolish and rush in blind. Instead, we shall develop a strategy as intelligence comes in."

"And how exactly do you propose we gather that?" Charlie said, disheartened.

Bawb smiled. "As I told you before, I have paid my spies *very* well. Now that foresight shall bear fruit. We will know exactly what we are up against soon enough. But for now, you must rest and regain your strength."

Charlie leaned back and took a deep breath, all the possibilities of where Ara could be, and what they might be doing to Leila, running through his head.

"Oh, shit. Hunze!"

A flash of emotion crossed Bawb's face. "Trapped in the castle, with the others."

"But if they find her—"

"Thomas and his people will protect her. And remember, there were a lot of temporary faces helping in the kitchen due to the illness going around. With what has happened, I must admit, I now have to wonder if the sickness was natural in origin."

"I'd begun wondering the same thing. But if someone could cause an outbreak like that, we're dealing with more than just trace magic, aren't we?"

"I'm afraid so. But my original point is that it is something that also plays to our advantage. Hunze will blend in with the kitchen staff. They adore her, and I am confident she will be protected as best they can. And remember, she has learned to bake, so not only is her disguise fleshed out, she is actually good at it. She has value to them."

"So they'll likely add their own to the staff to oversee, but let those already there stay on so long as they do a good job."

"Precisely. But now, you rest. You will be safe here, and I have things I must attend to."

CHAPTER THIRTY-SIX

It wasn't much by Wampeh standards. Or by those of pretty much anyone from his galaxy, for that matter. But Bawb had been generous with the seized kingdom's coin, and it had paid off.

Kind words of appreciation, and a very hefty payday when there was nothing pressing motivating it, had made him very popular with his spy network. They'd all become rather well off, thanks to the newcomers, and that had earned him more than a little loyalty.

King Horgund had now taken the throne, but long before he ever set foot in their land, the men knew his reputation. Tight with his money, and reined in by his mistress. Ever since his queen's passing, he had been an ever more difficult ruler, and taking a new lover--even one who would finally provide him a son, as his queen had been unable--hadn't diminished his ire.

He wouldn't seek out and execute the spies. Every kingdom had them, and every ruler knew it. That's why they kept their aides and trusted associates close. But while they wouldn't be punished, neither would they have employment. It would be back to scraping up coin by whatever means they could, and *that* was not a pleasing prospect.

Bawb had been in constant contact with his network before the duel between the two kings, but since they had fled, his normal channels of communication were simply not an option. He had other means at his disposal, but it would require the use of the last of the magical charge in the lone konus he had secreted on his person.

Had it not been for his desire to help Hunze in her baking adventures, he might not have even possessed it at all. She was having a bit of trouble with baking temperatures, and more than a few loaves of bread had burned in the process. But she was so enthused, he found himself unable to resist the urge to help her.

It was a small konus, but with its help, he adjusted the ovens while she worked, a little boost while she improved her trade. From what Thomas had said, she had mastered much of the baking arts. Now she just needed to be able to do it on her own.

Unfortunately, her unknown magical lifeline was cut a few days sooner than Bawb had planned, interrupted by the untimely invasion.

"Very well," he muttered as he slipped into the peasant's clothing he had stolen from the dead, slaughtered and left on the roadside when the invaders arrived.

The blood had come out with a little rinse, but he hadn't dared give the attire a full washing. To do so would not only remove the camouflaging stench of old sweat, but would also make the fabrics stand out amongst the commoners.

So it was that Bawb layered the stinking clothing upon his frame, carefully hiding his musculature with additional bits of fabric, making him seem a bit larger—and softer—than he really was. No one was terribly intimidated by a fat man. Especially not a fat drunk. And *that* persona was one that had served him well on countless occasions.

The assassin slid the konus onto his wrist.

"*Occulo,*" he said, forming a reflection on a piece of broken glass.

It wasn't perfect, but it would have to suffice. Carefully, he began layering a series of spells, a closely held secret of disguise known only to a handful. He had to modify as he went, given the constraints of the rapidly draining konus, but it would work well enough.

In a few short minutes, his pale complexion had darkened to that of a ruddy-cheeked field worker, his hair and eyes shifted to a mousy brown. Even his teeth had taken on the stained look of a peasant, though he could still summon his fangs, should he require.

A fully charged konus would have afforded him so much more to work with, he noted as he stared at his transformed visage in the reflection. But this would do. This would do quite well. Only one more thing remained.

He took a bottle of cheap wine and pulled the cork, then liberally poured it down the front of his clothes.

"Sweat, filth, and wine," he said, satisfied at the resulting slurry of stinking grime. He gave a fake little hiccup and tipped his hat to the man in the reflection.

"Binsala, my friend," he slurred to himself. "Nice to see you again."

Binsala the trader stumbled his way through the realm, a bottle in one hand, a half-eaten loaf of dirt-crusted bread in the other. Bawb originally worried he might be going a bit far with the act, but the general mood of those he came across was one of despair. And what better way to deal with that than with alcohol?

His seeming drunkenness fit right in with the others drowning their sorrows. He could go where he pleased, for the most part, because a drunk of Binsala's demeanor was never seen as a threat.

Just as planned.

He covered a great deal of distance that day, staggering up to familiar faces, giving the secret passphrase of the king's aide to the incognito spies.

"*You* work for the king's aide?"

"Aye, thass right," he slurred in reply. "Wass told to pass along whatever news there was."

"Are you sure you can keep the message straight?" the spy asked. "Perhaps I should carry the news."

"Nah. Thass okay. I'll be fine," the assassin said.

"Very well. I have news of the forces and their numbers. And of the queen, as well. But if you need my help delivering the message, you need only ask."

Bawb was impressed. The man seemed legitimately concerned about his ability to carry out his task. He made a mental note. If they survived this ordeal, this man would see a bonus for his performance and loyalty.

The disguised Wampeh repeated the process several times when he managed to find one of his spies in their usual haunts. The news was the same from all of them, give or take a few minor variations. King Horgund had claimed victory after Charlie fled the duel, his men dispatching many of the king's guard before subduing the rest.

Apparently, Captain Sheeran had survived, apparently convincing his men to lay down arms and embrace the new king. Thus, the castle had been turned over without a fight. It raised his ire, the lack of spine, but there was a silver lining. Hunze would be safe. Had the castle fallen in a siege, her circumstances would be far less stable.

Having gathered as much information as he thought possible for the day, Bawb turned and cut through the trees, heading back via a much more direct route. He was making good time, and when he came to a small clearing on a hill, he paused, looking out over the land.

The skies were starting to shift to shimmering pre-dusk hue. Despite the current circumstances, Bawb did have to admit this planet's golden hour truly was a thing to admire.

"Hey, you," a gruff voice called from the treeline across the clearing.

Bawb had seen the half dozen soldiers as they made their way through the woods, but as King Horgund had already taken the castle, he hadn't placed much concern in his men's appearance. The battle was won, and their king was victorious, hence, no need for a fight.

Unfortunately, the men didn't seem to be the sort to pay attention to that kind of detail.

"I'm talking to you, peasant," the man said again, lumbering toward Bawb, his men in tow.

"Shorry," Bawb said, with a drunken slur. "I dinn't hear you over there. I'm Binsala. Nice to meetcha. Issn't it a nice evening?" he slurred.

"It'll be nicer when you hand over that wine."

"But iss mah lasht bottle."

The soldier snatched it from his hand, uncorking it with his teeth and taking a deep swig. "This wine is piss!" he griped. "How the hell do you stomach such swill?"

"I told you. Iss mah last bottle. The good shtuff is loooong gone."

The soldier's men formed a circle around the drunken peasant.

"You have any coin on you, *friend*?" one asked, his hand resting on the pommel of his sword.

"Only enough fer a bottle and a loaf," Bawb replied.

"I'll take that, then."

Bawb looked around. They were far from the roads, and they were alone. He staggered and fell against the man, his stench rubbing off on him, causing him to step back a stride. The soldiers had assumed this drunk was weak. A victim.

They assumed wrong.

"Stupid drunk. You'll regre--"

The soldier was cut short when the knife he'd been reaching for in his belt--and found mysteriously missing--sliced through his neck, nearly severing his head from his body. Bawb mused that perhaps he had a little more aggression to work out of his system than he had first realized. And what better way than this?

Two more soldiers fell before they even drew their swords, the vital arteries the stolen knife found its way home to rapidly draining them of their blood as they were opened in fountains of gushing crimson.

That left three, and Bawb had to remind himself this was a *unique* situation. He had to hold back. This had to look sloppy. Like the work of resistance during the takeover. In other words, he had to use all of his skill to make his strikes appear as if he had no skill. He smiled in amusement at the thought as he stole the men's lives as crudely as possible. This was a most unusual, and surprisingly welcome, challenge.

Twenty seconds after the first man had fallen, the other five had joined him, lying on the ground, their organs rapidly cooling to match the evening air.

Bawb scavenged anything of value, as anyone else would have done, then made sure he was clean of all traces of blood and turned to head back to his temporary home. The dead soldiers would be found, eventually. Just a few more casualties on the field of battle, lost in the confusion of the takeover. The Wampeh assassin would be long gone by then.

CHAPTER THIRTY-SEVEN

A shakily cast disabling spell just missed the pale Wampeh, his sixth sense reflexes instinctively jerking him aside.

"Jesus, Bob. Knock first. Or whistle or something. I could have killed you."

The assassin began shedding his disguise, dumping the captured weapons and valuables on a low table.

"First, you were nowhere near killing me. Second, whistle? You do realize we are trying to avoid attention, not draw it to ourselves."

"Point taken," Charlie grumbled.

"And third, do you realize what you just did?"

"I know, I know. Don't use magic in public, it'll freak out the locals if they see."

"That too," Bawb agreed. "But more importantly, you just cast a defensive spell at me."

"Yeah? And?"

"And you are still without a konus. And recently poisoned, no less."

Charlie paused, staring at his bare wrists.

"Holy shit."

"Yes. Holy shit, as you are so fond of saying." Bawb pulled up a stool and sat, removing his boots with a firm tug. "You are still not fully recovered from the poisoning, and your mind is obviously a bit clouded still yet, but your inner power seems to be growing."

"I'm a spell-casting badass," he replied with a grin.

"Yes. Such a badass," Bawb joked.

Charlie crinkled his nose, then mock-gagged a little. "What in the world is that smell? Is that you?"

"Part of the disguise. One must blend in, and when among filthy farm workers, the smellier the better," he said, then stood and dropped his trousers.

"Whoa! Hey, now!" Charlie blurted, turning away from the naked, pale man.

"This prudish reaction to nudity is ridiculous, Charlie. And you lived among pirates, slaves, and gladiators. I know for a fact none of those living situations lend themselves to much privacy, especially come bathing time," he said, grabbing a cloth and bucket of water to scrub the stink and grime away.

A quick dip in the nearest stream would have been far preferable, but given their situation, a public appearance of that nature was most definitely not in the cards.

"Yeah, well, fine," Charlie said. "But that doesn't mean I want to spend my first moments of healthy sight staring at your frosty, white, Wampeh junk."

"One, you are not healthy yet. I estimate it will take at least until tomorrow for the remainder of the poison to be processed out of your system. And two, it may be frosty and white, but I assure you, the women I have bedded would agree, it is *not* junk," Bawb said with a wry grin.

"Oh, man. I did not need the visual," Charlie said with a pained laugh. "If it's all the same to you, I'll just face the wall for now."

"It matters not to me, one way or the other," Bawb replied, giving himself a good scrub.

The wall was nothing special to look at, but for the moment, Charlie found it quite interesting. "So, what news out there? How screwed are we?"

"The kingdom has been taken, as you have already deduced, especially given the outcome of your duel with King Horgund."

"So, no casualties? I blacked out just as things started heating up."

"Unfortunately, there were. Many of your guard were lost in the aftermath of that fight, but the remainder of your subjects and troops gave up peacefully, as was agreed. For the most part, at least. There were those who fought the usurper, regardless, and there were casualties had on both sides. Mostly ours, though, I'm afraid. Horgund had far more men hidden than we were aware of."

"And how the hell did that happen? I mean, I get sneaking in and having some troops ready to go, but that was a full-fledged army out there. No way they just marched all the way here but no one happened to see them."

"Agreed. Something is not right," Bawb agreed.

"And why didn't Ara see them? I've been trying to reach her, but the poison must have really done a number on my head. I still can't connect with her."

"I do not know why she did not see the forces coming, but I'm afraid we will not be able to ask her. Ara is still missing."

Charlie felt his blood run cold.

"Missing? She's a giant, red dragon. How the hell can she be missing?"

"It is just as it sounds. None have seen her since Horgund arrived."

Charlie closed his eyes and *felt* with his senses, reaching out for that familiar connection. He couldn't reach his friend, but to his core, he knew she was still alive. Just somehow, some way, out of touch.

"She's alive. I'm sure of it."

"I am glad to hear this news. But without her presence, and power, we are at a terrible disadvantage," Bawb said as he patted himself dry and slid into clean clothes. "But there is another problem, Charlie."

"Great. What else?"

"You must remain calm. Promise me you will control your emotions."

Charlie felt a spike of panic in his chest. "I'll keep myself in check, Bob. But what's wrong? What haven't you told me?"

"They have Leila. It has been confirmed. She is being kept in the dungeon."

Hearing they were keeping her in the dark space beneath the castle, King Charlie, formerly the most powerful man in the realm, felt his knees buckle slightly. Then he felt something else. His rage flaring dangerously hot. "So it wasn't a trick, the fabric Horgund waved."

"No, it was not."

"But Baloo?"

"Hurt and kept from her when she was taken, according to my sources. Caught in a trap of some sort."

"But not killed?"

"Not while my spy was there, but he had to flee, lest he be taken as well. The last he saw, they were making off with her while Baloo was still trapped in the woods."

"He just let them take her?"

"If he'd been free, I am certain he would have laid waste to a great many of her assailants rather than allow it."

"But she *was* taken, Bob."

"I know."

"Which means Baloo is dead. And Leila is a prisoner in our own castle." He felt the anger bubbling up, but forced himself to keep his rage in check. Bawb was right. He couldn't fly off the handle. Not if they were going to save her. He couldn't let his feelings get in the way of sound planning and tactics.

"Oh, shit. Bob, what about Hunze?" he asked. "Were your spies able to get word?"

Bawb's brow furrowed slightly, but he otherwise seemed at ease. Or as much as one could be after his home had been taken from him by an invading army.

"She is unharmed," he replied. "As we had hoped, Thomas secreted her among his staff. She is safe, at least for the immediate future."

Charlie studied his friend. The Wampeh pretty much never showed emotion, but for some strange reason, when it came to the young Ootaki woman he'd saved from slavery, and likely demise, something shifted in him. If you didn't know him, you'd miss it, but Charlie had been spending a lot of time with the deadly assassin. Enough to pick up on the minute tells when Hunze's name arose.

"We'll get her back. We'll get both of them," he reassured his friend.

"That is my intention," Bawb said, sliding his feet into his clean, proper-fitting boots, shoving the scavenged disguise into a rough sack and stowing it in the corner of the room.

"So now what?"

"Now? Now you get healthy. Purge the rest of that poison from your system and regain your strength. We dare not break into the castle until you are back to one hundred percent."

Charlie cocked his head. "I'm sorry, I must be confused still. It sounded like you said we would be breaking into the castle. I'm sure you meant to say, 'after we round up the men and form an army,' right?"

"No. Just you and me, sneaking into the castle."

"As glad as I am that you're so confident in your abilities, need I remind you that there are only two of us, and the castle is where the enemy is."

Bawb smiled, his pointed canines gleaming menacingly. "Yes. But that is also where all of our weapons are hidden."

"But you said——"

"Ara is gone. Baloo is dead. Leila is captive, and Hunze is trapped within those walls," he said, a wicked gleam in his eye. "I think the time for subtlety is past. I think it is time to break out some magic. A lot of it. A can of whoop-ass, as you are fond of saying. I hope you agree with my assessment."

Charlie pictured brutally smiting the invaders with his magic. It would be a bloodbath.

"Oh, I agree," he said. "I agree wholeheartedly."

CHAPTER THIRTY-EIGHT

The king's guards, along with a handful of other men who had fought the invading army, felt the hard ground of the courtyard dig into their flesh, where they'd been forced to kneel for the better part of an hour. King Horgund had wasted no time flushing out those loyal to King Charlie, segregating them from the rest of the men.

He would normally have made a public spectacle of them. A warning to others not to follow their foolish ways. But this was a somewhat unique situation. Out of sight and earshot of his longtime advisers, his very pregnant mistress had pulled him aside, giving him a far different bit of counsel.

In the end, she appealed to his kinder side––or at least his more logical one––and convinced him that he should punish the men in private. She was so near her time, and if he executed the men in public, the possibility of a full-fledged uprising was very real. Best instead to dispatch them in a manner that did not rile up the locals in a single, large instance. She did not want her child born in war.

Smitten with his lover, and anxious to meet his new son, the conquering king acquiesced.

But that didn't mean men would not be dying this day.

Seated on an elevated platform, King Horgund drank deeply from his chalice of wine. It seemed King Charlie had a fondness for quality drink, he had been pleased to learn. After a more thorough examination of the cellars, he would have to remember to take his men to visit the winemaker and relieve him of several more casks. A tax, due the new king of the realm.

In the meantime, however, there was bloody business at hand. He nodded to the captain of his men, a brute of a fellow named Sykes.

"For sedition against the rightful king, as determined by individual combat, and for inciting others to violence against their new ruler, you are found guilty. Have you any statement?" the new king's captain asked the man kneeling before him.

"Fuck you! Bloody filth! You're nothing but—"

The captain's sword plunged downward through the man's neck, piercing his heart, putting an abrupt end to his words.

Sykes pulled his blade free and wiped it on the dead man's tunic, then moved down the line to the next prisoner.

"Please, sir. There must be a mistake. I gladly welcome King Horgund to our lands. I would never take up arms against him," the man said.

"Yet here you are. Captured in battle along with these other men," the captain countered.

"I'm just a soldier. I swear, I had nothing to do with that. We just follow orders. If you want to blame someone, blame him!" he begged, pointing to Captain Sheeran.

"At least have the decency to die with honor, you pathetic oaf," Sheeran growled.

Captain Sykes drove his sword into the man's chest, then walked to the former king's captain. "A man of action, I see."

"As are you. Begging does not become us."

"It does not," Sykes agreed, eyeing the man before him.

While Sheeran might have been on his knees, it was only in

body. His spirit stood as tall and strong as ever. Captain Sykes had to respect the man's spine. He also recognized him from the battle upon the dueling field.

"On your feet. The king would have words with you."

Captain Sheeran rose as best he could with bound hands and followed his captor to the raised platform. King Horgund leaned forward and studied him a moment, a curious look in his eye.

"You were present at the contest with your former king, were you not?"

"Yes, Sire."

"And your men attacked mine when my victory was at hand. Is that not correct?"

"Yes, Sire. That too is correct."

"These are your men. Loyal to you. Loyal to your king. Yet I remember you ordering them to halt their attack. Why is that?"

Sheeran shifted on his feet, well aware of the scrutiny he was under.

"Your Highness was engaged in an agreed-upon contest. To intervene, even if King Charlie was losing, would be dishonorable."

"And you are a man of honor, then?"

"I am, Sire."

"Yet you would let your king die at the hands of an invader."

Sheeran spat on the ground. "That bastard Charlie was no king of mine. I served, aye, but not because I was loyal to him. Have you heard the tale? How he came to seize the throne from my rightful king?"

"Refresh my memory."

"He killed him. Didn't even use his own hands, like an honorable man would. Instead, he had his infernal dragon devour him. Burned him alive, then ate him whole. That is no way for a king to die, and no way for another to claim the crown."

"Yes, I heard of this event," King Horgund said.

"And you are not afraid of his mighty beast?" Sheeran said, eyes darting toward the sky, as if he expected her to swoop down at any moment and burn them all.

King Horgund smiled, utterly relaxed in his seat. "I'm not worried about the creature," he said. "It has been handled."

"Sire?"

"I have counsel of a powerful wizard of my own, you see. One who helped rid me of the winged obstacle to the throne."

Sheeran seemed shocked. "The dragon is truly gone?"

"Yes."

"Then I humbly offer my service to you, Sire. King Horgund, the rightful king, who claimed the throne by legitimate combat."

The king laughed. "You shed your king and offer your loyalty to me so easily, Sheeran?"

"My loyalty was never King Charlie's to have, Sire. I'd be proud to serve you."

Horgund glanced at Captain Sykes. The armored man nodded ever so slightly. Sheeran was well respected and known throughout the realm. And if he was on their side, perhaps they had an option besides executions for the others.

At least, for most of them. Some would still need to be made examples of, naturally.

"Very well, Captain Sheeran. Kneel, and swear your fealty."

His hands were unbound, and his sword returned to him, which, as he had done when Charlie claimed the throne, he unsheathed and planted in the soil before him, kneeling in front of his new king. He swore his oath, then rose to his feet, free and restored in rank.

"Now, your first duty is to empty the barracks. My men will be taking up residence there."

"Of course, Sire."

"And then I wish for you to weed out the loyal from the traitors. Can you do this for me?"

"Yes, Sire. But if I may, can I request the assistance of my loyal man to aid me in my duties?"

"Granted. Which one is he?"

"Owen. Come here, lad," Sheeran called out. The beaten youth scrambled to his feet and joined his captain. "We serve King Horgund now."

"Aye, Captain."

"I want you to spread the word among the men." He took his sword and freed the youth's hands. "You're serving the new king under me, understand?"

"Aye, Captain."

"Good lad. You'd best get to work, then. Go on, now."

Owen took off to find the others, leaving Sheeran before the king.

"Well done, Captain. Your men obviously respect your judgment. But, where were we? Oh, yes," the king said, rising to his feet and speaking loudly to the prisoners. "I would have all of you see what happens when you are loyal to me. You can be restored to your former positions, like the captain, here. You can have a good life. Feed your families. But only if you are loyal to me, and me alone." He nodded to Sykes.

Captain Sykes swung his sword, neatly decapitating a wounded captive who had fought at the dueling field. The headless body trickled blood onto the ground, while the others awaited their fate.

"The same will happen to any who help this rogue criminal. Your former king, Charlie." Horgund paused a long moment, the silence hanging uncomfortably in the air. "But, for whosoever finds and turns him in," he continued, "there will be a hefty reward of golden coin and prominent rank in my castle. Now, those who fought my men as they took the towns and castle are free to go, for you were unaware what had occurred between your king and I. Tell the others of my mercy."

Sykes moved down the line, freeing the group of men taken as they claimed the castle after the king's duel.

"The rest of you," he said to the remaining men, kneeling in the dirt. "You dishonored yourselves, attacking despite the agreement between your king and I. For this, you shall be made an example of, that others will not make the same mistake."

Several hours later, the men's bodies lay in a shallow, mass grave just outside the castle. Their heads, however, remained above ground, a gruesome reminder to all who would doubt the new king's resolve.

CHAPTER THIRTY-NINE

"Haven't seen him. Nope," the man on the road said. "Why? Is the king alive?"

Captain Sheeran scanned the road and adjacent fields with his sharp eyes from atop his horse, then turned them back to the man standing at the side of the road.

"The old king is exiled, long live the new king."

"Long live the king!" Owen exclaimed from atop his adjacent horse.

"Who? Horgund?"

"*King* Horgund. It would do you well to remember it, for others may not be so understanding of your words."

"Sorry, Captain. *King* Horgund. But it's true, then? King Charlie's beast is missing, along with the man himself?"

At the mention of the dragon, all three couldn't help but glance upward, expecting that familiar shape to soar overhead at any time. But the skies remained empty.

"We'll find him," Owen said. "Me an' the captain are riding the entire kingdom if we have to."

The younger man had ridden out with Captain Sheeran that morning, and the pair had covered a sizable swath of the kingdom in a very visible search for the renegade king. Word had spread that they were looking high and low.

King Horgund had been particularly pleased to hear his new man was performing so zealously when his spies reported in. Sometimes the transition of power did not go so smoothly, but with the realm's longtime captain leading the search, locals were far more likely to fall in line. It was a pleasing turn of events, and one that allowed him more time with his mistress as her time grew near.

A son. An heir. After his former queen's failure to produce one for so many years, this passionate young woman he'd taken to his bed shortly after his queen's untimely death had provided him not only comfort and warmth in the darkest of hours, but now the one thing his bed's former occupant could not. Offspring.

And thanks to the efforts of a certain local turned to his side, he was now free to focus his attentions upon his lover when she needed them most.

Captain Sheeran had been a most fortuitous acquisition, and Captain Sykes wholeheartedly agreed. Things had fallen into place, just as his wizard had foretold. King Horgund had been confident. Overconfident, even. But the overthrow of Charlie's realm had gone even easier than they expected.

All that remained was the final elimination of the rogue king, and his victory would be complete. And he was confident his zealous new captain would leave no stone unturned. It seemed his dislike of King Charlie had only festered and grown since their first meeting, and it would serve King Horgund well.

"So, no sign of him, then?" Sheeran said to a passing shepherd.

"None. I'm sorry I can't help ye, Captain."

The captain and his aide nudged their horses and rode on. There were still a lot of farmers and peasants to visit. Their survey of the realm would take some time, of course, but they were making good progress regardless.

Late in the day, Captain Sheeran and Owen dismounted their horses at a flourishing farm. It was in better shape than most, the fields lush and thick with healthy growth. The farmer had also avoided destruction of his lands by immediately swearing fealty to the new king as his men rode past. As a result, aside from their taking several sheep and bushels of grain as a tax, his lands were left unscathed.

Farmhands worked the last hours of sunlight out in the fields, but Sheeran had another destination, riding toward the small cluster of buildings.

"Cap'n. Good to see you, sir," a deep voice said from the open farmhouse door.

"Likewise, Clay. It does my heart well to see you in good health. I take it all is well here?"

"Aye. King Horgund let us be, though his captain did tell us ta bring another dozen bushels of grain, as well as a sizable portion of tha crops just coming ripe."

"A tax, eh?"

"Aye," Clay said with a chuckle. "Rather ironic, isn't it? Me, the taxman's right hand now havin' ta produce taxes for tha new taxman."

"Hard labor the king had you doing."

"But honest labor."

"You would not wish to petition the new king for your old position back? He might have use for a man of your experience."

Clay paused, nodding a greeting to the recently hired help as they walked past. He had his suspicions they were on King Horgund's payroll, but then, he was just a laborer himself. What could he possibly say or do about it?

"I'm happy here, Cap'n. This life suits me. Far less stress, the food is good, tha air is fresh, and tha company is warm," he said, glancing at one of the farmer's daughters as she worked with the animals.

Sheeran smiled, knowingly. "I see. So, King Charlie's punishment suits you, then."

"It does, at that."

"And have you seen him, then?"

"No, I haven't," Clay replied in a loud voice. "Hey, you lot," he called out to the workers. "Any of you seen King Charlie around these parts? The Cap'n here is trying ta find 'im."

A murmur rose in the ranks, but none had seen the runaway king.

"Sorry we can't help ye, Cap'n."

"No worries, Clay. We will ride the land from end to end until we find him. King Horgund has a few others searching as well, but Owen and I know these parts well, and he has given us free rein in our task."

"Well, I don't know how much I'd believe the rumors," Clay said, "but I heard 'e was spotted up north, close to the border. But that's quite a long ride. Unless his dragon flew him there atop her back, of course."

Sheeran locked eyes with him. "The beast is gone. There has been no sign of it since the day King Horgund's army arrived. The king himself told me it was taken care of."

"Oh?"

"Yes. Apparently, the king has a powerful wizard working alongside him, though I haven't seen him with my own eyes."

"Well, that *is* news. A wizard, you say. A strange time we're livin' in, eh, Cap'n? Wizards and dragons roaming our lands."

"On that, we are in agreement," Sheeran said.

"And what of the queen? Rumor has it she was captured visiting the farm just over those hills."

"You heard right. She was taken the same day the dragon went missing."

"Killed?"

"No. The king's wizard had her placed in the dungeon. I have not seen her, but word in the castle is, she is still alive."

"Who keeps an innocent woman in a dungeon?" Clay grumbled.

The workers nearby looked at him curiously.

"What? You lot may be new to this farm, but the queen always treated us well. Their quarrel was with the king, not her. Do you louts think it's okay to lock innocent women in a dungeon?"

"She's a deposed king's queen," one said. "It's only natural."

Clay sighed, defeated. "I suppose you're right. An' I have no love for tha king. It's just, the queen was nice ta me."

"Well, you'll be pleased that she lives, yet, then," Sheeran said. "Be glad for that, for her king will undoubtedly not be so lucky once we find him."

"And her beast? The big furball?"

"Dead, from what I hear," Owen interjected.

Clay's shoulders sagged slightly. He was a massive man, and the queen's visits meant the rare canine large enough to play with him. It was a silly thing, but he would miss his furry friend.

"Well, I wish ye both luck on your quest. Can I offer ye something ta drink before ye ride out?"

"Appreciated, Clay, but we are well-provisioned for our task. Now, come along, Owen, we have much ground to cover before sunset."

Sheeran and his young aide nodded their farewell to the farm workers and trotted off down the road. Clay and the others went back to work, laboring with talk of the new information fresh on all of their lips.

The skies eventually began to darken, and all left the fields to clean up, Clay taking up the rear.

"Come, it's suppertime," the farmer's daughter said, brightly.

"I'll be right there," he replied, a warmth in his eyes as they met hers. "I forgot my spade out in the field."

"Clay, you know how Father gets about his tools."

"Aye. Go on and start without me. I'll be back soon."

She turned and went inside, while the large man trotted off into the fields as darkness fell. He retrieved his spade, which was exactly where he left it, along with a small bag of the day's harvest, then made his way to the small, disused hovel at the edge of the fields.

He placed the bag at the door and leaned against the wall, nonchalantly.

"They're gone," he said to the air. But he knew the air was listening. "The queen lives, but is in the dungeons. No sign of the dragon, and King Horgund has search parties riding the kingdom. I said to try north, but I don't know if it'll help any."

He pushed off from the wall and walked back to the farmhouse, his spade in hand, but the sack of food left behind. The door opened a crack, and a pale, white hand pulled it inside.

"Well," Bawb said as he closed the door behind him, "it seems we have a bit of news."

CHAPTER FORTY

"So these won't work?" Charlie asked as he stripped the weapons from the dead man at his feet.

"No," Bawb replied. "These are common soldiers. Look at the colors."

"I can't really see them very well in the dark, Bob. You're the one with the super Wampeh eyes."

"Use your magic, Charlie."

"Oh, yeah."

Charlie reached within himself and pulled a strand of power, then used it to cast the seeing spell the assassin had taught him. Ser Baruud's night vision spell was good, but Bawb's was even better. Of course, it was only natural an assassin should know all the best tricks for things of that nature, he figured.

He looked at the men they'd slain and dragged into the woods. Bawb was right. The uniforms weren't the ones they would need in order to blend in with the other castle guards. Of course, the men all knew one another, and the uniforms would only buy them a moment, but a moment would be all they needed.

"Shit, you're right," he grumbled. "We need to take a pair of the castle's guard."

"As I said."

"But we're *outside* the castle, Bob. How often do the castle guards come out here? And away from the walls, where we can ambush them, no less?"

"It *is* problematic," Bawb agreed.

"So what's the plan?" Charlie asked as they hid the bodies in a shallow grave. Just two more men gone missing in the night.

"I fear we may have to adjust our strategy. I assume there is still no contact from the Wise One?"

"Nothing. It's incredibly faint, but I can feel our connection. I know she's still alive. But beyond that, I can't reach her."

"Then it falls entirely upon us. I will have my spies dig up what information they can. We should know more by tomorrow night. For now, we need to leave this area. We are too close to the castle for prudence."

Charlie looked toward what had so recently been their home, but knew his friend was right. Without means to disguise themselves, going inside would be suicide.

The following night, Bawb returned from a nocturnal reconnaissance, a little blood on his hands.

"Trouble?" Charlie asked, seeing the telltale red.

"No," Bawb said, wiping the remnants with a rag. "I had *words* with one of the mercenary spies King Horgund had lurking around the woods."

"Lurking. Now that's funny."

"How so?"

"Not *funny*, funny. Just funny. Like, the poor guy probably thought *he* was the most dangerous thing out there, when he should have been afraid of what *else* was out there in the dark."

Bawb sat on the floor and rubbed his hands together,

warming them after his excursion in the cool night air. Charlie held up his hand and cast, igniting a small, blue flame. The size, and color, cast so little light, there was no fear of the dim glow drawing attention through any cracks in the hovel's walls.

"Thank you, Charlie. The water in the stream *was* a bit cold," Bawb said, warming his hands.

"My pleasure. I know it's got to be tough not having your gear for so long. I mean, you have all of these spells to keep you warm, or dry, and all that other stuff. But now you're stuck out here with me and can't access any of it."

Bawb grinned. "You know, the Wampeh Ghalian are not allowed to so much as touch a weapon or magical item for the first three years of our training."

"You never told me that."

"We train together, and I teach you as best I can. But there are many things I have not told you, Charlie. And I swore an oath to keep these things secret from all in the galaxy."

"But we're not *in* that galaxy anymore."

"A convenient loophole," the Wampeh agreed. "And seeing as Ara is gone, along with the spell she was working on to return us to the right time, and right galaxy, I feel a little sharing of this knowledge of the Wampeh Ghalian is acceptable. I don't think I shall ever see my home system again."

"But it's not *that* bad here, is it?"

"No, not at all. But nevertheless, it is a far different thing to visit a place, knowing you can return home at any time, than being stranded there."

Having been in precisely that circumstance for several years in the distant galaxy his friend called home, Charlie knew exactly how he felt. It was only when they were thrown back to Earth by a convergence of unlikely factors that he returned to his planet of origin. Just as he had finally accepted he would never come home again, that's exactly what happened.

Well, not *exactly*. He *had* arrived a few thousand years too soon. But aside from that little glitch, Charlie had made it back. And now he was king. Or, *was* king.

"Any more word on Hunze?" Charlie asked.

"As expected, she is still safe in the kitchens. Thomas and the others have her working with them as part of the staff."

"At least there's finally a bit of good news," Charlie said with a sigh. "But what else have you learned?"

"Most of the staff have remained in their same positions. The guards have changed, naturally, but King Horgund did not want to restaff the entire castle. Especially not as his mistress is so near to giving birth that her lady-in-waiting never leaves her side for a moment."

"A baby in the castle."

"Yes. And likely born in your former chambers. I'm sorry, but they have taken over your rooms and destroyed much of what was in them."

"It's just stuff, Bob. Things can be replaced. Not people. Which is why we need to figure out a new plan to get in there, get our gear, and rescue our women."

"Hunze is not my––"

"You know what I mean. Now, do you think Gwendolyn could maybe slip some poison into Horgund's food? Give that bastard a taste of his own medicine?"

"I do not believe she will make a move against the new king. And besides, that is assassins' work. And if the king truly does have a wizard at his side, poisons would be detected, anyway."

"So we're stuck with some asshole living in our house, eating our food, imprisoning our friends, and having a happy little family life. Just great. And now he's getting an heir too. Next thing you know, he'll try to take the girls as concubines and pop out more of them."

A dark look crossed Bawb's face. "This will be his first child," he said, an icy tone in his voice. "And I intend to see to it that it will also be his last."

Charlie had seen that look on his friend's face before. For a split second, he almost felt sorry for Horgund.

"I'm afraid it is a bit premature, but I need to harvest a most particular tool," the pale man said. "We need to make an outing."

"Harvest?"

A knowing smile crept onto the assassin's lips. "You'll see."

CHAPTER FORTY-ONE

The path was hard to see, even with the help of the vision-enhancing spell, and Charlie found it difficult to keep up with his Wampeh friend. The man became a part of the night, moving with great speed and stealth in the dark as his sure feet followed the near-invisible path that he alone knew so well.

They were going fast. Far faster than either would have preferred in the murky light––or lack thereof––but Bawb was making the trek without his familiar shimmer cloak, and despite his razor-sharp senses scanning for any sign of danger, he couldn't help but feel almost naked as he walked the familiar trail. And so, they sped on.

They finally arrived at the base of a rocky, granite face, where the back side of a hill had sloughed off millennia prior. Charlie followed Bawb through the fallen rocks to an almost invisible crack running up the face.

Without hesitation, the Wampeh jammed his hands in and began climbing.

Just like bouldering back in J-Tree, Charlie mused. Only this climb was quite a bit higher, and they had no crash pads to cushion their fall should they tumble. *So don't fall*, he told himself, then followed his friend up the stone face.

After the first ten meters, the climb became far easier, with multiple outcroppings of dirt and vegetation breaking up the ascent. They made good time, until they reached the halfway point. There, Bawb stopped.

"What is this place?"

"A natural growth," Bawb replied. "Saplings took root here some time ago, and managed to find purchase in the soil and rock."

The tiny cluster of trees seemed to have done well from the slight elevation, the location affording them more direct sunlight than if they were competing for its rays with a forest full of neighbors. But one tree in particular stood out, even in the dim light of the moon.

It had a warmer color to its bark, and its leaves were likewise a deep, rich green. It almost radiated health and strength. And Charlie recognized the feeling tingling his senses.

"The waters?"

"Yes," Bawb said, examining one of the tree's low branches.

"You've been feeding this tree with the Balamar waters we brought from the Wasteland?"

"Yes."

"But you'll combust if you touch them."

It was true. While the waters were healing to the skin of nearly all they touched, Wampeh were a different matter entirely. In fact, if splashed with the liquid, they would combust, much like vampires reacted to holy water in those old-timey videos.

Bawb chuckled at his friend's concern. "I was *very* careful, Charlie."

Nevertheless, Charlie shuddered at the thought of his friend going up in flames. The healing waters he and his ship's second-in-command, Rika, had stumbled upon shortly after crashing on the first alien world a human had ever set foot on had such amazing healing properties for non-Wampeh. In fact, having drunk deep of them, he had found himself almost invulnerable to smaller injuries.

Cuts would heal in a day. Bruises in hours. The waters were safe for most species to touch, but would kill almost any creature from that galaxy that was foolish enough to drink them. But Charlie and Rika were not from that galaxy.

The memory of his friend twisted a knife in Charlie's gut. He hadn't thought about her in ages. But there was good reason. While she hadn't been killed, exactly, their slave trading captors had lobotomized her, and not even the healing powers of the Balamar waters could restore her mind. The pilot and mech driver became a shell of herself, sold into slavery, never to be seen again.

Charlie shook his head clear. *Not the time to get sentimental.*

"Good thing we keep the waters very well hidden. I would hate to imagine the staff accidentally serving you a glass of it," he managed to joke.

"Yes, that would be...unfortunate."

The assassin pulled a sharp blade from his hip and carefully carved the branch he had been examining free from the tree. Something was different about that one, and when he looked closer, Charlie could see what appeared to be a lone, long strand of Ootaki hair, golden as ever, poking out through the wood itself. It seemed as though the hair was coming from *inside* the branch, the tree growing and healing around it.

The remainder of the strand had been carefully, and tightly, woven around the wood. It seemed amazing it had survived the elements up in the exposed location, but Ootaki hair was far stronger than it looked, and required a sharp blade to cut.

"It was feeding off of the sunlight up here," Charlie realized.

"Totally exposed, all day long, with nothing to block it from absorbing the rays."

"Correct."

"And you had it running *inside* of the branch, feeding the wood with the absorbed power from the sun's energy. That, plus the waters, means you healed the branch and made it stronger than ever. And we saw with Hunze and Ara that this system's sun is very nourishing to their power."

"Again, correct," Bawb said with a smile. "Very good deductive reasoning, Charlie. But you missed a few of the finer points."

"Such as?"

"Such as, I had Ara help me reforge a charged konus into a power rod. It was delicate work, but with her abilities, it was a success. *That* is what I implanted in the core of the branch, wrapped in the most powerful of Ootaki hair."

"Of course. Helping it heal, while absorbing power from the sun and channeling it into the heart of the wood, and therefore, the embedded konus."

"Exactly. But there is one final detail."

"Oh? It gets better?"

"You know Hunze, Charlie. Her hair has never been shorn."

"Making it the most powerful it will ever be."

"Yes. The first cut. And the Council of Twenty has been feeding power into it her entire life."

"Impressive, I know. But even as a first cut, it's still just a strand."

"Yes, but not just any strand. A *freely given* one."

Charlie knew the implications. Ootaki hair was powerful on its own, and even more so if fed additional magical energy, as the Council had done for decades. But as potent as it was, and even if they managed to capture an Ootaki before they'd had the first cut of their hair, the locks, when taken, would lose a large portion of their power.

It was why the Council fed so much into their captives over the years. Overcharging the hair, knowing there would be power loss, as all cuts caused. But hair freely given suffered no such diminished magic. And as a strand that had never been cut, that lone, golden thread contained more power than many konuses combined.

"You forged a mixed-magic weapon into a tree," Charlie said.

"Inspired by you."

"By me?"

"Yes," Bawb replied, gently carving the far end from the branch, making it a portable size. "It still needs quite a bit of shaping, and I have to be careful to keep the blade from Hunze's hair, but I have made an experimental weapon out of live wood. I have made what you call a *wand*."

Charlie remembered telling him about the fictional tools of the fictional wizards of his world. But now, standing on Earth's soil, a wand actually existed. And though it still needed finishing, he could feel the power it contained.

Bawb took a strip of leather and wrapped it tightly, protecting Hunze's golden strand while he whittled the smaller twigs from the branch for easier transit. If his theory was correct, the hair would recharge the wand if it were drained, refilling it endless times as the strand pulled in energy from the sun.

"You know, Charlie, this was only meant as a test to see if it would even work. But now it seems this is our only magical device outside the castle walls. Though we have no idea what it is capable of. Or if it will even work, for that matter."

"Then you should try it out."

"Not yet. First it must be shaped, and carefully at that. As you once said, the taper focuses the power, and I wish to be certain nothing interferes with that."

"Well, I was speaking hypothetically. Magic and wands don't actually exist on my world."

"And yet, here we are," Bawb said as he tucked away the unfinished wand and sheathed his knife.

The pair then carefully climbed down the stone face and made their way back to their shelter under cover of night.

CHAPTER FORTY-TWO

The slightest crackling of twigs caught the sharp ears of the captain's aide as he silently walked the woods. Owen had known *something* was going on out in the trees at night, but had never managed to see for himself. Tonight, he hoped, would be different.

There had been whispers of strange creatures lurking, attacking, and bodies were found as often as they weren't. He suspected it was just bandits, or even rebel troops holed up and avoiding King Horgund's men, but there were actual dragons afoot. With that in mind, he put his disbelief in the people's superstitions aside. Nowadays, anything, it seemed, was possible.

He padded through the foliage on silent feet, wearing his softest-soled boots for the night's excursion. Captain Sheeran had outfitted him with them himself, showing him how best to shift his weight as he walked to avoid making a sound. The captain had shown him a lot, actually. He'd never had a son of his own, and Owen liked to think the older man had adopted him, in a way, passing along skills to the heir he'd never had.

The feel of the rocks and twigs through the pliable leather

was odd at first. But once he had become accustomed to the sensation, he found himself able to walk quite comfortably in the stealthy attire. They wouldn't do for daily wear, but in the dark of night, they were perfect.

It wasn't far ahead, where he'd heard the noise. It was probably a deer, or perhaps a wild pig, but it could just as easily be something—or someone—else. He kept his hand on the pommel of his new short sword—a part of his weaponry since King Charlie had arrived—but did not draw the steel.

Another of Sheeran's teachings, that had been.

"They'll see the reflections," he had said, showing the younger man how easily the bright metal could catch the light in even the darkest of locations. "Movement is what draws the eye, and it's damn near impossible to hold a blade perfectly still unless you've got it planted in the ground. But a body in dark clothing, *that* can move, slowly, and not draw attention."

Owen had taken the lesson to heart, and was applying it, as well as the myriad others he had learned, as he stalked his prey, whatever it may be.

The sound had shifted, he realized. Someone was moving quickly, and away from him, toward the deep woods. If they reached the stream, he'd lose them in the noise of the flowing water.

He picked up his pace as best he could, trying to close the distance without giving himself away. His ears strained to track the path of his quarry, but they were exceptionally stealthy. Ordinary men didn't move like that, he realized, a little flush of adrenaline surging into his system. Fortunately, he was in the middle of his pursuit, so the flight aspect of his visceral response had no time to kick in.

Faster and faster he went, desperately trying to catch a glimpse, but even his sharp eyes could not pick them out in the dark. The sound of water soon reached his ears. Any moment, he would lose them to the rushing noise of the stream. It wasn't much, just a small rivulet, really, but for prey as skilled as this, it would be enough. Enough for them to make good on their flight.

He moved quickly, but the adrenaline was wearing off, and the annoying realization that he would be returning empty-handed began to set in. Standing on the muddy bank, he looked for some trace. A footprint, anything. But there was none. He waited, motionless another minute, then, with a frustrated sigh, turned and began the walk back to the castle.

Captain Sheeran wouldn't be mad, but Owen had hoped to impress him this night. Sadly, it was not meant to be.

Had the lad opted to venture out in the opposite direction that night, things might have taken a much different turn, for at that very moment, just a few miles away, a far noisier group was traipsing through the woods.

The new king's troops were confident in their demeanor. Cocky. King Horgund had made an example of the former king's men, and they now had the run of the land. Soon, they would begin the king's process of new taxation, which always afforded them the opportunity to acquire a few niceties for themselves in the process.

It was with this invincible swagger that they found themselves fallen upon by a band of armed men in the dark of night. Men with not just standard weapons, but some armor as well. Not bandits at all, it seemed.

"Rebels!"

It was all the soldier managed to say before taking a cudgel to the throat, effectively silencing him for the rest of his brief life.

The odds were roughly even, a handful of men on either side, all trying to kill one another in the confusion of darkened battle. The newcomers wore their protective armor, but King Charlie's rebel soldiers were engaging them in an unusual means of combat.

Rather than battling sword-to-sword, as was the norm, the

surprisingly nimble men were dodging the heavier blades of their opponents, parrying them aside and slipping beneath the weapon's arc, attacking the weak points in their armor. The shorter swords the men used were proving most effective, and more than one man found himself bleeding, despite his protective metal shell.

But in the dark of night, and on uncertain footing, the tables turned repeatedly, with both forces incurring injuries and losses. Organized fighting soon devolved into a sharp-bladed brawl. A scramble for their lives, where kicking, stabbing, and everything in between was fair game.

King Charlie had made the point clear in one of his training speeches weeks prior. In melee combat, there is no such thing as honor and fair play. Either you live, or you do not. He strongly suggested they do whatever necessary to achieve the former.

It was seeming as if the rebel forces might actually prevail, King Horgund's men finding themselves forced to fall back as best they could, when a hooded figure stepped from the shadows. How long he had been there, none could say, as he had seemed to simply appear from the woods out of nowhere.

The surviving members of both the king's troops and the rebels paused their fight, unsure which side of the fight this new arrival was on. They needn't have worried about that, they soon learned, and moments later, all of them found out in the most horrible of ways.

Come morning, their bodies were found by one of the king's patrols as they searched for the rogue king.

"What the hell?" the highest-ranking soldier said as he surveyed the carnage. "Are those our men?"

"They are. And what appear to be rebel troops, as well," his lieutenant said.

They moved closer to inspect the men. "It's Cooper, and that one's Murphy," he noted as he turned the bodies over.

All of them, rebel and soldier alike, had one thing in

common. All were far cleaner and paler than one would expect, especially given their circumstances. The soldiers leaned closer, examining the gaping wounds in several of their necks. Clean and dry.

"I don't understand," the younger man said. "Where's all of their blood? They're drained dry."

CHAPTER FORTY-THREE

Charlie was enjoying a moment of quiet meditation in the hovel he was now calling home when a quiet knock roused him from his Zen. Bawb was at the door in a flash. An utterly silent flash that held a wicked blade in its hand.

"It's me," a voice said through the wood.

Bawb's shoulders relaxed. He unbolted the door and opened it a crack.

"Clay, what are you doing here? It's daytime. Someone might see you."

"Aye, so let me in."

The pale man stepped aside and let the massive man enter, glancing out from the shadows to make sure no one had been watching. So far as he could tell, they were unobserved.

"Everyone is off working tha eastern fields today," Clay said. "No one should be over here."

"You still have not explained what you're doing here," Bawb said. "It is of vital importance our presence remain secret."

"Ease up, Bob. Clay knows that," Charlie said, stepping in. "So, what's going on? Obviously something significant if you're stepping outside our normal procedures."

The big man shifted, uncomfortably. "I've heard from me contact in tha castle again. Tha men are spooked. Something is up in tha woods. Fighting and death."

"To be expected, given an invasion," Bawb said, returning to whittling the length of wood in his hands, removing the smallest of slivers with great care.

"Normally. But this ain't the usual kind we see from bandits and thugs."

"How so?"

"Mysterious, late-night murders. Men are dead. And it's *weird*. The way they were killed, it's not natural."

"Weird in what way?" Charlie asked.

Clay gulped hard. "Tha men, they were found the next day. Both tha king's men—sorry, the *invader's* men, as well as yours."

"Rebels still putting up a good fight, I see," Bawb said with a little smile. "I'm glad they took some of Horgund's men with them."

"But that's tha thing," Clay said. "They were *all* dead. No survivors. And they were drained of their blood."

Charlie flashed a quick glance at Bawb, but the Wampeh maintained his stone-like expression.

"You're sure of this?"

"Aye. My contact is never wrong."

"And who *is* your contact?"

"I can't say."

"I'm the king, Clay. And they're helping us. I think you can tell me," Charlie said.

"No, Sire. That's not what I mean. I don't know who they are. They just leave me messages in the night, hidden behind one o' tha rocks in tha low wall in the western field."

"But you have no idea who it is?"

"None. The messages are left at night, long after I'm asleep. Why? Do ye think they may be comin' for ye?" Clay said, a suddenly panicked look in his eye.

"Clay, they know I'm here. I think if they had ill intentions, we'd have seen troops at the doorstep by now," Charlie replied. "No, it seems we have a friend in the castle. Now to figure out what this warning means."

The large man moved back to the door. "Well, I'd best join tha others before they wonder where I've gone off to."

"Yes, a wise idea," Bawb agreed. "And, Clay, thank you for your continued help. You're performing admirably, and it is not unnoticed."

"Just doing what I can ta help," he said, blushing slightly.

"Well, keep it up," Charlie added. "And let us know if you hear anything else."

"Of course, Sire," he said, then ducked his head out the low door.

Bawb bolted it behind him and returned to his chair, whittling part of his wand while the Ootaki hair wrapped around it absorbed power from the shaft of light he'd placed his seat in. He was calm, but wore a perplexed look on his face.

"So. Blood-sucking fiends are afoot in the kingdom," Charlie finally said.

"It would appear that way."

A long silence followed.

"So, uh, you sure you didn't do it?" Charlie finally asked.

Bawb paused his work, the knife falling still in his hands. "I'm sure, Charlie. I don't just accidentally suck people dry, you know."

"I know. I'm sorry I asked, it's just this is so weird, and––"

"I understand it is weird. But I was with you last night. And besides that, why would I drain a human?"

"You tell me. If my planet's sun possesses a powerful magical radiation, maybe everyday people absorb it. It'd make a convenient power source."

"Your people absorb energy much the way people shift pebbles and sand searching for precious metals. Tiny flecks appear from time to time, but not enough to be of any real use. The energy I would acquire from humans would be minimal. And it would be of such low magical potential––even with your sun factoring into the equation––that it would be of no use. There's just so little energy in your kind."

"So, you actually *can* strengthen yourself by drinking from us."

"Well, I *could*, but it's not practical. Not sustainable. Simply eating food is a far more reliable energy source. Remember, Charlie, I am accustomed to dining on wmmiks and vislas. A human, even a dozen of them, would not equal a drop of the power from them."

Charlie pinched the bridge of his nose and shook his head. "You know what this means, Bob."

"Yes."

"By all appearances, there's another vampire out there."

"Well, not a Wampeh. I am unique in this galaxy. But is there another *something*? Yes, it would seem."

"That's just great. As if we didn't have enough to worry about. Now there's someone out there eating up people in the night."

"Things have just gotten far more interesting, I am afraid. And it is not a good thing."

Charlie let out a morbid chuckle. "You know, there's an old curse on my planet. 'May you live in interesting times.' Well, it looks like we're right smack in the middle of them."

Bawb gently shaved a sliver from the wand in his hand. The wood's tapering end made Charlie think of the classic end for vampires in Earth lore. A stake through the heart. Somehow, he didn't think a wand powered by extra-galactic magic was what they had in mind, though.

"How's that coming, by the way?" he asked.

"Surprisingly well. Though the outermost layer is dry, the center is still quite vibrant and alive. I've been feeding additional charge into it through the sun's rays, and I've sensed absolutely no decay, even though it was severed from its tree a day ago."

"So, the wand is alive?"

"In a technical sense, yes. It's not sentient, or enchanted, if that's what you mean."

"I didn't know that was even possible."

"Here? No. In my world? Oh, yes."

"May I?" Charlie asked, holding out his hand.

Bawb passed the wand over, and for a brief moment, Charlie felt a tickling hint of the power contained within.

"It had to be the waters. And the Ootaki hair. And maybe even the konus you put inside of it. I have to wonder, if you keep charging it in the sun, could this thing be immortal?" he asked, then handed the wand back to its owner.

Bawb considered the question a moment, then calmly set back to work, shaping the magical implement. "I don't know, Charlie. But given our current odds, it may well outlive you and me both."

CHAPTER FORTY-FOUR

Like a pumpkin.

Or perhaps a watermelon.

Whatever descriptor one would choose for the king's mistress's distended belly, *enormous* would suffice. She was pregnant, and very much, at that.

It had been an uneventful few days, and King Horgund was resting in his chambers with his love, his ear pressed above her navel, listening to his son kick. He was sure it was a boy. Wizardly soothsaying had assured him as much. And his son would be strong, and one day, King Horgund's line would be known throughout the stars.

For now, however, a healthy baby would suffice.

The pregnant woman's appetite was as enormous as her belly, and Thomas and his kitchen staff worked extra shifts to ensure there was always a variety of foods on hand to satisfy her cravings at all hours of the day or night.

Sweet, savory. Salty or sour. They never knew exactly what she would want, and thus, it had been something of a hectic time in the kitchens since the new king's arrival. The staff would all be relieved once the child was born and they could return to a more normal schedule. But for now, it was all hands on deck.

Lunchtime greeted them with a request for fresh breads and an assortment of meats from the queen's lady-in-waiting, a particularly strong woman with dark hair and taut muscles. To get close to the queen, you would have to get past her, and only the king was afforded that privilege.

The kitchen buzzed to life, quickly gathering a wide selection of meats, as well as several loaves of Hunze's fresh-baked bread. As a finishing touch, Thomas added a tray of cheeses and pickled vegetables, alongside some fresh fruit. He had learned early on, it was better to provide her with many options before she grew cranky and had to ask for them.

Gwendolyn hoisted the massive tray, but it was awkward, the bread threatening to topple off before it could be carried to its recipient.

"Hunze, be a dear and help me, would you?"

"Of course, Gwen," she said, glad to be of assistance.

She picked up a separate tray, and the two women split the load between them, then quickly made their way up the winding stairs to the hungry mother-to-be.

The cover provided by Thomas had worked perfectly, just as Bawb had thought it would, and Hunze was ignored by all. Merely another cog in the kitchen's machinery, unworthy of notice or comment.

The anonymity was actually quite enjoyable for the Ootaki woman. She was working, now. *Really* working. Not just being humored by the staff because of who she was. It was labor, and not easy. And she liked it.

The guards outside the royal chambers stepped aside as the women approached, granting them access to deposit their loads.

"No, my dear, the men have still not managed to find the rogue," they heard the king saying as the door opened.

"Not acceptable. So long as the former king is still roaming free, his allies will remain a thorn in your side, my love. You don't want that sort of distraction while raising your new son, do you?"

"Of course not, dearest," he replied, ushering the cleaning servant away with his armload of soiled linen. "Ah, at last," he said when he spied the women bearing trays of food. He deftly plucked a slice of cured meat from the tray as they walked into the room. "My lady is famished, aren't you, love?"

"Starving," she replied from her bed, where she reclined against a mountain of pillows. "Put the meats here, slave," she said, gesturing to the table beside her.

Her lady-in-waiting stepped aside, allowing the women to come closer.

"Servants, my dear. We call them servants," the king said from his chair.

"Servants, slaves, I don't really care, and I am far too hungry for semantics," she said, shoving several slices of cured meats into her mouth with relish.

The women deposited the trays and scurried out the door, but the cleaning servant lingered. He had possessed a higher calling before the former king had blundered into the crown. The king's tax collector had been his title, and it was a good job. That was, until Charlie stripped him of his rank and set him to work cleaning, like the lowest of servants.

He was a man of ambition, however, and this fortuitous convergence was his one chance to perhaps regain some status. He might be killed in the process, but given the condition of his life, he felt it was worth the risk.

The tax collector rushed toward the royal couple, "Sire, if I may, I think I can help you with the former king——"

He found his words abruptly cut off, and his perspective of the room shifted as he was suddenly on his back, the king's mistress's wiry-muscled lady-in-waiting's forearm pressed hard against his throat, a knife drawn and ready.

"Stay your hand," the king said.

She sheathed the knife and eased the pressure on the little man's throat.

"What was this you were saying? About helping with the renegade?" he asked.

"King Charlie still has friends residing within the castle walls," the pinned man said.

"Oh, do let him up. It's hard to understand him with your arm across his throat."

He found himself released and roughly hauled to his feet.

"Now, what was that?" the king asked.

The tax collector rubbed his throat and wiped his watering eyes. "I said he still has friends in the castle."

"Well, I would assume as much. You were all his staff, after all, so it's only natural."

"No, Highness, that's not what I mean. The serving wench, the one called Hunze. She was just here, dropping off those trays. She arrived here with King Charlie as part of his entourage. She ate at his table. She is not just serving staff. She is one of his close friends."

"Fascinating," the king said. "I wonder if—"

"Bring her to me!" his pregnant mistress shrieked, clearly agitated. She shifted in pain, her hands clutching her belly.

"Is it time, mistress?" her attending lady asked, quickly sheathing her knife. "Are you close?"

"No. Not yet," she replied, gritting her teeth. "Now go fetch me that woman."

Her lady-in-waiting darted from the room, returning moments later with the golden-haired servant, her arm held in a vise-like grip.

"Bring her to me."

Hunze was ushered close to the bed.

"Looks rather jaundiced to me," the king noted.

The pregnant woman noticed the unusual bulges in her clothing. "Open her coverings," she commanded.

Her lady did as she was asked, deftly unfastening Hunze's clothes, revealing the multiple, thick, long braids of golden hair wrapped all around her body. The king was astounded by the sight.

"I've never seen anything like it. How utterly odd."

"Shall I kill her, m'lady?" the wiry brunette asked.

"No, nothing like that," she replied. "This one is a friend of Charlie's. That makes her valuable to us. Lock her in the eastern tower."

"It is only four levels high. Aren't you worried she might try to escape?"

"No. The fall would kill her, and the trees outside are far too low for any to hope to reach her. She will be secure there until we need her," the mistress said.

"But, my love, what good can she be to us? We already have his queen, yet still he has not surfaced," the king noted.

"True, but we will find use for her yet, my love." She turned to the taxman, eyeing his modest attire. "And you."

"Yes, Highness?"

"You have served us well, little man. And you shall be rewarded for it. Servants who prove their loyalty can see their position rise quite high in this castle. A lesson you shall teach the others by example. But for now, your first task is to accompany this woman to the tower. Bring a guard with you, and should anyone ask, tell them it is by command of the king."

"Love, shouldn't *I* be the one saying that?" the king said, eyebrow arched.

"Yes, of course, dearest. I'm so sorry. Please, forgive my impertinence. With your son so close to being born, I forget my place in all the excitement."

The king smiled at the mention of his heir, his brief ire

soothed. "Do as she says," he instructed. "And tomorrow, you shall begin the day in a new position."

Soon thereafter, the poor Ootaki slave girl found herself once more confined against her will. Locked in a high tower, alone and afraid. She looked out the window across the land, hoping at least her friends were okay, then curled up on her bed and wept herself to sleep.

CHAPTER FORTY-FIVE

It was dark.

Not nighttime dark, where stars and planets cast a faint illumination from light years away, but proper *dark*. The air was cool and remaining somewhat fresh despite the dragon's body heat, though the temperature was due to the millions of tons of rock pressing down from above.

The trickle of cold water that still seeped through the collapsed chambers in a rivulet not only helped even out the temperature, but the hydrogen and oxygen broke their bonds as they flowed, providing a boost to the faint trickle of fresh air finding its way in through fissures and gaps.

It was this slow erosion of the stone, its seemingly impenetrable mass being eaten away by the gentlest of liquid pressures over thousands upon thousands of years, that had carved out the caverns in the first place. And now, something far more solid than a stream had taken up residence within them.

Ara was deep underground. Far too deep to attempt to claw or blast her way out—at least, not without bringing down the rest of the imposing weight above her. The mighty Zomoki had tried at first, of course, instinct commanding her to break free at all cost, just as a younger Zomoki might, but this dragon had the benefit of age and wisdom. Instead of frantically digging and casting powerful spells, she surveyed the chamber she was confined to, then sipped at the trickle of water and curled up to think.

The walls were far, and the ceiling was still relatively high. High enough to allow her to stand at full height. She could even stretch out her wings if she positioned herself just right. But that was about it. She had miraculously been spared when the series of magical bursts set off the tunnel collapse, but she was a realist. Ara did not for a moment believe her survival had been intentional.

Lady Luck had her eye on her just this once. Though, being trapped, far from the sun, and the skies, and her friends, she couldn't help but wonder just how lucky she was. At least there was fresh water for her to sip, though not a rushing stream as she would have preferred. But the gentle flow was enough. Enough to keep her hydrated and healthy.

And, more importantly, it carried a tiny trace of the soothing radiation emitted by the planet's sun. Drinking it was akin to feeding an elephant with a thimble, but the only magic she was expending in her imprisonment was from the continual attempts to reach her friend on the surface.

But no one answered.

The veins of iron running through the rocks undoubtedly blocked her magic, as she had learned soon after their arrival on this planet. This metal ore apparently disrupted proper use of spells and power, for whatever reason. She and Charlie had spent some time experimenting with ways around the issue, but it appeared there were none to be had.

Interestingly, one day, Charlie had remembered something from old Earth legends. Tales of witches and warlocks—Earth terminology for a subset of users of power—being bound with iron chains to break their ability to connect with and use their magic.

While she was not in chains, the iron around her seemed to be doing precisely that. The legend, apparently, was based in fact, though how it even became a legend on a planet with no native magic users she had no idea.

What she did know was there were still gaps in the stone. Air seeped in, and water, too, so there was a faint thread of connection to the surface. Now, if only she could somehow tap into it. Piggy back a message on it and get her warning out. Though she feared by now Charlie was well aware of the threat to the kingdom.

Over and over, she tried to reach him, and every time, she failed. He was alive––she could sense the faintest flicker of his life energy still connecting with hers––but beyond that they were cut off. With practice, however, she might be able to alter her sending to bend and adjust to the obstacles in its path. She didn't know if it could be done, but there was nothing to lose in the effort. She might be lost, but she could still try to help her friends return home.

Silently, the mighty dragon began sending the same message over and over, humming it rhythmically in her head the way Charlie did in hopes he would somehow pick it up. It wasn't her location, or a plea for help. It was the spell she had been working on since they arrived. The one she hoped would someday take him back to the future. Back to when he belonged.

Before becoming trapped, Ara had hoped that perhaps from there––or, more appropriately, *then*––she and Bawb could combine forces, using their cache of powered devices, and a little help from Charlie and his system's powerful sun, to hopefully jump back to their own galaxy.

It was a long shot, of course, but she had been alive a very long time, and the tricks she knew were enough to fill many men's sleeves. And as for the Wampeh known as the Geist, she was certain he had a few tricks up his own sleeves to contribute.

But now it appeared she would not be able to test the theory with her friends, and there was no way they had the power to jump to a distant galaxy on their own. Not without her. But she thought the time problem might be a far easier one. Just tap into the original mess of forces that threw them backward a few thousand years, and use the strained magic as a sort of rubber band, snapping it back into place and returning them to the correct time. Forward to where they belonged.

That much, she hoped, they could do without her.

So, in what she believed to be her final contribution to their friendship, Ara settled in to hibernate in her prison, but instead of simply singing herself to sleep, she began sending the quiet message of her farewell spell to get the rest of them home, over and over. If nothing else, at least it would help pass the time until she finally managed to slip into a slumber.

"Go without me, my friend. I'll show you the way."

"Did you hear that?"

"Hear what?"

Charlie rushed from the trees they were using for cover until he found a clearing where he could look skyward. He strained his eyes, along with his mind, searching for his missing friend.

"What is it?" Bawb asked, walking to his side, one hand gripping his wand, the other resting on the pommel of his sword. "Trouble?"

"No. Something different. Like a song in my head."

Bawb's gaze sharpened as he squinted, surveying the dark skies. "Do you feel her, Charlie?"

"I thought I did."

They both stood stock-still for several minutes as Charlie reached out with all of his mind and power. That tune was stuck in his head now, a strange melding of words that sounded distinctly magic, but it wasn't clear. Not in focus. But it was there, just the same. And every so often, it repeated.

"I-I don't know what it is," he finally said. "But I think she's trying to reach me."

"Then she is okay."

"I don't know," Charlie said, haltingly. "But she's still alive."

The assassin felt his stomach relax slightly at the words. Their friend was in trouble, no doubt, but the Wise One still drew breath. But they would have to focus on that later.

"Come. We have much to do," he said, leading the way from the clearing.

Reluctantly, Charlie eased his focus, the strange melody slipping from his conscious mind to his subconscious as he turned his attentions back to the task at hand.

CHAPTER FORTY-SIX

The next night, Charlie and Bawb crept to the castle dressed in peasants' garb. The castle, they were glad to find, looked more or less the same. The banners had changed, naturally, as had the guards along the walls, but otherwise things seemed more or less as they had been.

Except the two men were on the outside, and did not dare sneak in. Not yet.

A light shone from a window high above, and a flash of gold brightened it as the occupant walked past, catching Bawb's eye.

There were groups of men positioned around the grounds, Charlie noted as they quietly crept through the shadows. It seemed, for some reason, they had added to the perimeter guards. And recently, at that. A throng of two dozen men stood at attention, apparently an impromptu inspection of sorts, though why they would do one at this late hour was beyond him. Bad for morale, that. But the new king worked in mysterious ways.

A short man in ill-fitting armor seemed to be the group's leader. Or at least, he thought he was, given the way he spoke to them. But even in the dark, Charlie could read the men's body language. Whoever this little man was, he apparently grated on their nerves. For a moment, he seemed familiar, but then Bawb nudged Charlie and signaled him to follow.

"What did you see?" he asked his pale friend.

"I spied Hunze in the tower window."

"So she's okay."

"Yes, but locked away, high above the treeline. But the path to the shimmer-hidden doorway remains unobstructed."

"Good. I didn't think they'd find it, but that doesn't mean they wouldn't set up a tent or something right in front of it, with our luck."

"It seems our good fortune remains intact," Bawb noted. "At least for the time being." His sharp eyes scanned the men coming and going around the castle.

There was a fair amount of foot traffic this evening, and that would help hide them from prying eyes as they made their survey. There was simply no way to stay totally out of sight near the castle walls, so it was far better to be easily seen, but unnoted.

Bawb had applied a fair coating of dirt to darken his complexion, and Charlie had put on a peasant's ragged cloak, going so far as to smear actual feces on the outside of it. No one wanted to get too close to a man who smelled, literally, like shit.

Disguised as best they were able, the two men made their way closer. It took only a short time to skirt the castle, all the while moving casually, appearing to be no more than peasants walking the path. But these peasants had just made careful note of the number and position of guards, the paths they followed, and what reinforcements might be lurking behind the parapet above.

They had just about finished their loop when the short man and his troops were passing them, heading the other direction. The little fellow was riding atop a horse that seemed too big for his diminutive stature, but he appeared to revel in it anyway.

Bawb and Charlie quickly exited the path and headed into the woods. The little man was staring after them from atop his steed.

"Come with me," he said, diverting the men from their prescribed route.

"But, sir, we are to patrol the——"

"I give the orders," he snapped. "And I order you to come *this* way." He turned his back and stormed ahead, fully expecting the men to follow, which, reluctantly, they did.

The tax collector was already reveling in his new power. He commanded two dozen men, and the king was pleased with him. But now, so soon after his promotion, he had an opportunity to once again show his worth. To achieve an even higher position.

He couldn't be entirely sure of it, and he didn't dare risk calling out the full castle guard, but he could have sworn that was the deposed king and his cowardly aide he just saw darting into the trees.

Alone, he would stand no chance. Even with a handful of men, he had doubts. He had seen the king spar, and knew he was a skilled fighter. His pale aide was a useless hanger-on, but King Charlie would be a handful.

Fortunately, he had over twenty men backing him up now. And if he managed to take the former king to his new one, oh, the rewards that would be showered upon him.

"Quietly, you idiots!" he hissed at the clanking soldiers behind him.

Of course, silence was difficult in armor, but the men did the best they could as they hurried deep into the woods.

"We are being followed," Bawb noted as they crested a low hill not far from the castle.

"I know," Charlie replied. "How many, do you think?"

Bawb strained his ears and listened. "Twenty. Perhaps thirty. With armor."

"I heard that part. Not terribly quiet, are they?"

"No, but they are following our trail rather effectively. I think it is time to discard that foul thing."

It took Charlie a moment to realize what he meant. He'd been wearing the stinking cloak for so many hours, he had actually become accustomed to the stench.

Shit. Of course. They're following the smell. Stupid, Charlie, he scolded himself as he shed the cloak.

"Come on. We can widen the gap if we hurry."

The duo raced ahead, putting another low hill between themselves and the castle as they fled. The men on foot behind them were falling behind, but the sound of a horse's hooves was growing louder. Their leader, it seemed, had ridden ahead.

Charlie was about to suggest they quickly eliminate the pesky pursuer when the sound of clanking weapons greeted them from ahead. It was another group of soldiers, returning to the castle, and they'd just blundered right into them in their haste.

"Well, this is rather unfortunate," Bawb muttered.

Bawb pulled his cloak farther over his head, but Charlie had discarded his. He could only hope the newcomers didn't recognize the king in peasant garb.

"You, there. What are you two doing out in these woods?" the leader of the approaching men called out.

"We live here, sir," Charlie said, as meekly as possible. "Just over those hills."

"Only bandits and rebels use the forest trails. Honest people use the roads."

"But, sir, it is a much longer walk if we take the road. This path saves us a lot of time. I assure you, we're not bandits, and we are certainly not rebels. We have no armor, as you can see. We are just simple folk."

The soldier looked them over a long moment. He was traveling with at least twenty men of his own. Hunting rebel soldiers, no doubt. Charlie just hoped he would buy his tale. Finally, the man nodded, satisfied.

"All right, get home. But from now on, stick to the roads. Even if it is a longer walk."

"Of course, sir. Thank you, sir," Charlie said as he and Bawb moved past the men.

It was just looking like they were in the clear when a shrill voice called out, "Stop them! That's the renegade king!"

Charlie spun. The pest on horseback had caught up with them during the delay. And, he realized, he did know the man.

"The fucking taxman," he grumbled as he drew his sword. "Goddamn death and taxes, eh, Bob?"

The Wampeh had no idea what he was talking about, but it didn't much matter with the men surrounding them.

"Yes! It *is* you," the little man crowed. "The king will reward me greatly for this. Even more than when I turned in your friend hiding in the kitchen."

Bawb bristled, and Charlie knew the man well enough to know what was coming next. They drew their swords, putting their backs to one another for defense.

"They didn't say we had to bring you back alive," the taxman said.

Then all hell broke loose.

It was chaos in the woods. Charlie and Bawb were horribly outnumbered, nearly thirty to two, but the spacing of the trees at least granted them some respite from the charging attackers. Nevertheless, they were each facing several men at once.

They swung and stabbed, dispatching men as quickly as they were able, but the tax man's reinforcements soon arrived, and there was simply no way they could overcome nearly sixty men on their own.

Bawb, though likely about to die, was nevertheless smiling as his arms spun in a deadly windmill of carnage. If it was his time to go, *this* seemed a fitting manner.

Charlie fought as hard and fast as he was able, but eventually took a blow to the arm, miraculously struck largely with the flat of the man's blade. The panic of battle had made the man careless, and that saved Charlie's arm. It hurt, though, and he cried out in pain and frustration.

Surprisingly, a ferocious growl replied to his utterance.

The soldiers spun, and the taxman's horse reared in fear as his feisty passenger was ripped from his back by a blur with powerful jaws. The beast easily ripped the taxman's head from his body and turned on the other soldiers. Despite their armor and weapons, the men turned to flee.

Many were not fast enough.

Limbs flew, heads were crushed. It was utter carnage, and moments later, a dozen men lay dismembered at the massive canine's feet.

"Baloo! You're alive!" Charlie gushed.

"Charlie, they're spreading out. We can't stop them all from reaching the castle and sounding the alarm," Bawb realized as he skewered the last living man at his feet.

He was right. There were over thirty men scrambling back toward the safety of the castle. And once they were there, the king's entire army would ride out after them. And heaven help their friends in captivity.

Charlie had some magic at his disposal, and he managed to take down a few of the fleeing men, but there were too many.

"I can't get them all!"

A realization flashed on Bawb's face.

"I have an idea," he said, drawing the strange, wooden implement from his hip.

He had no idea if it would even work, but there was simply no time for tests.

"Stand behind me. I do not know if this will fly true," he said.

Charlie pulled Baloo to him and stepped behind his friend. The Wampeh then pointed his wand and cast his spell. One of the most deadly and powerful of the Wampeh Ghalian's secret arsenal.

The wand crackled with power, spitting out a flash of hot death. The men in its path turned to sprays of blood and bone, obliterated in their tracks. Of the thirty soldiers, only a handful at the very perimeter of the spell escaped harm.

Charlie stood stock-still, mouth hanging open with shock. Bawb too was temporarily stunned by what had happened. By what he had just done. His assassin's reflexes kicked back in, and he quickly fired off a rapid series of much smaller, individually targeted spells, dropping the remaining men one by one, like a sniper, as they fled.

The wand glowed a second longer, then returned to normal. For all intents and purposes, it seemed to be no more than a tapered stick in the pale man's hands.

"Did you know it would do that?" Charlie finally managed to say.

"No, I certainly did not."

"Holy shit, Bob. That was... I don't even know what to call that."

"Amazing works. Or incredible."

A relieved grin spread across Charlie's face. "So, the wand idea. Not a bad one, eh?"

Bawb smiled and examined his new toy. "Completely intact and unscathed, though it feels largely drained of power. At least so far as I can tell."

"But if you put it in the sunlight tomorrow––"

"Yes, I believe it will recover full potency, or at least much of it. And I shall certainly use it far more sparingly in the future."

Charlie scratched Baloo behind the ears, the muddy, bloody beast panting happily from the long-absent affection.

"That spell. That was horrific. *Impressive*, but..."

"Yes, I know. A spell of last resort, though never meant for that particular purpose. I had no idea the power contained in this wand, so I cast the most powerful one I could draw upon without preparation. Apparently, this device is *far* more powerful than I ever expected. I still need to learn its limitations and quirks, but it would seem we now have at least one powered weapon at our disposal."

Charlie looked over his canine friend with joy. Baloo was filthy, but he seemed well-fed. Given his proclivity for hunting game, that was no surprise. What was, however, was his being there in the first place.

"Wasn't he supposed to be trapped and killed?" Charlie said, searching for any injuries on Baloo.

"There. His leg," Bawb said. "The fur is growing back slightly off-pattern. Right where a trap would have broken it."

"But that was just days ago," he said. Then it hit him. "Oh, of course. Back in the Balamar Wastelands, when Baloo was just a pup, he played in the mist when we hosed down Ara with the healing waters."

"I do not recall this."

"No, of course not. She flew you back to the campsite so you wouldn't accidentally get sprayed and blow up."

"Which was appreciated."

"So he must still have that in his system. No wonder it's healing so quickly. And if we can get to our stash of the waters hidden in the castle, we can easily fix him up the rest of the way."

Baloo, for his part, was just happy to be with his pack, his hind leg twitching with joy as he received abundant scratches.

"What about these bodies? We can't leave them like this," Charlie said as he surveyed the carnage.

"Allow me," Bawb said, waving his wand and lifting the remains into several piles. He separated the weapons and armor from the corpses, then, with another flick of his wrist, covered the bodies with dirt and leaves. "Primitive, but it will have to suffice for now."

"Agreed. And enough excitement for the night."

Quietly, and with the unexpected companionship of their furry friend, the pair made their way back to their hideout to eat, plan, and rest. Given the events of the evening, things were going to get interesting in these parts, and soon.

CHAPTER FORTY-SEVEN

The pile of weapons Bawb had brought back with them to their hideout in the disused hovel was rather impressive. Of course, they each had only two hands, so Charlie wondered just how much good the massive stash would do them.

It had actually been quite a load to move all the way to their base of operations, but Bawb's new toy apparently had a bit more juice remaining than he'd first estimated. With a simplified lifting spell, combined with a bit of help from Charlie's growing internal magic, the pair had managed to lug all of it back with little trouble.

They'd have whipped up a makeshift carry sack for Baloo, as Leila sometimes did, but both were so happy to see the filthy beast that they thought it best to simply have the overjoyed animal pad along with them unencumbered. It was as much for their benefit as his, truth be told. They'd seen the carnage the full-grown animal could inflict when riled up.

That he had been sidelined long enough for them to have captured Leila said something about the strength of the trap he'd been snared in. That was likely why his leg had still not healed fully.

"You know, he must've damn near torn his foot off pulling free from that trap," Charlie noted, scratching the good boy as he contentedly lapped up a dish of the fresh milk Clay had left for them earlier that afternoon. "And after that little display in the woods, heaven help the men who set it if he ever catches up with them."

The assassin looked up from his work, the weapons now sorted into piles based on quality, length, and heft.

"I would think, with a nose like his, they might not have a choice about his finding them, you know. We'll need to keep him on a short leash for the time being. If he goes tearing through Horgund's men, they'll lock down the castle grounds even tighter."

"But he's all the way out here. And he hadn't ventured near the castle yet. We'd have heard."

"I know. But he found us, Charlie. And we are his family. His pack. Where we go, he will want to go as well, and we will have to dissuade that urge."

"He'll listen to me," Charlie said.

He didn't know why, or how, for that matter, but with his strengthening magic, he found he had picked up some of Leila's gift with animals. He had no use to really pursue it, not with her around, but the latent talent was there. He just had to practice a bit.

"Baloo," he said, focusing on the canine as he reached out with his mind. "Leila is okay. We're going to get her back," he said both with and without words.

Baloo's tail sprang to life, wagging merrily.

"So, he *does* understand you," Bawb noted. "Fascinating."

"Add it to the day's list," Charlie replied. "I mean, that wand of yours is one helluva potent device."

Bawb twirled the length of wood deftly in his hand.

"Hey, careful with that!"

"I'm not casting, Charlie. We're fine."

"You say that, but after seeing what that thing was capable of, I'd still rather you treated it like a loaded gun."

"As you wish," the Wampeh replied, holding the wand gently. "It is a remarkable thing you inspired, and I'm glad I fabricated it. The efficacy with which it cast, it was as if the living wood understood and amplified the spell."

"Hang on a second. You said you had Ara reshape a konus to form the core."

"Yes. And?"

"And did that konus have an active translation spell tied to it at the time?"

"It's one of my standard spells. All of my devices carry one in some form or another."

Charlie nodded his head. "That explains it. I have no idea how, but it looks like you may have given the tree the means to understand you. And if that's the case, it very well may be echoing back your spells, both through the konus, as well as the Ootaki hair."

A look of astonishment grew on the pale man's face. It was something he hadn't considered in all the months he'd been carefully watering the plant, strengthening the branch with carefully applied magic, and even talking to his tree as he tended it.

"Admittedly, it seems you may actually be correct, which would be a fascinating circumstance, and one previously undocumented in any of the systems."

"But this isn't one of your systems. Here, your magic reacts differently. Hell, just look at the sun. It does nothing for us humans, but Hunze and Ara suck up that energy like a sponge with water."

Bawb carefully unwrapped the length of hide protecting the Ootaki hair wrapped around the shaft. He placed it atop a low table near the eastern-facing wall. Every day, a shaft of light would poke through a gap in the wall, and now, come morning, his wand would begin absorbing the sun's first rays, replenishing its power.

"You know, much as I have hope for this new tool, I have to say, I still miss my regular gear. My armlets. My slaaps. And especially my enchanted blades. All equipment I have used for more years than I care to count. And all safely hidden away within the walls of the castle."

"Safe from everyone, but that includes us, at the moment."

"Precisely."

"Hey, man, I get it," Charlie said. "The stuff you're familiar with. Yeah, muscle memory is a big thing. That level of comfort using your gear without having to even think about it takes a long time to reach. And I think we may be able to get our stuff, now that we have captured armor from Horgund's men. They were castle guards, and their gear will allow us some freedom of movement once we get inside."

"I agree, but we will need to come up with more of a plan than merely sneaking in our hidden entry point and rushing to retrieve our equipment. It is only a matter of time before the missing men are noticed. That was a *lot* of them. Far too many for their absence to slip through the cracks."

Charlie looked over at the pile of weapons and thought about the bodies and armor still buried in the woods. Bawb was right. It was only a matter of time before the alarm would be raised. They'd need support if they were to succeed.

"I have an idea. We hide this stuff out in the treeline. When Clay comes by in the morning, we tell him where it is, as well as the gear buried with the bodies back toward the castle."

"There were very few bodies left."

"You know what I mean," Charlie shot back. "Anyway, he knows the people on the neighboring farms and seems to have made friends with them, so he's the perfect person to distribute weapons and armor to those he can trust. I don't know if they'll even need them, but if things go tits up, it'll be far better the locals are armed rather than unarmed."

"On this, we agree," Bawb said. "And this will give us a force should we need to rally men to arms."

"Exactly."

"And this gave *me* an idea, as well."

"Oh?"

"Yes. I'm thinking, with a fair amount of creative planning, we can have our allies infiltrate and disrupt the castle's perimeter guards. Because if we hope to get inside, retrieve our gear, and save our friends, we're going to need quite a distraction."

"No, Bob. We'll need a miracle."

CHAPTER FORTY-EIGHT

The plan had gone more or less as intended the following morning. Clay had acquired the location of not only the large cache of weapons hidden just outside the farm in the treeline, but also that of the buried equipment from men slaughtered the night before.

Despite his intimidating appearance, as well as his former profession as the now-deceased tax collector's muscle, the burly man expressed his reservations. Even with the reappearance of Baloo, whom he hugged gleefully as his face was licked with enthusiasm, he still seemed unsure about farmers and common folk taking up arms in any assault on the castle. Even confronting the king's troops outside of its walls was a concern.

It took a lot of talking things through before Charlie, with Bawb's subtle help, brought him around to their way of thinking. Things were still in limbo in the kingdom, but once King Horgund had cemented his power and installed more and more of his people in key positions, the locals would be at terrible risk.

"Do you truly believe he'll leave all of the farms to their own devices, Clay?" Bawb had inquired, casually. "You worked for the tax man and are intimate with how those collections are made. If you had to guess, what do you think Horgund will do once people fall into complacency once again? Will he leave you as you are, or will he begin squeezing for all he can extract?"

"Well, I hadn't really thought of it like that," Clay admitted.

"But that's why we're asking your input now, Clay," Charlie joined in. "You're a smart man, and you know this part of a king's business."

"Aye, but ye didn't force tha people ta pay if they couldn't, Sire."

"But that's *me*, Clay. What would the old king have done? Or the one before him? Or Horgund, now that he's seized the throne?"

The enforcer-turned-farmer mulled it over a long while. "Yer right, Sire. He'll likely start overtaxing just as soon as people's emotions stop running so high."

"Precisely. And while those emotions are high, we must arm those who are willing to fight to keep what's theirs, if necessary. Now, Bob and I sincerely hope to end this without requiring farmers to fight, but if our plans are not enough, that time may come."

Clay nodded his assent. "I'll speak with tha others."

After that, Charlie and Bawb spent the day planning out an elaborate ruse involving their remaining loyal troops still hiding in farms and the woods around the kingdom. The spy network had done their job admirably, and at Bawb's urging, they'd stealthily connected a small network of loyal men, able to mobilize their forces on no more than a day's notice. When the time came, give them twenty-four hours and they'd be ready. Ready to fight, and even die, in the name of their king.

It was enough to make Charlie well up with pride. He was a stranger to this land, but after his rather startling arrival, he had finally been accepted. At least by many. And now, in just a few days, they would all fight together.

. . .

"Sire! Sire!" Clay hissed outside the hovel door a few hours before evening fell.

"Get inside before someone sees you," Bawb ordered, ushering him inside. "We aren't to reconvene until the morning. What are you doing out here? You should be with the others. It's nearly dinner time."

"I know, but they're finishing up in the eastern fields, out of sight."

"But why are you here?"

"Because a rider just came to the house. He came for *me*."

"Oh, shit. What happened?" Charlie asked.

"Happened? He gave me this," he replied, handing over a tightly wrapped roll of parchment.

Charlie read it quickly, then handed it to Bawb, who likewise took in the hastily jotted words.

"It seems we have a dilemma," he said.

"Yeah, no shit, Bob." The king turned to the messenger. "This isn't your usual arrangement, Clay. You said messages were *always* left for you behind a stone in the wall."

"They are. But tha horseman said it were urgent, then handed me this an' left. It's the same as the others. I know the man's hand, and this is his."

"But no one would risk direct contact with you unless it was either incredibly urgent, or a trap," Charlie noted.

"Agreed," Bawb said. "I would presume this to be a trap, if not for the fact they could have just surrounded the farm and taken us, if they knew we were here."

A long pause hung in the air, the silence growing more uncomfortable by the second as the men mulled over the situation.

"*Unless* they didn't actually know our location, only who

brought us the news," Charlie said, hurrying to the shuttered window.

He peered out the gap in the slats, but all appeared calm outside. "Bob, do you sense anything?"

"No, I do not. But hold for a moment," he said, picking up his wand from where it sat soaking in the day's sunshine, freshly recharged, though he was still unsure exactly how much.

"What's that?"

"A wand," Charlie said, abandoning all subterfuge.

"Wait, your aide is a wizard?" he asked, eyes going wide.

"What? No, Bob's not a wizard. He just...knows a few wizard tricks, is all, right Bob?"

"Oh. Yes, quite correct," Bawb said.

"And hopefully this little trick might just save our skins, so hush, now."

Bawb quietly cast his spell, probing the surrounding woods for any signs of hostiles. The spell wasn't precise, but it would give you a rough idea of the forces you were facing. For an assassin, it was often enough to make the difference between success and failure.

"Nothing," he finally said, lowering the wand. "We are still alone here."

"Then maybe this isn't a trap."

"I shall reserve judgment, for now," Bawb said, sheathing his wand and strapping on his weapons.

"So, we're going, then?"

"I think given what we just learned, we have no choice."

Clay watched the two, utterly confused at what was happening. "Wait, so are we going to battle? Do I need to tell the others?"

Charlie felt a flush of pride in his chest. The man who had hated his guts not so long ago was now arguably one of his most trusted followers. If they survived this ordeal, he'd be sure to find a suitable way of rewarding him for his service. But for now, they had a task.

"There's no time, Clay. Come morning, pass the word and tell them to keep their ears open and be ready for a call to arms. But, for now, they must carry on as normal. But Bob and I have something we must do."

He joined his assassin friend in strapping on his weapons and gathering his set of stolen armor. Baloo was watching with great curiosity, his massive tail slowly swishing side to side. It gave Charlie an idea.

"Clay, can you *send* a message to your contact?"

"I-I think so, Sire. If I can catch up to tha man who delivered his note on tha road. He only left a short while ago."

"Excellent. And could you get us a cart? One large enough to hide Baloo and our armor in?"

"Aye, but it may raise a few questions."

"We'll have to risk it. Pull it to the far west end of the farm, next to the road. We'll be out to collect it shortly."

"They might see you, Sire."

"We'll stick to the woods and go the long way around. Trust me, we're good at being stealthy when we want to be."

Clay headed for the door, a man on a mission.

"Clay, wait," Charlie called after him. He strode to the man and clasped his hand in a firm grip. "Thank you, my friend. For all you have done, you forever have my gratitude."

The large man was glad the lighting was dim, lest his king see him blush from the praise. He nodded once, then stepped out into the late afternoon sun.

Bawb looked at Charlie with a curious expression on his face. "The timing seems a bit, *suspicious*, wouldn't you agree?"

"Yeah, but you saw the note. And you said it yourself, if they knew we were here, they would have just come for us." He unrolled the parchment and read the words again. "If Horgund's mistress truly has been in labor all day, then by now the household must be in utter chaos. And Horgund and his guards will all be tired and stressed."

"Agreed. The pending birth of the king's heir will lead to great distraction within the castle walls. But once the child is born, and the household returns to normal, the opportunity will be lost."

"So we hurry," Charlie said as he tucked the note back into his pocket and picked up his gear, donning a ragged cloak. "We'll have to keep our pace slow enough to not draw attention, but we should reach the castle just after nightfall."

"If not slightly before."

"Well, then. So much for our carefully thought out diversion," Charlie said with a laugh. "As they say, 'The best laid plans of mice and men oft go awry.'"

Bawb smiled his pointy-toothed grin. "I like that one. But you are neither mouse, nor man. You are king. And the time has come to reclaim what is yours."

CHAPTER FORTY-NINE

Rumbling along the bumpy road, two peasant farmers made their way along the outskirts of the forest surrounding the castle's vast grounds. Piled in the back of their cart was a mound of hay, along with a small collection of goods for market, covered with a dirty tarpaulin.

They had passed several of the king's men as they led the tired pony down the road, but with the buzz of the goings-on within the castle in the air, they had been largely ignored. The king's mistress was giving birth, and the castle was in a frenzy.

Naturally, word spread quickly, and this new bit of chatter now quickly passed from the lips of the king's men. Would things calm once the child was born? Would he at long last marry the lady and make her his official queen? What was to happen to the endless searching for the escaped, rogue king?

The peasants they passed were particularly interested in that last question, but if the pair were successful in their infiltration of the castle, the king and his aide would no longer need to walk the realm in disguise.

They parked the cart off into the woods less than a mile from the castle and piled branches and leaves against it, hiding it from casual view, though a more thorough search would find it relatively easily. But the sky was darkening, and once night had fully fallen, it would be invisible right up until you stumbled into it.

Charlie flung back the tarp and moved aside the produce covering their stolen armor. "Time to gear up," he said, strapping on the metal skin.

They'd selected the lighter armor used by the guard on patrol. It was less protective than full battle armor, but it also allowed a far greater range of motion, and would let the men run if need be.

Baloo poked his head from the pile of hay and sniffed the air.

"That's right, boy. We're home," Charlie said, affectionately scratching that sweet spot behind his ears. "Now listen. We're going to get Hunze and Leila, but we need you to stay here and guard our escape path."

Baloo's tail began wagging at the mention of his mama's name.

"Stay out of sight, Baloo. And don't eat anyone. At least, not until we get them out of the castle. Is that clear?"

The massive canine rubbed his muzzle on Charlie's hand, then licked it.

"I believe he understands the task at hand," Bawb said.

"So, this is it," Charlie said, starting off down the path.

Bawb cocked his head, straining his ears. "I'll follow a few minutes behind you."

"Something wrong?"

"Likely not, but I don't want to take any chances."

The screams of pain rang out across the castle, hanging in the air like an invisible warning to stay away or die. Someone was *not* having a good time of it

King Horgund paced the antechamber, while his mistress's lady-in-waiting helped the nursemaid tend her lady. The swollen-bellied woman's water had broken many hours prior, but she had been slow to dilate, and as a result, the baby was taking its time in coming.

The contractions were unlike any pain she had ever endured, and she swore she would kill the bastard who had done this to her. Had the king heard her words, he would have taken them for the pained rants of childbirth. And maybe they were, but for a moment, when the nursemaid saw the raging look in the woman's eyes, she had her doubts.

It had been nearly fourteen hours since she began the process when the king's heir finally slipped out into the world, his lungs filling with his first breath of air, then crying out mightily. The staff in attendance quickly headed off to spread the word, while the two women at her bedside cleaned the infant and handed him to his mother.

She took the bundle and looked at it with exhausted eyes. There was no joy on her face in that moment of unguarded honesty. But she had cemented her bond with the king, and that was what mattered.

With weary arms, she raised the child to her breast and allowed it to suckle for the first time, while the final contractions expelled the placenta.

"It is done, my lady," her loyal aide said.

"Good. I've been confined to this bed for too long," she said, trying to rise.

The nursemaid put her hand on her shoulder, only to find it snatched away most painfully by the icy-eyed lady-in-waiting.

"But she's weak," she managed to squeak. "You must rest!"

"Weak?" the new mother scoffed. "I assure you, I am *not* weak."

She slid her legs to the edge of the bed and tried to stand, only to fall back onto the bed. Shock hit her as she realized that no matter how stubbornly strong her mind might be, the rest of her was utterly drained, just as the nursemaid had said. It seemed she was indeed weak, and incapacitated to a disconcerting degree.

"Very well," she relented, reclining on the bed once more. "I shall rest a bit longer." She looked up at her aide. "Bring in the king. He'll want to meet his new son."

CHAPTER FIFTY

Charlie dashed through the woods, his Wampeh friend following not far behind. The shimmer-guarded door was just across the small clearing at the side of the castle, and it was a clear shot. Charlie paused at the edge of the treeline and scanned the dusk-lit area.

Not a soul, he was pleased to note. *Perfect.*

Crouching as low as his stolen castle guard's armor allowed, he darted to what seemed to be an ordinary section of stone wall, the multiple layers of shimmer camouflaging the secret door. He took one last look around, ensuring no one was watching, then slipped into the castle, leaving the door cracked open behind him.

It would still be invisible unless you stumbled right upon it. More importantly, it would save Bawb precious seconds, should he need them. Charlie had learned plenty under the assassin's tutelage. Including just how close he sometimes came to capture or death. Seconds could make the difference between success and failure.

Charlie was banking on the chaos of the pending birth within the castle's walls to help mask his presence. The new king's guards would be afoot, but most of the old staff—those who knew him on sight—should hopefully be in their chambers or off performing their jobs. He knew the path he had to take, and if the stars aligned, he should be able to pass unnoted.

All he needed was to make it to the little storage closet up the stairs from the kitchen. There he would wait until Clay's insider made contact. From that point, it would be a quick dash to rescue the queen, and hopefully recover one of their caches of magical weapons in the process. Now all he needed to do was make it there unseen.

As if the universe had been listening, and thought he needed more of a challenge, a pair of guards rounded the corner at that moment, walking straight toward him.

Shit. Eyes forward, Charlie. Act normal, he reminded himself. *Just keep walking.*

"You, there. What are you doing in this area? You're in perimeter guard's attire," the nearest man called out as they neared.

"Uh, I was told to go to the kitchen and get some, uh, wine."

"You don't come into this part of the castle," the man said, eyeing him curiously. "I don't know you. What's your name?"

"Smith, sir. John Smith. I'm not from your kingdom. I was brought on to the ranks here when that horrible King Charlie fled like a coward."

Laying it on a bit thick, Charlie.

The man's expression softened a bit.

"Ah, a local smithee's son, eh? Then you're ignorant of how things work here now that a *real* king is on the throne. I'm glad to hear you appreciate the difference between our honorable King Horgund and that yellow coward."

Or not *too thick, apparently.*

"Oh, yes. King Horgund is such an improvement, long may he rule. But I really should get that wine."

"No perimeter guard has the authority to request such a

thing. Especially not from the king's cellars. What fool sent you on this task?"

"Uh, I'm sorry, I don't remember his name."

A suspicious look crept back into the man's eye. Charlie's mind raced.

"He was a really short fellow," he blurted. "I believe he was the former king's tax collector."

The soldier relaxed, a look of exasperation flashing across his face. "Oh, *that* one."

"You know him, then?"

"Yes. The king's mistress's new favorite. He helped them find that blonde bitch that was hiding in the kitchen."

"Oh? I hadn't heard," Charlie said, a flush of adrenaline leaking into his veins.

"She's been handled. Locked away in the tower now. But that obnoxious little man is to have whatever he wants. Apparently, he has earned the lady's favor, and thus, the king's," he said, stepping aside. "Off with you, then. You'd best do as you were bade."

"Thank you, sir. I will, straightaway. And a good evening to you," Charlie said, hurrying on his way.

He covered the rest of the way with no further incidents, moving a few sacks of flour into a makeshift seat, settling himself in the closet to wait. He just hoped things were as uneventful for his Wampeh friend.

Bawb slashed and stabbed, dispatching the king's guards who had stumbled upon him just as he neared the castle with great violence. His cloak's hood had fallen back, and his fierce, pale visage struck terror in the hearts of the men he fought. Until his blade pierced said vital organ before moving on to the next man.

The ambient lighting was dim, but not full night. As such, the dozen men could quite clearly see what was befalling their comrades. The pale assassin was giving a master class in death and power.

The poor men falling at the ends of his blades stared in dying shock as their skills—which they had formerly thought were rather impressive—were bypassed with the slightest of effort by the deadly man in their midst. They had felt cocky and sure when they first drew steel on the man, possessing a great numerical advantage. But very quickly they realized they were *not* at an advantage at all.

Three of the poor men had held back, standing clear of the fray, watching with eyes wide as the other nine were slaughtered wholesale before their eyes. The Wampeh's blades finished the others and turned on them, but stopped just short, blood dripping from the metal as the fierce assassin stared hard at the trio.

"I know you," he said through clenched teeth, the points of his fangs showing, extending as they so often did when he was in battle. "You served in the king's guards before Horgund came to our lands."

"Aye, we did," the one man still capable of speech replied.

The others remained silent, and a whiff of the air made it clear at least one appeared to have soiled himself in fear.

"And are you with the king?" Bawb asked. "The *rightful* king. Do not lie to me. I will know."

It was clear what would befall a wrong answer.

"Aye, we still support King Charlie. But we were absorbed into Horgund's ranks, demoted, and forced into foot patrol."

Bawb had been in the death business a long time, and as an assassin, he'd heard many at the point of his blades tell tales in hopes of saving their skin. As such, he had become quite proficient in reading men. These, he saw, were true to their word. At least, the word of the one still in possession of faculties enough to speak.

"Very well," he said, sheathing his blades.

The men continued to stare in disbelief. The king's aide, the meek and soft-spoken man they'd ignored as no more than a hanger-on, had been playing possum the entire time, hiding his true nature. Their king was a formidable fighter, capable of besting any in the realm. And now it was clear, his pale friend was even better.

"Close your mouths, lest you ingest a fly," Bawb said with a wicked grin.

He was actually enjoying the moment. It was exceedingly rare for anyone to witness his true skills, and if they did, even by accident, he almost never left them alive to tell of it. But here, in this time and place, the fast-spreading rumors would serve them well.

"I need you to come with me," he said to the man still capable of speech. "You two have a different task. Are you with me?" he asked.

At that moment, a soldier who had hidden himself beneath a fallen comrade pushed the body from atop himself and took off toward the castle at a full run. He was out of knife-throwing range, and a chase would put his secrecy at risk. Without hesitation, Bawb drew his wand, aimed, and cast a smiting spell. The man simplhy exploded in a red mist.

It was excessive, and far more power than he wished to expend, but the impression it made on the men was worth it. The king was retaking his throne, and he had a deadly wizard backing him. If there had been any lingering doubt as to their loyalties, they were erased in that instant.

"Aye, we're with you. What do you need of us?"

Bawb turned to the silent pair. "You two, spread word among the people, get notice to your other comrades hiding in the ranks. King Charlie is back, and we are retaking the kingdom, starting tonight."

The two nodded their understanding, then took off into the night to spread the word.

"And me, sir?"

"What's your name?"

"Simon, sir."

"Well, Simon. You shall help me rescue my friend."

"But the king? The queen?"

Bawb smiled. "Do not worry, friend. That is being taken care of."

CHAPTER FIFTY-ONE

Charlie's ass was beginning to fall asleep. Sitting on compressed sacks of grain, it turned out, was not the most ergonomic or comfortable of positions to be in. A cushy lounge chair, it most certainly was not.

He'd been waiting there for quite a while. Or at least, it felt like it. Stuck in a dark closet, it was kind of hard to tell exactly how much time had passed. Like that isolation tank he'd once floated in on a whim, only minus the saline, pitch-darkness, and tranquility.

Funny, I used to like spending afternoons in here, getting some quiet time. A nice respite from all that king business, he mused with a wry grin. *Look at me now.*

The closet door rattled without warning, then abruptly flew open. Standing there in the doorway, towering over the seated king, stood Captain Sheeran.

Charlie leapt to his feet, ignoring his numb buttocks, and moved to draw his sword in the tight space.

"Sire, wait! Clay sent me," Sheeran blurted, hands held out in front of him, open and without weapons.

Charlie hesitated, his blade halfway out of its sheath. "*You're* the insider? But you can't stand me. I thought you—"

"You're a good man, Sire. And, despite my initial concerns, you have proven to be a good king. It was difficult to admit my error in judgment, but you care deeply for the people. And despite having only just arrived to this realm, you have taken the position seriously and placed its people under your protection and care."

"You say this, but you're still a captain in Horgund's ranks. You flipped, Sheeran. And you tried to stop the men from engaging during the duel."

"Aye, and I would do so again, given the same circumstances. An agreement was made, and to intervene would sully the honor of our men," he said. "As well as yours, Sire."

"Even if I died."

"Yes. Even if you died. Those were the terms agreed upon. For the good of the men. Of the people. But as you fought, it was also clear to all watching that something was wrong. Only, I had no way to prove it."

"I was poisoned. Damn near killed me, too. One of Horgund's lackeys infiltrated my staff and laced my water skin."

"Ah, that would explain it, then. I've been at the receiving end of your sword—though in training—and knew there was no way you would lose to Horgund unless foul play was afoot."

"But as I said, you serve him now."

"To draw close to our enemy, yes. Men have died because of my choice that day, but the greater good was at stake." He paused, reflecting on the dead weighing on his soul. "I was forced to make some unsavory choices, Sire. But as I said, I would do it again if I had to."

"The needs of the many outweigh the needs of the few," Charlie said.

"Well put, Sire," he agreed. "And the many need their king."

"And their queen."

"Yes. The next order of business," Captain Sheeran said. "Are you ready, Sire?"

"Ready as ever," Charlie replied, reaching out and clasping the captain's forearm in a firm shake. "Thank you, Captain."

"Don't thank me yet, Sire. We have a hard fight ahead of us, but you have many loyal men within the ranks, all of them awaiting my word. We are outnumbered, yes. But this is our soil. Our castle. Our home."

Charlie felt a surge of pride in his chest. They'd had their disagreements, yes, but the captain had always been a man of honor. Now it was clear just how deep-seated that honor was. That, and he gave a pretty darn good pep talk.

"But that battle is yet to begin. For now, you must fetch your queen," Sheeran continued. "She is being held in the dungeon. The smaller chamber, to the far end once you reach the bottom of the stairs."

"Wait, you're not coming with me?"

"No, Sire. I must rally the men. They will only respond to my word directly. There are turncoats in our midst, and caution is required. But do not fear, I have assistance ready." He gave a low whistle.

Owen jogged down the hall from where he'd been standing watch at the top of the stairs, covering Captain Sheeran's back should they be disturbed.

"Sire," he said, bowing slightly.

"You too?" Charlie asked. "You're with me?"

"Aye. To the death, Sire," he replied, standing tall with readiness.

Another man Charlie had thought hated his guts, now proving to be one of his most loyal followers. Again, that feeling. He was proud of his men. And if they survived this ordeal, there would be some changes around this place. Promotions, for one. He'd think of more later.

If they lived, of course.

"Well, then," Charlie said. "Let's go get the queen."

CHAPTER FIFTY-TWO

The revelation that Hunze was being held in the castle's tower had not deterred Bawb from his goal. He would free her at all cost, no matter how difficult the task may be.

Simon followed the pale man as he approached the tower wall. It was a tall, smooth surface of interlocked stones rising up four stories above the ground. It was in the window of the topmost level that Hunze had been spotted.

Unfortunately, Bawb knew full well just how difficult access to that chamber would be. The lone staircase spiraling upward was easy to defend, those guarding the topmost levels able to launch projectiles down upon any who tried to ascend without their permission. What he needed was another way in.

Fortunately, a fear of heights was not one of his shortcomings.

After seeing Hunze in the high window the prior evening, Bawb had set to work on a backup plan to reach her, and now it seemed that plan's time had come. The devices he had cobbled together were crude, but he felt they should be effective enough for his purposes.

Affixed to each boot he wore a pair of small straps with short metal claws on the tips. They wouldn't provide much of a grip on the stone face, but the Geist didn't require much.

He just needed to get close enough to the window to call to his friend and have her lower herself down to the treetop he'd attached a crude tether to. From there, they would descend via the tree's branches until they were safe on the ground.

Bawb made quick time up the lower trunk of the tree, easily sliding between the well-spaced branches. It was only toward the topmost that the going got tough, the proximity of the limbs hindering his progress until, finally, he was at the last that could support his weight.

From there, he tied off his short rope, securing one end to the tree, the other to his waist. He then edged out on the branch until his hands met the stone face.

"Are you okay up there?" Simon whispered up to him.

"Yes. Now keep your eyes peeled for patrols."

"What? Ice peels?"

"No. Your *eyes* peeled," he repeated, a bit louder.

"Ah. I understand," the man on the ground called back up.

Bawb dug his fingertips into the small gaps in the stone and began his careful ascent. In another world, he'd have had his entire kit at his disposal, including sticky-soled, flexible-toed boots that allowed him to cling to the smallest of irregularities in an otherwise smooth face. But this was not that world, and he was forced to make do with what was at hand. It was slow work, dragging his feet up until he could find purchase with one of the metal tips, then push his body higher until he could find another fingerhold.

Simon watched the man scale the building with awe. The king's aide was so much more than any of them had previously imagined. And no, he was literally climbing a sheer face to rescue the poor maiden in distress.

"Hunze!" Bawb hissed toward the open window a good six meters above him. "Hunze!"

A shadow passed across the window, then the golden-haired woman leaned out, a confused look on her face. She could have sworn she'd just heard her name, but she was in a tower, several levels up from the ground.

"Hunze, down here!"

"Bawb? What are you doing?"

"Coming to rescue you. Do you have sheets in your room?"

"Yes. But why?"

"I want you to tie them together and rappel down to me."

"You want me to *what*?"

"Rappel, Hunze. Climb down to me."

Far below, Simon strained his ears to catch the exchange. It sounded like the king's aide was calling the blonde woman, but he couldn't quite make out the rest.

"Bawb, the sheets aren't long enough to reach you."

"Try!"

"No, I'm sure of it. But wait, I have an idea. Hold fast, I'll be right back," she said, disappearing back into the window.

"Not as though I have anywhere to go," he muttered, clinging to the rock face.

A braided, golden rope fluttered down to him from above.

"What in the worlds—?" he wondered, then realized what she had done. "This is your hair, Hunze."

"Obviously," he heard her call out from inside her room. "I've braced myself as best I can. Climb up to me."

"It's your *hair*."

"Yes, and it is far stronger than it looks. Now, come on."

"You're far up, Hunze."

"What?"

"I said, you are far up, Hunze," he repeated, amazed at the length of her hair. He had never before seen it fully unraveled. An entire lifetime of growth—nearly three decades worth—braided and hanging for him to climb, gleaming brightly against the gray stone.

"Just do it," she ordered.

Bawb, surprised by the firm tone of her voice, obeyed, grabbing the braid and quickly scaling to her window. It was an unbelievable sight to see, but one that had only been witnessed by one man.

Simon had seen and heard the exchange from far below. Well, he'd seen it. His hearing, however, was questionable.

"What did he say?" he mused. "Rap something? Was it, 'Rapunzel'? Was that it? Whatever he said, the woman threw down her golden hair to him, and he climbed right up, just like it was some kind of golden stair."

It was an extraordinary thing he'd seen. "Wait till I tell the wife," he mused. "And the kids! They'll be amazed."

And so they would. And the story would pass from them to his children's children, and theirs as well. Generations upon generations, spreading the tale of what Simon had seen that one night. The night when Rapunzel lowered her golden hair to her noble suitor, come to rescue her from the high tower she'd been imprisoned in.

That was as far as his version of the tale would go, but his heirs would add to it, in their own time. Bawb and Hunze, however, did not have the luxury of waiting generations. They had to escape, and now.

No sooner had Bawb's feet cleared the windowsill than the golden-haired woman wrapped him up in a fierce embrace, hugging him tightly, her hair lying in a coil on the floor. Unsure exactly how to react, Bawb gently returned the embrace, holding her close, her warmth radiating into him, even through his clothes.

After a long, silent moment, they both loosened their grips, stepping back to take in the sight of each other.

"You are alive," she said, tears of joy in her eyes as she wrapped her lengthy braids around her body and secured them in place once more.

"As are you," Bawb said, a little flush now coloring his pale cheeks. "Did they mistreat you?" he asked, a brief glimpse of the man known as the Geist flashing through his eyes. "If they did, they will suffer. *Immensely.*"

"No, I am unharmed," she said, taking him by the hands. "You came for me. You climbed a tower for me."

"I would climb far greater heights than these, if need be," he replied, allowing himself to be caught up in the moment. But a moment was all he could spare. "Come. Time is short. We will have to make our way down the tower."

Fortunately, the guards would never hear him coming. Their attention was always focused on attacks from below. Never would they expect their demise to rain down on them from above.

Bawb knew their rough number and positions. This would be almost comically easy after all they'd been through.

He moved to the door, Hunze's hand in his.

"Wait."

"What is it, Hunze? We must hurry."

"I know. But it's the king's mistress. There's something you should know."

CHAPTER FIFTY-THREE

Charlie raced down the familiar hallways of the castle, following Owen as he quickly scanned the way for guards, then gestured for him to move ahead. Despite the speed with which they moved in this unusual, but necessary, way, Charlie was antsy. He needed to get to the dungeon, and fast. Captain Sheeran was quietly rallying the men for a fight. He just had to get Leila the hell out of there before it erupted.

Owen, for his part, was making good time, his keen eyes scouring for potential confrontations well before he motioned for the king to join him. The odds of their running into staff who knew the king at that particular time in that particular place was slim, but prudence was almost always the best course of action.

Charlie knew the thick stone walls would hide the sounds of fighting, but best save that for the dungeons, where he could easily hide bodies, rather than the hallways. They finally reached the heavy door to the dungeons and pulled it open, closing it behind them as they descended to the muffling depths of the subterranean chambers.

Unlike the halls above, the dungeon had several of King Horgund's men standing guard over the captive queen. From what Charlie could see, it looked like close to ten of them. Were he with Bawb, it would be easy odds, but with a novice at his side, he knew it was going to be a tough fight.

"Hey, you can't be down here," one of the guards called out.

"Oh, but we were told to report to the dungeon," Owen said.

"You're one of Sheeran's men, aren't you?"

"Aye."

"Well, get out of here. Only Horgund's guards are allowed."

Charlie kept walking.

"Didn't you hear me?" the guard growled.

"You ready?" Charlie asked Owen, his hand drifting to the pommel of his short sword.

"I am, Sire."

"And you remember the new moves I showed you?"

"Been practicing every day since you've been gone."

"Good man. I'll be grading you after," Charlie said with a wink, then drew steel and dove into battle. The first two guards didn't even have time to react before they lay bleeding out on the stone floor.

The young man at his side showed no hesitation, joining him in the fray, and in moments, both of their blades were flashing in the torchlight of the dungeon. The guards reacted with a bit more urgency when they saw their comrades fall to the ground, and in no time, the fight had erupted to full force.

Charlie watched Owen from the corner of his eye as he battled a trio attempting to pin him to a stone column.

They're going to flank him, he realized.

Rather than press on, Charlie quickly dropped into a roll to the side, which seemed to be a tactically unsound move so far as his adversaries could tell. But his aim was not them, and he rolled to within arm's reach of the men hectoring his young companion.

Charlie's blade flashed out, low and fast. Two of Owen's attackers cried out as their Achilles' tendons were severed by his

277

blow, dropping them to their knees despite their best intentions to remain upright.

Owen seized the opportunity to part one of the guards from his head, the other likewise downed by a slice to the neck.

Four down.

The Dragon King snatched up one of the fallen men's blades and swung it into action, windmilling his arms in a flurry of attacks. Another guard fell, but there were five remaining, and they'd fallen into a more defensive stance.

"Get help!" the leader of the group ordered the man in the rear of the formation.

He started to run, and with the wall of men between them, there was no way Charlie or Owen could reach him.

"Fuck it," Charlie growled. *"Azokta!"*

The Wampeh Ghalian killing word flowed from deep within his body, calling upon his own internal magic, drawing energy from his bond to his mighty dragon friend. It wasn't the most powerful spell he'd ever cast, but seeing as he had no konus and no slaap, it would have to do.

The fleeing man dropped to the ground, stone dead, his armor hitting the hard ground with a dull clank. The other men's faces paled.

"The king is a wizard," one gasped.

"That's right, bitches. And he's had enough of this bullshit," Charlie said, casting a series of small, distracting spells to throw the men off guard.

He would have preferred to kill them from a distance, or at least immobilize them enough to safely finish the fight, but he still didn't know exactly how much internal power he possessed, and if it really was tied to Ara, with her missing, he just couldn't risk it. And after Bawb's display in the forest, suffice to say, he had learned to play it safe when it came to the ways of magic.

The remaining guards fought back as best they could, but their spirit had been broken. The visceral terror of realizing they were very much *prey* and not equal combatants took the fire from their fight. They did not surrender, however, and Charlie had to grudgingly respect them for it, though it did not stop him from slaying every last one of them.

"Check them. Make sure they're dead," he commanded Owen.

The young man stared at him, jaw hanging open.

"Yes, Owen. I used magic. You can freak out about it later, okay? We have work to do."

Owen stopped gawking, his brain kicking back into gear. "That. Was. Amazing! Can you teach me that?"

Charlie couldn't help but pause.

"You're not afraid?"

"No. You're my king. Why, should I be?"

"Well, no. But most people freak out a bit, is all."

A woman's muffled voice was shouting, and close.

"Leila!"

Charlie ran the length of the room to the thick door from which he'd heard the cries. He unbolted the heavy iron rod and swung the weighty wood open.

Leila sat tied to a chair, a sweat-soaked burlap sack over her head. Charlie whipped it off, his queen squinting uncomfortably in the glare of the torchlight.

"Charlie?"

"Yeah, babe. I've got you," he said, wrapping his arms around her, his hands deftly slicing through the ropes binding her as he held her tight.

"Is she okay?"

"Yeah, Owen. We're good. Clear the stairwell. I'm going to help her up."

"I can walk, Charlie," she said stubbornly, immediately stumbling on weak legs.

"Leila, they've been mistreating you for days. Accept the help, please."

279

She paused a moment, noting both the lack of strength in her limbs and the concern in his eyes. "Okay," she relented.

Charlie helped her across the dungeon, careful to avoid the slippery red mess he'd made.

"All this fuss for me?" she said, eyeing the carnage.

"Anything for my queen," he softly replied.

They had just made it to the top of the stairs and were heading down the hallway toward the hidden door Charlie had left ajar when fifteen of King Horgund's men rounded the corner, blocking their exit.

"Surrender or die!" their captain called out.

"What do we do, Sire? Can you use your magic on them?"

"You showed him your spells?" Leila asked, shocked.

"Just one. And it was an emergency."

"This seems like an emergency, too."

"Yeah, but Ara is missing, and I don't know how much of my juju is tied to her," he said. Despite the odds, a small grin began to spread on his lips.

"What?"

He leaned over and whispered into Leila's ear. She smiled as well, then took a deep breath.

"Baloooooo!" she called out at the top of her lungs.

"What's she on about?" the captain asked.

"Oh, you'll see," Charlie replied, a knowing grin spreading on his lips.

He had been a good boy, patiently waiting out in the woods like Charlie asked him to. But when he heard his mama's voice, calling him with urgency, Baloo took off from his hiding spot in a flash, a gray blur speeding from the trees right into what appeared to be a solid stone wall.

But his nose told him it wasn't. It was a door. And the door was open.

The enormous canine leapt onto the men, his jaws ripping them to shreds in a cathartic display of aggression and fury.

They had taken Leila. Hurt her. Kept her from him. If Charlie had killed with anger and efficiency, Baloo's revenge was an outright slaughter.

The guards stumbled back, unable to draw weapons, as they had foolishly come charging into the corridor in tight formation. But Baloo had no such problem. No swords to draw, merely tearing teeth, bringing all of them a swift demise. In a matter of minutes, all of the men lay dead or dying.

"Oh, come here, baby!" Leila called as her boy trotted over to her, covered in blood and gore, but none of it his own.

Leila ignored the sticky mess and hugged him tightly around his massive neck. Baloo's eyes met Charlie's, content and whole. They were finally a family again.

"You need to get out of here," Charlie said. "Bawb and Hunze will meet us in the woods. Baloo knows the way. And if you get separated, find Clay. He will shelter you."

"No, Charlie. I want to stay and fight."

He hugged her tight, then pushed her away. "You're weak, and I can't be effective in battle if I'm worried about you as I fight. Please, go with Baloo. You'll regain your strength, and you'll have your revenge. But not tonight. Please."

She hesitated, eyes welling up with emotion. "Fine. I'll go," she said, turning to leave. "And Charlie?"

"Yeah?"

"Don't die."

He smiled, his heart shining through his eyes. "Love you too."

As soon as his queen was out of sight, he turned to the young man fighting by his side. "Owen, the captain has rallied the men to fight by now. Are you ready to retake the castle?"

"Aye, Sire. And with your magic, I know we'll win the day. There's no way King Horgund's wizard will dare oppose us."

Charlie hesitated. "Owen, have you even *seen* this wizard?"

"Well, no. But I've heard the others talk about him."

"And have any of them actually seen him?"

"Uh, not that I know of, actually."

They'd have used their magic by now if they actually had it, Charlie realized with pleasure. *The whole thing was a ruse.*

"All right, then. Gird your loins, sonny boy, it's clobberin' time."

"Sire?"

"Never mind. Come on. Let's retake what's ours."

CHAPTER FIFTY-FOUR

The sounds of fighting grew louder as Charlie and Owen ran. Being men of action, they ran *toward* the conflict rather than away from it. There was a full-scale uprising underway, and the commotion in the hallways as they raced to join Captain Sheeran was merely overflow from the main battle in the courtyard.

Soldiers in King Horgund's colors were fighting one another, they noted. As they drew near, Charlie saw their faces and realized he recognized many of them. Men he had helped train. Men from his own kingdom and loyal to Charlie, absorbed into Horgund's ranks, now turning against the invaders.

The odds were still against them, however. A great many of their comrades had fled and were in hiding, though they'd gladly join the fray once word reached them.

But this was a few thousand years before wireless comms, and by the time those reinforcements heard of the battle, it would already be over.

"I've got to get to my weapons," Charlie grunted, slashing down a pair of Horgund's men.

SCOTT BARON

"Seem to be doing just fine with those," Owen joked as he landed a killing blow on his own opponent.

"You don't understand, Owen. They're *magic* weapons."

A light went on in the young soldier's head. "Oh. Well, then. Point the way, Sire."

They pushed through the thickening combat, trying to make it closer to the wing of the castle that housed Charlie's former chambers. They would never keep their hidden cache of weapons there, of course. That would be the first place any thief or invader would look for valuables. But one of their two caches was tucked away in that part of the castle, hidden in plain sight on the lowest level behind months upon months of shimmer spells.

"This way," Charlie said, leading them down a smaller corridor to one of the servants' common areas.

The shortcut was abruptly blocked by the cacophonous roar of heavy battle spilling into the room. From the hallway Charlie had intended to take, no less. Behind them, sounds of combat were also closing in.

"Shit. Looks like we have to make a bit of a stand, Owen. You ready?"

The young guard just smiled as if he were having the time of his life. If they made it through this ordeal, he was going to set him up with Bawb for some one-on-one training. He certainly seemed to be of the right mindset for it.

The combat was thick, and both sides seemed to be evenly matched, more or less.

We can take them. We just need to position that group to block their—

A particularly violent fighter caught the king's attention out of the corner of his eye. A strong fighter with long, dark hair. And aggressive. A woman, he realized, as he caught a better glimpse of her shape as she mowed through his men. There was no denying it, the berserker of a woman with her dark hair falling out of her quickly pulled ponytail was a formidable combatant.

She was taking his men out with brutal efficiency, he was distressed to see, and there was something strangely familiar in her movements. He just couldn't put his finger on why.

"Look out, Sire," Owen said, engaging a trio of men charging his king. One of them was swinging a spiked club, which narrowly missed Charlie's head.

"Good looking out," Charlie said with a grin, pivoting and slicing the man's club arm from his body, then running him through.

Owen used the techniques Charlie had taught him, bending and twisting to gain access to the less-protected joints in his more heavily armored opponents' equipment. The first went down in a heap as the artery in his upper thigh was sliced open. Charlie knew it would only take seconds before he blacked out from blood loss.

That left the third man. Owen was still bent low and vulnerable, so Charlie rushed past him to engage. The exchange of sword blows was fierce. The man obviously knew how to fight, and was giving the king far more of a challenge than any of the others he'd faced so far.

But Charlie was better, and he knew it. With a feint to the left and a step to the right, he passed the man's sword and buried his dagger in his chest, the reinforced tip making its way through the layer of metal and driving straight into his heart.

"Sire! Look out!"

Charlie spun as Owen fell into him, blood gushing from his side, where the berserker bitch had planted her sword.

"No!" he shouted, swinging his own sword high, blocking her follow-up blow as he lowered the youth to the ground.

"I'll be fine. Fight," he said, blood bubbling from his lips.

Given the intensity of the woman's attack, he had no choice

but to fight. He also knew Owen would not live to see the end of the battle.

"Fucking bitch! I'm going to end you!" he roared, swinging his sword and dagger in a tandem assault, wailing on the strange woman.

It was chaos, the battle raging all around them, but Charlie was focused on this one opponent with a deadly anger. Again, he pounced, but she was ready, her blades meshing with his in a test of strength and resolve. She struggled against him, the two drawn close, face-to-face. Her hair shifted aside, and Charlie got a clear look at her face.

And his world went sideways.

"Rika?" he managed to say in utter shock.

She paused, the briefest flash of what seemed to almost be recognition. Familiarity. Then it was gone, replaced by pure aggression, along with a solid kick to the chest.

Charlie reeled, falling over, his sword parrying defensively, his tactics suddenly shifting one hundred eighty degrees from offense to defense. It was Rika. *His* Rika. His mission's second-in-command, and pilot of their massive mech. But that was impossible. It simply couldn't be.

She'd been lobotomized, and a few thousand years in the future in a galaxy far away, sold off as a common house slave. He'd seen it with his own eyes, the only other survivor of his ship's crash in that distant part of the universe.

But it *was* her. He knew it without a doubt.

"Rika, what the hell are you doing?"

"How do you know my name?" she growled, stabbing fiercely at his torso.

Charlie deflected the blow, but now found himself having to not only defend himself, but also protect his attacker from his own men trying to help their king.

"No, this one is mine!" he shouted, knocking one of his guards back as he tried to engage alongside him.

"As you wish, Sire," the man said, a confused look on his face as he turned to find another opponent in the melee.

Charlie had to find out what was going on, but the middle of a life-and-death battle was not the ideal place for it. He glanced at the expired youth, bled out on the floor. Owen had died saving him. And now, he was saving his killer.

One way or another, he knew he had to get her out of there. Somewhere safe. Somewhere he could find out what the hell was going on. Charlie shoved Rika and dashed into an adjacent room.

No one here. Good.

His friend-turned-assailant rushed after him.

Charlie stood in the middle of the room, his hand raised, a determined focus in his eyes.

I know I have the power, he told himself. He just hoped he was right.

"Dispanus," he silently cast, the major stun spell flowing from within.

He did have the power after all. And while he didn't know how much remained, at least it was enough for this.

Rika took the full force of the spell, knocked violently unconscious, dropping to the floor in a heap. Charlie was just glad she didn't accidentally land atop one of her blades. The spell would have her out for some time, but this was something strange, and he didn't intend to take any chances.

He quickly bound her hands. Tight. Then he hauled his apparently not dead friend over his shoulder and made for the door at the far end of the room, heading out to the courtyard, where the rest of King Horgund's soldiers were engaged with Captain Sheeran and his loyal men.

CHAPTER FIFTY-FIVE

Charlie fought one-handed, his unconscious friend slung over one shoulder as he slayed another half dozen men on the way to the courtyard. The path to his hidden weaponry was sadly blocked from reach, well behind a rather sizable group of King Horgund's men. He only hoped Bawb had better luck than he did.

Captain Sheeran broke off from the fighting to join his king when he saw him approaching. He was more than a little surprised to see him carrying a woman over his shoulder.

"Horgund's bitch's lady-in-waiting?" Sheeran exclaimed when he saw Charlie's load. "What is she doing here?"

"We came upon her in the fighting. Over in the west wing. She was going all berserker in there."

"But that makes no sense. I've seen her around the castle. She's the mistress's aide. She never leaves her side, especially not with the child coming."

"But she did, obviously."

Sheeran looked at her sleeping face. "Almost pretty. When she's not actively trying to kill you, that is. But you know what this means, Sire. The child has been born. With that distraction removed, Horgund will assemble his men and provide the leadership they require to form a more cohesive attack. We need to regroup immediately, before they fall upon us."

"Agreed. Fall back to the far end of the courtyard. Our forces are heavier there. It should be a better place to prepare. Plus, we'll have stone at our backs and an escape through the gate if things go wrong."

"Aye, Sire." Sheeran shouted orders to the men, who quickly started shifting their position, as ordered. He looked around the combatants, scanning their faces. "Where's Owen, Sire? I don't see him."

Charlie was silent a long moment, and Sheeran knew what had befallen the lad before he uttered a word.

"He died well, Captain. He was brave and true. He saved my life at the cost of his own."

Sheeran nodded, his jaw flexing as his emotions welled up. "How? Did you slay his killer?"

Charlie looked away. This was not going to be easy.

"No, though if it were anyone else they'd have found an unmerciful fate at the end of my sword."

"But why?" he asked, the pain clear in his voice.

"Because she was the one, Sheeran. *She* killed him."

He drew his dagger. "A cruel and heartless bitch. Leave her to me, and I will avenge him."

Charlie's heart ached. He knew exactly how the grieving man felt, but he couldn't hand over his friend, no matter what she'd done.

"I'm sorry, I truly am. But I can't do that, Captain."

"Why not?" the man replied, his fists fighting to unclench as he spoke to his king.

"Because not too many years ago, this woman was my friend. Lost to me. Sold into slavery in a land so very far away. She shouldn't be here. There is no logical way she *can* be here, but she is. And she doesn't even know me. A friend for years, just tried to take my life. I have to know why. To find out what the hell is going on."

Captain Sheeran struggled with the emotions raging within him, slowly pulling them back under control.

"I want her dead, Sire."

"I know. And so would I, under any other circumstances."

Sheeran stood silent a long moment. "Your situation, it is...difficult," he said, drawing a long breath. "And if I am to be honest with myself, were I in your boots, I would do the same."

Charlie grasped him by the shoulder and locked eyes with his loyal guard. "Thank you, Sheeran. You're a better man than most, and you have my gratitude."

Men cried out in agony as their lives were violently taken from them, jarring both men from their moment of contemplation.

"I think we need to see to the battle, Sire."

"I think you're right."

Charlie and Sheeran rushed to the rear of the ranks, tucking Rika's unconscious form well out of harm's way, then returned to the battle.

"Do you think we can retake the northern wing while holding the courtyard?" Charlie asked as they fought through the waves of Horgund's troops.

"If they are all as poor fighters as these, then yes. I believe it is possible. And watching our men fight, I am glad to say I was mistaken about your training regimen. They are far better conditioned than the invaders, and your new fighting technique has indeed proven a formidable weapon against Horgund's men."

Charlie smiled. "Thank you, Captain. Now, let's see about taking back this castle."

The battle raged, and Charlie and Sheeran fought side by side, plowing through Horgund's men, their forces moving with them en masse, driving the newcomer soldiers back.

Charlie scanned the combatants as they moved, Rika's impossible presence weighing upon his mind.

No time for that now. First win, then *freak out.*

A wave of heavily armored men suddenly broke through the ranks of disorganized soldiers, piercing Charlie's defensive line and scattering his men. A rapid retreat to the courtyard was called, an unanticipated regrouping in the face of the new tactics.

They pulled back quickly, forming a new line, when a familiar sight strode into battle, barking orders as he came.

Horgund.

The invading king locked eyes on Charlie across the battleground, pointing his sword at him in challenge.

"Oh, yes, bitch. It is on," Charlie growled, then rushed toward the heavily armored king.

Their swords clashed in a shower of sparks, the force of the blow nearly making Charlie's hand go numb. Horgund was strong, no doubt, and he was fresh. But worse than that, Charlie was simply getting tired. His muscles had been put to such use over the past hour that it made the torturous obstacle course workouts Rika used to put him through years ago—way back before they had even launched their ill-fated space mission— seem like a mere warm-up.

But this was it. Two kings fighting for the ownership of the realm. Charlie would have to dig deep if he expected to come out victorious. And deep he would dig. The only question was whether it would be enough.

CHAPTER FIFTY-SIX

Bawb held Hunze's hand tight as the rushed down the last level of the tower's staircase. It had taken them longer to pass the guard than he had originally anticipated. That's not to say the assassin had any problems with the men whose lives he took, just that there were far more of them than he expected.

Hunze had stayed a good twenty steps behind him as Bawb instructed, ensuring she didn't unintentionally draw attention by making a sound as they descended the stairs. This served dual purpose, as Bawb also didn't want her to see him do his deadly work.

He was well aware that she knew who he was. *What* he was. But the stealthy killer had found himself unexpectedly not wanting her to actually see what he did. Though she'd seen a lot, and would see more before the day was done, assassination was one thing he wished to spare her.

By the time she joined him on the lower level, she had stepped over nearly twenty bodies, carefully laid out against the walls of the stairway, leaving her a clear path to travel. Bawb was nothing if not a considerate killer.

When he took her hand as she joined up with him, she was

surprised to find it free of any blood whatsoever. Though given what he had just done for her, she wouldn't have minded had there been. But the Wampeh had been careful in his work, leaving no unnecessary sanguine traces anywhere on his person.

"We have to hurry," she said as they stepped onto the lowest level. "We must warn Charlie!"

She pulled Bawb's hand, but found the man immovable.

"What are you doing, Bawb? There's no time to waste!"

"I agree. However, my task is not a waste, I assure you. Come with me. There is one thing we must do while the guards are occupied elsewhere."

He led her at a run down the hallway, rounding the curved stones of the tower's staircase to the point where it disappeared in a ninety-degree angle into the castle's thick walls.

"There's nothing here, Bawb. We need to––"

The pale man reached out to the stone, and his hand disappeared. Hunze heard a faint click of a latch unfastening.

"A shimmer door?"

"Yes."

"I didn't know you had placed a shimmer in this part of the castle."

Bawb smiled as he withdrew a pair of packs, loaded with magical weaponry and a few bottles of iridescent water. Aside from the ones tucked in the other cache, these were the last of the Balamar waters in the galaxy. He reached into the larger of the bags and pulled out a pair of very familiar tools. His armlets, fully charged with magic and ready for battle. He smiled as he felt their reassuring warmth on his skin.

"That was the point, dear Hunze," he said, sliding the heavier bag onto his back, the other slipped over his shoulder. "No one was aware of its existence. Only Charlie and I know of the locations of our weapons. Hopefully he has gathered the rest from the other wing of the castle."

"So, *now* we warn him?"

"Yes," he replied, tightening the straps of the packs. "Now we warn him."

"Great. But the castle is big. How do we know where to find him?"

Bawb grinned. "Just follow the sound of fighting."

The two took off at a run, heading toward the din of battle. Bawb hoped they wouldn't be too late.

A small cut had opened on Charlie's cheek, where the tip of King Horgund's sword had managed to get just a little too close. It was minor, though, and with his healing abilities, would be gone in a day. But for the moment, the sheen of red gave Charlie the crazed look of a madman.

He had been battling the man who had stolen his throne for nearly ten minutes at this point. The difference in skill between the king and his men was massive, and while Charlie could have taken him in single combat, the rules and decorum of a duel were not in play today.

Both had their captains and men fighting at their sides, protecting them from sneak attacks, as killing a king would earn the slayer a mark of glory and hefty reward. Several times Charlie had overcome his exhaustion and had Horgund on the ropes, only to be forced back when the man's troops rushed to his aid, forcing Charlie to pull away.

It was this back and forth that kept the fight fluid, constantly changing. Neither man held the advantage for long, and the carefully placed lines of defense were scattered on both sides.

Charlie read the battlefield and made a decision. He pulled Captain Sheeran aside a moment.

"You need to get Rika out of here. Take her to the safehouse. Don't say its name, but I know you know where."

"But, Sire, I cannot leave your side."

"If they take her back, I'll never find out what's going on here. Please, Captain," he urged.

The captain was a man of honor, and his king had given him an order. Yet his king was in immediate peril as well. Finally, he made a decision.

"There are men here I would trust with my life. I shall have *them* take her. I vouch for their honor and trust their discretion."

"Fine. Just hurry," Charlie said, leaping back into the fray as Horgund made another charge.

Sheeran raced to one of his men and carefully issued his order into the man's ear. He nodded, then grabbed his fellow soldier to help in his task. The pair fought their way toward the back of the courtyard to where the king's prisoner lay unconscious.

Charlie and Horgund made their way through the battle and clashed once more, each of the two kings trying his best to part the other from his head. Horgund, while fresher than Charlie, was also far less conditioned and was showing signs of fatigue. All of Charlie's seemingly obsessive training was paying off as the advantage began to shift yet again.

The two were left to fight unaided and uninterrupted for a moment as the battle shifted around them. The space they were suddenly afforded was a welcome respite, and they were able to focus solely on killing one another, not worried about those around them.

"Give me back my kingdom, you bastard!" Charlie shouted, swinging his sword at the invader's head. "Get out of my castle!"

Horgund deflected the attack and launched a counter. "*Your* castle? You were defeated on the dueling field. Your men violated the agreement. You have no honor!"

"Honor?" Charlie growled, unleashing a flurry of blows, each of which Horgund barely deflected. "You're the one with no honor. You never would have won that fight if you hadn't poisoned my water skin."

Horgund hesitated, a look of genuine shock on his face. "What lies do you speak? I would never stoop to such a dishonor."

"Lies? I think not. I *was* poisoned that morning."

The two continued to engage, but the intensity had diminished, the revelation taking the fight from both men.

"I swear on my honor, I had no part of such a deed."

From the look in his eye, and despite the fact the two men had been trying to kill one another for some time now, Charlie could see he was telling the truth.

"But if it wasn't you who poisoned me, then who?"

"I did," a voice called out, cutting impossibly through the din of battle like a hot knife to butter.

Both men turned, the battling men around them likewise pausing their combat.

"My love! You should be resting!" Horgund called out to his mistress.

The new mother stood there casually in the midst of blood and death, calmly suckling her newborn. She looked at the two men, pulling the infant son from her breast and handing him to the wet-nurse attending at her side. She then took her sweet time covering her exposed chest, staring at the *rightful* king the whole time. She flashed him a wicked smile.

"Hello, Charlie."

CHAPTER FIFTY-SEVEN

"Hello, Malalia," Charlie said, feet locked in place with shock.

"You know this man?" Horgund asked, confusion spreading where rage had formerly resided.

"You could say that," she replied, surveying the battlefield surrounding her.

"And who is Malalia?"

"I am."

"My love? That is not your name."

"Oh, but it is."

All of the combatants had ceased fighting, unsure exactly what was happening, but suddenly far more interested in the goings-on of their kings than their own individual clashes. It was eerie, the silence her presence commanded, and she reveled in it.

The king's mistress saw movement across the courtyard. Her lady-in-waiting being carried out the gate, it seemed.

"So," she said with a wicked grin, "I see you've met my little pet."

She watched Charlie's face, reveling in the confusion she found there.

"I have to tell you," she continued, "after you killed my father, I knew I would eventually have my revenge. Somehow, some way, I would make you pay."

"Your father was still alive when he was last seen, Malalia. What did you do to him?"

"Silence!" she shrieked, a wave of angry magic rippling out from her across the courtyard. "*You* and your friends killed him. And that was all it took to get the Council of Twenty to back me in my plans."

"You took your father's place," Charlie realized. "You became the new Visla Maktan."

"You always were so very clever, Charlie," she cooed. "And sentimental. Always with the stories of your poor friend, taken from you after you crashed. And your home world, so far away. It was your own doing, you know. Your tales led me to her. Mind you, it took quite some time finding your Rika, and acquiring her cost me a fair amount of coin. Then there was the process of breaking her down and remaking her. It took a great many spells, applied over time. She's quite fearsome, now, you know."

"I've seen," he replied. "But that battle was only months ago, Malalia. In another galaxy. And you weren't even pregnant then."

"No, I was not," she grumbled. "That little bundle of discomfort was courtesy of our friend, here. Apparently, my pessary spells do not work with human physiology. Imagine my surprise when my flow ceased."

"Quite a surprise, I'd imagine."

"Indeed, it was. But we can call it a happy accident."

"I never took you for the mothering type."

"Oh, I'm not. But it did serve to bind this one closer to me," she said, gesturing to her king. "Men. So sentimental about having a son to carry on their line. And taking a king as a lover? How better to control his forces?"

"My love, I do not understand," Horgund said.

"No, I suspect not."

Charlie couldn't believe his eyes, but she really was there. *Somehow,* she had followed him all the way to Earth.

"It makes no sense. You didn't come through the wormhole with us. We would have seen."

"No, I did not," she replied. "In fact, I spent nearly two years fighting the Council's battles in my father's place. Cementing my position atop their ranks. It was tiring work, fighting the rebellion you started."

"Me?"

"Yes, you. Nearly every inhabited system in the galaxy heard about your little performance at Tolemac."

"*You* were there?" he realized. "You were the one who destroyed the planet."

"Because of *you,* Charlie! It was all *your* fault. And it sparked a revolution. So I did what I had to. I fought it, gaining power, seizing control of Council assets. So long as I was victorious, what did they care?"

"But you had another plan, didn't you?"

"Oh, my clever human. Pity you will die horribly once I drag you and your friends back home. Back to the *right* time and galaxy. And it will be slow, I assure you, while your companions will live the rest of their lives in torment and agony."

"You're fucking nuts. You do know that, right?"

"Always the joker. But answer me this. Would a crazy person have been able to achieve the greatest feat of magic ever performed in the entire galaxy?"

"Killing a planet doesn't make you great."

"Not that, Charlie. That was child's play. But with your precious Rika in my possession, I was able to peel through her mind, pinpointing this pathetic rock you call home. And there was more in there," she said with a wicked smile. "You know, she was quite fond of you. A shame the Tslavars scrambled her brain, or maybe you could have had a nice life together."

Charlie gritted his teeth, but didn't take the bait. She wanted an excuse to react, and he wouldn't give it to her.

"And with your friend's memory of where your home was, it was then just a matter of crafting the right spell to recreate your little escape hatch trick. It took quite a long time, and even then I had to use the last of the Council's Ootaki hair to power it. The most powerful spell ever cast in the systems."

"You stole your people's power stores and left them high and dry? In the middle of a rebellion?"

"For revenge? It was worth it. Though I admit, your world was far more primitive than I imagined."

"There's a reason for that, Malalia. It wasn't an escape hatch. It was an accident. We had no intention of coming to this planet, and especially not this time."

"Yes, I gathered as much when my craft nearly tore apart, dumping me on this wretched rock, and almost a full year before you even arrived here. Had I realized it was a time-shifting spell as well, I would perhaps have foregone your destruction."

Suddenly, it all became clear. Charlie realized what had happened after so much head-scratching confusion.

"That was what Ara sensed. She sensed *you* on the planet. But you'd been layering shimmers, hadn't you? Hiding yourself long before we ever got here."

"Clever boy."

"And you're why she couldn't see your forces as they gathered in the kingdom. You cast a shimmer over them as they advanced, didn't you?"

"Again, correct."

"But even you aren't that powerful, and your konuses would have drained long ago."

"Yes, that is true," she said, magic crackling across her fingertips. "But I learned a thing or two from your Wampeh friend."

"But that's impossible. Your physiology isn't Wampeh. Your kind can't absorb power."

"No, we cannot. But once I finally captured my very own Wampeh Ghalian—and it cost me over a hundred men to do so, I might add—I drained him nearly dry, over and over and over for more than a year. You see, it was something my father had said in a fit of anger. Something about soiling my blood. His insult proved to be my rebirth."

"What the hell are you talking about?"

"I added small amounts of the Wampeh's blood to my own, until I slowly began to acquire his gift for taking another's power. And then I fed. On such a variety of power users. I'm quite strong now, Charlie. Far more than ever before."

She pointed her finger and zapped a man dead with a word. It was an impressive show of sheer power, but Charlie saw her wince from the effort. Childbirth had weakened her. For the moment, at least.

"Your human friend was the only other survivor of our crash, so when I charmed the king into taking me as his lover after his wife's unfortunate demise—"

"At your hands, I assume?"

Malalia merely smiled.

"As I was saying, I kept your Rika as my chambermaid and finished making her what she is. Quite a fighter too," she added with a wicked smile.

King Horgund, having finally transitioned from utter shock, looked horrified. "My-my queen. You killed her? And the talk of this Dragon King threatening my kingdom? The reason I marched to war? This was all predicated on lies?"

"You always were slow on the uptake, Horgund," she said, bored with the man.

The king flushed red with rage, but not at Charlie this time. He turned to the wet-nurse.

"Take my son inside," he growled. "I would not have him see his treacherous mother slain."

The wet-nurse blanched and quickly ran back into the castle with her precious bundle.

"Now to deal with you," he said, spinning on his now former lover.

"Oh, Horgund. I'm afraid you've outlived your usefulness, *my love*," she cooed, then raised her hand, smiting him dead with a killing spell, then igniting his body in flames just for shits and giggles.

Jesus. She's fucking crazy. Crazy, and strong.

Charlie raised his hand, quickly casting a silent *slovera* spell, extinguishing the flames.

"Without a konus," Malalia noted with great curiosity. Charlie, it seemed, had power after all. "My, my. Isn't that interesting."

Captain Sheeran stared in disbelief at the smoldering remains of King Horgund. Magic, treachery, deceit. Much had been wrong in the invader's household, but he apparently had no idea just how much. He turned to his men, holding his sword aloft, commanding their attention.

"The king is dead. Long live the *rightful* king!" he bellowed.

"Long live the king!" his men echoed.

"Not for long," Malalia said, raising her hands, preparing to cast her deadly spells.

A blast of magic spun her around. Then another landed, knocking her to the ground. The new mother scrambled back to her feet, fury in her eyes.

"You!" she hissed.

Charlie turned to see Bawb and Hunze standing in the courtyard entry. The Wampeh assassin had shed his timid disguise, Charlie noted. And he was armed. To the teeth. He cast a major disabling spell, the power flowing from his konuses with ease.

Malalia, however, countered his spell, stopping it dead in its tracks despite not wearing a konus or slaap. She had always been a powerful visla, but this was something new. Something *more*.

Bawb's eyes went wide as she recovered and started casting her own attacks, actually pushing him back. Her internal magic was so much greater than before. It was utterly massive. If not for her recent childbirth draining her energy, she would have overpowered him easily, he realized.

Charlie raced to his friend's side and quickly donned a pair of heavy konuses from the bags he carried. He then slipped on a pair of slaaps for good measure, then joined the fight.

Their combined spells plowed through Malalia's attacks, shattering her spells, physically throwing her back with enough force to blast her right through the castle's stone wall. The two lowered their weapons and looked at one another with shock in their eyes.

"Malalia––" Bawb said.

"I know. We have to go. Now! Sheeran, get your men out of here and meet us at *the place.*"

"But surely, she must be dead, Sire."

"I wouldn't count on it," Charlie replied. "Shit just got weird, and there's a *lot* I need to fill you in on. Things you need to know. But there's no time, and this is not the place. This is a battle that you and your men *cannot* win. Now run, before she recovers. We'll regroup when all are clear. You know where."

"Aye, Sire," he said, reading the concern in his king's eyes. "Men, we are leaving. Fall back and follow me!" he shouted, leading his troops from the castle as fast as they were able.

To his amazement, the rubble that had collapsed atop the crazy bitch woman actually seemed to be shifting.

"Faster!" he shouted.

His men, tired as they were, had no trouble increasing their pace as they fled into the night. Whatever horses were saddled nearby were immediately mounted, darting off down the darkened road.

"She'll take time to recover," Bawb said as he cast layer upon layer of containment spells atop the pile of debris.

"But she'll get out. And weak as she is, we're still not ready for this," Charlie replied.

Bawb nodded and took Hunze by the hand.

The trio then fled the castle, unsure if they would ever return.

CHAPTER FIFTY-EIGHT

In the wake of the battle, people had fled the castle grounds as fast as their legs would take them, and not just King Charlie's troops and staff. Word of what had happened spread like wildfire, and the king's mistress's brutal murder of their king—and the horrific, dark magic manner in which she did it—chilled them to the core.

The resulting exodus left only the most loyal of troops in the castle walls, along with those who felt their odds of survival were simply better on the side of the crazed witch than the former king. The others had scattered to the wind.

Charlie and his friends took the road toward their hideout, shifting to the woods a few miles away. It didn't really matter, he supposed. Now that Malalia had given up all pretext of normalcy, she'd likely unleash all of her power in her efforts to find them. It was only a matter of time. But they wouldn't make it easy for her.

Captain Sheeran came to them shortly after they had arrived back in their hideout, where they had discovered Rika had been deposited and restrained prior to their arrival, as requested. Leila had let the men in when they brought Charlie's old friend, and it was she who pensively sat guard over the sleeping woman from her king's home.

Rika was conscious now, and her eyes shot daggers at all around her, but she was still tightly bound, as well as gagged, for good measure. The men had been cautious, and rightly so. After a few years with Malalia pumping hate and foul magic into her, there was no telling how much damage the crazed witch had done, though Baloo would likely have put a stop to anything before she caused much harm.

"Is what she said true, Sire? About the other galaxy?" Sheeran asked, though he already knew the answer. He was not a stupid man, and the facts were plain, once Malalia had laid out the circumstances.

Charlie sighed and offered the captain a large cup of wine, and on this occasion, the soldier accepted.

"Yes, Captain. We arrived here from another world," he finally said.

The captain nodded slowly. "I figured as much. The dragon, and your unusual friends. You're all from a distant place and not of this planet."

"Well, to be fair, I actually *am* from Earth, just not from this time."

"Oh? Well, that's good to hear," Sheeran said, only half joking.

"Why's that? I mean, the whole thing is kind of a mess."

"Aye, that it is, but I at least feel a little better serving a king who is human. No offense to your friends."

Bawb chuckled. "No offense is taken, Captain."

"You know, that was quite a display you put on back there. You're quite an actor, Bawb. I never would have guessed you had that in you."

"Thank you, Captain. It took many years of practice to attain that particular skill."

"Appear weak when you are strong, eh?" Sheeran said with a

grin. "It seems a lesson you took to heart far more than most. But, Sire," he said, turning back to Charlie. "What would you have of your men? They are scattered throughout the woods, scared, but awaiting your command."

"There will be a reckoning. Tomorrow. Now that her presence is known, Malalia will not dally with subterfuge. She will come for us."

"But she doesn't know where you are, Sire."

"Given the magic she unleashed, I think the pregnancy was the only thing keeping her from finding us and laying waste to the entire area. Now that she's had the child, her strength will return."

Sheeran stared at the floor a moment, mulling over their options. "I will have the men prepare for battle, then. Tomorrow, we will either be victorious, or die valiantly in battle."

"Thank you, Captain. You're a good man, and I hope to see you alive and well at the end of this."

"It's in fate's hands now, Sire," he said, then stepped out of the hovel.

"He's a good soldier," Bawb said. "We are fortunate to have him as an ally."

"I know," Charlie agreed. "But against Malalia? With her power?"

"Where is Ara?" Hunze asked. "She is mighty. I'm sure she could stop her."

"I don't know, Hunze. I've tried searching for her every day since she vanished, but only the tiniest of whispers of her reach the edges of my mind. She's alive, *somewhere*, but I don't know where."

"I can clear that up," Leila said, crossing the small room and sitting with her king. "They had me wearing a hood, but the men in the dungeon were still somewhat loose with their lips. I heard one mention a trap. A magical device to lure her into a cave far away, where they had entombed her."

Charlie's stomach sank. "Far away to them might not be far by her standards. But buried alive?"

"That's what it sounded like," Leila replied. "But her kind can survive underground for years, right? She said they had been known to hibernate for long stretches."

"Even so, if she is truly trapped without the ability to escape, all she can do is wait. And we must face Malalia on our own."

"About that," Bawb said, a concerned look on his face. "Her power. It...it is impossible, Charlie. I mean, I've *felt* her power before, but this was so much more."

"Yeah, you missed that bit."

"What bit?"

"Her bad guy exposition speech. It sounded like she'd been practicing it for months while she waited for everything to line up for her. The thing is, she is *not* the same woman we left behind months ago. In fact, she spent a few *years* filling her father's shoes and biding her time."

"Years? And biding for what?"

"For when she would steal their remaining Ootaki hair and use it to chase us across space––and much to her surprise––*time*. You said it yourself, while Hunze was the only survivor on their doomsday ship, several of the seats were vacant. Malalia tracked down those Ootaki and used them to reach us."

"But the pregnancy?"

"Yeah, like I said, she didn't expect the whole time travel part. The spell she was attempting to create was iffy at best to begin with, and with that element thrown in, well, she wound up crashing here, but over a year too soon. She spent years preparing, then arrived another year too early. Time is a fickle bitch, I guess."

"Ah. That would explain the infant. She was stuck here. Stuck and unsure if we'd ever arrive anywhere near her own arrival."

"Pretty much. So she sank her hooks in a local king and

made herself a cozy home. Then we came a year later and got her back on her murderous track again."

"But that still doesn't explain her power, Charlie. It was immense. I've never sensed anything quite like it."

"Maybe a little like it," Charlie said. "Look, man, I know you're not going to like hearing this, but Malalia captured one of your people. A Wampeh Ghalian."

Bawb nodded grimly. "It is a peril of our work. Capture and death is a price we all risk paying."

"But she didn't kill him. Not outright. That's the thing. She drained his blood and added it to her own, slowly, over years. From there, it seems she's been feeding on others, taking their magic. Their power. That's why there were men drained in the forest. She took their essence to feed on. Must be the pregnancy making her even more power hungry than normal."

"Charlie, that shouldn't work. But even if it did, do you realize what that means? She is not a Wampeh Ghalian. If she has forced her body into a vessel for others' power, she will never be able to stop. If she does, she will die."

"So she's stuck chasing the dragon," Charlie mused.

"We know she is. And she caught her."

"Sorry, I meant figuratively. It's an old Earth figure of speech."

"This *is* old Earth."

"Yeah, but it's not *that* old. Anyway, we've got our weapons now, but I really don't know if even that will be enough to stop her."

"Agreed," Bawb said, his eyes darting to Hunze. He was worried about her more than himself, Charlie realized. The assassin had grown a heart, it seemed.

"Well, there is one thing I could try, but it might be ugly," Charlie said.

"Uglier than death?"

"Point taken," King Charlie said with a grim chuckle. "Ara

had been working on a new spell. One that might return us forward to the proper time. I think that's what she's been sending me since she's gone missing."

"But how does that help us?"

"Malalia wants to take us back to *her* galaxy. But she doesn't have the power to make a time jump. At least, I don't think she does. She said she used it all up getting here, not even knowing what she was doing. And this is a non-magical planet. She can't recharge. But if we used our magic to counter hers, what if, instead, we piggybacked on her spell. I think I finally know how Ara's spell works."

Bawb's eyes widened with understanding. "You're suggesting we use her to get back to my galaxy."

"Precisely. We get you all home and leave her stranded here, with no way to feed her addiction. You said it yourself, humans contain so little power, even an army of them would be a drop in the bucket for her needs."

"But you would be stranded back there with us. Far from your home once more."

Charlie looked at Leila. His queen. "Worth it."

"And what of the Wise One?" Bawb asked. It was a question all were thinking, but none had voiced.

"In this time. This place? We simply have no means of finding her. But I think she's been reaching out to me. Telling me something else."

"This is good news!"

"What I think she's been saying is to go without her."

The tiny rays of hope faded from their faces.

A low table fell over, breaking the moment.

Rika.

Her struggles against her bonds had interrupted and caught all of their attention. Charlie picked up the cup of water he'd had at his side for some time and walked over to her, squatting to look her in the eyes.

"Behave, okay? I know you have to be thirsty," he said, gently pulling the gag from her mouth. "Here, drink."

He held the cup to her lips, and Rika eagerly gulped it down until the cup was empty. Charlie watched her a moment. He couldn't be certain, but it seemed the anger in her eyes had diminished somewhat. Her mind might have been damaged, but she was his friend, and he owed it to her to see what, if anything, he could do.

Bawb noted the water had held a slight iridescence, but said nothing. Their supply was limited, but friendship was a noble cause.

Leila walked to the far end of the room and took a seat. Charlie sensed something was bothering her. After the time they'd spent together, he'd become attuned to her body language.

"Hey," he said, walking over to her.

"That's your friend. The one you came to my galaxy with."

"Yeah. An old friend from Earth. *My* Earth. The Tslavars took her from me years ago. I thought she was dead."

"But now she is returned to you."

"In a way. I don't think a happy reunion was Malalia's plan, though," he said with a little grin. Leila's mood was unimproved.

"And you two?" she finally said.

Oh, he realized.

"Us? No, we never—"

"It's okay, Charlie. I understand if you—"

"Leila, I love *you*, and nothing will change that."

He placed his forehead against hers, then pulled her into his arms and held her close. For just a moment, all was good in the world. Then Baloo joined the party, licking them both, and all was good, but also a bit slobbery.

Bawb and Hunze watched the couple, then locked eyes a long moment. Finally breaking their gaze, the Wampeh spoke.

"Charlie, if we do not stop Malalia tomorrow, many will perish beside us. We have to use everything we can to stop her."

"I know, Bob. And every last bit of it is all laid out here on the table. I just don't know if it'll be enough. I hope so, but I don't know.

A faint smile teased Bawb's lips. "There is *one* option we haven't yet considered."

CHAPTER FIFTY-NINE

Morning arrived with the musky stink of fear hanging in the early mist. It was as if the land itself knew what was coming and wanted no part of it. An animal reaction born of the most primal place.

But Malalia did not come.

It was not until early afternoon that the queen bitch of the realm rode out from the castle with every last one of her soldiers. The vast majority were at her side not out of loyalty or a sense of duty, but out of sheer terror. When she had forced her way out of the rubble atop her the night before, twenty men had perished horribly in her rage before she regained control of her emotions.

The ultimatum was simple. Fight for me or die. And it would not be a good death. So, they suited up in their finest armor, sharpened their swords, and marched to war. The four guards closest to her were now sporting thin golden bands around their necks. Originally taken by King Horgund when she had come to be his mistress, Malalia had reclaimed the magical collars as her rightful property, salvaged from the dead on her crashed ship.

No one else could use them, nor could they have melted

them down with their primitive technology. But *she* could put them to their original use, and as a result, the men guarding her would do her bidding without hesitation.

And so it was she rode to the farm where Charlie and his friends hid, her army at her heels, ready to engage his. Of course, the fighting of piddling little humans was of no real consequence. Men would die this day, but their deaths would just be for show. The real battle would play out between her and the two power-wielding men.

And Charlie, it seemed, now possessed some magic of his own. The residual feel of it on her body after his counterattack *smelled* like Zomoki. He was bonded with the mighty beast, but in her former, *lesser* state, she had simply been unable to sense it.

"Two miles!" the scout reported as he raced back to the farm.

Captain Sheeran sat on a bale of hay, enjoying what might be his last day's sun. After a surprisingly refreshing cup of cool water offered by his king personally, he had to admit, he felt good. Better than good, actually. Sheeran felt *great*. 'To your health, and a long life' they had toasted, and that was exactly as the king intended.

Charlie and Bawb sat with him, armed and comfortable in warm overcloaks. Hunze was waiting just behind them with Leila and Baloo. There was no sense in staying far away. A battle of this order would make such precautions moot anyway.

At their feet, the packs of magical weaponry lay waiting, ready to be handed off to Charlie and Bawb as needed. They would drain one dry and toss it into one bag, reloading, in essence, from the other. They also had the bottles of the healing Balamar waters, though Charlie wasn't sure how exactly they might use them. They healed, but against Malalia's onslaught, they might not be able to do so fast enough.

Leila had suggested they might try to devise a delivery method to launch at Malalia.

"Water balloons?" Bawb chuckled. "I have to admit, it is a clever thought. If she truly has absorbed Wampeh blood, perhaps she will react to it as my kind do."

"Yeah, it's a creative idea, Bob, I agree. But there's one little problem there. What if she doesn't?"

"Then she won't combust," Leila said.

"And we will have just healed her and made her even stronger," Charlie added.

The queen blushed slightly. "Oh, yeah. So, I guess back to plan A."

The four of them shared a laugh in the face of death, their bond as close as ever.

And then there was Rika joining the party. The violent woman was still bound and gagged, but surprisingly seemed far less feral than the night before. She sat on the ground, Baloo's massive form standing guard over her. After he gave her another drink of water that morning, Charlie insisted she be kept close at all times, and the others agreed.

It was odd, knowing they might all die this day, but strangely, they all were in good spirits. They had arrived on this world as mere friends, but whatever happened today, they would now face it together as family.

"There are men hidden on either flank, deep in the woods. It'll take them a good five minutes to reach us once the signal is given, but having them that far out is the only way to keep them from her scouts' eyes," Captain Sheeran said as the dust and rumbling of Malalia and her army grew closer in the distance.

"And the pits?"

"All dug and covered, Sire. Their cavalry will be slowed, and quickly, if they attempt a frontal charge."

"A damn waste of horses if they do," Charlie said, reluctant to harm the innocent animals.

"War is waste, Sire. Rarely does much good come of it, so we do what we can to minimize the losses. Horses are valued animals, yes, but given the choice between a horse and a man, I'll take the man."

"Unless it's one of Malalia's troops, of course."

"Well, naturally," he added with a laugh. "Though I doubt many are fighting of their own free will. Why, nearly a quarter of the men present at the battle last night fled with us, and those not still running stayed and joined our ranks."

"No traitors, among them?"

"I like to think I'm a good judge of character, Sire. After what they saw that woman do to their king last night, I do not believe a drop of loyalty to that tainted crown remains in them."

"Good."

"Aye, we need the men." Sheeran gazed at the forces hiding in the shadows of the woods. "And if they *do* turn on us, I've ordered all of our men to smite them with extreme prejudice."

Charlie couldn't help but laugh at the exclamation. "Oh, my. Thank you, Captain. I needed that."

"My pleasure to serve, Sire," he said with a wry grin.

The Dragon King scanned what would soon be a battlefield with his keen eyes. The troops were spaced out, a good portion of them hidden both behind the farm buildings, as well as in the fields. Others were obscured by the treeline, their exact numbers harder to gauge by their positioning.

Charlie wanted to give them the best chance he could, making it difficult for Malalia to target them. Or at least make it as difficult as was in his ability. This was Visla Yoral Maktan's daughter he was dealing with, after all, and who knew what she might try.

CHAPTER SIXTY

The column of armored men arrived at a leisurely pace, led by their queen, her collared guards surrounding her. Bawb's sharp eyes caught the glint of the golden metal from his galaxy, even from a distance.

"Control bands around some of their necks. The ones directly beside her at the least, though I can't tell if there are more."

"It doesn't matter. They'll all fight regardless. They know she'll just kill them herself if they don't," Charlie said, grimly.

"It will bring us no honor killing these men," Sheeran said. "But we do what we must to ensure victory. Even if that means harming those we would otherwise shelter. Once they take up arms against us, that is all that matters on the battleground."

Malalia sat there across the field that would soon be stained red with blood, casually watching them from atop her horse. She dismounted and strode to a hay bale to step upon for a better view. The horse would surely buck and flee when she started casting her spells, and that just would not do.

"I can feel it from here," Charlie said. "Can you feel that, Bob?"

317

The Wampeh's jaw flexed slightly. "Oh yes, my friend. She has recovered from her childbirth. And she is *strong*."

Malalia casually surveyed the area. Oh yes, she saw the men hiding in the trees, but they were of no real concern to her. What she wanted lay straight ahead. She raised her arm, and her troops drew their weapons.

Here we go.

"Ready!" Captain Sheeran bellowed.

Her arm fell, and with it, her men took off at a run, charging into battle. Charlie's forces waited, letting their adversary come to them.

"Now!" Sheeran said, the youth at his side blowing a shrill horn blast.

Spears and arrows rained down from the woods, striking the foremost soldiers and stopping them dead in their tracks. A return volley against the protected archers would be a waste of arrows, so Malalia's men raced toward their opponents. Once the combatants were engaged, archers could not target them without risking hitting their own men.

The battle swung into full gear, and the men of King Charlie's guard put on an impressive display of close-quarter tactics with the short sword, using the techniques the king had shown them, while throwing in a few new variations Captain Sheeran had taught them as well.

The men teamed into trios, operating as a single unit to overwhelm and separate the enemy from their comrades. Then, once there was only one broadsword to deal with, two would swing high, engaging the heavily armored man with overhead attacks, forcing him to defend his head.

At the same time, one of their number would scramble low—made possible by his modified armor's superior range of motion—and disable one, or both, of the man's legs. As he stumbled and fell, the other two struck at the joints, driving their daggers into the narrow spaces.

The blows themselves were not fatal. At least, not immediately. But they did serve to quickly disable and remove a soldier from the battle.

"Interesting tactic," Charlie said, watching from behind the lines. "Your creation?"

"Aye," Captain Sheeran replied.

"Well done, Captain. Way to think outside the box."

"Sire?" he said, confused. "What box?"

"It's just a––Nevermind. Just, nice job, is all."

"Thank you, Sire."

The battle raged, and men were falling from both sides. Charlie was sickened by the carnage, but he knew it had to be done. The stage had to be set. Finally, he had seen enough.

"Malalia!" he bellowed, using an amplification spell to boom his voice across the battleground. "Enough of this pointless bloodshed. Why waste these men's lives? It is us you want, not them."

The spell hadn't cost him an iota of power. The konuses lining his arms were his most powerful, and had cast it with no noticeable energy loss.

Malalia thought a moment. He could see her musing over something in her wicked mind, even from across the field. Then she waved her hand, casting a *yap zina* spell, knocking the legs out from all of the men before her, following it with another spell, flinging their bodies aside to the edges of the battlefield, wiping the area clean of the combatants from both sides.

"Holy shit. She is seriously strong."

"I told you," Bawb said.

"Yeah, but *damn*," Charlie replied.

Malalia stepped down from her hay bale and began walking straight toward him, relaxed and carefree.

"Are you challenging me, Charlie? Really? And here I thought you had gained a bit of common sense since I last saw you."

319

Charlie flashed a knowing glance at his Wampeh friend.

"You'll have to refresh my memory, Malalia. Did you mean that time when we kicked your ass, destroyed your fleet, and Bob here stuck a knife in your father's side? *That* time?"

He had hoped for a reaction, and boy did he get one.

Malalia flew into a rage, launching spell after spell in her fury. But Charlie and his friends remained unharmed, the attacks shattering and dissipating before they ever got close. Some spells even rebounded, ricocheting back into her own forces, taking out one of her personal guards in a most horrible way.

Charlie and Bawb smiled. It had been an exhausting night's work, but it was worth it, and now Malalia Maktan was falling for the same trick that had, in part, led to her father's defeat.

Taking turns in shifts, Charlie and his Wampeh friend had cast spell upon spell in the air, creating a densely layered protective field in front of, and above them. All they had to do was steer Malalia into the right place to ensure her attack would be directed at them.

"A hay bale?"

"Yes, Bob. A hay bale," Charlie had replied.

"Would you care to fill me in on this bit of strategic genius, my king?" he said, sarcasm in his voice.

"She's a megalomaniac. And a narcissist. Malalia will want to not only see the battlefield, but she'll want to be sure everyone sees her. She'll want to stand out. And what better way to stand out than to step up?"

Bawb had to admit, it was actually a very clever manipulation of their adversary's psychological shortcomings. "I'll bring one over," he said.

"Right here. This is the spot she should stand," Charlie replied, marking the spot.

And their plan had worked perfectly. While they were vulnerable from the sides, so long as she came at them head-on, they stood a chance. If she shifted her attack just a bit to either side, she'd smash right through it. But even with her attacking as planned, her power was going to be too much. Eventually, the spells would all fail, leaving the men to face her alone.

They were armed to the teeth, but it appeared to be a losing proposition in the face of her immense power.

Charlie turned to Captain Sheeran.

"You need to take all of the men and get them back. Get them to safety."

"But, Sire!"

"No buts, Sheeran. This is a magical battle. One your men can't hope to survive, and I won't have any more innocents fall in my name. This is my fight, and I'll handle it," he said, clasping the captain by the shoulder and locking his gaze. "Sheeran, if I should fall and she lives, you must take the men and flee. But if I fall, yet we prevail, then make sure the people are led well. By a good, and honorable man."

"By whom, Sire? You are king."

"And if I'm gone, you'll make an excellent one, my friend."

The few troops within earshot murmured their approval of the choice. Captain Sheeran held his gaze silently a moment longer, sharing a look of respect. Then he nodded and turned to the men.

"You heard the king. Fall back." He grasped his king's hand in a firm grip. "Good luck, Sire."

"Thank you. Now, get moving."

With that, Captain Sheeran and his men drew clear of what was surely to be the most spectacular magic battle his world had ever seen.

CHAPTER SIXTY-ONE

After her futile attack, Malalia had called her opponents out, seeking parlay to discuss the situation face-to-face.

Walking to meet their destiny, Charlie felt like one of those old-timey gunslingers from the films his granddad had shown him when he was a boy. Only, instead of guns, they had magical weapons and a wand. Actually, Charlie still had his guns, taken through time with him when they first arrived, but the ammunition had long since run out. A casualty of those first tumultuous weeks as ruler of a new land.

Should have taken more ammo, he had chided himself. But in the heat of battle, and in the midst of a panicked retreat, they were happy to have brought any supplies at all. In fact, escaping with their lives was good enough for one and all.

And now those lives might very well end. But not if Charlie could help it. And they did have their packs, loaded with magical weaponry, as well as the last of the Balamar healing waters. Given who they were facing off against, this was going to be interesting, to say the least.

"You ready for this?" he asked the assassin at his side as they walked past their defenses to confront the evil queen from another galaxy.

"As ready as one can be, given the circumstances," Bawb replied. "And if we fail, oh, what a glorious way to go out, you must admit."

Charlie chuckled, barely keeping his poker face affixed. "Ladies, make sure you stay close."

"Right behind you," Leila said, tugging the short lead that connected her to Rika. The formerly berserker woman was now quite docile, it seemed, but they were still taking no chances, and her hands remained firmly bound.

Hunze walked behind Bawb, a small pack over her shoulder, her hand gently touching the small of his back, letting him know she was close. Close, and safe. Protected.

Malalia had stopped her massive assault when she realized she was unable to find a weakness in their rather ingenious defense. She hated to admit it, but she had underestimated them. With limited resources, they had found a way to hold her far greater power at bay. But now, with the promise of parlay, they were walking out of their protective bubble and into her trap.

The Ootaki girl was with them, she noted, the woman's long, golden hair hanging loosely down past her ears, then pulled back and wrapped around her body. The sheer power contained within that one slave would be more than enough for her purposes when she slayed the others.

"So, Malalia. Here we are again," Charlie said, stopping a good thirty feet from the hateful woman. "Are you going to play nice this time?"

"Oh, Charlie. Ever the joker," she cooed. Coming from such a horrible person, the sweet tone was enough to make his skin turn cold. "I see you have brought my pet back to me. Hello, pet!"

"Rika's not yours anymore."

"We'll see about that," she replied. "And you even brought your Wampeh friend to do your dirty work for you once more. Perhaps I'll drain him dry this time," she taunted. "And Leila. Lovely to see you again. Feeling better since I tortured you, I take it."

"Ignore her. She's just trying to get a rise out of you," Bawb said.

"And what of you, assassin? Does it not offend your sensibilities, knowing the blood of one of your kin now flows in my veins?"

"It is an abomination, Malalia, and one brought on by your own hand. And that will be your undoing."

"Oh, please. I am stronger than ever."

"Yes, but you will never be able to stop feeding. Unlike me, you no longer have that choice."

Her smile faltered a split second, but Bawb saw it. Oh yes. It seemed she was well aware of the unintended consequence of her folly.

"It is of no matter. Soon enough I will feast upon all of you."

"So, your offer of parlay was to discuss eating us?" Charlie asked. "Not really in the whole spirit of the tradition, there."

"Idiots. You actually believed I would peacefully surrender to the likes of you?"

"Well, we were hoping––"

"It will never happen. And now you have foolishly been lured from your defenses."

"Yet we are not defenseless," Leila said, holding up her arm to display the konus she wore.

"Ah, I see you are all well-armed. How delightful. That will make this so much more satisfying."

She cast a spell skyward, a canopy of crackling power blocking the sunlight from above. It was all for show, of course. She wanted to play with her meal before eating them.

"It's funny, really. I am so far beyond your ability to engage, it is almost tragic. The overpowered versus the weaklings. And soon, I will cast the spell I've been working on since I arrived here. I shall break free of this pathetic little rock and drag you all back to my world, where you'll live the rest of your miserable existences in agony as I––"

"Sorry to interrupt, but are you going to be finished with that whole evil villain thing soon? You already monologued yesterday, and to be honest, it's getting kind of old," Charlie said, then flashed her his brightest smile.

"You've seen my power, yet still you mock me. Brave. Or foolish."

"Oh, come on, Malalia. We all know you don't have the power to make that spell work. You said so yourself, you drained all of your resources chasing us here. If you could have cast it, you would have done so already."

A cruel smile spread across Malalia's face. "Oh, but who said I would need my power alone? Once I take your Ootaki's hair, I will have more than enough for my spell. And then, you weaklings will be entirely at my mercy."

"Is that right?" Bawb said, dropping his long overcloak.

It took a moment for Malalia to register what she was looking at. A long, tightly woven golden braid wrapped around his body, in addition to the weapons on both arms and strapped to his waist.

"But where did you––?"

Hunze stepped from behind him, her hands lifting her hair high, revealing a close-shorn scalp all the way around, only the hair on top untouched. She was now sporting an Ootaki undercut. It had been hidden by her new hairstyle, and Malalia had failed to notice. That meant all that hair. That massively powerful *first-cut* hair was now the Wampeh's.

"I'm going to enjoy taking that from your cold, dead body," Malalia hissed, casting a killing spell at the assassin.

Bawb easily batted it aside.

"You'll drain that hair before I'm done," she said.

"I think not," he replied, a scary confidence in his voice. "And you won't be taking this from me."

"Oh? Is that so?"

Hunze smiled at Bawb, then looked at the evil queen. "Yes, it is so."

Suddenly, the reality set in. *It was freely given*, Malalia realized. The hair was now so much more powerful than she had ever imagined. If only she could get her hands—"

"*And* it was given *out of love*," the golden-haired girl added, gently kissing Bawb on the cheek.

The implications were ground-shaking, and Malalia actually felt fear for the first time in ages. Ootaki were slaves. Their first cut was by far the most powerful, and they could, on rare occasion, be coerced to freely give their locks, which also increased their potency. But slaves didn't do so out of love. It was unheard of. But if legend was correct, and she had truly done so, the power was off the charts. And more importantly, the locks were bound to the loved one they were given to for life. It was the Ootaki equivalent of giving your heart.

The jolt of fear flooding her body sent Malalia into survival mode, casting her transit spell despite being underpowered, and suddenly *very* outmatched.

"Now!" Charlie yelled, both he and Bawb reacting on instinct, countering her spell and piggybacking it, channeling the power the Wampeh now possessed with the transit spell Ara had been teaching Charlie.

The magic mixed, the conflicting spells and power sources clashing in a sparking ball of energy.

"I can feel it!" Bawb called out. "We're connecting to my galaxy!"

Charlie felt something as well. The folds of time were lining up, just as Ara had hoped they would. In a moment, he'd be dialed in, taking them back to the time they left. But Malalia had one last trick up her sleeve. Literally.

It was an Ootaki hair grenade. The last she possessed, made strong by the system's sun and saved for a last resort. That moment had apparently arrived, and she threw the magical device, detonating it into the mix of spells, throwing them into chaos.

The recoil snapped out violently.

Malalia screamed, then was abruptly cut off as she was physically ripped from the battlefield and flung through an unstable wormhole to parts unknown. Whether it led back to her galaxy, or somewhere else far away, they had no way of knowing. Even if they did, that quickly became the least of their concerns.

Leila felt something hot flare against her skin. A green glow was bursting from her chest.

"My Magus stone. But what is it––?"

She was cut off as they were caught up in a mix of tumultuous power as the unstable cascade of spells accelerated its decay, swirling together with her new addition to the mix. Then the entire ball of energy flipped and folded on itself, snatching up the group in a flash.

When the smoke and dust settled, they were nowhere to be found.

CHAPTER SIXTY-TWO

"This is still Earth," Bawb said, sniffing the air. "I recognize this smell." He wrapped his arms around Hunze protectively as he scanned for danger.

Charlie also looked at the land around them. Indeed, it certainly looked like Earth, though the smell of farming and cook-fires was nowhere in the breeze. It was funny, but he'd become so accustomed to it since becoming king, its absence now stood out more than its presence.

"Didn't it work?" Leila asked.

"I-I'm not sure."

"What did you do, Charlie? The farmhouse, the fields? They're all gone."

She was right, he realized. This wooded area had just been a farm only a minute ago, but now there was no trace of it. Nor was there sign of the carnage that took place, or the fate that had befallen all of those men.

Baloo didn't seem concerned. His attention was caught by something in the treeline, sending him off in a streak.

"Baloo!" Leila called out.

"Don't worry. He'll be back," Charlie said, somehow knowing what he was after.

"Yes, a rabbit," Leila replied.

"I didn't say anything about a rabbit."

"But you––" she paused, cocking her head. "Huh."

Charlie pulled her close. "What am I thinking now?"

She planted a warm kiss on his lips.

"Mind reader," he said, smiling.

Baloo returned to them a minute later, small flecks of blood on his muzzle.

"Well, at least we don't have to worry about *one* belly going hungry," Charlie joked. "Come on. I need to see something."

The five of them followed Charlie through the tall grass and into the woods, Rika at the rear, though as calm as she had become, the bindings hardly seemed necessary. The road was gone without a trace. Likewise, all of the trails they had come to know so well. In fact, all of the man-made landmarks were no more. It wasn't until they crested a hill a while later that Charlie's theory was proven.

"Is that––?" Hunze gasped.

"Yeah. That's our castle," he replied, staring at the ruins. "Come on," he said, the others following as the shock wore off.

"But what happened to it?" the Ootaki asked as they drew near. "The tower is toppled. And look! There are trees growing out of its walls!"

"Yeah, I know. It looks like it's been abandoned for quite some time, wouldn't you say?"

"Do you mean...?"

"Seems that way," Charlie said as they approached the familiar stone of the castle's base. "We didn't make it back to your galaxy, but it seems we did succeed it sling-shotting forward in time."

"I must admit, this has become an interesting situation," Bawb said. "If we can recreate Malalia's spell, perhaps we can now jump back to our own galaxy, now that the difficult part has been accomplished."

"Well, all of it is difficult, to be fair," Charlie noted. "It's just the time part was far harder and required a *ton* more power. If not for the strain caused by our arrival still existing in the air, we probably wouldn't have been able to use the rubber band effect to throw us forward through time."

"So you're saying we couldn't do it again if we wanted."

"That pretty much sums it up. But as for Malalia's spell, well, without Ara's expertise, it might take us a *long* time to make that one work. And we jumped without our space suits. They were stashed away in the—"

"What is it?" Leila asked, her eyes scanning for danger.

"I wonder," was all he said as he took off through a crumbled gap in the castle wall.

"Charlie, where are you going?" she called after him. "We'd better follow. No telling what might be in there."

"Agreed," Bawb said, drawing his sword, slaaps and konuses at the ready.

The former king of the realm made quick time through the familiar ruins of the castle. Walls had crashed to the ground, and not everything was aligned as it had once been, remodels and additions having been made over the thousands of years since they had inhabited it. But the basic layout was the same.

Charlie moved from the dark of the debris-choked corridor out into the courtyard, now lush and overgrown. He didn't stop to take in the sights, though, heading straight across it toward the west wing instead. Where he'd lain his head to sleep a couple of millennia ago.

Come on. Be there.

The western wing of the castle had seen a bit more abuse than the rest, likely when the castle had been sacked at one point or another. It made sense, the royal chambers would be a choice target for conquering forces. But it wasn't the chambers he was heading for.

"Help me move this," he said when Bawb and the others caught up.

"Use your konus, Charlie."

"Not here. I don't want to risk it setting anything off."

Bawb looked around the chaotic debris and realized where they were standing.

"You don't think it's still there, do you?"

"Why not? We hid it very, *very* well, after all."

The Wampeh did not hesitate, quickly putting his muscle into the effort, helping Charlie shift the tumbled stone aside, leaving a small gap leading into the long-abandoned section of the castle.

"Come on, baby. Please still be there," Charlie said as he slid through the opening.

A small crash rang out from inside.

"Charlie, are you okay?" Leila called after him.

"Yeah, I'm fine. Just tripped over some junk. It's a mess in here."

"What are you looking for?"

"Hang on a minute," he replied.

She could hear more junk being shifted around as he made his way toward whatever his objective was.

"Bingo!" his voice rang out through the hole.

A lot of rustling ensued, followed by a pair of bags being pushed out of the opening.

"I recognize these," Leila said. "But they should be rotted away by now."

"Nope," Charlie said, poking his head through the gap and climbing back out. "When Bob and I tucked this stuff away, we not only layered shimmers on the hiding place, but also put several wards and protections on the gear itself, just in case some unforeseen disaster befell us."

"Like a psychotic, magical queen bitch from another galaxy?"

"Well, we were thinking more along the lines of a fire, or flood. But yeah, that too," he replied. "Come on, let's get back outside. It's dark, it's damp, and it's kinda depressing in here."

They clambered out of the debris, back into the sunlight flooding the courtyard through the few trees that had managed to take root there.

"Moment of truth," Charlie said as he set down the packs and opened them. "Oh, yes. Come to Papa," he said, beaming as he pulled out several heavy slaaps and a konus.

Bawb tested one out. "Fully charged after all this time. Most excellent."

"And there are more in the bag," Charlie noted. "But let's see just how lucky we are."

He unfastened the flap of the other bag and gently pulled out a small bottle and pair of large jugs.

"You saved wine?" Hunze asked, confused.

"No, Hunze. Those are the Balamar waters," Bawb clarified.

Charlie took the small bottle and opened it, taking a little sip. A surge of well-being and healthy energy flushed his body. "Yep. Still potent. Hey, Bob. Are Ootaki sensitive to this stuff?"

"They should not be harmed by it," he replied. "Why?"

"She got a little banged up in the commotion. I know you can't touch this stuff, but do you mind if I—?"

"Please," the protective Wampeh said.

"Cool. Hunze, I'm going to pour a tiny bit onto that scrape on your neck. It should heal you up nicely, okay?"

"Of course." The golden-haired woman had been through more than enough to trust her friends by now.

Charlie poured a few drops onto the scrape. They all watched the water absorb into her skin, the injury already beginning to heal and fade.

"That was quick. I guess her kind are really sensitive to it," he said, moving to recap the bottle.

A few drops of water landed on her hair, and the entirety of her locks suddenly seemed to almost glow in the nourishing rays of the sun's light.

"Whoa. Wasn't expecting that," Charlie said. "You feel okay?"

"Yes. I feel fine. Why?"

"Your hair. It kinda went a little crazy on us there. Got super bright."

"A particularly powerful energy can do that sometimes. I've seen it when the vislas would channel their magic into the other slaves."

"Huh. Cool." He turned to Rika, who was standing beside Leila, still bound tight.

She had resumed struggling against the restraints since they reached the castle. Something about seeing the place had set her off. There was still some fight in her eyes, but the bruise on her head from just the other day was gone. Healed. Charlie took one of the large jugs and walked over to her.

"Her *mind* was damaged, Charlie. There's no fixing that."

"Yeah, but she's human. And we can do something the rest of you can't."

He pulled the gag from her mouth, then uncorked the jug and held it to her lips.

"Go on, I know you're thirsty."

She looked at him with an angry stare, then greedily gulped down the water, the furrows on her brow relaxing with every mouthful. When she was sated, Charlie finally recorked the jug and placed it with the rest of their gear, watching his damaged friend as the waters did their work.

"Even if you can heal the flesh, the memories that were taken from her will likely not return. They heal physical ills, but *that* may be beyond even their capabilities," Bawb said softly.

"I know, Bob. But I have to try. I mean, she'll never be the same. I get that. And who knows what memories are still in there, all scrambled up from the Tslavars and Malalia's mindfuck. But she's my friend. And if anything might help her, I have to try."

"Just so long as you aren't setting yourself up for disappointment, my friend."

"Thanks, man. I know, and I appreciate the concern."

Charlie stowed the recovered gear with the rest of their supplies, first taking one more swig of the Balamar waters before tucking them away. They ignited something inside of him. Something more than just that healthy feeling. A familiar, visceral buzz tickling his senses all the way to his blood.

"You there?" he silently asked. He sensed a faint *something*, but there was no reply.

"Come on. Something tells me civilization is this way," he said, then headed out, following his senses across the land nature had reclaimed.

CHAPTER SIXTY-THREE

The trek had not been nearly as arduous as any of them had worried. In fact, the land was bursting with life, fecund and healthy, and Bawb had no trouble catching ample game. On top of that, Leila's time with the locals––albeit a few thousand years prior––had familiarized her not only with the regional crops, but also the wild vegetables and berries that sprang up across the land.

Fresh water was abundant, the region having shifted to a somewhat rainier clime since they had last set foot on the lands. The resulting waters available to them were fresh and clear. Better yet, they appeared to have had the benefit of being in a non-industrial region. The skies had no odor of industry, and there wasn't a trace of pollution in the soil.

Baloo was having a wonderful time as well, having actually worn himself out chasing deer through the woods. He had only been playing. Mostly, anyway. By the end of the day, as night started to fall, he finally took one down, filling his belly before drinking himself to satiation from a small stream.

"Now there's a happy boy," Charlie said as the enormous

canine padded into their camp and lay down beside their magical fire.

Baloo happily accepted the loving scratches of his friends, even allowing the newcomer to pet him. Charlie and Leila shared a look when he did.

Rika's initial arrival had been met with growls and bared teeth. Baloo was an excellent judge of character and intentions, and at that time, hers had been most foul. But now, a change had taken place. Whether it was distance from Malalia's influence, or the healing waters finally repairing the damage done to her, Rika had turned a corner, and Baloo, it seemed, knew it.

The scratches and petting finally ceased, and rather than curling up for a nap, he first leaned over and licked her face. The gentleness of the gesture brought unexpected tears to her eyes, though she didn't quite know why. Rika sat there quietly crying as she stared at the dancing flame.

It was nice, being able to cast a fire spell after so many months having to burn smoking wood to fit in with the locals. The safe, clean flame could be left burning all night long, courtesy of Bawb's wand. And the tiny drop of power used in casting would recharge in the first moments of sunlight.

He could have just pulled power from any of their devices, but only the wand would recharge on its own. The others would require some effort to replenish, and he hadn't yet learned how to, or if he even could, use the locks Hunze had gifted him for that purpose. As for starting a fire, he dared not pull from their power. A single hair could have incinerated the entire valley, for all he knew. The power within them was beyond any he had ever experienced, a gift of the heart from the unusual Ootaki. The only woman he had ever cared about.

Bawb curled up with Hunze beside the fire, his arms wrapping around her and holding her close as they drifted to sleep. A big spoon to her smaller one, who would give his life to keep her safe.

. . .

"What the hell is that?" Charlie gasped the following afternoon as they crested a hill after a long day of hiking.

What lay before them was a welcome sight for all of their eyes. Civilization.

"It is your world, Charlie," Bawb said with an uncharacteristically warm laugh. "You tell us."

"No, Bob. You don't get it. I have no idea what we're looking at. I mean, we had skyscrapers and residential towers back home, but nothing like this. *This*? I've never seen anything like it."

The city below them was a glistening marvel to the off-worlders' eyes. Bright spires that climbed into the sky, clad in gleaming glass and metal. Thin walkways passed between them at impossible heights, somehow connecting the buildings without plummeting to the ground.

Amazingly, Bawb could tell, there was absolutely no magic.

Long roadways stretched across the land, their vast stretches winding among the buildings, occasionally passing below or within them through what seemed to be a localized network of small tunnels, likely designed to allow conveyances to enter and exit to avoid foul weather.

And then there were the public gardens. Beautiful plots of green interspersed within the gridwork of development. But not for agricultural purposes, it seemed. They appeared to have been placed purely for aesthetic reasons. The entirety of the scene was beautiful to the visitors' alien eyes.

"Astounding, Charlie. You described the technology of your world, but having not seen it with my own eyes, I did not fully appreciate the scale, the wonder of what your people were capable. This rivals even the marvels of Tolemac." He fell silent a moment, realizing what he had said. "That is, before its fall, obviously," he added, a hint of color rising to his cheeks. Hunze had indeed sparked something of a change within the deadly assassin.

"But this isn't how stuff should be. Something's wrong," Charlie said, adjusting the straps of his pack and beginning the descent to the city below. "Come on, you guys. We need to get down there. I've got to find out exactly what the hell is going on."

CHAPTER SIXTY-FOUR

Charlie felt like a fool, walking through the incredibly modern city with a sword in his hand. He had his slaaps and konuses now, of course, but had become so accustomed to carrying the bladed weapon in the past months that it had become something of a second nature to him.

The outskirts of the area had been a shock to him. It was home, obviously, but different. Futuristic, but deconstructed. As if the incredibly advanced society had collapsed in on itself. Had given up the ghost and simply ceased to be. It was incredibly perplexing.

"What is all of this, Charlie?" Leila asked.

"I don't know. Something happened here."

"It's like it was taken apart. Scrapped for parts," Rika said.

Charlie looked at her curiously. She had been improving by the hour, and now, in an Earth city, something had seemed to click back into place. She was still damaged goods, no doubt, but more than a little trace of his old friend seemed to be making a reappearance.

"Yeah, I think you're right, Rika. What else do you see?"

She scanned the area, her eyes bright and alert.

Oh yeah, that's the Rika I know. Sharp and analytical. Ready to take on the world.

"There are signs of some sort of cleanup. Fairly recently, by the look of it. Over there, see?" she said, pointing to an empty stretch of roadway.

"What? I don't see anything," Hunze said.

"No, she's right," Leila chimed in. "The road's surface has been gouged. As if something heavy had been dragged across it. See? It happened over there, too."

Charlie had been looking at the big picture, but now, zooming in on a much smaller level, he could see it clearly. They were right. *Something* had been going on. Maybe not in the past few weeks, but the marks were recent, no more than a few months old.

"Let's keep moving. The buildings toward the center seem to be intact. I think we'll probably find a lot more answers once we get there."

The others nodded their agreement, moving out as a single unit, eyes scanning all around as they left the deconstructed outskirts for the impressive structures at the heart of the city.

Bawb stared up at the marvels that presented themselves to them. Up close, the man-made structures were even more impressive, if that was possible.

"Incredible," he said. "All of this, done without the use of any magic. Astounding."

Leila was also impressed. Hunze, having lived her life in captivity, really didn't know what to think, but she had to agree, the sight was indeed a breathtaking one. Baloo, on the other hand, didn't much care for the buildings, but his nose was twitching, something in the air having caught his attention.

"Do you hear that?" Bawb asked.

Charlie and the others strained their ears. The gentle breeze was rustling the leaves of the nearby trees, but there didn't seem to be anything else. Or was there?

"Hang on. Are those voices?" Charlie asked.

"It appears to be. English, from what I can tell, though I cannot make out that odd vocalization in the mix."

"Why isn't the translation spell working?"

"It was designed for all known tongues, including yours. But this must be something new. I will have to modify it. Give me a moment. The change to the spell should kick in momentarily."

"Hang on. Something *new*? What the hell does that mean, Bob? We're on Earth. We've been here for ages. There can't be anything——"

Charlie felt his stomach drop and adrenaline spike at the sight of a seven-foot-tall, four-armed creature with grayish skin and eyes both on the front, *and* back of its head walking toward them, accompanied by a human——sporting a metal arm from the elbow down——and what appeared to be an android. An android in a fine suit.

"What in the ever-loving fuck is going on?" Charlie blurted in shock.

The newcomers stopped in their tracks, as surprised at the sight of a sword-wielding man and his band of oddly-dressed friends as they were at the sight of them. Especially the pointy-toothed vampire man and the enormous wolf-like thing that stood growling at their side.

"Is that a vampire?" the human gasped.

"In daylight? Really, Edward? Should I get a stake?" the fedora-wearing cyborg joked.

"He's *carrying* a stake, Carlos," the man replied, gesturing to Bawb's wand. "This makes no sense."

"I thought no one was in this sector," the metal man mused. "Naraaxik, you said it had been surveyed."

"It had been, Carlos. I do not know where these people came from."

"*English*, Naraaxik, please. You need to practice."

"Apologies. I forget and slip into my native Chithiid sometimes."

"Understandable," the human said. "And I don't mind. I need to practice my Chithiid, if I'm going to visit Taangaar on my next vacation."

Charlie lowered his sword, as Bawb did with his wand. Obviously, these were not a threat. Or if they were, they were the variety that would be better handled by a slaap than a shiny bit of metal.

"Who are you people?" he asked, staring at the four-armed alien.

"We might ask you the same," the human said. "No one's supposed to be out here. The survivors were relocated years ago. Did you come from the London colony?"

"London? So, we're in the UK?"

The man glanced at his friends, the three sharing a confused look. "Uh, yeah. This is the UK. How exactly do you not know where you are? And where's your ship? Did you take one of the loop tubes here? I didn't think this branch was operational yet."

"What's a loop tube? And what on Earth is that thing?"

"Thing? I am a Chithiid, thank you very much," Naraaxik replied.

"Sorry, no disrespect intended. It's just, I've never seen your species before."

"And I've never seen any of those three," Naraaxik replied, gesturing to Bawb, Leila, and Hunze. "But we Chithiid have been here on Earth for hundreds of years. And ever since the war with the Ra'az ended, we've been——"

"Hang on. What war? And what's a Ra'az?"

"Charlie, what's going on?" Leila asked. "And what is that *thing*?" she said, pointing to the android.

"You see a seven-foot-tall, four-armed alien walking down the street, and the one thing that gets your attention is the android. Of course," he said with a chuckle.

"Well, *technically,* I'm a cyborg," Carlos replied. "I just chose not to replace my flesh covering. After so many years 'au naturel,' I grew rather accustomed to living without it."

"But we're decades from having a functional AI."

"You're obviously mistaken," the tin man countered with a chuckle.

"Charlie?" Bawb said, his eyebrow arched high with both amusement and questions.

"I know, Bob. I'm working on it."

The human of the group stepped forward toward Charlie and his friends, holding out his hand. "I think we're all getting off on a somewhat confused footing. Let me start by saying my name is Edward. This big fella is Naraaxik, and the shiny bloke is Carlos. We're in charge of the rebuild survey of this area."

Naraaxik nodded his head in greeting. "Your Chithiid is excellent, I might add."

"He was speaking English," Edward said.

"No, he wasn't. It was Chithiid, I heard it."

"Actually, it's a little more complicated than that," Charlie said. "I'm Charlie, by the way," the Dragon King said, shaking the offered hand, but omitting his title. He felt that might seem a little snobbish, given the circumstances. "That's Bob, and Hunze over there. And she's Leila. They're all from other planets. Rika, back there, she's human, like me."

Baloo let out a little *whumpf.*

"Yes, I know. I haven't forgotten you. And that's Baloo," he added.

"Three new alien species? And *here*, of all places? It makes no sense," Carlos said. "How in the world did they get here? And why on Earth are you wearing those, uh, *colorful* outfits?"

Charlie couldn't help but laugh. "Yeah, about that. It's a long, loooong story. But the abridged version is we just got here."

"Oh, well, in that case––"

"From about two thousand years in the past," he added.

The Chithiid and others looked at one another, but, surprisingly, not freaking out.

"You need to speak with Cal and the others," Naraaxik said.

"Yeah, we need to call the boss," Carlos agreed.

"Hang on. Cal? Who's Cal?"

"He's one of the leaders. Part of the AI conglomerate helping guide the reconstruction of post-Ra'az Earth."

"AI? Reconstruction? What happened here?"

"One moment, please," Carlos said, cocking his head to the side as he connected to his internal comms device. "Okay, they've been informed and have passed the message along. We have to finish our survey of the area, but you'll get a lift out of here in fifteen minutes."

Charlie shook his head in confusion. "None of this makes any sense. What's going on?"

"Don't worry," Edward said. "It will all be made clear when you talk with Cal and the others. Rip is on her way to pick you up, now."

Out of the frying pan again, Charlie thought. *I just hope the fire isn't too bad.*

CHAPTER SIXTY-FIVE

Their ride came, not in the form of a car, truck or even flight-car, but rather, a sleek ship that looked more like something out of a futuristic movie than the planet Charlie had left behind. That it had hover and vertical landing capabilities was impressive in and of itself, but when it did so with no visible thrust signature was when Charlie began to think things were *far* more complicated than he'd originally thought.

Then a teenage girl came bounding down the ramp.

And that's what she was. At least to Charlie's eyes, though at what he guessed was seventeen or eighteen, she was really far closer to a woman than a child. But after all he'd been through, she just seemed, well, *young* to be a high-ranking liaison for the AI that appeared to be running the planet in the few years since his departure.

"Hey, I'm Rip," she chirped, rushing up and shaking Charlie's hand.

"Oh, cool! That's a sick haircut!" she said, hopping over to Hunze. "Rip," she said, sticking out her hand again in greeting.

Confused by the rather gregarious young woman, Hunze shook her hand.

SCOTT BARON

"Greetings. Welcome to Earth," she said with a mock-somber voice as she gave Bawb a Vulcan hand salute.

He held up his hand, respectfully mirroring her gesture. "What is this greeting?" the Wampeh asked.

"Just for funsies. Something my aunt taught me. She and my uncle are totally into all that old-time video stuff."

She then greeted Leila and Rika both with a smile and a fist bump before turning her attention to Baloo.

"Oh my God! Look at you!" she squealed, rushing up to the massive beast and plunging her hands into his fur, scratching him all over with obvious glee.

"Uh, yes, of course. Please, run up to the dangerous-looking attack monster over there. He doesn't bite. Much," Charlie said, astonished.

"Oh, he won't bite me. He's a good boy, isn't he? Yes, you are. Yes, you are!" she said, smothering Baloo with affection. The huge canine actually flopped onto his back to better receive belly rubs.

"Okay, then. She obviously passes the Baloo test," Leila said with a grin. "Some guard animal you are."

Baloo looked at her and just whumpfed contentedly.

"Look, I hate to interrupt your cuddle time, Rip, but you're supposed to take these people to LA," Edward interjected. "I believe Cal's going to talk to––"

"Yeah, I know," she said, interrupting him. "No worries. Eddie here just passed his flight check and is clear for space travel. We'll just make a quick hop to orbit and be there in no time."

"You named your ship Eddie?" Edward asked, blushing.

"Yeah. After you, ya big doofus."

"My name is Eddie, not Edward," the ship corrected.

The newcomers were having a hard enough time following the hyperactive teen, but it was the talking ship that really threw them for a loop.

"My dad used to call me Eddie," he replied.

"Really? You actually think *you're* my namesake?" the ship chimed in.

"Hey, now. Play nice," Rip chided. "And no, not really, Ed. You know nascent AIs get to pick their own names and genders––or lack thereof––these days."

"Yes, we do," Eddie chimed in. "I wanted to call myself Ed two-oh-nine, but Rip said that was lame. So Eddie it is. Why? You don't like it?"

"Fine by me," Edward replied, shaking his head. The ship was just as loony as its pilot. "It was just a bit surprising."

Charlie was barely keeping up with the rapid-fire exchange, and adding a talking ship to the mix didn't make it any easier.

"Uh, Earth to crazy girl. You mind filling us in on what's going on?" Charlie asked. "And is that an actual AI-powered ship?"

"Oh, right. Sorry. I was just out taking Eddie here for a test spin. You know, working out the kinks and all that, when Cal asked us to divert and give some newcomers a ride to LA."

"Why LA?"

"It's our base of operations these days. Home. Only makes sense they'd want to talk to you in person." She turned to the Chithiid and spoke to him in his native tongue. "Anyone else coming? Or is it just these five? And the big doggie, of course."

Despite the translation spell Bawb had cast, there was still the slightest of accent present as the magic learned its way around the new language.

"Just these," the four-armed man replied. "And Rip, no scenic route, please. Cal is very interested in speaking with them."

"Fine, Naraaxik. You suck all the fun out of things."

The Chithiid chuckled and smiled. "Happy to be of service, Rip. Now, you should be on your way, yes?"

"All right," she griped. "Come on, you guys, load up. You can stow your gear in the lockers just to the right, by the seats."

Charlie and the others looked at one another with a bit of shock on their faces. The girl was a steamroller of energy, but the others seemed to defer to her, and her ship was more advanced than anything Charlie had ever seen. Odd as it might be, young Rip was to be their chauffeur.

"Incredible," Charlie said, admiring Eddie's sleek interior. "What kind of material is this? A titanium alloy? Or is that a carbon fiber?"

"Carbon? Please. I'm made of a high-tensile composite reinforced with a nanite repair matrix," Eddie said with a laugh as he closed his doors and took to the sky.

There was no sound, Charlie realized. No engine noise. Whatever tech this was, it was far more advanced than anything his design team had ever laid eyes on, and they had been led to believe their work was the absolute bleeding edge of the planet.

The ship quickly exited the atmosphere, flying high and fast before dropping back into a descent path right over Los Angeles. The whole trip had taken a meager thirty minutes.

They stepped out into the morning sun, having hopped continents and time zones as easily as changing their shoes. Los Angeles was a different sight altogether. It was still largely empty, but aliens, humans, and androids alike could be seen on the streets.

"Come on. We'll hop on the tube and be there in a few minutes," Rip said, leading them to an escalator to descend into the belly of the city.

As they dropped underground, Charlie and his friends got one last look at the gorgeous city of skyscrapers before being swallowed up into the ground for the last leg of their most unusual journey.

CHAPTER SIXTY-SIX

The tube station at the center of town was essentially empty, though there were a few people––alien and human alike––making their way to other loop tubes as they passed. The newcomers' unusual attire, as well as the aliens among them, were something of an attention-getter in the otherwise tranquil terminus.

"Up this way. It's one of the communications hubs in the area. It'll let Cal tie in Zed and the others more easily," Rip said, leading them to a bright room furnished with some small potted trees, warm lighting, and plush couches.

Rika flopped down onto one, melting happily into the soft comfort of the first modern Earth furniture she'd seen in years. Leila shrugged, then joined her. The others took chairs, sitting until this Cal fellow showed up.

"Welcome to Los Angeles," a voice greeted them.

"Uh, hello?"

"Hi, Uncle Cal!" Rip said cheerfully.

"Hello, Ripley. And greetings to our new friends. My name is Cal. With me on this conversation is Zed, lead AI in the orbiting fleet, and Sid, strategic AI on the Dark Side moon base."

"Hey there," Zed greeted. "Welcome to town."

"Greetings," Sid chimed in.

"We wished to first have a little chat with you ourselves before bringing the full council together to—"

"The Council is here?" Bawb said, leaping to his feet, ready for a fight.

"Of course it is. The Council of Earth's AI, human, and Chithiid overseers has been in place since the war ended. But if your story is true, I suppose you wouldn't know that."

"Which part of our story?" Charlie asked. "The part where they're aliens, or the part where we just got here from about two thousand years ago?"

"All of that, actually. But while your friends are obviously alien in origin, you and your female companion are entirely human."

"You sure about that?" Charlie asked, jokingly.

"Of course. We scanned you as soon as you arrived."

"Hey, invasion of privacy, much?" he grumbled.

"A necessary precaution. There was a great plague that spanned the globe. We finally eradicated all traces, but we are cautious, nevertheless. Regardless, you have my apologies. But if you would, can you please clarify this time jump you mentioned to our men in the UK?"

"You familiar with the concept of an Einstein-Rosen bridge?" Charlie asked.

"Of course we are," Zed replied. "Every AI knows about that technology, isn't that right, Cal?"

"Indeed. The Asbrú flight was the very basis for generations of research. Why, in fact—"

"The *Asbrú*?" Charlie blurted. "That's our ship!"

"Your ship? Impossible. It was destroyed during a test flight in Earth's orbit," Sid said. "The historic records are extensive. The mission was taught to every engineer and space pilot who followed it."

"Wait," Cal interrupted. *"What is your last name, Charlie?"*

350

"I think you know it, Cal," he replied. "Gault. Charlie Gault."

"My word. I would never have thought this possible."

"But you died. You all died," Zed noted.

Charlie turned to his friend on the couch. "Hey, Rika. We dead?"

"I don't feel dead."

"Me either. So, nope. To answer your question, definitely not dead."

"Rika? That is Rika Gaspari?"

"Damn, you guys really *do* know us," Charlie replied.

The AIs silently conversed, the revelation hanging thick in the air.

"So, you're the crew of the *Asbrú*?" Ripley said. "Like, for real?"

"Yeah."

"That's so cool! You're famous. That mission is taught to everyone in first-year pilot's training. It's textbook," the teen said.

"That's pretty cool," Charlie said with a grin. "I suppose you want our autographs."

Ripley laughed. "Well, it's textbook on what *not* to do," she added. "Isn't that right, Uncle Zed?"

"Oh, most definitely," the AI replied with amusement.

Charlie sighed. It really was going to be one of those days.

"Great. I'm famous for screwing up. That's just fantastic," he grumbled.

"There is much to discuss," Cal said, rejoining the conversation. *"Many new questions have arisen in light of this information. But first, do you know when your ship first vanished, Charlie?"*

"Yeah. Given how long we've been out there, and if I count my time with the Tslavars, and Ser Baruud, I'd have to say it's been a little shy of four years."

"No, Mister Gault. More like eight hundred."

Charlie felt the world spin a little beneath him.

Talking ships. Genius AIs. Aliens living on Earth in a post-war reconstruction.

"We didn't jump back to my own time then, did we?"

"I am afraid not."

"Charlie, what does this mean?" Leila asked, alarmed by the look on her king's face.

"It means we overshot the mark by nearly a thousand years. We arrived in my future."

"I'm glad you understood so quickly. Truly, you are the mind you were made out to be in the historical documents. But you are here now, and questions still linger. Such as, how did you arrive where you did? There was not any trace of a ship touching down in the UK, nor were there any readings of wormhole energy anywhere in the system."

"Perhaps I can answer that," Bawb replied.

"And you are the one called Bob, right?" Zed asked.

"Yes, I am Bawb, of the Wampeh Ghalian."

"The what?"

"It's a sect of deadly space vampire assassins," Charlie said with a chuckle. "There's more to the story, but that's the very basic bit."

"Vampires? But you guys were in the sun. I saw you," Ripley said.

"Charlie has taken to likening me to your 'vampires,' but I can assure you, the Wampeh Ghalian are not of your world."

"So how did you get here, then? Was it a Wampeh Ghalian cloaking device of some sort hiding your ship?" Sid asked.

"Nothing so crude. We arrived by magic."

Ripley started laughing. The AIs, however, were not amused.

"This is a serious question, Mister Bob. We need to know precisely how you traveled through time to arrive here, undetected by any of our scanners."

"And I have told you," he replied.

"Please, there is no reason for these make-believe stories. You can trust us, here. How did you really do it?" Zed asked.

"Bob, would you please?" Charlie asked with a knowing glance.

"My pleasure," the Wampeh replied, rising to his feet.

In a fluid motion, he drew his wand and cast a minor spell, the small potted tree across the room bursting into flame before he cast the extinguishing spell, snuffing it out. Bawb sheathed his wand and sat back down.

"I just had that planted," Cal said.

"My apologies, Cal," he said, the little smile on his lips not diminishing.

"That was unlike any energy signature I've ever seen," Zed interjected. "And almost undetectable with our normal scans. If we hadn't been actively monitoring the room, it would have gone unnoticed."

"Like the man said. Magic," Charlie said. "Same way we can all understand each other. A user-linked translation spell."

The magical expenditure of the wand sparked that odd feeling in his head again. In his blood. A connection.

"And speaking of magic and things you all won't believe," he continued, "I have another friend I think you'd *love* to meet. I haven't seen her in a while, but I know she's out there, and we need to find her."

"She walked off from your party before you met our people?" Cal asked. *"We can send a search flight to find her and—"*

"That won't quite work," Charlie interjected.

"Why not?"

"Well, she was kind of buried under a mountain," he replied.

"A mountain? Then even if she had ample oxygen, I'm afraid she's not going to have long," Zed said.

"Yeah, about that," Charlie said. "Uh, she's already been down there a really, *really* long time."

"How long?"

"About two thousand years."

Ripley sat up in her chair. "Uh, hang on. Did you say two thousand years? No way *anyone* can survive being buried for––"

"*And* she's a dragon."

Had record players not gone out of use a thousand years earlier, the needle would most certainly have abruptly skipped across this most unusual tune.

"I'm sorry, a *what*?"

"Yeah. Exactly what it sounds like. Wings, fire-breathing, the whole shebang."

Ripley and the AIs fell silent, utterly unsure how to process that piece of information. Finally, it was not the city-sized AI, or the leader of the fleet, or the base on the moon who spoke up. It was the stunned teenage girl, sitting cross-legged on her chair.

"I'd better get Aunt Daisy."

CHAPTER SIXTY-SEVEN

As it turned out, Ripley's somewhat legendary aunt was off-world at the moment, but Cal and the other terrestrial AIs had been more than happy to help their unexpected visitors track down their lost friend. It would be a search and rescue of unprecedented scale, and a lot of people volunteered to be a part of it.

No one had ever tried to dig up a live dragon before.

Of course, no one knew exactly where Ara had been trapped. Sheeran's intelligence had only been that Malalia's people had lured her with a magically brimming konus, left deep within a system of caverns, the power enhanced and directed outward just right. Just enough to catch the attention of the mighty dragon.

Her kind were powerful and wise, but the one downfall of so many species held true for Zomoki as well. They were curious. And what better to arouse their curiosity than traces of an impossible magical power on a world where it shouldn't exist?

"She couldn't have been more than a few hundred miles from the castle," Charlie determined, extrapolating the rough area of the search based on the fact that, while Ara could fly,

Malalia and her henchmen were on horseback. There was only so far they could travel to carry out their little treachery. Ara was somewhere in the UK. They just had to find out where.

It made sense, Charlie had mused. A real dragon buried in the land that had long held myths of them throughout history. He had to wonder if Ara herself hadn't inspired more than a few of those tales.

A plan was devised, utilizing Charlie's tenuous link with his buried friend. It would be time-consuming, and was iffy at best, but they hoped he would *feel* her presence as they flew near her, like a human divining rod.

Chithiid salvage crews had put out the request for volunteers to help rescue a creature trapped some two thousand years prior by an evil power. They had no idea what a dragon was, nor did they owe any loyalty to the strange people from the past, but within mere hours, offers of assistance began flooding in. Chithiid and human alike were ready to help.

The mechanicals were pitching in as well, cyborgs helping rebuild across the globe offering to catch the next tube or flight out when the time came. Now, it all rested on Charlie.

It was exhausting. Technically, all he was doing was flying around, comfortably seated in a cushioned chair. But emotionally, viscerally, he was being spread increasingly thin. After four days of it, he finally accepted Leila's offer to join him.

"This macho, lone bindoki thing isn't a good look," she had said.

"Honey, we say 'lone wolf' on this planet."

His queen slapped him playfully. "Just shut up and let me help."

"All right," he relented. "But you'll just wind up as bored as everyone else on the flight."

Leila was definitely not bored as she marveled at the land from their aerial vantage point. They had spent a pair of lengthy days making low passes over yet another series of mountains, this time heading farther west in their search for any sign of their friend.

Charlie had briefly sensed something, but then, as every time before, it slipped from his grasp, like a fistful of sand held in rough surf. One moment he had it, the next it was gone.

"Guys, I appreciate the hard work, but this is the twentieth mountain we've surveyed in the last few days. I think we can call it a day," he said to the pilots.

"All right, Charlie. It's your call."

"Then I'm calling it. It's getting late."

"You know, if you want to stick around for another half hour, I know a beautiful spot on the Welsh coast where you could catch the sunset," the pilot said, nodding toward Leila, who sat quietly staring out the window. "Might be a nice recharge," he added.

Charlie smiled, gratefully. "Excellent idea. Thank you."

The pilot merely smiled, then shifted course for the far reaches of Wales.

Charlie shifted his seat, pulling Leila close and draping his arm across her chest as they took in the sights of the scenic flight.

"It really is beautiful," she said quietly. "I was sad to leave my home, but this place, it's magical, in its own way. And it was actually beginning to feel like home."

"I know," he replied, kissing her temple. "Not a bad life, eh? King and queen of the realm."

"Well, a part of the realm, anyway."

"With you as my queen, it was more than enough."

A warmth began to spread in Leila's chest.

Then it heated up Charlie's arm as well.

"What the hell?" he blurted as he pulled his arm back.

Leila's Magus stone was glowing, triggered by Charlie's

contact, Ara's blood mingled in his veins. But now the stone was reacting on its own, having slowly absorbed traces of Ara's power over the time Leila had spent in close proximity to the magical creature.

"It's getting stronger," she exclaimed. "That way!"

"Turn right!" Charlie shouted into the cockpit. "We've got a hit!"

They banked right and followed the glowing stone as it drew them to their hidden friend.

"This can't be right. There's no mountain here," Charlie said, confused.

"No mountains, but there are some pretty extensive caverns all throughout this area. Maybe your friend was buried, but in a quarry cavern, not under a mountain."

It all made sense. Limestone was porous, and the waters from the wet region would have eroded miles upon miles of caverns over millions of years. The perfect place to trap a dragon.

"There!" Leila called out. "Put the ship down!"

They landed in a clearing and headed out on foot until she stood atop a large mound of rubble, the ancient trace of where a tunnel opening once stood.

"We've found it, Charlie," she said, eyes wet with joy. "We've found her."

All that remained was digging their friend out.

Those who had volunteered their services leapt into action, and within a day, a round-the-clock effort to excavate Lord knew how many miles of collapsed stone was underway. Charlie was there the entire time, watching with eager anticipation.

"You need proper sleep and a hot meal. Go join your friends in London and get some rest, Charlie. You look exhausted," the dig foreman said. "We'll call you the moment we find something."

Reluctantly, he hopped the next flight out, and within an

hour was showered and shaved. His queen made sure he ate a good meal and tucked him into bed. Within minutes, he was fast asleep.

The following days Charlie introduced his friends to the comforts of his world. As much as he could, that is. He was being introduced to them as well, being hundreds and hundreds of years into his own future. And the tales he heard were astonishing.

Apparently, there had been a global attack by a hostile alien species. It had wiped out nearly all of humanity, stopping their culture dead in its tracks for centuries, until, finally, a woman named Daisy and her friends saved humanity, putting a stop to the war once and for all. Compared to his own story, he felt she had him beat, hands down.

As for his friends, they were astounded at the comforts of this world as much as the miracles technology could provide. Hot water on demand, and without the need for a spell cast from a magic-storing device that had to be constantly recharged. It was marvelous.

Then there was the food. So many varieties, and such creative uses of ingredients. Ripley's father had taken particular pleasure in feeding the newcomers, having flown all the way from his restful home in Los Angeles to personally greet them. He was quite a character, and a skilled chef on top of that. Charlie thought his dear friend Tuktuk would have liked meeting him.

But that friend was dead, and many hundreds of years ago at that. A sad loss at the hands of time travel. He just hoped his life had been a happy one. If he'd remained with his dearest Magda, he was pretty sure it was.

As for the other human in the group, Rika had been scanned in the most advanced medical facilities Charlie had ever seen, and the prognosis was both heartening and sad. Severe damage had been done to her frontal lobes when the Tslavar slave dealers had lobotomized her. Then, adding Malalia's mindfuck on top of that, and it was a miracle she had any gray matter intact at all.

But that was precisely what she had, though the AIs studying her had no explanation how. Her brain was healthy and healed, the damaged areas, quite impossibly, regrown as if new.

What she had stored there in the last several years was gone, however, and given what she'd been through, maybe that was for the best. But she also now had the tools at her disposal to form new memories. To start fresh.

Bawb hadn't commented on Charlie's continued use of the Balamar waters on his friend. Their supply was limited, and once it was gone, there would be no replenishing it. However, this was someone close to Charlie. Harmed by Malalia in ways that made his blood boil in sympathy for his friend. His friend could use all of the water, if need be, so far as he was concerned.

"Charlie?" Rika said a few days later, when he came to see her in her suite.

"You remember?"

"Not exactly," she said haltingly. "But we were friends, weren't we?"

"Yes, we were."

She sat silently in thought a long moment.

"Will you come talk to me again tomorrow?"

"Every day. I'll even take you for a run, if you like," he said, remembering how she had tortured him on the base obstacle course to prepare him for their mission.

Rika smiled at the suggestion. "I'd like that, Charlie. I'd like that a lot."

He left her a little while later, joining Leila for dinner, the pair taking a long stroll after, then retiring to their bed, wrapped tightly in each other's arms.

In a different suite, Hunze sipped a mug of tea, while Bawb carefully cleaned his magical weapons and stowed them away, along with the radiant braid of Hunze's hair. He ran his fingers over the golden locks, then closed the case, sliding it under the bed before walking to sit with the young woman staring at him so intently.

"You know," he finally managed to say. "We haven't talked about what you did back there. On that day."

"I did what was necessary, Bawb. And I would do it again without hesitation."

"I know you would. But..." He hesitated. "We also have not discussed what you said when we faced Malalia."

Hunze's warm smile broadened. "What more is there to say?"

"It's just that, you said it was freely given, your hair."

"And it was."

"Yes. But you also said something else."

Hunze placed her mug on the low table and slid close, looking deep into his eyes. If anyone had been watching, they would have sworn the deadliest assassin in thirty systems trembled slightly as she placed her hands atop his.

"I did, Bawb. And those words were true. It was given of love."

The tension between the two crackled as strongly as any spell might, until the dangerous man known as the Geist, for once, and finally, let his guard down, pulling his love in close with a kiss.

CHAPTER SIXTY-EIGHT

Two more weeks of excavation had passed, and enough limestone to build their own mountain had been removed from the collapsed caverns, while workers carefully shored up the walls, protecting against collapse. Charlie visited frequently, Leila at his side, the two helping guide the work in the right direction.

It was astonishing, the hand-in-hand work put in by Chithiid, humans, cyborgs, and AI-powered machinery—all of it collaborating to save their friend. They had arrived in a time unfamiliar to them all, and had been embraced with open arms. This was the kind of future world Charlie could live with.

He was standing just outside the mouth of the excavation site when a powerful rumbling shook the ground, nearly knocking him from his feet.

"Cave in!" a man yelled, running from the gaping maw of the caverns.

A massive plume of dust, forced up from the depths of the earth spewed out into the sky, accompanied by a giant burst of flame.

"They hit a gas pocket! Everyone get clear!"

Charlie breathed deeply and smiled, savoring that familiar charred odor hanging in the air. That wasn't gas smoke. Oh no. He knew that smell quite well.

With an explosion of rock and debris, the form of a massive dragon burst into the sunlight, wings flapping hard for the first time in millennia.

"Ara, it's me!"

Nothing but noise and confusion filled his head, like the shrieking of a hundred maniacs locked in their cells, howling a chorus of insanity. The Zomoki turned her feral eyes on him and roared, landing hard on the ground in front of him.

"Aranzgrgghmunatharrgle!" he shouted into her mind, using the damn near impossible name he'd forced himself to finally learn. *"Ara, it's Charlie. You're free. Please, calm down."*

The mighty dragon flapped her wings and spewed flame into the air, but then, slowly, she settled down, the soothing energy of the sun's rays soaking into her for the first time in so very long.

"Is it really you?" she asked, blinking in the bright light, a shaky unease in her voice.

"Yes, it's really me."

"But what are all of these creatures around me? And these tech-magic machines?"

"We're on my world, Ara. Remember? And these are the people who live here. They've all banded together to help rescue you."

A tear formed in one massive, golden eye, then rolled slowly down her cheek. *"Then this is not another dream?"*

"No. You're really free."

Ara slowly calmed herself further, forcing deep breaths into her lungs. Her first truly fresh air in millennia. The tension and panic around her eyes gradually relaxed, and when she turned her golden gaze on her friend once more, Charlie recognized the warmth behind those eyes.

"I have something for you," he said, taking the last jug of the Balamar waters from his pack. *"Open wide."*

The men, aliens, and AIs all watched in fascination and horror as the terrifying monster's enormous mouth opened wide. Her teeth were enough to fuel more than one man's nightmares for quite some time. Then, impossible for them to comprehend, Charlie leaned into the beast's mouth.

"You're not going to curl up into a hardened ball again, are you?" he asked as he emptied the jug onto her tongue.

Ara swallowed the small taste of the waters, a shiver of pleasure running through her body. *"No, Charlie. This is far less water than before."*

"Good."

"And I've been absorbing energy from the small rivulet that has been trickling through the cavern all this time. It brought me traces of the sun's energy every day, and, though I may not look it, I am actually stronger than before. I've just been stuck in a cave for... How long has it been?"

"About two thousand years, give or take."

Ara fell silent. Even for a Zomoki as powerful and old as she was when captured, a hibernation that long had never been heard of. She let out a little sigh, accepting the news as best she could. *"That has got to be some kind of record,"* she joked.

Charlie beamed, tears of joy on his cheeks.

"It's good to have you back."

"It's good to be back," she said, sitting up and shaking mightily, the dried old scales flaking off and falling away, revealing her gleaming red form, bright in the sun's light.

"What ever did happen, Charlie?"

"That is a long story, my friend. And boy, do I have a lot to tell you. But you're free for the first time in ages. How about you and I go for a little flight? I would love nothing more than to show you around my world."

Ara lowered herself to the ground, and the men surrounding the excavation site watched in awe as the tiny human climbed up onto the massive dragon's back.

"Thank you all!" Ara bellowed, shocking the onlookers as she took to the skies.

Several of the AI ships that happened to be flying in the region that day had thought they were perhaps having a processor malfunction when they saw what appeared to be an actual dragon soaring alongside them.

"Is that a man on its back?" one asked in utter confusion before making a beeline for the nearest service depot to have its synapse relays checked.

But indeed, it was. A man and a dragon, flying free. In time, they would learn all about her, the mythical being, from a galaxy far away. But for now, the dragon named Ara and her bonded friend reveled in their reunion, flying free in the Earth's sun's warming glow.

BUT WAIT, THERE'S MORE!

Follow Charlie on his continuing adventures in the fourth book
of the Dragon Mage series: Magic Man Charlie

THANK YOU

Reader word of mouth is an independent author's lifeblood. So if you enjoyed this book and have a moment to spare, please consider leaving a rating or review on Amazon or on Goodreads, or even sharing it with a friend or two. Your support is greatly appreciated.

Thank you!

~ Scott ~

ALSO BY SCOTT BARON

Standalone Novels

Living the Good Death

The Clockwork Chimera Series

Daisy's Run

Pushing Daisy

Daisy's Gambit

Chasing Daisy

Daisy's War

The Dragon Mage Series

Bad Luck Charlie

Space Pirate Charlie

Dragon King Charlie

Magic Man Charlie

Odd and Unusual Short Stories:

The Best Laid Plans of Mice: An Anthology

Snow White's Walk of Shame

The Tin Foil Hat Club

Lawyers vs. Demons

The Queen of the Nutters

Lost & Found

ABOUT THE AUTHOR

A native Californian, Scott Baron was born in Hollywood, which he claims may be the reason for his rather off-kilter sense of humor.

Before taking up residence in Venice Beach, Scott first spent a few years abroad in Florence, Italy before returning home to Los Angeles and settling into the film and television industry, where he has worked as an on-set medic for many years.

Aside from mending boo-boos and owies, and penning books and screenplays, Scott is also involved in indie film and theater scene both in the U.S. and abroad.

Made in United States
North Haven, CT
23 September 2024

57784082R00225